Crit...
THE BO...

"Dunning weirdly and wonderfully intersperses publishing arcana with fisticuffs, gunplay, and an impossibly dense plot, until he has you believing the unspeakable things his obsessional cast would do for a single precious book."

—*Kirkus Reviews*

"Dunning is a hugely talented writer. . . . *THE BOOK-MAN'S WAKE* is the book we've all been hoping it would be: even richer, better and stronger than its predecessor. . . . Even more memorable than the plot are Dunning's characters and the harsh secrets they keep, which must be unraveled before the mystery can be solved . . . nail-biting suspense."

—Tom and Enid Schantz, *Denver Post*

"The author, himself a former rare-book dealer, immerses the reader in this intriguing, little-known milieu without losing sight of the page-turning yarn he's spinning. In the end you may be disappointed that the last plot twist has finally played itself out."

—Pam Lambert, *People*

"Bless us all, Dunning and Janeway are back. As before, Dunning's text is enlivened with fascinating tidbits on first-edition prices. . . . Nothing bookishly sedentary here."

—Charles Champlin, *Los Angeles Times Book Review*

"This 'don't miss' mystery was definitely worth waiting for. . . ."

—*Kansas City Star*

Critical Acclaim for
Booked to Die

"A joy to read for its wealth of inside knowledge about the antiquarian book business and its eccentric traders . . . A soundly plotted, evenly executed whodunit in the classic mode . . . Cliff Janeway makes a honey of a debut."

—*The New York Times Book Review*

"Dunning is an amazingly assured writer, willing to head off down narrative side streets, secure that his readers will follow. He's never wrong. *Booked to Die* joins the select ranks of specialist crime fiction that works on all levels."

—*Booklist*

"Crisp, direct prose and nearly pitch-perfect dialogue enhance this meticulously detailed page-turner."

—starred review in *Publishers Weekly*

"I am . . . an unabashed admirer of John Dunning's *Booked to Die*. No one . . . can fail to be delighted by the sort of folkloric advice Janeway carries with him."

—*Boston Sunday Globe*

More Praise for
John Dunning

"A standout masterpiece of crime fiction. The characters are involving, the writing direct and forceful—though unashamedly tender in places—the plotting irreproachable . . . compelling page-turning stuff with a bonus. The author himself is a rare-book dealer. He evokes that arcane world as only an insider can."

—*Philadelphia Inquirer*

"Dunning, twice nominated for the Edgar, deserves to win one for this Denver cop-turned-bookman tale—a lively, seductive primer on how to open a bookstore, spot a first edition, warehouse it, price it, and enjoy it for its own sake."

—starred review in *Kirkus Reviews*

"Dunning's assured and muscular prose illuminates the fascinating byways as well as the possibilities for fraud and violence in the bookseller's world."

—*San Francisco Chronicle*

Books by John Dunning

For orders other than by individual consumers, Pocket Books
grants a discount on the purchase of **10 or more** copies of
single titles for special markets or premium use. For further
details, please write to the Vice-President of Special Markets,
Pocket Books, 1230 Avenue of the Americas, New York, NY
10020.

For information on how individual consumers can place
orders, please write to Mail Order Department, Paramount
Publishing, 200 Old Tappan Road, Old Tappan, NJ 07675.

THE
BOOKMAN'S
WAKE

JOHN
DUNNING

POCKET STAR BOOKS
New York London Toronto Sydney Tokyo Singapore

This book is a work of fiction. Names, characters, places and incidents are products of the author's imagination or are used fictitiously. Any resemblance to actual events or locales or persons, living or dead, is entirely coincidental.

A Pocket Star Book published by
POCKET BOOKS, a division of Simon & Schuster Inc.
1230 Avenue of the Americas, New York, NY 10020

ISBN: 0-671-56782-9

First Pocket Books printing March 1996

10 9 8 7 6 5 4 3 2 1

POCKET STAR BOOKS and colophon are registered
trademarks of Simon & Schuster Inc.

Cover design by Rich Hasselburger

Printed in the U.S.A.

Again, prices on actual books discussed by characters in the story may be a year or two out-of-date. In a time of madness, when a new novel can bring ten times its cover price a year after publication, prices become obsolete almost as they're published. Janeway remains a cynic when people pay too much too soon and glorify the trendy. But he is an equal-opportunity cynic who saves his deepest skepticism for me, when he and I are alone at four-thirty in the morning.

Another tip of the hat to Warwick Downing, who bullied me for three years. To George Fowler for turning me left and right in the Seattle rain. To Pat McGuire for long friendship and a kick in the duff when I needed it. And a kind word for the small-press publishers of today. Some still struggle valiantly in the great lost cause.

THE
BOOKMAN'S
WAKE

The man in St. Louis died sometime during the afternoon, as near as the coroner could figure it. It happened long ago, and today it is only half-remembered even by old-timers who follow crime news. The victim was eccentric and rich: that, combined with the inability of the police to identify either a motive or a suspect, kept it on front pages for a week. Then the press lost interest. Reporters had been charmed by the puzzle, and by the colorful background of the deceased, but they could only sell that for a few days and then something new had to happen. It didn't—the case slipped off the front pages and became history, perhaps to be resurrected periodically in anniversary pieces or in magazine accounts of unsolved mysteries. On the news desk at the *St. Louis Post-Dispatch,* an editor ripped and read an AP squib about a triple murder in Phoenix, fifteen hundred miles to the southwest and thought—not for the first time—that the world was getting dangerously crowded with crazy people. He considered using it as a two-graph filler on page eight: then he thought, Christ, we've got enough crazy people of our own, and the Phoenix murders got bumped by a UPI account of a squabble along the Chinese-Russian border. In Phoenix, that day and for the rest of the week, the case was front-page news. The cops didn't have a clue. If murder had to happen, said the cop in charge of the

1

Phoenix case, it should at least be logical. It's not the garden-variety passion killer we find scary, the cop said, it's the guy who kills for no good reason and then disappears into the night. The police hardly ever catch him because he strikes without reason and has no motive. The trouble with random murder is that all the common denominators are superficial. The killer may break in the same way, he may use the same weapon, but there is never anything that hints of a motive because there isn't any. Give me a motive, other than craziness, said the cop, and I'll clear this case. That cop didn't know, because it didn't make the papers in Phoenix and was one among many brutal homicides on the national teletype as the long weekend began, that a Baltimore man had just been killed in much the same way. This time there was a survivor—his wife, blind from birth and left babbling madly in the killer's wake. She was useless as a witness and was soon committed to a state institution, but perhaps even then she might have had something to tell an investigator with knowledge of Phoenix and St. Louis and the perspective to see them all as a single case. But computers weren't yet in broad general use: communities separated by vast distances weren't linked as they are today; murders weren't grouped electronically by such factors as weaponry, forensic matching, and killer profiles. There was the teletype, with its all-points bulletins advising that murders had been committed, but what else was new? The term *serial killer* had not yet entered the common lexicon, and to most people it was inconceivable that a killer might strike in St. Louis on Monday, Phoenix on Wednesday, and in a Baltimore suburb on Friday night. On Sunday there was a double murder in Idaho—a rancher and his wife killed just as they were sitting down to dinner. This was big news in Boise, but it made hardly a ripple in St. Louis, Phoenix, or Baltimore. On the ninth day the killer struck for the last time—an elderly woman living alone in New Orleans. This time he set fire to the house, hoping, police theorized, to cover up his crime. In each of the five cities teams of detectives worked their local angles and found nothing. They sifted false clues, chased down rumors, and slowly over the weeks watched their final leads disappear into the big blank wall. The one common denominator remained hidden by the vast expanse of geography and by the often cryptic methods of police teletyping.

No one knew it then, but in each of the death houses lived a book collector.

That's how I got into it, more than twenty years later.

BOOK I

ELEANOR

1

Slater wasn't my kind of cop. Even in the old days, when we were both working the right side of the good-and-evil beat, I had been well able to take Mr. Slater or leave him alone. He had played such a small part in my life that, for a moment, I didn't know who he was. I was working in my office, a small room in the rear of the used-and-rare bookstore I owned in Denver, writing up books for my first catalog, when Millie buzzed me from the front. "There's a Mr. Slater here to see you," she said, and the last person I would've thought about—did think about—was Clydell. This was annoying. My work was going slowly: I was an absolute novice at bibliography, and even with modern books there are pitfalls everywhere. Open on the table before me was a copy of *Nickel Mountain,* by John Gardner, as fresh and crisp as the day it was born in 1973. Gardner had signed it on the half title, a nice little touch, since he won't be signing any more, that almost doubled its value. It's not yet an expensive book—about $25–40 unsigned, in fine first edition—the kind of book that should be a snap to describe and price. The publisher was Alfred A. Knopf, who not only puts out fine books but also gives you the straight bibliographical poop. He's not like Lippincott, who states *first edition* most of the time, or McGraw-Hill, who states it when the guy in the back shop feels like putting it on: if Knopf says it's a first edition, you can take it to the bank and cash it . . . although I do remember one or two Willa Cathers that might or might not follow tradition. Let's face it, all these houses are dotted with land mines. William Morrow was a model of consistency, but on one pricey little Harry Crews title, instead of noting *second printing* as always before, he put two tiny dots at the bottom of the copyright page. Cute, Morrow. That little piece of camouflage cost me $40 for a spectacular nonfirst last year. Doubleday always, and I mean *always,* puts the words *first edition* on his copyright page and takes it off for later printings. But on one John Barth he didn't: he put no designation whatever, instead hiding a code in the gutter of the last two pages. The code must say H-18—not H-38 or H-Is-for-Homicide or H-anything-else—or it's not a first. Harper and Row was as reliable as Knopf over the years, except in one five-year period, circa 1968–73, when for reasons known only to Messrs. Harper and Row in that great bookstore in the sky, they started putting a chain of numbers on the *last* page, for Christ's sake, in addition to saying *first edition* up front. Figure that out. The only way I can figure it out is that people who publish books must hate and plot against people who cherish them, make collectibles of them, and sell them. I can just see old Harper and Row, rubbing their translucent hands together and cackling wildly as some poor slob shells out his rent money, $700, for a *One Hundred Years of Solitude,* only to discover that he's got a later state, worth $40 tops. Harper really outdid himself on this title: in addition to hiding the chain of numbers (the first printing of which begins with "1"), he also published a state that has no numbers at all. This is widely believed to be the true first, though there can still be found a few keen and knowledgeable dealers who would beg to differ. The one certainty is that on any Harper title for that era, the back pages must be checked. Thus concealed are points on early Tony Hillermans in the $750-and-up range, some Dick Francis American firsts (the numbers on one of which seems to begin with "2," as no "1" has ever been seen), a good Gardner title, and, of course, *Solitude,* a fall-on-your-sword blunder if you make it, the rent's due, and the guy who sold it to you has gone south for the winter.

So I was stuck on *Nickel Mountain,* with a guy I didn't want to see storming my gates up front. I was stuck because I seemed to remember that there were two states to this particular book, A. A. Knopf notwithstanding. I had read somewhere that they had stopped the presses in the middle of the first printing and changed the color on the title page. God or the old man or someone high in the scheme of things didn't like the hue, so they changed it from a deep orange to a paler one. Technically they are both first editions, but the orange one is a first-first, thus more desirable. It's no big deal, but this was my first catalog and I wanted it to be right. The title page looked pretty damn orange to me, but hot is hot only when you have cold to compare it with. Go away, Slater, I thought.

I took an index card out of my desk, wrote *check the color,* and stuck it in the book. I told Millie to send the bastard back, and I got ready to blow him off fast if he turned out to be a dealer in snake oil or a pitchman for a lightbulb company. Even when he came in, for a moment I didn't know him. He was wearing a toupee and he'd had his front teeth pulled. The dentures were perfect: you couldn't tell the hairpiece from the real thing, unless you'd known him in the days when the tide was going out. His clothes were casual but expensive. He wore alligator shoes and the briefcase he carried looked like the hide of some equally endangered animal. His shirt was open and of course he wore a neckchain. The only missing effect was the diamond in the pierced ear, but I knew it was only a matter of time before he'd get to that too.

"You fuckhead," he said. "Lookitcha, sittin' there on your damn dead ass with no time to talk to an old comrade-in-arms."

"Hello, Clydell," I said without warmth. "I almost didn't know you."

He put his thumbs in his lapels and did the strut. On him it was no joke. "Not bad, huh? My gal Tina says I look twenty years younger."

Tina, yet. An instant picture formed in my mind—young, achingly beautiful, and so totally without brains that she just missed being classified as a new species in the animal kingdom.

"You're the last guy I'd ever expect to see in a bookstore, Clydell," I said, trying to keep it friendly.

"I am a doer, not a reader. It's good of you to remember."

"Oh, I remember," I said, sidestepping the gentle dig.

"My deeds of daring have become legends among the boys in blue. I'm still one of their favorite topics of conversation, I hear. So are you, Janeway."

"I guess I can die now, then. Everything from now on will just be downhill."

He pretended to browse my shelves. "So how's the book biz?"

I really didn't want to talk books with a guy who—you could bet the farm on it—couldn't care less. "Have a seat," I said reluctantly, "and tell me what's on your mind."

"Listen to 'im," he said to some attendant god. "Same old fuckin' Janeway. No time for bullshit, eh, Cliffie? One of these days they'll make a movie about your life, old buddy, and that's what they'll call it: *No Time for Bullshit.*"

It was all coming back now, all the stuff I'd always found tedious about Slater. His habit of calling people old buddy. The swagger, the arrogance, the tough-guy front. The false hair on the chest, as some critic— probably Max Eastman—had once said about Hemingway. The glitz, the shoes, the bad taste of wearing animal hides and buying them for his wife. Then bragging about it, as if going deep in hock on a cop's salary for a $4,000 mink was right up there on a scale with winning the Medal of Honor for bravery. Some of us thought it was poetic justice when the Missus took the mink and a fair piece of Slater's hide and dumped him for a doctor. But there was still light in the world: now there was Tina.

"It's just that I'm pretty sure you didn't come in here for a book," I said. "We sold our last issue of *Whips and Chains* an hour ago."

"You kill me, Janeway. Jesus, a guy can't even stop by for old times' sake without getting the sarcasm jacked up his ass."

"To be brutally honest, you and I never ran with the same crowd."

"I always admired you, though. I really did, Janeway. You were the toughest damn cop I ever knew."

"I still am," I said, keeping him at bay.

He made dead-on eye contact. "Present company excepted."

I just looked at him and let it pass for the moment.

"Hey, you know what we should do?—go a coupla rounds sometime. Go over to my gym, I'll give you a few pointers and kick your ass around the ring a little."

"You wouldn't last thirty seconds," I said, finally unable to resist the truth.

"You prick," Slater said in that universal tone of male camaraderie that allows insults up to a point. "Keep talking and one day you'll really believe that shit." He decided to take my offer of a chair. "Hey, just between us old warriors, don'tcha ever get a hankering to get back to it?"

"You must be out of your mind. No way on this earth, Clydell."

He looked unconvinced. "Tell the truth. You'd still be there if it wasn't for that Jackie Newton mess. You'd go back in a heartbeat if you could."

"The truth? . . . Well, what I really miss are the Saturday nights. I hardly ever got through a whole shift without having to wade through guts and pick up the pieces of dead children. It's pretty hard for something like this"—I made the big gesture with my arms, taking in the whole infinite and unfathomable range of my present world—"to take the place of something like that."

We looked at each other with no trace of humor or affection. Here, I thought: this's the first honest moment in this whole bullshit conversation—we've got nothing to say to each other. But the fact remained: Slater hadn't come waltzing in here to show off his togs and tell me about Tina.

He lit a cigarette and looked at the bookshelves critically, the way a scientist might look at a bug under a microscope.

"Is there any money in this racket?"

I shook my head. "But it's so much fun we don't care."

"Yeah, I'll bet," he said dryly.

I felt my temperature rising. Slater had about twenty seconds left on his ticket and he must've known it. Abruptly, he switched directions.

"Y'know, there are some jobs where you can have

fun and still make a buck or two. Maybe you've heard."

I think I knew what he was going to say in that half second before he said it. It was crazy, but I was almost ready for him when he said, "I could use a good man if you're ever inclined to get back in the real world."

I let the full impact of what he was saying settle between us. He raised his eyebrows and turned up his palms, pushing the sincere look. It probably worked like a charm on children and widows and one-celled organisms like Tina.

"Let me get this straight, Clydell . . . you're offering me a job?"

"More than a job, Cliffie . . . a lot more than that."

"I don't think so."

"Don't jump too fast, old buddy, till you hear me out." He took a long drag and blew smoke into the air. "Last year I paid tax on a quarter of a million dollars."

"Somebody's gotta pay for those two-hundred-dollar toilet seats the Pentagon keeps buying."

"Listen, you asshole, just shut up and listen. The best thing I ever did was take early retirement and go out on my own. Right now I'm the hottest thing Denver's ever seen. I may branch out into radio. I was on two shows last week and the program director at KOA says I took to it like nobody she ever saw. Are you listening to me, Janeway? I could make a second career out of this if I wanted to. It's so easy it oughta be against the law. None of those guys work more than two or three hours a day, and I'm just gettin' warmed up then. It's all bullshit. I can bullshit my way out of anything, and that's all you need in radio. I found that out after the first five minutes. It ain't what you know, it's what you got between your legs. You hear what I'm saying?"

"Clydell, what's this got to do with me?"

13

"Keep your pants on, I'm getting to it. This is all by way of saying that your old buddy is leading a very full life. They invite me on to talk about the detective business and find out I can hold my own on anything. I'm filling in for the morning drive-time host next week. *Denver Magazine* is doing a piece on me, a full-blown profile. They're picking me as one of Denver's ten sexiest men over fifty. Can you dig that?"

I could dig it. Any magazine that would come up with a horse's-ass idea like that deserved Slater and would leave no stone unturned in the big effort to find him. I hoped they'd shoot their pictures in the morning, before the town's sexiest man got his hair off the hat rack and his teeth out of the water glass.

Slater said, "On radio they're thinking of billing me as the talking dick."

"This also figures."

"I can talk about any damn thing. Politics? . . . Hell, I'm a walking statistical abstract. Ask me something. Go ahead, ask me a question . . . about anything, I don't care."

"Oh, hell," I said wearily.

"I've got an answer for everything and *you* can't even come up with a fuckin' question."

I looked at him numbly.

"Here's something you didn't know. They skew those microphones in my favor. If I get any shit from a caller, all I've gotta do is lean a little closer and raise my voice and he just goes away." He gave me a grin and a palms-up gesture, like a magician who'd just made the rabbit disappear. "I'll tell you, Cliff, I'm really hot as a pistol right now. I'm at the top of my game. There's even talk about them doing one of my cases on the network, on *Unsolved Mysteries.*"

"If you're such a ball of fire, how come you didn't solve it?"

"I *did* solve the goddamn thing, that's why they

want to do it, you goddamn moron, as a follow-up to a
story they did last year about all the meatheads who
couldn't solve the damn thing. Get this straight,
Janeway—there is no case I can't solve. That's why
I'm cutting Denver a new rear end, because I guarantee everything. I get results or I don't cash the check.
You got a missing person? . . . I'll find the son of a
bitch. If he owes you money, I'll drag his ass back
here, and before we're through with him, he'll wish
he'd never laid eyes on you, this town, and most of all
me. I can find anybody in a day or two—it's just a
matter of knowing your guy and using the old noggin.
We've got a computer database with access to seventy
million names in every state in the union. If the
bastard's got a MasterCard, works for a living, or has
ever subscribed to a magazine, I've got his ass in my
computer. I can tell you his home address, phone
number, the size of his jockstrap, and how many X-
rated videos he watched last week. I can tell you stuff
about yourself that you didn't even know."

"Clydell . . ."

"Okay, the point is, I can't keep up with it. I've got
three legmen and three tracers on my payroll full-
time, and I still can't keep up with all the work. I
could put on three more people right now and we'd
still be a month behind in our billings. I turn down
more jobs now than I take on: I take on any more, I
won't be able to do the sexy ones myself. I'll just be a
paper man, shoveling shit and passing out assign-
ments. Not the life for your old buddy, if you know
what I mean. This is where you come in."

"Uh-uh," I said, shaking my head.

"You'd be second-in-command. Write your own
ticket. I guarantee you'd make fifty grand, rock bottom, your first year. You'd have your pick of all the
interesting cases, you'd be the go-between between me
and the staff. You'd get a staff car and all expenses

paid. I'm telling you, old buddy, my people go first-cabin all the way. My liquor cabinet opens at four and the staff has all the privileges. And if you're lonely at night, we've got three secretaries with world-class t-and-a, and they do a helluva lot more for a guy than take his dictation. I know you're not crazy about me, Janeway, I got eyes in my head. But you ask anybody who works for me, they'll all tell you what a pussycat I am. A guy does it my way, he's got no problems. You're gonna love this, and you'll love me too before it's over. Even if you don't, nobody says we've gotta sleep together."

With that sorry premise, I excused myself and went to the bathroom.

He was still there, though, when I came back.

"Think about it," he said.

"I already have."

"Think about it, you dumb schmuck." He looked around critically. "You're like me, Janeway, a man of action. What the hell are you doing here?"

I'll give it one try, I thought, see if I can make him understand the tiniest truth about the world he's blundered into. But I couldn't find the words even for that. You'll never convince a doorknob that there's anything more to life than getting pushed, pulled, and turned.

"I appreciate the thought," I said, "but I've got to pass."

"This job's tailor-made for you, it's got your name stamped all over it. You want proof? . . . I'll toss you a plum. Two days' work, you pick up five grand. There's even a book angle, if you're interested."

I stared at him.

"Do I finally have your attention?" he said, grinning. "Did I just say a magic word or something?"

"You might've started with that, saved yourself a lot of time."

"Shut up and listen. I need somebody to go pick up a skip. My staff's booked solid for the next two weeks; I'm so tight right now I can't even send the janitor out there. This lady needs to be delivered back to the district court in Taos, New Mexico, ten days from tomorrow, absolute latest. The bondsman's out fifty grand and he's willing to grease our cut to fifteen percent for dragging her back. I've already done the arithmetic: that's seventy-five big ones, just for taking a couple of plane rides. I pay your freight out there, you go first-class all the way, *plus* I give you the big cut."

"Where's out there?"

"She's in Seattle."

"How do you know that?"

"I went to Madame Houdini and looked in a crystal ball, you fuckin' schlemiel. I play the odds, that's how. This gal comes from there, she's still got people there, where else is she gonna go? I called a guy I know and put him on her case. Just sit and watch, you know the routine. Yesterday, around four o'clock, there she comes, bingo, we got her. My guy just gives her plenty of rope, and after a while she leads him to the Y, where she's staying."

"Where's your guy now?"

"Still on her tail. He called me from a phone booth an hour ago, while she was getting her breakfast at the bus station lunch counter."

"Why not just have him pick her up? Seems to me that'd be the easy way."

"It's not him I'm trying to impress, meatball. Let me level with you, Janeway: I don't give a rat's ass about this case, it's just a way for you to make some quick and easy dough and see how much fun workin' for your old buddy really is. I swear to God, when I thought of you last night, it was like the answer to some prayer. I've been needing somebody like you as

17

a ramrod in my office for at least a year now, but nobody I talked to seemed right for the job. Then this Eleanor Rigby thing popped and it came to me in one fell swoop. Cliff Janeway! What a natural."

"What Eleanor Rigby thing?"

"That's the skip's name."

I blinked. "Eleanor *Rigby?*"

"Just like the song," Slater said in the same tone of voice. But his eyes had suddenly narrowed and I sensed him watching me keenly, as if, perhaps, I might know Eleanor Rigby as something other than a song of my youth.

"Eleanor Rigby," I said, staring back at him.

"Yeah, but this little baby's not wasting away to a fast old age."

I blinked again, this time at the picture he showed me.

"Not bad, huh? You make five big ones and you get to ride all the way home handcuffed to *that*. I'd do this one myself, old buddy, if it wasn't for a radio date and *Denver Magazine.*"

Then, very much against all my better judgment, I said, "Tell me about it."

2

Eleanor Rigby had gone to Taos to steal a book: that, at least, was how the betting line was running. On the night of September 14, four weeks ago, she had by her own account arrived in New Mexico.

Five nights later she had burglarized the country home of Charles and Jonelle Jeffords. While tossing the house, she was surprised by the Jeffordses sudden return; a struggle ensued and shots were fired. According to a statement by Mrs. Jeffords, the Rigby woman had shot up the place in a panic and escaped the house. The law came quickly and Rigby was flushed out of the surrounding woods. She had initially been charged with aggravated burglary, a violation of New Mexico statute 30-16-4: then, after further interviews with the victims, the DA had added the more serious business—aggravated assault, assault with a deadly weapon, and attempted murder. I didn't know what the penalties were in New Mexico, but it probably wasn't much different from Colorado. The whole package could get her ten years in the state penitentiary. The judge had set a standard bail: the DA had probably argued that Rigby had no ties to the community and was not a good risk, but judges, even in the punitive era we seem to be heading into, are reluctant to throw away the key before a defendant has had her day in court. Bail was $50,000: Rigby had put up as collateral a property she owned, a wooded tract near Atlanta that had been left her by her grandfather. The bondsman had posted the cash bond and had taken title to the property as a guarantee that she'd appear for her court date.

But Rigby did not appear. She returned to the Jeffordses' house, broke in again, stole some papers and a book, and this time got away.

"That's where we come in," Slater said. "The Jeffords woman wants her book back; it's one of those things, you know how people get over their stuff. A few days later she heard from the cops that Rigby had been seen in Denver; Jeffords got pipelined to me. It didn't take us long to figure out that Rigby had been here for one night only, just passing through on her way to Seattle. The rest is history. My guy's got a bead on her and she's sittin' in the bus station, waiting for one of us to come pick her up. That's when I thought of you, old buddy. I'm sittin' at my desk thinking about this crazy dame and her book, and all of a sudden it hits me like a bolt of lightning right in the ass. *Janeway!* And I wonder where the hell my head's been the last two years. I didn't give a damn about the case anymore, I've got bigger problems than that on my mind, and you, my good old buddy, are the answer to all of 'em."

I looked at him, wondering how much of this bullshit I was expected to swallow at one time.

"Think of it this way, Cliffie. You got nothing to lose, and you can buy a helluva lot of books for five grand."

It was almost uncanny: that's exactly what I was thinking, almost to the word. It was as if Slater had drilled a hole in my head and it had come spilling out.

"And while you're up there, you can double your money if you happen to stumble over that little book that Jeffords wants back so bad. Best deal you've had in a month of Sundays. You get five grand guaranteed, just for getting on the airplane. Get lucky and make yourself another five."

"What's the name of this book you're looking for?"

He got out his wallet and unfolded a paper. "You familiar with a thing called *The Raven?*"

"Seems like I've heard of it once or twice. It's a poem. Written by Edgar Allan Poe."

"This one was by some guy named Grayson. Does that make any sense to you?"

"Not so far."

"All I can tell you is what the client told me. I wrote it down real careful, went back over it half a dozen times, and it's still Greek."

20

"Can I see the paper?"

He gave it up reluctantly, like a father giving away a daughter at a wedding. The paper was fragile: it was already beginning to wear thin at the creases. I didn't say anything about that, just unfolded it gingerly and looked at what he had written. "Actually, I do know the book," I said. "It's a special edition of *The Raven,* published by the Grayson Press."

I sensed a sudden tension in the room, as if I had caught him stealing something. Our eyes met, but he looked away. "I don't understand this stuff," he said.

"What about it don't you understand?"

"What makes these things valuable . . . why one's worth more than the others. You're the expert, you tell me."

"Supply and demand," I said in a masterpiece of simplicity.

Slater was probably a lifelong Republican who was born knowing the law of supply and demand. It's the American way. If you want something I've got, the price will be everything the traffic will bear. If I've got the only known copy, you'd better get ready to mortgage the homestead, especially if a lot of other people want it too. What he didn't understand was the quirk of modern life that has inflated ordinary objects and hack talents into a class with Shakespeare, *Don Quixote,* and the Bible. But that was okay, because I didn't understand it either.

But I told him what I did know, what almost any good bookman would know. And felt, strangely, even as I was telling it, that Slater knew it too.

"The Grayson Press was a small publishing house that dealt in limited editions. I've heard they made some fabulous books, though I've never had one myself. Grayson was a master book designer who hand made everything, including his own type. He'd take a classic, something in the public domain like

21

The Raven, and commission a great artist to illustrate it. Then he'd publish it in a limited run, usually just a few hundred copies, numbered and signed by himself and the artist. In the trade these books are called instant rarities. They can be pretty nice collector's items, though purists have mixed feelings about them."

"Mixed feelings how?"

"Well, it's obvious they'll never take the place of the first edition. Poe's work becomes incidental to this whole modern process. The books become entities of their own: they're bought mainly by people who collect that publisher, or by people who just love owning elegant things."

He gave me a nod, as if waiting for elaboration.

"It's not an impossible book to find, Clydell, that's what I'm telling you. I think I could find your client one fairly easily. It might take a month or two, but I could find it, assuming the client's willing to spend the money."

"The client's willing to spend ten grand . . . which I'd be inclined to split with you fifty-fifty."

"The client's crazy. I could find her half a dozen copies for that and still give her half her money back."

"Don't bullshit me, Janeway. How do you find half a dozen copies of a rare book like that?"

"People call them instant rarities: that doesn't mean they're truly rare. My guess is that this Grayson *Raven* is becoming a fairly scarce piece, but I still think it can be smoked out."

"You guys talk in riddles. Rare, scarce . . . what the hell's the difference?"

"A scarce book is one that a dealer might see across his counter once every five or ten years. A rare book— well, you might spend your life in books and never see it. None of the Grayson books are really rare in that sense. They're scarce just by the fact that they were all limited to begin with. But they're all recent books, all done within the last forty years, so it's probably safe to say that most of them are still out there. We haven't lost them to fire, flood, war, and pestilence. As a matter of fact, I can tell you exactly how many copies there were—I've got a Grayson bibliography in my reference section."

I got the book and opened it, thumbing until I found what I wanted.

"'*The Raven and Other Poems,* by Edgar Allen Poe,'" I read: "'published by Darryl Grayson in North Bend, Washington, October 1949. Four hundred copies printed.' It was one of Grayson's first books. The last time I saw one in a catalog . . . I'm trying to think . . . it seems like the dealer was asking around five hundred dollars. That's pretty steep, actually, for a book like that, but I guess this Grayson was a pretty special bookman."

"And you really think you could get your mitts on half a dozen of these?"

"Well," I hedged, "I could find her one, I'm sure enough of that."

"How do you go about it? I mean, you just said you'd only get to see one of these every five or ten years."

"Across my counter. But I won't wait for that, I'll run an ad in the *AB*. That's a booksellers' magazine that goes to bookstores all over the country. Somebody's bound to have the damn thing: if they do, they'll drop me a postcard with a quote. I might get one quote or half a dozen: the quotes might range from two hundred up. I take the best deal, figure in a fair profit for myself, your client pays me, she's got her book."

"What if I decide to run this ad myself and cut you out of the action? Not that I would, you know, I'm just wondering what's to prevent it."

"Not a damn thing, except that *AB* doesn't take ads . from individuals, just book dealers. So you're stuck with me. *Old buddy,"* I added, a fairly nice jab.

It was lost on him: his head was in another world somewhere and he was plodding toward some distant goal line that he could only half see and I couldn't imagine.

"My client wants the book, only the one she wants ain't the one you're talking about."

"I'm not following you."

"This Grayson dude was supposed to've done another one in 1969."

"Another what?"

"Raven."

"Another edition of the same book? That doesn't sound right to me."

I thumbed through the bibliography, searching it out.

"There's no such book," I said after a while.

"How do you know that?"

"It would be in the bibliography."

"Maybe they missed it."

"They don't miss things like that. The guy who put this together was probably the top expert in the world on the Grayson Press. He spent years studying it: he collected everything they published. There's no way Grayson could've published a second *Raven* without this guy knowing about it."

"My client says he did."

"Your client's wrong, Clydell, what else can I tell you? This kind of stuff happens in the book world . . . somebody transposes a digit taking notes, 1949 becomes 1969, and suddenly people think they've got something that never existed in the first place."

"Maybe," he said, lighting another smoke.

A long moment passed. "So go get Rigby," he said

at the end of it. "Pick her up and cash your chips. At least we know that's real."

"Jesus. I can't believe I'm about to do this."

"Easiest money you ever made."

"You better understand one thing, Slater, and I'm tempted to put it in writing so there won't be any pissing and moaning later on. I'm gonna take your money and run. You remember I said that. I'm happier than I've been in years. I wouldn't go back to DPD for the chief's job and ten times the dough, and listen, don't take this personally, but I'd rather be a sex slave for Saddam Hussein than come to work for you. Can I make it any clearer than that?"

"Janeway, we're gonna love each other. This could be the start of something great."

3

For an hour after Slater left I browsed through the Grayson bibliography, trying to get the lay of the land. I had owned the book for about a year and had never had a reason to look at it. This is not unusual in the book business—probably 90 percent of the books you buy for your reference section are like that. Years pass and you never need it: then one day a big-money book comes your way and you really need it. There's a point involved and you can't guess, you've got to be sure, and the only way to be really sure is to have a bibliography on the book in question. In that shining moment the bibliography pays for itself five times over. Bibliographies are not for casual browsing or for bathroom reading. They are filled with all the technical jargon, symbols, and shorthand of the trade. The good ones are written by people with demons on their backs. Accuracy and detail are the twin gods, and the bibliographer is the slave. A bibliography will tell you if a book is supposed to contain maps or illustrations, and on what pages these may be found. It will describe the binding, will often contain photographs of the book and its title page, will even on occasion—when this is a telling point—give a page count in each gathering as the book was sewn together. If a printer makes an infinitesimal mistake—say the type is battered on a *d* on page 212, say the stem is fractured ever so slightly, like a hairline crack in a skier's fibula—it becomes the bibliographer's duty to point this out. It matters little unless the printer stopped the run and fixed it: then you have what is called in the trade a point. The bibliographer researches relentlessly: he gets into the printer's records if possible, trying to determine how many of these flawed copies were published and shipped before the flaw was discovered. Those copies then become true firsts, hotly sought (in the case of hot books) by collectors everywhere.

Bibliographies are among the most expensive books in the business. A struggling book dealer on East Colfax Avenue in Denver, Colorado, can't possibly buy them all when the asking price is often in three figures, so you pick and choose. I remembered when the Grayson book was published: it was announced with a half-page spread in the *AB*, an ad that promised everything you ever wanted to know about the Grayson Press. I had torn out the ad and stuck it in the book when it arrived. The title was *The Grayson Press, 1947–1969: A Comprehensive Bibliography*, by

Allan Huggins. The blurb on Huggins identified him as the world's top Grayson scholar and a collector of Grayson material for more than twenty years. The book looked substantial, one for the ages. It was thick, almost eight hundred pages, and it contained descriptions of every known book, paper, pamphlet, or poem ever issued by the Graysons. It had come in a signed limited edition at $195 and a trade edition at $85. To me it was a working book. I took the trade edition, and now, as was so often the case, I was damn glad I had it.

It was divided into four main sections. First there was a narrative biography of Darryl and Richard Grayson. This, combined with a history of their Grayson Press, took sixty pages. The second section was by far the biggest. It attempted the impossible, the author conceded, to catalog and annotate every scrap of Grayson ephemera, all the broadsides that the brothers had printed over a twenty-two-year career. This consumed more than four hundred pages of incredibly dense copy. The third section was called "Grayson Miscellany": this contained the oddball stuff—personal scraps, Christmas cards (the Graysons had for years printed their own cards, charming pieces that, today, are eagerly sought), special announcements, trivia. Even the commercial jobs they had taken on—posters, menus for restaurants, brochures for the Oregon Fish and Wildlife Department —all the unexciting ventures done purely for cash flow, are now avidly collected by Grayson people. There would never be a complete accounting: a fire had destroyed the printshop and all its records in 1969, and it's probably safe to say that previously unknown Grayson fragments will be turning up for a hundred years.

It was the final section, "Grayson Press Books,"

that was the highlight of the bibliography. Grayson had made his reputation as a publisher of fine books, producing twenty-three titles in his twenty-two years. The books were what made collecting the scraps worthwhile and fun: without the books, the Grayson Press might have been just another obscure printshop. But Darryl Grayson was a genius, early in life choosing the limited edition as his most effective means of self-expression. When Grayson began, a limited edition usually meant something. It meant that the writer had done a work to be proud of, or that a printing wizard like Darryl Grayson had produced something aesthetically exquisite. Scribners gave Ernest Hemingway a limited of *A Farewell to Arms,* 510 copies, signed by Hemingway in 1929 and issued in a slipcase. But in those days publishers were prudent, and it was Hemingway's only limited. Covici-Friede published *The Red Pony* in a small, signed edition in 1937, with the tiny Steinbeck signature on the back page. Perhaps the nearest thing to what Grayson would be doing two decades later was published by a noted printer and book designer, Bruce Rogers, in 1932: a limited edition of Homer's *Odyssey,* the translation by T. E. Lawrence. People can never get enough of a good thing, and around that time the Limited Editions Club was getting into high gear, producing some classy books and a few that would become masterpieces. The Henri Matisse *Ulysses,* published in the midthirties, would sell for eight or ten grand today, signed by Matisse and Joyce. Slater would find that interesting, but I didn't tell him. It would be too painful to watch him scratch his head and say, *Joyce who? . . . What did she do?*

Like almost everything else that was once fine and elegant, the limited edition has fallen on hard times. Too often now it's a tool, like a burglar's jimmy, used by commercial writers who are already zillionaires to pry another $200 out of the wallets of their faithful. There are usually five hundred or so numbered copies and a tiny lettered series that costs half again to twice as much. The books are slapped together as if on an assembly line, with synthetic leather the key ingredient. As often as not, the author signs loose sheets, which are later bound into the book: you can sometimes catch these literary icons sitting in airports between flights, filling the dead time signing their sheets. Two hundred, four hundred, six hundred . . . the rich get richer and God knows what the poor get. The whole process has a dank and ugly smell that would've horrified the likes of Bruce Rogers, Frederic Goudy, and Darryl Grayson. According to Huggins, Grayson was the last of the old-time print men, the printer who was also an artist, designer, and personal baby-sitter for everything that came off his press. Look for him no more, for his art has finally been snuffed by the goddamned computer. Grayson was the last giant: each of his books was a unique effort, a burst of creativity and tender loving care that real book people have always found so precious. The Thomas Hart Benton *Christmas Carol* had been Grayson's turning point: he had worked for a year on a new typeface that combined the most intriguing Gothic and modern touches and had engaged Benton to illustrate it. The book was sensational: old Charles Dickens was covered with new glory, said a *New York Times* critic (quoted in Huggins), the day the first copy was inspected by the master and found fit to ship. The *Times* piece was a moot point: the book was sold-out, even at $700, before the article appeared, and it mainly served to make the growing Grayson mystique known to a wider audience. People now scrambled to get on Grayson's subscription list, but few dropped off and Grayson refused to increase the size of his printings. The *Christmas Carol* was limited to five hundred, each signed in pencil by Benton and in that pale ink that would later become his trademark by Grayson. There were no lettered copies and the plates were destroyed after the run.

I skimmed through the history and learned that Darryl and Richard Grayson were brothers who had come to Seattle from Atlanta in 1936. Their first trip had been on vacation with their father. The old man had their lives well planned, but even then Darryl Grayson knew that someday he would live there. He had fallen in love with it—the mountains, the sea, the lush rain forests—for him the Northwest had everything. After the war they came again. They were the last of their family, two boys then in their twenties, full of hell and ready for life. From the beginning Darryl Grayson had dabbled in art: he was a prodigy who could paint, by the age of eight, realistic, anatomically correct portraits of his friends. It was in Atlanta, in high school, that he began dabbling in print as well. He drew sketches and set type for the school newspaper, and for an off-campus magazine that later failed. He came to believe that what he did was ultimately the most important part of the process. A simple alphabet, in her infinite variety, could be the loveliest thing, and the deadliest. Set a newspaper in a classic typeface and no one would read it: use a common newspaper type for a fine book and even its author would not take it seriously. The printer, he discovered, had the final say on how a piece of writing would be perceived. Those cold letters, forged in heat, sway the reading public in ways that even the most astute among them will never understand. Grayson understood, and he knew something else: that a printer need not be bound to the types offered by a foundry. A letter *Q* could be drawn a million ways, and he could create his own. The possibilities in those twenty-six letters were unlimited, as long as there were men of talent and vision coming along to draw them.

Personally, the Grayson brothers were the stuff of a Tennessee Williams play. They had left a multitude of broken hearts (and some said not a few bastard offspring) scattered across the Southern landscape. Both were eager and energetic womanizers: even today Atlanta remembers them as in a misty dream, their exploits prized as local myth. Darryl was rugged and sometimes fierce: Richard was fair and good-looking, giving the opposite sex (to its everlasting regret) a sense of fragile vulnerability. In the North the personal carnage would continue: each would marry twice, but the marriages were little more than the love affairs—short, sweet, sad, stormy. The early days in Seattle were something of a career shakedown. Darryl got a job in a local printshop and considered the possibilities; Richard was hired by a suburban newspaper to write sports and cover social events— the latter an ideal assignment for a young man bent on proving that ladies of blue blood had the same hot passions as the wide-eyed cotton-pickers he had left in Atlanta. Having proved it, he lost the job. Huggins covered this thinly: an academic will always find new ways to make the sex act seem dull, but I could read between the lines, enough to know that Richard Grayson had been a rake and a damned interesting fellow.

A year of this was enough. They moved out of town and settled in North Bend, a hamlet in the mountains twenty-five miles east of Seattle. With family money they bought twenty acres of land, a lovely site a few miles from town with woods and a brook and a long sloping meadow that butted a spectacular mountain. Thus was the Grayson Press founded in the wilderness: they built a house and a printshop, and Darryl Grayson opened for business on June 6, 1947.

From the beginning the Grayson Press was Darryl Grayson's baby. Richard was there because he was Darryl's brother and he had to do something. But it was clear that Huggins considered Darryl the major figure: his frequent references to "Grayson," without the qualifying first name, invariably meant Darryl, while Richard was always cited by both names. Richard's talent lay in writing. His first book was published by Grayson in late 1947. It was called *Gone to Glory,* an epic poem of the Civil War in Georgia. Energetic, lovely, and intensely Southern, it told in nine hundred fewer pages and without the romantic balderdash the same tragedy that Margaret Mitchell had spun out a dozen years earlier. Richard's work was said to have some of the qualities of a young Stephen Crane. Grayson had bound it in a frail teakwoodlike leather and published it in a severely limited edition, sixty-five copies. It had taken the book four years to sell out its run at $25. Today it is Grayson's toughest piece: it is seldom seen and the price is high (I thumbed through the auction records until I found one—it had sold, in 1983, for $1,500, and another copy that same year, hand-numbered as the first book out of the Grayson Press, had gone for $3,500). Huggins described it as a pretty book, crude by Grayson's later standards, but intriguing. Grayson was clearly a designer with a future, and Richard might go places in his own right. Richard's problems were obvious—he boozed and chased skirts and had sporadic, lazy work habits. He produced two more poems, published by Grayson in a single volume in 1949, then lapsed into a long silence. During the years

1950–54, he did what amounted to the donkey work at the Grayson Press: he shipped and helped with binding, he ran errands, took what his brother paid him, and filled his spare time in the hunt for new women. He freelanced an occasional article or short story, writing for the male pulp market under the pseudonyms Louis Ricketts, Paul Jacks, Phil Ricks, and half a dozen others. In 1954 he settled down long enough to write a novel, *Salt of the Earth,* which he decided to market in New York. E. P. Dutton brought it out in 1956. It failed to sell out its modest run but was praised to the rafters by such august journals as *Time* magazine and *The New Yorker.* Amazing they could find it in the sea of books when the publisher had done what they usually did then with first novels—nothing at all. The *New York Times* did a belated piece, two columns on page fifteen of the book review, just about the time the remainders were turning up on sale tables for forty-nine cents. But that was a good year, 1956: Grayson's *Christmas Carol* rolled off the press and Richard had found something to do. He wrote a second novel, *On a Day Like This,* published by Dutton in 1957 to rave reviews and continued apathy from the public. One critic was beside himself. A major literary career was under way and America was out to lunch. For shame, America! Both novels together had sold fewer than four thousand copies.

His next novel, though, was something else. Richard had taken a page from Harold Robbins and had produced a thing called *Warriors of Love.* He had abandoned Dutton and signed with Doubleday, the sprawling giant of the publishing world. The book was a lurid mix of sex and violence, a roaring success in the marketplace with eighty thousand copies sold in the first three weeks. The critics who had loved him were dismayed: the man at the *Times* drew the inevitable comparison with Robbins, recalling how in his first two books Robbins had seemed like a writer of some worth and how later he had callously sold out his talent for money. The only critic in Richard's eyes was his brother, though he'd never admit it or ask for Grayson's judgment. It was clear, from a few surviving pieces of correspondence, that Grayson had had nothing to say beyond a general observation that whoring—a noble and worthy calling in itself—ought to be confined to the bed and never practiced at the typewriter.

Richard never wrote another book. His big book continued making money throughout his life. It was filmed in 1960, and a new paperback release again sold in vast numbers, making an encore visit up the bestseller charts. Huggins viewed Richard as a tragic literary figure, lonely and sensitive and often mean, ever seeking and never finding some distant personal El Dorado. He continued to live in North Bend: had a house built on the property for his wife, who soon left him for another man. But there were long periods when he disappeared, absorbed into the decadent life of Seattle and Los Angeles and New York. In North Bend he filled his nights with classical music, so loud it rocked the timbers. Often he would drift down to the printshop, where he sat up all night composing poems and bits of odd prose for nothing more than his own amusement. Sometimes he would set these pieces in type, striking off one or two or half a dozen copies before dismantling the layout and staggering to bed at dawn. Old acquaintances might receive these in the mail, lyrical reminders of a time long past. One poem, containing four stanzas and lovingly printed on separate folio sheets in Grayson's newest typeface, was fished out of the garbage by a neighbor. It remains, today, the only known copy. An occasional piece might be sent to a childhood friend in Atlanta, a girl he once knew in Hollywood, an old enemy in Reno who, inexplicably, kept it, only to learn later that it was worth real money. These would arrive out of the blue, the North Bend postmark the only hint of a return address. In an apologia, Huggins described the bibliographer's nightmare of trying to include it all—there was simply no telling how many had been done and completely destroyed, and new scraps were turning up all the time. At least one Grayson collector had assembled more than two hundred unpublished poems and bits of prose, set in type by Richard in his odd moments. There had been talk of getting these writings published, if rights could be determined and the heirs could ever agree. A dual biography had been published three years ago: titled *Crossfire* with the subtitle *The Tragedies and Triumphs of Darryl and Richard Grayson,* it had been written by a woman named Trish Aandahl and brought out by the Viking Press. The Graysons died together in a fire that destroyed the printshop on October 14, 1969. Both had been drinking and apparently never knew what happened to them. Aandahl was cited by Huggins as the chief source of information on Grayson's final project, which had been destroyed in the fire. It had engaged him for years, off and on around other work. Reportedly he had designed two intricate, separate-though-compatible alphabets for the two parts, English and French. Based on a few surviving letters and the recollections of people who knew him, Huggins was able to pinpoint the French volume as Baudelaire's *Flowers of Evil.*

I remembered that Baudelaire had been one of Poe's biggest fans in his lifetime. In fact, Baudelaire had translated Poe's works into French.

4

I flew to Seattle the same afternoon. The job was a piece of cake, Slater said at the airport. The kid had no priors and had offered no resistance to the deputy who arrested her in the woods. No weapon had been found, either in Rigby's possession or in a search of the vicinity. The shooting was believed to be an act of panic, and Rigby had ditched the gun immediately afterward. At the bond hearing her lip had described her as a sweet kid committed to nonviolence. She was either Mother Teresa or Belle Starr, take your pick. I took my gun along for the ride. I wasn't about to shoot the kid, but when you've been a cop as long as I was, you don't leave home without it. I cleared it through the airline and tucked it in my bag, which I checked through luggage. I was also carrying a certified copy of the bench warrant and an affidavit describing in detail the Rigby woman's crime. I read it all through again on a bumpy two-hour flight.

Slater had arranged everything. I had a car waiting and a room at the Hilton downtown. My plan was short and sweet: I would bust the Rigby woman, park her for safekeeping in the Seattle jail, cut a swath through the Seattle bookstores tomorrow, and deliver her to New Mexico tomorrow night. The ghosts of Poe and Baudelaire were my companions, but I shook them off. I was not going to get into that, I promised myself. Poe sat beside me as the plane circled Seattle:

36

the gaunt little son of a bitch just wouldn't go away. The hell with you, I thought: I'm taking this woman back to New Mexico. Poe gave a crooked little smile and fastened his seat belt, and the plane dropped into the dense cloud cover and rumbled its way down-ward.

My contact was a guy named Ruel Pruitt. Slater had used him on several cases with Seattle angles and found him to be "a good guy at what he does. He hates the world," Slater said, "but he's like the damn invisible man, and there's nobody better at this cloak-and-dagger shit." I was to check into my hotel and wait in my room until Pruitt called, then go pick up the girl. After that I was on my own. I had never done any bounty-hunter work, but I knew the routine because I had cooperated with enough of them when I was a Denver cop. Some were okay, highly profession-al: then there were the goofballs right out of a Chuck Norris movie. All I needed for this job, Slater assured me, was a sturdy pair of handcuffs, and he had given me a set of good ones from the trunk of his car.

I got into Seattle at three-thirty Pacific time. Of course it was raining. Perry Como might think the bluest skies you ever saw were in Seattle, but all I've ever seen there is rain. I almost missed the hotel—the Seattle Hilton has its check-in lobby on the ninth floor, and only a garage entrance and elevator at street level. By four-thirty I was settled in my room, on the seventeenth floor with a window into rain-swept Sixth Avenue. At 5:05 the telephone rang. A velvety voice said, "Janeway?" and I said, "Yeah," and he said, "I'm in a bar near the Kingdome." He gave me an address and said he'd be outside in a blue Pontiac. He read off his plate number and I got it down the first time. "Don't let the door hit you in the ass on the way out," he said. "I got no idea how long this little dyke's gonna sit still."

Wonderful, I thought, listening to the dead connection—just the kind of charmer I'd expect to find working for Slater. I slipped the cuffs into my jacket pocket and ten minutes later I pulled up behind the Pontiac on First Avenue. The plate matched the number he'd given me, and I could see two people sitting inside. One of them, I thought, was a woman. The bar nestled at the foot of an elevated double-decker viaduct, looking like a cliff dwelling at Mesa Verde. It was triangular, squeezed in where the street slashed through on a kitty-corner layout. The rain was heavy now. I sat waiting for a break, but the rain in Seattle isn't like the rain in Denver: a guy could grow a long white beard waiting for it to slack off here. At 5:45 by the digital in my car, I decided to run for it. I flicked up my parking lights, got his attention, hopped out, and ran to his car. The doors were locked. Pruitt and his ladyfriend sat smoking, chatting as if I weren't there. I rapped on the backseat doorglass and Pruitt looked around, annoyed, and pointed to his custom seatcovers. I stood with water running down my nose and looked at them through the glass, said, "Son of a bitch," and hoped they could read my lips. Eventually he got the message: he leaned over the seat, found an old blanket, and spread it over his seatcovers. By the time he was ready to open the door, I was drenched.

I pushed the blanket roughly out of the way and flopped down on the backseat.

"Hey, cowboy," Pruitt said, "are you trying to piss me off?"

The woman giggled and we all looked at each other. Pruitt was an ugly pockmarked man. His face had been badly pitted long ago, the way you used to see on smallpox victims, and it gave him a look of rank decay. He smelled of cedarwood aftershave and peppermint, which on him had a faintly sickening effect.

He was in his late forties: his girlfriend was younger, a brassy-looking blonde. But it was Pruitt. who commanded the attention. His coat was open so I could see the gun he wore. He was an intimidator, I knew the type well, it had crossed my path often enough when I was a cop in Denver. Give him an inch and he'll walk all over you. He'll bully and embarrass you and make life miserable. I never give guys like him an inch, not even when I could see, like now, the eyes of a killer.

"Where the hell did Slater dig you up?" he said.

"He used to date my mother. I hear he found you the same way."

The blonde gave a small gasp: one didn't, I was supposed to believe, talk to the man in that tone of voice. Pruitt's eyes burned holes in my head. "We've got a real smart-ass here, Olga. Ten thousand guys in Denver and Slater sends me a smart-ass."

"Tell you what," I said evenly. "Let's start over. I'll go back to my hotel and dry out, have a drink, get a good dinner, maybe find myself a friend of the opposite sex to help me pass the time. You sit here in the rain, follow Slater's girl, and call me when you want to pass the torch. How does two weeks from tomorrow sound?"

"A real smart-ass. You're getting water all over my car, for Christ's sake, didn't your fucking mother teach you anything? Where were you raised, in a back alley behind some Denver whorehouse?"

"As a matter of fact, yeah. I seem to've missed all the advantages Mrs. Hitler gave you."

He burned me with his killer eyes. The blonde seemed to be holding her breath, waiting for him to crawl over the seat and kill me.

"Just for the record," I said pleasantly, "I'm about this close to pushing what's left of your face right through that windshield. Do we understand each other yet, Gertrude? . . . or do I have to take that gun away from you and empty it up your ass?"

We sat and stared. I was ready for him if he came, and I thought he might. The rage simmered in the car and fogged up the windshield. In the end, he had a higher priority than teaching a cowboy from Denver who was boss.

"You want to tell me about this woman?" I said.

"You've got her picture. She's in there, it's your job now."

"I'll tell you when it's my job. If I have any more trouble with you, I'm out of here, and you and Slater can figure it out by yourselves."

"Shit."

I couldn't improve on that, so I let it ride. We sat in the car for a few minutes without talking. "Go inside," he said to Olga as if I weren't there. "See if our pigeon's getting lonely." She got out and ran through the rain, disappearing into the bar. Pruitt sat in silence, his collar turned up to his ears, his eyes riveted on the neon lights in the window. He lit a cigarette but put it out without comment when I cracked the window and the rain came in on his seats.

"Let's get this over with," he said. He got out in the rain and walked to the bar. I trailed along behind him. He tapped the hood of an old roadster parked at the front door—Rigby's, I was left to conclude. It was a true jalopy, with current Washington plates and bad tires. We went inside. Pruitt didn't want to go past the dark aisle that led into the barroom. We stood there a moment in the pitch, trying to adjust our eyes. It was still early, but already the bar was crowded with happy-hour zombies and refugees from various wars. Music was playing loudly on the jukebox: "Sea of Love." Maybe thirty people were at the bar and at tables scattered around it. The bartender was a fat

40

man who looked like Jackie Gleason. Olga sat on a stool at the far end. Two stools away was Eleanor Rigby.

"There she is," Pruitt said.

We stood for another moment.

"Is it your job yet, or am I supposed to stand here all night?"

"Go on, blow."

He motioned to Olga, who left an untouched beer and came toward us. "I'll probably meet you again sometime," he said to me. "The circumstances will be different."

"I'm in the Denver phone book, if you ever get out that way."

"Maybe I'll make a point of it."

Asshole, I said, not entirely under my breath.

I ambled to the bar and sat on the only empty stool, directly across from Rigby. The bartender came; I ordered a beer and sucked the foam off. Ten yards away, Eleanor Rigby had another of whatever she was drinking. I watched her without looking. I looked at two guys having a Seahawks argument and I watched her with peripheral vision. I watched the bartender polishing glasses and I looked at her. She looked bone weary, as if she might fall asleep at the bar. I stole a frontal look. There wasn't much danger in it, she was just another good-looking girl in a bar and I was a lonely, horny guy. She'd be used to gawkers, she must get them all the time. She was twenty-one, I guessed, with thick hair pinned back and up. "Eleanor Rigby." I shook my head and tried to clear away the Victorian spinster the song conjured up. I wondered what it does to people, being named after something like that and having to carry that baggage all your life.

I was in it now, committed to the deed. I told myself she was nothing more than a cool five grand, waiting to be picked up. I wasn't sure yet how to take her—probably later, on the street. I didn't like the smell of the crowd in the bar. It was a blue-collar crowd, a sports crowd, and there's always some ditz ready to rise up out of a crowd like that and defend a pretty woman's honor no matter what. Never mind my court papers, never mind the cheap-looking ID Slater had given me as I left. The ID identified me as an operative of CS Investigations of Denver, but there was no picture of me on it and it gave me no authority beyond what Slater had, what anybody has. What I could use right now was a state-issued license with my kisser plastered all over it. But the state of Colorado doesn't require its private detectives or its psychotherapists to have special licenses: all a bozo needs is an eight-by-twelve office, the gift of gab, and the power of positive thinking. I was making what amounted to a citizen's arrest, and I had the law on my side because she had jumped bail and was now a fugitive. But if you have to explain that to a crowd in a bar, you're already in trouble.

I nursed my beer and waited. She sat across the waterhole, a gazelle unaware of the lion's approach. The stool had opened to her immediate left. I was tempted, but a shark moved in and filled it. Story of my damn life: the studs make the moves while I sit still and consider the universe, and I go home to a cold and lonely bed. I thought about Rita McKinley and wondered where she was and what she was doing with herself. In a way that was difficult to explain, Eleanor Rigby looked a little like Rita, like a younger model. Actually, she looked nothing like Rita at all. The stud to her left was already hitting on her. In happier times she might've been thrilled, but now she just looked tired and bored. The bartender drifted down and asked if I wanted another brew. I said I was okay, I'd send up a flare when the need became great. At the front table the Seahawks flap was still raging, a real-life commercial for Miller Lite. Across the way, Mr. America said something and gestured to her drink. She shook her head and tried to go on with her life, but he remained doggedly in her face. She swished her ice and sipped the watery remains while her hero worked his way through the first twelve chapters of his life story. He was one of those loud farts, the kind you can't insult: he probably couldn't be killed, except with a silver bullet. He was halfway to his first million and nobody to share it with. I couldn't imagine any interesting woman falling for that line, but interesting probably wasn't what he was after. The guy was a moron, either that or I was. I didn't have time to dwell on it because just then Eleanor Rigby got up and left him flat, halfway between the big deal he had just pulled off and all the bigger ones coming down the pike.

I liked her for that. In a way it was a shame I was going to have to bust her. I left two bills on the bar and followed her down the hall to the johns. She disappeared into the ladies'. I checked to make sure there was no other way out, then I drifted back into the bar and took up a position where I couldn't miss her. I was standing near the only window, which looked out into the street. Heavy black drapes were closed over it, but I parted them slightly so I could see out. I was staring at her car, my hand suspended between the curtains. Someone was sitting behind the wheel. I saw a light, very faint: he was looking for something, rummaging through the glove compartment. He put on his hat and got out in the rain. Pruitt. He stood for a moment, oblivious to the rain that had bothered him so much before. He gave her door a vicious kick, leaving a dent six inches across. I saw the snap of a blade, a wicked stiletto, and he bent over and poked a hole in her tire. Then he walked away and I watched the car go flat.

Just then she came out of the hallway. She walked past, so close I could've touched her. I let her go, following her out through the narrow foyer. By the time I got to the door she had run to her car. I stood watching her through the tiny pane of glass. Yes, she had seen the flat tire: she was sitting in her car doing nothing. I could imagine her disgust. Time for Lochinvar to appear, as if by magic: a knight with a bouquet in one hand and a set of shackles in the other. Bust her now, I thought, walking out into the rain: bust her, Janeway, don't be an idiot. But there was Poe, grim and pasty-faced, lurking in the dark places under the viaduct.

I stopped at the curb and pointed to her tire. She cracked the window ever so slightly.

"You got a flat."

"No kidding."

"Hey," I said in my kindest, gentlest voice. "I can't get any wetter than this. Gimme your keys, I'll get out your jack and change it for you."

5

She sat in the car while I changed her tire. I jiggled her up, took off her lugs, and hummed a few bars of "Singin' in the Rain." Her spare tire was like the others: it had been badly used in at least three wars, the alleged tread frequently disappearing into snarls of frayed steel. I hauled it out of the trunk and put it gently on the curb. The street was as deserted as a scene from some midfifties end-of-the-world flick, but it fooled me not. Pruitt, I thought, was still out there somewhere, I just couldn't see him. If this were *Singin' in the Rain,* he'd come on down and we'd do a little soft-shoe routine. I'd be Gene Kelly and we'd get Eleanor Rigby out of the car to play Debbie Reynolds. Pruitt would be Donald O'Connor, tap-dancing his way up the side of the viaduct and out onto the highway, where he'd get flattened by a semi. Suddenly I knew, and I didn't know how, that there was a joker in the deck: Slater hadn't hired me for my good looks after all. A far greater purpose was hidden under the surface: what had been presented as an interesting side dish was in fact the main course, and the big question was *why the camouflage?* I was told to play lead in *Singin' in the Rain,* and now, well into the opening number, I learned it was really *West Side Story* we were doing. In a minute Pruitt would come down and we'd do one of those crazy numbers where the good guys sing and dance with the hoods, just before they all yank out their zip guns and start zipping each other into hoodlum heaven. I scanned the street again, searching for some sign of life, but even Poe had disappeared into the murky shadows from whence he'd come.

I tossed Rigby's flat tire into her trunk and contemplated the spare. I resisted the inclination to laugh, but it was a close call: she must've searched the world to've found five tires that bad. *I'll take your four worst tires and save the best of my old ones for a spare.* You gotta be kidding, lady, there ain't no best one. *Oh. Then throw away the three worst and give me whatever's left.* You know the routine, Jack Nicholson did it in a restaurant in *Five Easy Pieces:* four over well, cooked to a frazzle, and hold the tread. Pruitt didn't need a knife, a hairpin would've done it for him. I hummed "I Feel Pretty" in a grotesque falsetto as I fitted the tire onto the wheel, but it didn't seem to brighten the moment. Crunch time was coming, and I still didn't know what I was going to do. It was that goddamned Poe, the wily little bastard: he had cast his lot with Slater and was waxing me good. That one line about Baudelaire in the Huggins bibliography had been the hook, and I was too much the bookman to shake it free.

Was it possible that Darryl Grayson had been working on a two-book set, Poe and Baudelaire, English and French, at the time of his death, and that one copy of the Poe had been completed and had survived? If you read "Dear Abby" faithfully, as I do, you know that anything is possible. What would such a book be worth, quote-unquote, in today's marketplace? . . . A unique piece with a direct link to the deaths of two famous bookmen, snatched from the blaze just as the burning roof caved in. Was it truly the best and the brightest that Darryl Grayson could make? If so, it was worth a fair piece of change. Ten thousand, I thought, Slater even had that right: it was worth just about ten grand on the high end. But with one-of-a-kind pieces, you never know. I could envision an auction with all the half-mad Grayson freaks in attendance. If two or three of them had deep pockets, there was no telling how high such a book might go.

I tightened the last of the lugs with my fingers. Not much time left now, and it wasn't going to end with the whole company out in the street singing "Maria." I needed some quick inspiration and got it—the thin point of my filing-cabinet key shoved into her air valve brought the spare hissing down flat. She didn't hear a thing: the rain was drumming on her roof and her window was up. I got up and walked around the car, looking at her through the glass. She cracked the window and gave me a hopeful smile.

"The news is not good. Your spare's flat too."

She didn't say anything: just took a deep breath and stared at her knuckles as she gripped the wheel. I fished for a legitimate opening, any bit of business that might make her trust a half-drowned stranger on a dark and rainy night. "I could call you a cab," I said, and my luck was holding—she shook her head and said, "I don't have enough money left for a cab." That was a cue, but I didn't leap at it like a sex-starved schoolboy, I let it play out in a long moment of silence. "I could loan you the money," I said cheerfully, and I thought I saw her doubts begin to vanish in the rain. "Hey, you can mail it back to me when you're flush again." She gave a dry little laugh and said, "That'll probably be never." I shrugged and said, "You're on a bad roll, that's all. Look, I don't want you to get any wrong ideas, but I've got a car right across the street. I could drive you home . . . as long as you don't live in Portland or someplace."

She seemed to be considering it. I knew I didn't look like anything out of the Seattle social register, so sincerity was probably the best I could hope for. I leaned in close, crossed my arms against her window, and talked to her through the crack. "Look, miss, you can't stay out here all night. If you're broke, I'll loan you the money for a place . . . a cheap place, okay? . . . no strings attached. Call it my good deed for the year, chalk it up to my Eagle Scout days. If you're worried about me, I can understand that, I'll slip you the money through the window and give you an address where you can send it back to me when your ship comes in. What do you say?"

"I thought Good Samaritans were extinct."

"Actually, I'm your guardian angel," I said, trying for a kidding tone to put her at ease.

"Well, you've sure been a long time coming."

"We never show up until the darkest possible moment."

"Then you're right on time."

"I could spare thirty dollars. You won't get much of a room for that, but it's better than sitting in your car all night."

She leaned close to the crack and studied my face. "Why would you do something like that?"

"Because you look like you've just lost your last friend. Because I know you'll pay me back. Because once or twice in my life, I've been so far down it looked like up to me."

"Richard Fariña."

I didn't say anything, but I was surprised she had made that connection.

"That's the title of a book by Richard Fariña. *Been Down So Long It Looks Like Up to Me.*"

I said, "Oh," and pretended not to know it. I'd have to watch that, keep the literary metaphors out of my talk until I saw where we were heading.

"So what do you say?" I asked.

"I won't take your money . . . but, yeah, maybe a ride. . . . I could use a ride if you're going my way."

"I'm sure I am."

I told her to stay put and I'd drive up close so she wouldn't get wet. Then I had her, snuggled in the seat beside me. No wonder monsters like Ted Bundy had it so easy. That thought crossed her mind too and she said, "I guess I'm a sitting duck if you're some wacko from a funny farm." She shrugged as if even that wouldn't matter much. I gave her the big effort, a smile I hoped was reassuring. "Ma'am, I don't blame you at all for thinking that, I'd be thinking it myself if I were in your shoes. All I can tell you is, you're as safe with me as you'd be in a police station."

I hoped this wasn't laying it on too thick, but it didn't seem to bother her. "My name's Janeway."

Her hand was warm and dry as it disappeared into mine. "Eleanor Rigby."

I was surprised that she'd use her real name: she probably hadn't had time yet to get used to being a fugitive.

"Eleanor Rigby," I repeated. "You mean like . . ." and I hummed the staccato counterpoint.

She tensed visibly at the melody. For a moment I was sure she was going to get out and walk away in the rain. "You've probably heard that a million times," I said, trying to make light of it. "I imagine you're sick of it by now." Still she said nothing: she seemed to be trying to decide about me all over again. "Look, I didn't mean anything by that. I grew up on Beatles music, it was just a natural connection I made. I sure wasn't relating you to the woman in the song."

Her eyes never left my face. Again I was certain I was going to lose her, she seemed that ready to break and run. "We can start all over if you want. My name's Janeway, and I'll still loan you the thirty if you'd rather do it that way."

She let out a long breath and said, "No, I'm fine."

"And your name is Eleanor Rigby, I understand. It's a great name, by the way. Really. How'd you come to get it?"

"The same way you got yours, I imagine. I come from a family of Rigbys and my father liked the name Eleanor."

"That's as good a way as any."

Now she looked away, into the rainy night. "This is going to be a lot of trouble for you."

"Trouble's my middle name. Which way do you want to go?"

"Get on the freeway and go south. Stay in the left

lane. When you see I-90, branch off to the east, take that."

I turned the corner and saw Interstate 5, the cars swirling past in the mist. I banked into the freeway, glancing in my mirror. No one was there . . . only Poe, interred in the backseat.

"You'd better turn that heater on," she said. "God, you're so wet."

"I will, soon's the car warms up."

She gave me a look across the vast expanse of my front seat. "I guess you're wondering what I was doing in a bar if I was so broke."

"I try not to wonder about stuff like that."

"This is the end of a long day, in a very long week, in a year from hell. I was down to my last five dollars. The only thing I could think of that I could buy with that was a margarita. I had two and killed the five. Sometimes I do crazy things like that."

"So now what do you do? Do you have a job?"

She shook her head.

"At least you're not stranded here. I couldn't help noticing the Washington plates on your car."

"No, I'm not stranded. Just lost on planet Earth."

"Aren't we all. I'm not so old that I don't remember what that feels like."

"You're not so old," she said, looking me over. "You must be all of thirty."

I laughed. "I'm not doing you that big a favor. I'll be forty years old before you know it."

"Almost ready for the nursing home."

"You got it. Where're we going, by the way?"

"Little town called North Bend."

Ah, I thought: Grayson country.

She sensed something and said, "Do you know North Bend?"

"Never been there."

"I'm not surprised. It's just a wide place in the

road, but it happens to be where my family lives. You know what they say about families. When you come home broken and defeated, they've got to take you in."

She was still tense and I didn't know how to breach that. Food might do it: I'd seen that happen more than once.

"Have you had dinner?"

She looked at me. "Now you're going to buy me dinner? Jeez, you must really be my guardian angel."

"So what do you say?"

"I feel like the last survivor of the Donner party. That means yes, I'm starving."

I saw an intersection coming up, filled with neon promise.

"That's Issaquah," she said. "There's a Denny's there. It was one of my hangouts when I was in high school. Can you stand it?"

I banked into the ramp.

"You look terrible," she said. "I don't suppose you have a change of clothes. Maybe they'll let you in if you comb your hair."

"If I get thrown out of a Denny's, it'll be a bad day at Black Rock."

Inside, we settled into a window booth. I ordered steaks for both of us, getting her blessing with a rapturous look. I got my first look at her in good light. She was not beautiful, merely a sensational young woman with world-class hair. Her hair sloped up in a solid wall, rising like Vesuvius from the front of her head. It was the color of burnt auburn, thick and lush: if she took it down, I thought, it would reach far down her back. Her nose was slightly crooked, which had the strange effect of adding to her appeal. She could stand out in a crowd without ever being a pinup. Her looks and ready wit probably made job-hunting easy, if she ever got around to such things.

"So what do you do for a living?" I asked.

"Little of this, little of that. Mostly I've been a professional student. I'll probably still be going to college when I'm thirty. I graduated from high school at sixteen and I've been in and out of one college or another ever since. I go for a while, drop out, drift around, go somewhere else, drop out again. I transfer across state lines and lose half my credits, then I have to start up again, learning the whole boring curriculum that I learned last year and already knew anyway, just to get even again. Schools shouldn't be allowed to do that—you know, arbitrarily dismiss half your credits just so they can pick your pocket for more tuition. But that's life, isn't it, and I'm sure it's nobody's fault but my own. It drives my family nuts, the way I live, but we are what we are. My trouble is, I've never quite figured out what I am. This is a mighty lonely planet, way off in space."

It was the second time she had said something like that. I was beginning to wonder if she had been star-crossed by her name, doomed to play out the destiny of a lonely woman whose entire life could be told in two short stanzas.

"I do what I can, but then I get restless," she said. "My mom and dad help out when they can, but they don't have any money either. For the most part it's on my shoulders."

"So what do you do?" I asked again.

"I'm versatile as hell. I know a lot of things, some of them quite well—just survival skills, but enough to buy something to eat and a room at the Y. I can work in a printshop. I wait a dynamite table. I mix a good drink—once I got fired for making 'em too good. I type like a tornado and I don't make mistakes. I'm a great temporary. I've probably worked in more offices as a Kelly girl than all the other Kellys put together. I could get in the *Guinness Book of World Records.* Do they pay for that?"

"I don't think so."

"Probably not. They make a fortune off us freaks and pay us nothing."

"You could probably get on full-time in one of those offices if you wanted. Law office maybe. Become a paralegal. Then go to law school."

"I'd rather lie down in a pit of snakes. I find the nine-to-five routine like slow poison. It poisons the spirit, if you know what I mean. About three days of that's about all I can stand. But that's most likely what I'll do tomorrow—get my dad to take me into town, go on a temporary, fill in somewhere till I've got enough money for a few tires and some gas, then drift away and do it all over again."

There was a pause, not long, while she seemed to consider something. "If I feel lucky, I might look for books tomorrow."

I tried not to react too quickly, but I didn't want to let it get past me. "What do books have to do with working in an office?"

"Nothing: that's the point. The books keep me out of the office."

I stared at her.

"I'm a bookscout." She said this the way a woman in Georgia might say *I'm a Baptist,* daring you to do something about it. Then she said, "I look for books that are underpriced. If they're drastically under-priced, I buy them. Then I sell them to a book dealer I know in Seattle."

I milked the dumb role. "And you make money at this?"

"Sometimes I make a lot of money. Like I said, it depends on how my luck's running."

"Where do you find these books?"

"God, everywhere! Books turn up in the craziest places . . . junk stores, flea markets . . . I've even found them in Dumpsters. Mostly I look in book-stores themselves."

"You look for books in bookstores . . . then sell 'em to other bookstores. I wouldn't imagine you could do that."

"Why not? At least sixty percent of the used-book dealers in this world are too lazy, ignorant, and cheap to know what they've got on their own shelves. They wouldn't invest in a reference book if their lives depended on it. They might as well be selling spare parts for lawn mowers, that's all books mean to them. Don't get me wrong: I love these people, they have saved my life more times than you would believe. I take their books from them and sell them to one of the other book dealers—"

"One of the forty percent."

"One of the *ten* percent; one of the guys who wants the best of the best and isn't afraid to pay for it. You bet. Take from the dumb and sell to the smart."

"That's gonna be hard to do tomorrow, though, if you've got no money."

She opened her purse. "Actually, I've got a little over three dollars in change. Pennies, nickels, and dimes."

"I don't think you could buy much of a book with that."

She finished her soup and thought it over. "I'll tell you a story, and you see what you think about it. I was down and out in L.A. I was broke, just about like this, down to my last bit of pocket change. So I hit the bookstores. The first one I went to had a copy of *Let Us Now Praise Famous Men*. You ever hear of that book?"

I shook my head, lying outrageously.

"A guy named James Agee wrote it and another guy

named Walker Evans illustrated it with photographs. This was a beautiful first edition, worth maybe three or four hundred dollars. The dealer was one of those borderline cases—he knows just enough to be dangerous, and he had marked it ninety-five. He knew he had *something,* he just wasn't sure what. I figured my friend in Seattle might pay me one-fifty for it, but of course I didn't have the wherewithal to break it out of there. I also knew it wouldn't last another day at that price—the first real bookman who came through the door would pick it off. I drifted around the store and looked at his other stuff." She sipped her water. "You ever hear of Wendell Berry?"

The poet, I wanted to say. But I shook my head.

"The poet," she said. "His early books are worth some money, and there was one in this same store, tucked in with the belles lettres and marked three dollars. I counted out my last pennies and took it: went around the corner and sold it to another dealer for twenty dollars. Went back to the first store and asked the guy if he'd hold the Agee for me till the end of the day. The guy was a hardass: he said he'd hold it if I put down a deposit, nonreturnable if I didn't show up by closing time. I gave him the twenty and hit the streets. My problem was time. It was already late afternoon, I had only about an hour left. What I usually do in a case like that is sell some blood, but they'll only take a pint at a time and I was still seventy dollars short. So I worked up a poor-little-girl-far-from-home hustle. It was the first time I'd ever done that, but you know what? . . . it's easy. You guys are the easiest touches; I guess if you're a young woman and not particularly hideous, you really can make men do anything. I just walked in cold off the street and asked twenty shopkeepers in a row if they could let me have two dollars for something to eat. One or two of them snarled and said, 'Get out of my life, you effing little deadbeat,' but you get a thick skin after the first two or three and then it all rolls off. One guy gave me a ten. In a café on the corner I got money not only from the owner but from half the guys at the counter. I could probably make a living doing that, but it has a kind of self-demeaning effect, except in emergencies. You don't learn anything, and one day you wake up and you've lost your looks and can't do it anymore. So I made a pact with myself, I would never do it again unless I had to. I got back to the store right on the button and bought my book. And my luck was running like a charm, I didn't even have to call Seattle, I found a guy in east L.A. who gave me more than I'd counted on—one seventy-five. He specialized in photo books and I thought he might be good for this one."

"That's amazing."

"Yeah, but that's not the end of the story. Even while he was paying me, I noticed a box of books on his counter, new stuff he'd just gotten in. On top of the stack was a first edition that damn near stopped my heart. I finally worked up my courage and asked him, 'Hey, mister, whatcha gonna want for this?' He got a stern, fatherly look on his face and said, 'I think that's a pretty nice book, sweetie, I'm gonna want twenty to thirty bucks for it.' And I almost died trying to pay him with a straight face. The next day I called my friend in Seattle and he sent me a good wholesale price, four hundred dollars. And there I was, back in the chips."

"Incredible," I said, and I meant it. I didn't know many bookscouts who could pull off something like that.

"Oh, yeah! . . . yeah! And *so* much more fun than working in some accountant's office or typing dictation for a lawyer. I mean, how can you compare *typing* all day with bookscouting. The only trouble with it is, it's not reliable. You can go weeks without making a real score, and the rest of the time you're picking up small change. So it all depends on how I'm feeling. If I think I'm gonna be lucky, I'll hit the stores: if not, I'll go to work for Ms. Kelly again."

I knew I shouldn't ask, shouldn't be that interested in the specifics. But I had to.

"What was that book, that was worth so much?"

She grinned, still delighted at the memory and savoring each of the title's four words. *"To . . . Kill . . . a . . . Mock-ing-bird!"*

I tried for a look that said, *It means nothing to me,* but what I wanted to do was close my eyes and suffer. Jesus, I thought . . . *oh, man!* That book is simply not to be found. Stories like that are what make up the business. A dealer in photography hands a pretty ragamuffin a thousand-dollar book, so desirable it's almost like cash, and all because he hasn't taken the time to learn the high spots of modern fiction.

The waitress brought our food. Eleanor reached for the salt and I saw the scar on her wrist. It was a straight slash, too even to have been done by accident.

At some time in her past, Eleanor Rigby had tried to kill herself, with a razor blade.

"So," she said, in that tone people use when they're changing the subject, "where were you heading when I shanghaied you in the rain?"

"Wherever the wind blows."

"Hey, that's where I'm going! Are you married?"

"I don't think so."

"Ever been?"

"Not that I can remember. Who'd put up with me?"

"Probably one or two girls I know. D'you have any bad habits?"

"Well, I don't smoke."

"Beat your women?"

"Not if they do what I tell them."

She laughed. "God, a nonsmoker with a boss complex. I may marry you myself. Don't laugh, Mr. Janeway, I've lived my whole life on one whim after another. Have you ever been at loose ends?"

"Once, I think, about twenty years ago."

"Well, I live that way. My whole life's a big loose end. I go where the wind blows. If the natives are friendly, I stay awhile and warm myself in the sun. So where's the wind blowing you?"

"Phoenix," I said—the first place that popped into my mind.

"Oh, lovely. Lots of sun there—not many books, though, from what I've heard. I'd probably have to work for a living, which doesn't thrill me, but nothing's perfect. How would you like some company?"

"You've decided to go to Phoenix?"

"Why not, I've never been there. Why couldn't I go if I wanted to?"

She was looking right down my throat. She really is like Rita, I thought: she had that same hard nut in her heart that made it so difficult to lie to her.

"What do you suppose would happen," she said, "if we just turned around and headed south. Strangers in the night, never laid eyes on each other till an hour ago. Just go, roll the dice, see how long we could put up with each other."

"Would you do that?"

"I might." She thought about it, then shook her head. "But I can't."

"Ah."

"I've been known to do crazier things. I've just got something else on my agenda right now."

58

"What's that?"

"Can't talk about it. Besides, it's too long a story. My whole life gets messed up in it and I don't think you've got time for that."

"I've got nothing but time."

"None of us has that much time."

She was feeling better now, I could see it in her face. Food, one of the most intimate things after the one most intimate thing, had worked its spell again. "Oh, I needed that," she said. "Yeah, I was hungry."

"I'm glad you decided to stick around."

"Sorry about that. I just have a bad reaction to that song."

"I think it's a great song."

"I'm sure it is. But it gives me the willies."

"Why would it do that?"

"Who's to say? Some things you can't explain."

Then, as if she hadn't been listening to her own words, she said, "I've got a stalker in my life."

She shook her head. "Forget I said that. I'm tired . . . at the end of my rope. Sometimes I say things . . ."

I stared at her, waiting.

"Sometimes he calls me and plays that song."

"Do you know who he is?"

"I know him by sight, I don't know his name. Obviously he knows mine." She shivered deeply. "I don't talk about this. But you've been such a dear . . . I can't have you thinking I'm crazy."

"Have you called the cops?"

She shook her head. "Cops don't seem to be able to do much with people like that."

"If he's harassing you on the phone, they can catch him. The time it takes to trace a call these days is pretty short; damn near no time at all."

"So they'd catch him. They'd bring him in and

charge him with something minor, some nothing charge that would only stir him up."

"How long has he been doing this?"

She took a deep breath, let it out slowly, and said, "Not long, a few weeks. But it seems like years."

"You can't put up with that. You've got to protect yourself."

"Like . . . get a gun, you mean?"

I let that thought speak for itself.

She sighed. "I've never fired a gun in my life."

The strange thing was, I believed her.

"Do you have any idea what he wants?"

"I think I know what he wants. But just now I would like to please change the subject. Let's get back to happy talk." She cocked her head as if to say, *Enough, already.* "Those wet clothes must feel awful."

"I've been wet so long it feels like dry to me. What was that guy's name?"

"That's more like it. His name was Richard Fariña."

"Is his book worth anything?"

"Mmmm, yeah," she said in a singsong voice. "Hundred dollars maybe. I wouldn't kick it out in the rain."

The waitress came and left the check.

Eleanor looked at me hard. "So tell me who you really are and what you're doing. I mean, you appear out of the night, kindness personified, you walk into my life when I've never been lonelier, you're going where the wind blows but you don't have a change of clothes. What are you running away from?"

"Who said I'm running away?"

"We're all running away. Some of us just don't get very far. Yours must be some tragic love affair for you to run with only the clothes on your back. What was her name?"

"Rita," I said, suddenly inspired. "It's funny, she was a book person, a lot like you."

"No kidding!"

"The same only different." I fiddled with the check. "She'd love that story you told me."

"The book world is full of stories like that. Books are everywhere, and some of them are valuable for the craziest reasons. A man gets put on an Iranian hit list. His books go up in value. A guy writes a good book, a guy writes a bad book. Both are worth the same money on the collector's market. A third guy writes a great book and nobody cares at all. The president of the United States mentions in passing that he's a Tom Clancy fan and suddenly this guy's book shoots into the Hemingway class as a collectible. And that president is Ronald *Reagan*, for God's sake. Does that make any sense?"

"Not to me it doesn't."

"It defies logic, but that's the way it is today. People latch onto some new thing and gorge themselves on it, and the first guy out of the gate becomes a millionaire. Maybe Clancy *is* a master of techno-babble. Do you care? To me he couldn't create a character if his damn life depended on it. You watch what I say, though, people will be paying a thousand dollars for that book before you know it. Then the techno-babble rage will pass. It'll fade faster than yesterday's sunset and the focus will move on to something else, probably the female private detective. And that'll last a few years, till people begin to gag on it. Meanwhile, it takes a real writer like Anne Tyler half a career to catch on, and James Lee Burke can't even find a publisher for ten years."

"How do you learn so much so young?"

"I was born in it. I've been around books all my life. When I was fourteen, I'd ditch class and thumb my way into Seattle and just lose myself in the book-stores. So I've had six or seven years of good hard experience. It's like anything else—eventually you meet someone who's willing to show you the ropes. Then one day you realize you know more about it than your teacher does—you started out a pupil, like Hemingway with Gertrude Stein, and now you've taken it past anything the teacher can do with it. And it comes easier if you've had a head start."

"Starting young, you mean."

She nodded. "At sixteen I had read more than a thousand books. I knew all the big names in American lit, so it was just a matter of putting them together with prices and keeping up with the new hotshots. But it's also in my blood. I got it from my father: it was in his blood. It took off in a different direction with him, but it's the same stuff when you get to the heart of it. Books . . . the wonder and magic of the printed word. It grabbed my dad when he was sixteen, so he knows where I'm coming from."

"Does your father deal in books?"

"He wouldn't be caught dead. No, I told you his interest went in another direction. My dad is a printer."

She finished her coffee and said, "I'd give a million dollars if I had it for his experience. My father was present at the creation."

I looked at her, lost.

"He was an apprentice at the Grayson Press, in this same little town we're going to. I'm sure you've never heard of the Grayson Press, not many people have. But you can take it from me, Mr. Janeway, Grayson was the most incredible book genius of our time."

6

There wasn't much to see of North Bend, especially on a dark and rainy night. I got off at Exit 31 and Eleanor directed me through the town, which had long since rolled up its awnings for the night. The so-called business district was confined to a single block, the café, bar, and gas station the only places still open. But it was deceptive: beyond the town were narrow roads where the people lived, where the Graysons had once lived, where Eleanor Rigby had grown from a little girl into a young woman. We went out on a road called Ballarat and soon began picking up numbered streets and avenues, most of them in the high hundreds. It was rural by nature, but the streets seemed linked to Seattle, as if some long-ago urban planner had plotted inevitable annexations well into the next century. We came to the intersection of Southeast 106th Place and 428th Avenue Southeast: I still couldn't see much, but I knew we were in the country. There was a fenced pasture, and occasionally I could see the lights of houses far back from the road. "Here we are," Eleanor said abruptly. "Just pull over here and stop." I pulled off the road across from a gate, which was open. My headlights shone on a mailbox with the name RIGBY painted boldly across it, and under that—in smaller letters—THE NORTH BEND PRESS. We sat idling. I could hear her breathing heavily in the dark beside me. The air in the car was tense.

"What's happening?" I asked her.

"What do you mean?"

"Is there a problem?"

"Not the kind of problem you'd imagine. I just hate to face them."

"Why would you feel like that?"

"I've disappointed them badly. I've done some things . . . stuff I can't talk about . . . I've let them down and suddenly it's almost impossible for me to walk in there and face them. I can't explain it. The two people I love best in the world are in there and I don't know what to say to them."

"How about 'hi'?"

She gave a sad little laugh.

"Seriously. If people love each other, the words don't matter much."

"You're very wise, Janeway. And you're right. I know they're not going to judge me. They'll just offer me comfort and shelter and love."

"And you shudder at the thought."

"I sure do."

We sat for another minute. I let the car idle and the heater run and I didn't push her either way. At last she said, "Let's go see if Thomas Wolfe was right when he said you can't go home again."

I turned into the driveway. It was a long dirt road that wound through the trees. The rain was beating down steadily, a ruthless drumbeat. In a moment I saw lights appear through the trees. A house rose up out of the mist, an old frame building with a wide front porch. It looked homey and warm, like home is supposed to look to a tired and heartsick traveler. But Eleanor had begun to shiver as we approached. "Th-there," she said through chattering teeth. "Just pull around the house and park in front." But as I did this, she gripped my arm: my headlights had fallen on a car. "Somebody's here! Turn around, don't stop, for God's sake keep going!" Then we saw the lettering on the car door—THE VISTA PRINTING COMPANY—and I could almost feel the relief flooding over her. "It's okay, it's just Uncle Archie," she said breathlessly. "It's Mamma's uncle," she said, as if I had been the worried one. A light came on, illuminating the porch and casting a beam down the stairs into the yard: someone inside had heard us coming. I pulled up in front of the other car at the foot of the porch steps. A face peered through cupped hands at the door. "Mamma," Eleanor said, "oh, God, Mamma." She wrenched open the door and leaped out into the rain. The woman met her on the porch with a shriek and they fell into each other's arms, hugging as if they hadn't seen each other for a lifetime and probably wouldn't again, after tonight. I heard the woman yell, "Gaston! . . . Get out here!" and then a man appeared and engulfed them both with bearlike arms. I had a sinking feeling as I watched them, like Brutus might've felt just before he stabbed Caesar.

Now Eleanor was waving to me. I got out and walked through the rain and climbed the steps to the porch. "This is the man who saved my life," Eleanor said dramatically, and I was hooked by the woman and pulled in among them. The man gripped my arm and the woman herded us all inside. "This place is a shambles," she said, picking up a magazine and shooing us on. I was swept through a hallway to a well-lit kitchen where a tall, thin man sat at the table. He got to his feet as we came in, and we all got our first real look at each other. The woman was young: she might easily have passed for Eleanor's older sister, though I knew she had to be at least my age. But there wasn't a wrinkle on her face nor a strand of gray: her only concession to age was a pair of small-framed granny glasses. The man was burly: my height and

heavier, about the size of an NFL lineman. His hair
was curly and amber and he had a beard to match.
The man at the table was in his sixties, with slate-gray
hair and leathery skin. Eleanor introduced them.
"This is my father, Gaston Rigby . . . my mother,
Crystal . . . my uncle, Archie Moon. Guys, this is Mr.
Janeway." We all shook hands. Rigby's hand was
tentative but his eyes were steady. Archie Moon
gripped my hand firmly and said he was glad to meet
me. Crystal said that, whatever I had done for their
daughter, they were in my debt—doubly so for bringing her home to them.

There was more fussing, those first awkward moments among strangers. Rigby seemed shy and reserved: he hung back and observed while Crystal and
Eleanor did the talking. Hospitality was the order of
the moment: Crystal wanted us to eat, but Eleanor
told her we had stopped on the road. "Well, damn
your eyes, you oughta be spanked," Crystal said. She
asked if we'd like coffee at least: I said that sounded
wonderful. Eleanor said, "I think what Mr. Janeway
would like better than anything is some dry clothes,"
and Crystal took my measure with her eyes. "I think
some of your old things would fit him close enough,
Gaston," she said. "Get him a pair of those old jeans
and a flannel shirt and I'll get the coffee on."

Rigby disappeared and Crystal bustled about. "Get
down that good china for me, will you, Archie?" she
said, and Moon reached high over her head and began
to take down the cups. Eleanor and I sat at the kitchen
table, lulled by the sudden warmth. Impulsively she
reached across and took my hand, squeezing it and
smiling into my eyes. I thought she was probably on
the verge of tears. Then the moment passed and she
drew back into herself as Moon came with the cups
and saucers and began setting them around the table.

"None for me, honey," he said. "I been coffeed-out

since noon, won't sleep a wink if I drink another drop."

"I got some decaf," Crystal said.

"Nah; I gotta get goin'."

"What've you gotta do?" Crystal said mockingly. "You ain't goin' a damn place but back to that old shack."

"Never mind what I'm gonna do. You don't know everything that's goin' on in my life, even if you think you do."

They laughed at this with good humor. They spoke a rich Southern dialect, which Crystal was able to modify when she talked to us. "This old man is impossible," she said. "Would you please talk to him while I get the coffee on?—otherwise he'll run off and get in trouble."

Moon allowed himself to be bullied for the moment. He sat beside Eleanor and said, "Well, Mr. Janeway, what do people call you in casual conversation?"

"Cliff sometimes brings my head up."

"What line of work are you in?"

"Why is that always the first thing men ask?" Crystal said.

"It defines them," Eleanor said.

"So, Mr. Janeway," Moon said loudly. "What line of work are you in?"

"Right now I'm between things."

"An old and honorable calling. I've been in that line once or twice myself. Sometimes it can be pretty good."

"As long as you come up smiling."

"Just for the record," Crystal said in her Southern voice, "we don't care what you do for a living. I'm just glad you were in the right place at the right time, and I'm grateful to you and we're so glad you're here with us."

"That was gonna be my next comment," Moon said, "in more or less that same choice of words."

"Where're you staying, Mr. Janeway?" Crystal asked.

"He's going where the wind blows, Mamma," Eleanor said, as if that explained everything.

"Tonight the wind dies here," Crystal said. "I won't hear any argument about it, we've got a fine room in the loft over the shop. It's warm and dry and there's a good hard bed. Best of all, it's private."

"You'll love it," Eleanor said.

"In fact," Crystal said as Rigby came in carrying some clothes, "why don't we get that done right now?—get you into some dry duds and checked into your room. We're putting Mr. Janeway in the loft," she said to Rigby, who nodded. To me she said, "The only thing I need to ask is that you not smoke over there. Gaston doesn't allow any smoking in the shop. I hope that's not a problem."

"Not for me."

"Good. I'll whip us up some cinnamon rolls to go along with the coffee. You get yourself thawed out and come back over in half an hour so we can all get acquainted."

"Me, I gotta go," Moon said.

"You ornery old cuss," Crystal said. "Damn if you're not the unsociablest one man I ever met."

"I'll take Mr. Janeway over to the loft while I'm goin' out," Moon said to Rigby. "No sense you gettin' wet too."

I followed him back through the house. We popped open two umbrellas and went down into the yard. Moon pointed out the path with a flashlight he carried, leading the way to an outbuilding about twenty yards behind the house. The first thing I noticed, even before he turned on the light, was the smell . . . the heavy odor of ink mixed with something else. The light revealed a long room, cluttered with machinery and steel cabinets. Two large ancient-looking presses stood against the far wall, a smaller handpress on a table near the door, and, nearer the door, was a vast, complicated machine from another century, which I thought was probably a Linotype. It was. "That smell shouldn't bother you any," Moon said. "It's just the smell of hot type. Gaston must've been working out here till just before you showed up. You shouldn't even notice it upstairs."

He flipped on the lights. Our eyes touched for less than a second, then he looked away. "I'll leave you a slicker here by the door, and the flashlight and the umbrella too. If you need anything else, there's a phone upstairs, you can just call over to the house."

The first thing I saw was a NO SMOKING sign. Moon moved me past it, onto the circular staircase in the corner opposite the presses, then up to the loft, a spacious gabled room with a skylight and a window facing the house. In the middle of the room was a potbellied stove, which looked to be at least a hundred years old. Moon stoked it and soon had a fire going: "This old bastard'll really dry out your duds. And it's safe, Gaston has it checked every so often. It'll run you right out of here if you let it get too hot on you." He walked around the room looking in corners. Opened a door, peeped into an adjacent room. "Bathroom. There's no tub, but you've got a shower if you want it."

He made the full circle and stood before me. He radiated power, though his was wiry, a leaner brand than Rigby's. His voice was the prime ingredient in the picture of hard male strength that he presented to the world. It was a deep, resonant baritone, bristling with Southern intelligence. He'd be great on talk radio, I thought, and I was just as sure that he'd have nothing to do with it. "The phone's here beside the bed," he said. "It's on a separate line, so you just call over to the house just like any other phone call." He bent over the end table and wrote a number on a pad. Then he stood up tall and looked at me. "I can't think of anything else."

"Everything's great."

He turned to leave and stopped at the door. "Crystal kids around a lot, but I really do have to go. There's a waitress in Issaquah who's got dibs on my time. You look like a man who understands that."

"I do have a faint recollection of such a situation, yes."

He gave a little half-laugh and asked if I'd be around tomorrow. "If you are, come see me. I run the newspaper, my shop's over in Snoqualmie, just a few minutes from here. Anybody in either town can tell you where I'm at. If the sun comes out tomorrow, I'll show you some of the best country in the world. I've got a cabin up in the hills about an hour's drive from here. Built it forty years ago and it's been swallowed up by national-forest lands, about a million acres of it. That'll keep the Holiday Inn bastards at bay, at least for the rest of my life. It's yours if you'd like to unwind in solitude for a few days."

Again he paused. "I can't quite put my finger on it, Janeway. I've got the feeling we owe you more than we know. Does that make any sense?"

"I can't imagine why."

"I don't know either, it's just a feeling I've got. Like maybe you came along in the nick of time, not just to keep our little girl from getting herself wet."

"If I did, I don't know about it. But I'm glad I could help her."

He looked at me hard. "The kid doesn't tell us much anymore. She's all grown-up, got a life of her own. She never had a lick of sense when it came to strangers. Hitchhiked home from L.A. when she was eighteen, damn near drove her mamma crazy when she told us about it that night at dinner. Today she got lucky and found you. Don't ask me how or why, but I know we're in your debt."

I made a little motion of dismissal.

"All of us. Me too. Hell, I've known that kid since she was born, she used to hang around my printshop for hours after school, asking questions, pestering. 'What's this for, what's that do?' She's such a sweetheart, I couldn't think any more of her if she was my own daughter. And I know that anybody who helped her out of a tough spot could walk in here and the Rigbys would give him damn near anything they owned. So rest easy, I guess that's what I wanted to say, just rest easy. These people aren't kidding when they say they're glad to see you."

Then he was gone, clumping down the stairs, leaving me with one of the strangest feelings of my life.

I sat at the stove in Gaston Rigby's clothes, goldbricking.

What the hell do I do now? I thought.

7

A few minutes later I climbed down the stairs to the printshop and stood there in the quiet, aware of that primal link between Gaston Rigby's world and my own. It was there, huge and fundamental—amazing that I could live a life among books and be so unaware of the craftsmen who made them. Darryl Grayson had worked in a shop much like this one, and not far from this spot. Here he had practiced his voodoo, making wonderful things on quaint-looking equipment, just like this. I felt a strange sense of loss, knowing that someday we would attain technological perfection at the expense of individualism. This magnificent bond between man and machine was passing into history. I was born a member of the use-it-and-throw-it-away generation, and all I knew of Grayson's world was enough to figure out the basics. The big press was power driven. The plate identified it as CHANDLER AND PRICE, and it was run by a thick leather strap that connected a large wheel to a smaller one near the power source. On a table was a stack of leaflets that Rigby had been printing for an east Seattle car wash. I looked at the handpress. It had been made long before the age of electricity, but it was still, I guessed, what Rigby would use for fine work. It had a handle that the printer pulled to bring the paper up against the inked plate. The table beside it contained a few artistic experiments—poems set in typefaces so exotic and disparate that they seemed to rise up on the paper and battle for attention. It's like beer, I thought foolishly. I had once been asked to help judge a beer-tasting, and I had gone, thinking, *this is so damn silly.* Beer was beer, wasn't it? No, it was not. I learned that day that there are more beers in heaven and earth than mankind ever dreamed of. And so it is with type.

Rigby seemed to have them all, yet instinctively I knew that this was far from true. Still, his collection was formidable. They were stacked in tiny compartments of those deep steel cabinets: there were at least fifty cabinets set around the perimeter of the room, and each had at least twenty drawers and each drawer held a complete and different face. I pulled open a drawer marked COOPER BLACK and saw a hundred tiny compartments, each containing twenty to fifty pieces of type. I looked in another drawer farther along: it was called CASLON OLD STYLE. I did know a few of the names: recognized them as pioneers of type development, but the names conjured nothing in my mind as to what their work would look like. I didn't know Caslon from a Cadillac, and most of the names were as foreign to me as a typeface of old China. There were DEEPDENE and BODONI, CENTURY and DEVINNE, KENNERLEY, FUTURA, BASKERVILLE, and GRANJON. Each took up several drawers, with compartments for various point sizes. There were some that Rigby himself didn't know—entire cabinets labeled UNKNOWN in all point sizes. UNKNOWN ANTIQUE FACE, C. 1700, FOUND NEAR WHEELING, WEST VIRGINIA, 1972. WHEELING, Rigby called it, and it seemed to have come, or survived, in only one size. At the far end, nearest the presses, was a cabinet marked GRAYSON TYPES, each row subtitled with a name—GEORGIAN, PACIFIC, SNOQUALMIE. On the other side were cabinets marked DINGBATS and WOOD-CUTS. I opened the first drawer and took out a dingbat. It was a small ornament, which, when I looked closely, became a fleur-de-lis that could perhaps be the distinguishing mark of a letterhead. In the far corner was a paper cutter: next to it, coming down the far wall, a long row of paper racks. Then the Linotype, an intricate but sturdy machine the size of a small truck. This was the world of Gaston Rigby. Enter it and step back to the nineteenth century, where—forgetting its sweatshops and cruelties and injustices—man's spirit of true adventure, at least in this world, made its last stand.

And there was more. I came to a door halfway down

the far wall and opened it to find a room almost as large as the first. I flipped on a light and saw what looked at first glance to be another workshop. But there was a difference—this had neither the clutter nor the workaday feel of the other. It looked like the workplace of a gunsmith I had once known, who also happened to be the world's most vigorous neat-freak. There was a long workbench with rows of fine cutting tools—chisels, hammers, and files of all sizes. There were several large anvils, a row of powerful jewelerlike eyepieces, two strong and strategically placed lamps. This is where he does it, I thought: does it all by hand. I realized then that I was thinking of Grayson, not Rigby, as if I had indeed slipped back in time and somehow managed to saunter into Grayson's shop. I saw the sketches on the wall—an entire alphabet, each letter a foot square and individually framed, upper and lower case. The drawings ringed the entire room. I looked closely and decided that they were probably originals. Each was signed *Grayson,* in pink ink, in the lower-right corner. At the end of the workbench I found a large steel plate. It was a die or matrix, a foot square, containing the letter *G* in upper case. It corresponded exactly to the *G* framed on the wall. Just beyond the matrix was a long device that looked like a draftsman's instrument: it had a swinging arm that could trace the *G* and, I guessed after examining it, scale it down. Suddenly I could see the process. Grayson would first sketch his letters on paper. Then he would cast a die in metal. Then, using his one-armed machine, he could scale it down to any point size, down to the type on an agate typewriter if he so chose. He was the Compleat Printer, with no need of a type foundry because he was his own typemaking factory. Rigby had saved a set of his sketches and some of his equipment: he had maintained the working environment of Darryl Grayson, almost like a museum.

When I looked around again the world had changed. My calling had shifted at the foundation, and I knew I would never again look at a book in quite the same way. I lingered, hoping for some blazing enlightenment. At the far end of the room, half-hidden in shadows, was a door I hadn't noticed before. Perhaps it was in there, the answer to everything. But the door was locked, so I had to forgo the pleasure.

I heard a bump up front: someone, I imagined, coming to fetch me. I turned out the light and went back through the shop to the front door. But when I opened it, whoever had been there was gone.

8

At the end of my universe is a door, which opens into Rigby's universe. Either side must seem endless to a wayward traveler, who can only guess which is the spin-off of the other. We sat at the kitchen table, talking our way through their high country and along my riverbeds, and if much of what I told them was fiction, it was true in spirit and gave them little cause to ponder. I discovered that I could tell them who I was without giving up the bigger truth of why I was there. Occupation, in fact, is such a small part of a man that I was able to frame myself in old adventures and bring them as near as yesterday. Crystal served sweet rolls steaming with lethal goodness, the butter homemade, the sugar flakes bubbly and irresistible. Rigby sat across from me at the kitchen table, his face ruddy and mellow, cautiously friendly. Eleanor had excused herself and gone to the bathroom. Crystal pushed another roll toward me with the sage comment that nobody lives forever. That was one way of looking at it, so I took the roll while Rigby considered going for a third. "Ah, temptation," he said in that soft, kind voice, and he and Crystal looked at each other and laughed gently as if sharing some deeply personal joke. I reached for the butter and said, "I'll have to run for a week." Crystal told me about a bumper sticker she had seen that said: DON'T SMOKE . . . EXERCISE . . EAT FIBER . . . DIE ANYWAY. And we laughed.

In twenty minutes my dilemma had been honed to a razor-thin edge. Something had to give, for deception is not my strong point. There was a time when I could lie to anyone: the world I went around in was black-and-white, I was on the side of truth and justice, and the other side was overflowing with scum-sucking assholes. Those days ended forever when I turned in my badge. I could like these people a lot: I could open a mail-order book business in a house up the road and be their neighbor. Every morning at eight I'd wander into Rigby's shop and learn another secret about the universe beyond the door, and sometimes in the evenings Crystal would invite me for dinner, where I'd give them the true gen about my rivers and deserts. Shave about eight years off my age and you could almost see me married to their daughter, raising a new generation of little bookpeople in the shadows of the rain forest. They were the real stuff, the Rigbys, the salt of the earth. Suddenly I liked them infinitely better than the guys I was working for, and that included all the judges and cops of the great state of New Mexico.

They were not rich by any means. The microwave was the only touch of modern life in the house. The refrigerator was the oldest one I'd ever seen still working in a kitchen. The stove was gas, one step up from a wood burner. The radio on the shelf was an Admiral, circa 1946; the furniture was old and plain, giving the house that rustic, well-lived look. Whatever Darryl Grayson had taught Gaston Rigby all those years ago, the art of making money was not part of the mix. Grayson's name had come up just once, in passing. Fishing, I had cast my line into that pond with the offhand remark that Eleanor had told me of a man named Grayson, who had taught Rigby the business. His hand trembled and his lip quivered, and I knew I had touched something so intrinsic to his existence that its loss was still, twenty years later, a raw and open wound. Crystal came around the table and leaned over him, hugging his head. "Darryl was a great man," she said, "a great man." And Rigby fought back the tears and tried to agree but could not find the words. Crystal winked at me, encouraging me to drop the subject, and I did.

"What's all this?" Eleanor said, coming in from the hall. "What're we talking about?"

"I was just asking about the Linotype," I said, making as graceful a verbal leap as a working klutz can expect to achieve.

"There hangs a tale," Eleanor said. "Tell him about it, Daddy."

Rigby tried to smile and shook his head.

"You tell 'im, honey," Crystal said.

Eleanor looked at her father, then at me. "It's just that we had a kind of an adventure getting it here."

"It was a damned ordeal was what it was," Crystal said. "What do you think, Mr. Janeway, how does ten days without heat in weather that got down to twenty below zero sound to you?"

"It sounds like kind of an adventure," I said, and they laughed.

"It was our finest moment," Eleanor said, ignoring her mother, who rolled her eyes. "Daddy heard from a friend in Minnesota that a newspaper there had gone broke and they had a Linotype in the basement."

"It had been sitting there for twenty years," Crystal said, "ever since the paper converted to cold type. Hardly anyone there remembered what the silly thing had been used for, let alone how to use it."

"It was ours for the taking," Eleanor said.

"Craziest damn thing we ever did," Crystal said.

"Who's telling this, Mamma? Anyway, it was the middle of winter, they were gonna tear down the building and everything had to be out within two weeks."

"It was one of those instant demolition jobs," Crystal said. "You know, where they plant explosives and bring it all down in a minute."

"So we drove to Minneapolis," Eleanor said.

"Nonstop," said Crystal.

"The heater in the truck went out in Spokane . . ."

"Didn't even have time to stop and get it fixed. We took turns driving, sleeping when we could."

"Hush, Mamma, you're spoiling the story. So we get to Minnesota and it's so cold my toenails are frozen. The snow was piled four feet deep, the streets were like white tunnels. You couldn't even see in the shops at street level."

"They had this thing stored in a basement room that was just a little bigger than it was," Crystal said. "They must've taken it apart and rebuilt it in that room, because right away we could see that we'd never get it out unless we took it apart and carried it piece by piece."

78

I looked at Rigby. "Had you ever done anything like that?"

He shook his head.

"He had to figure it out as he went along," Eleanor said.

"Gaston can do anything, once he sets his mind to it," said Crystal.

"Anybody can, with a little time and patience," Rigby said.

"We spent two days in that basement," Eleanor said, "tearing down this machine, packing the parts, and putting them on the truck. It was so cold your hands would stick to the steel when you touched it, and all around us the wreckers were stringing explosives."

"But we got the damn thing," Crystal said, "and sang Christmas carols all the way home . . . in February."

"We thought of getting the heater fixed in Montana," Eleanor said, "but by then, hey, it was up to ten degrees—a major heat wave."

"And we could smell home," Rigby said.

I could almost feel the satisfaction and joy of getting it set up here in working order, and I said something to the effect.

"Yeah," Crystal said, "even I can't deny that."

"You can't put a label on it," Rigby said.

"Somehow you mean more to each other," Eleanor said, "after you've done something like that."

A sudden silence fell over the table. The evening was over, and I knew that, once again, I was not going to bust her. I didn't know why—it certainly wasn't Poe anymore—but I was ready to live with it, whatever happened.

"You'll find a lot of books over there if you'd like to read," Crystal said. "Sorry there's no TV."

I made a so-who-needs-it gesture with my hands.

"Breakfast at six-thirty," she said. "That's if you want to eat with us. I'll rustle you up something whenever you come over."

She walked me to the door, leaving Eleanor and her father alone at the kitchen table. On the porch she took my hand. "Thank you," she whispered. Then she hugged me tight and disappeared back into the house. I stood on the porch listening to the rain. The night was as dark as it ever gets, but I felt as if a huge weight had been lifted from my back. There would be no bust, no handcuffs, no force. I watched my five grand grow wings and fly away into the night. Half the puzzle was finished.

Now that I knew what I was not going to do, I thought I could sleep.

9

I opened my eyes to the ringing of the telephone. It was five after three by the luminous clock on the table beside me: I had been asleep almost five hours. Par for the course, I thought, staring into the dark where the phone was. I let it ring, knowing it couldn't be for me, but it kept on until I had to do something about it. When I picked it up, Eleanor was there in my ear.

"I'm coming over. Is that okay?"

"I don't know . . . what'll your parents say?"

But she had hung up. I rolled over and sat on the bed. When five minutes had passed and she hadn't arrived, I groped my way to the window and looked across at the house. It was dark except for a faint light on the side facing away from me. Soon that too went out—someone in a bathroom, I thought—but then another light came on in the opposite corner. Something moved in the yard: I couldn't tell what as I tried to see through the rain-streaked glass, but it looked like some critter standing under the window had moved quickly back into the darkness. A deer maybe, or just a mirage thrown out by a brain still groggy from too little sleep. But I hadn't forgotten about Eleanor's stalker and I sat on the sill and watched the yard. The light went out and again I swam in an all-black world. I sat for a long time looking at nothing.

At ten to four I decided that she wasn't coming and I went back to bed.

I heard a sharp click somewhere, then a bump. *There she is,* I thought. But nothing happened. The drumming of the rain was the only reminder that I could still think and I could still hear. The minutes stretched toward the dawn. There was not yet a hint of light, which, given the clouds covering the state, was at least ninety minutes away. Again a light flashed. This one brought me up with a start—it was here in my room, inches away. As my eyes focused, I saw that it was the extension button on the telephone— someone had picked up the phone downstairs in the printshop and was having a conversation at four o'clock in the morning. This went on for some time, at least two minutes, then the line went dark. I rolled out of bed and went to the door, opened it, and listened down the circular staircase. *Nothing.* No sound, no light, not a hint of movement anywhere.

I lay on the bed staring up into the dark. Eventually, though I wouldn't have believed it possible, I began to doze off.

* * *

It was almost as if she had stepped out of a dream. I was drifting, somewhere between worlds, when my eyes flicked open and I knew she was there. "Hey," I said, and I felt her sit beside me on the floor. I reached out and touched her head: she had laid it across her folded arms on the bed. "Thought you'd never get here." She still didn't speak: for several minutes she just lay there under my arm, her breathing barely audible above the rain. Then she said, "I didn't come because I felt stupid. I am stupid, waking you up in the middle of the night."

"It's okay, I was awake anyway," I lied.

"The truth of the matter is, I've just been through the loneliest night of my life. It got so desolate I thought I'd die from it."

There was a long pause. She said, "I keep thinking that maybe my mom and dad can help me when I get like this, but they can't. I know they love me, but somehow knowing it just makes the loneliness all the stronger. Does that make any sense?"

"You're not their little girl anymore. You've lost something you can't ever get back, but you haven't yet found what's gonna take the place of it in the next part of your life."

"The next part of my life," she said with a sigh.

I could hear the pain in her voice. "I'll help you," I said, "if you'll let me."

She seemed to consider it. "Just talk to me, help me get through the night. I know you want to sleep and I'm being a thundering pain in the ass. But you have no idea how much it would help, Mr. Man from Nowhere, if you'd just talk to me for a little while."

"Listen and believe it. There's nothing I'd rather do, right this minute, than talk to you."

"Oh, Janeway." Her voice got thick, and broke. "I hurt so bad. I hurt so bad and I can't talk to anyone."

"Talk to me."

"I don't know, maybe somebody like you, who's just passing through and doesn't know me. I can't talk to Mamma and Daddy, there's just too much in the way. I don't know what it is, we can't get past the facts of the matter and get down where the real trouble is."

"What are the facts of the matter?"

"How completely and beyond redemption I've fucked up my life."

"Maybe it just seems that way."

"I've done a stupid thing. Don't ask me why, it was just insane. I felt compelled, like I had no choice. Then they said I'd done something worse, and one thing led to another and I did do something worse . . . only it wasn't what they said I'd done. But they locked me up for it, and now they want to lock me up again, maybe for years. If they do that, I will kill myself, I swear I will. I couldn't live in a cage."

"None of us can. That's not really living."

"But some people survive. I couldn't even do that, not if we're talking about years." She shook her head: I felt the movement. "No way."

Gently, I prodded her. "What did you do?"

She was a long time answering, and at first the answer was no answer at all. "I can't tell you either."

"I won't judge you."

"It's not that. There are pieces of the story missing. Without them I just look like a fool."

"Take the chance. Maybe I can help you find the pieces."

"No one can. None of it makes sense. I'm like that guy in *The Man Without a Country,* I've got no roots, nothing solid to hold on to. I love my parents but I have an awful time talking to them."

"Everybody does. It means you're one hundred percent normal."

She chuckled, a sad little noise. "And all the time I thought I was crazy. I have the worst time trying to talk to them. And I know I've got to, I don't think I can let another day pass without doing that. But how can I?"

"Try it out on me first."

She didn't say anything. I let her alone for a few minutes, then I nudged her arm. "What happened to you?"

"I was in New Mexico," she said at once, as if she'd been waiting for me to ask it one more time. "I got in trouble. . . . I can't tell you about that. But I've been carrying it around for weeks now. If I don't tell somebody . . ."

I gave her a little squeeze: nothing sexual, just friendly encouragement.

"That's where I picked up my stalker, in Taos." Again she tried to lapse into silence. But then she said, "I had a room there. I'd come home and things would be moved."

"Ransacked?"

"No . . . but yeah, maybe. I had the feeling he'd done that, been through all my stuff and then put it all back, just so. But he'd always leave one little thing out of place, something obvious like he'd wanted me to see it. Once he left a cigarette, still burning in a Styrofoam cup. He wanted me to know he'd just left. Then he started with the phone. It would ring late at night and I'd hear him breathing . . . or humming that song."

"You told me before: you knew what he wanted."

"He told me. But I can't explain it now, so don't ask me."

"Explain what you can."

"I felt like something evil had come into my life. I'd turn a corner and he'd be there, right in my path. He looked like a cadaver, his eyes were all sunken and he had holes in his face, deep pits across both cheeks. Scared me deaf and dumb. I can't tell you what it was like. I'd walk down to the phone booth and call home and he'd come up behind me, rip open the door, and stand there staring. He said he could kill me, right there at the telephone—*kill you and go up to North Bend and kill your mother too*. God, I just freaked. Then one night he got into my room when I was sleeping. When I woke up the next morning there was a dead . . . rat . . . on the bed beside me. And I really freaked."

I was listening to her words, trying to figure how and when this had all happened. It had to be some-time after the first Jeffords break-in, but before the second. Whatever else her stalker had done, he'd pushed her onto that next level of desperation. She had failed to get what she'd gone after at the Jeffords place—what the stalker also wanted—and had gone back for another run at it. Then what?

Then she took it on the lam: jumped bail, struck out for home. "So how'd you get back here?" I asked. She had driven her car, she said in that flat tone of voice that people use when you ask a stupid question. But I was trying to get at something else, something she couldn't yet know about. "What roads did you take?" I asked, and she laughed and wondered what possible difference it could make. "I came across the Sangres, up the Million-Dollar Highway to Grand Junction, then took the freeway home."

Slater had lied about her coming through Denver. He had probably lied about other things as well. The pockmarked man sounded like someone I had met quite recently, and my whole involvement felt sud-denly dirty.

I couldn't get her to say any more. "I've already said too much," she said. "If I keep on, I'll feel worse than ever. Maybe I should just take poison and save us all the grief."

"That, of course, would be the worst thing you could do." I calculated my next line and said it anyway. "I hope you're not one of those people who turn suicidal on me."

"Have you known people like that?"

"One or two. It's always tragic, especially when they're young."

"I saw you looking at the scar on my arm. Back in the restaurant."

"No use lying about it. I couldn't help noticing."

"Well, you're right. I did that to myself."

"Why?"

"Loneliness," she said without missing a heartbeat. "Desolation, the undertow, the barren landscape. I can't explain it. The loneliest times come when I'm adrift in a big city, or here with people who love me. When I'm really alone, up on a mountaintop somewhere, I'm fine. I go up to Archie's cabin and I can go for a week without seeing another living soul. The feeling of peace is just incredible. Too bad we can't live our lives on mountaintops. I really like being with people until I actually am, then I can't stand them. Maybe I should try to find Jesus; people say that works, though I can't imagine it working for me. I'm just not spiritually oriented. So I drift. Sometimes I don't even know where the road's gonna take me."

"Talk to me, Eleanor. You got in trouble in New Mexico, then you came back here. What happened then?"

"Nothing. That's the stupid part of it. I came fifteen hundred miles and I couldn't go the last mile home. Instead I drove out to see Amy. But she wasn't home and I couldn't find her."

"Who's Amy?"

"Amy Harper. She was my best friend till she married Coleman Willis. The cock that walks like a man. Our relationship got a bit strained after that. It's hard to stay friends with someone when her husband hates you."

"How could anyone hate you?"

"I wouldn't go to bed with him. To a guy who wears his brain between his legs, that's the last word in insults."

In a while I said, "So you went to see Amy but Amy wasn't there. You wouldn't want to kill yourself over that. Amy'll be back."

"How do you know?"

"People always come back."

"Maybe so, but I won't be here."

No, I thought: you probably won't be.

"What did you do then?" I said.

"Drove out to my parents' place. Stood in the rain watching the house, afraid to come up and talk to them. God, I've never been so alone in my life. Then I saw them come out and drive off—going to town, I figured, for the week's groceries. I went over to the house and sat on the porch. I wanted to die but I didn't know how. I thought if I could just lie down and close my eyes and not wake up, I'd do it. But it's not that easy. It's impossible, in fact; I don't want to *die,* for God's sake, I never wanted to die. I thought maybe I could find some peace in the printshop. I used to do that when I was a little girl. When I'd get blue, I'd go back in the shop and put my cheek against that cold press and I could feel the warmth come flooding into me, especially if there were books back there and if they were books I loved. I could take a book and hold it to my heart and the world was somehow less hostile, less lonely."

"Did that work?"

"It always works, for a while. But it's like anything else that has fantasy at its roots. Eventually you've got to come back to earth. Now I'm running out of time. Something will happen, today, tomorrow . . . something'll happen and I'll be history."

She pulled herself up on the bed. I heard her shoes hit the floor.

"Would you do something for me, Mr. Janeway?"

"If I can."

"Hold me."

"I don't think that'll be any great hardship."

"That's all I want . . . just . . . just . . ."

"Sure," I said, taking her into the cradle of my arm.

She was shivering. I drew the blanket up under my chin and the body heat spread around us. Her hair smelled sweet, as if she had just washed it. I knew I had no business smelling her hair. She snuggled tight against me and I had no right to that either. Maybe she'd go to sleep now. Maybe I could forget she was there, just like the people at Lakehurst forgot the *Hindenburg* when it was blowing up in front of them. Somewhere in the night Helen Reddy was singing "I Am Woman" and I was thinking *you sure are,* to the same driving melody. I had been what seemed like a very long time without a woman, and this one was forbidden, for more reasons than I could count.

We lay still on the bed, and slowly the dark gave way to a pale and ghostly gray. Saved by the dawn. It was five-thirty: the Rigbys would be getting up for the new day. I patted her shoulder and rolled out of bed, moving to the window for a look at the house. It was peaceful and ordinary in the rainy morning, nothing like the den of tears I had blundered into last night. I turned and looked at Eleanor. Her face was a white blur in the half-light: her eyes, I thought, were open. We didn't say anything. I hit the john, and when I came out, she had not moved from her spot on the bed. I looked out the window. Someone in the house had turned on a light, the same one I had seen earlier. I knew then what I was going to do.

"Listen," I said, still looking out the window. "I've got to tell you something." But I never got the words out. A car came out of the misty woods and up the road toward the house. I felt heartsick watching it come. Only when it had pulled in behind my rental and stopped did the cop behind the wheel turn on his flasher.

It filled the room and colored us a flickery red and blue. Eleanor lay still as death. Down in the yard, two county cops had stepped out in the rain. One walked up the steps, meeting the Rigbys as they came out on the porch. The other came up the path to the printshop.

"Judgment day," Eleanor said. "I had a feeling it would be today."

10

N ext case."

"The matter of Eleanor Jane Rigby, Your Honor. Filing number one three seven five nine six."

"Is this the prisoner? . . . are you Eleanor Jane Rigby?"

"Yes, ma'am."

"Do you understand the nature of this proceeding?"

"I think so."

"Let's be sure. This is an extradition hearing, to determine whether you will be returned to the state of New Mexico to face criminal charges outstanding there. Do you understand that?"

"Yes, ma'am."

"You may contest the extradition or waive that right. Do you have an attorney?"

"A public defender, in Taos."

"But here, in Seattle?"

"No, ma'am."

"Would you like to consult with an attorney here?"

"I don't see any point in it."

"You wish to waive that right?"

"Sure . . . might as well."

"Do you understand, Miss Rigby, that commencing any legal proceeding without an attorney is a risky and unwise decision?"

"It won't matter."

"So you wish to go ahead."

"Sure. I just want to get it over with."

"Very well. Mr. Wallace?"

"Yes, Your Honor. All we want to do is get her out of here."

"I can understand that. Do you have the extradition waiver form?"

"Yes, Your Honor."

"Thank you. For the record, I am now handing to the prisoner, Eleanor Jane Rigby, the consent form as required by Revised Code of Washington, title ten dash . . . uh, eighty-nine dash . . ."

"Uh, oh three oh, Your Honor."

"Thank you, Mr. Wallace. Will the prisoner please sign where the bailiff indicates?"

"What happens if I don't sign this?"

"We will hold you here for up to sixty days, New Mexico will make a formal filing of its demand, and there will be a full hearing."

"And in the end I'll go back anyway."

"The court cannot advise you of that, Miss Rigby. That's what an attorney would do."

"Where do I sign? . . . Here?"

"Let the record show that the prisoner is signing the waiver consent form in the presence of the court."

"And at this time I am tending the document to the court for your signature, Your Honor."

"Thank you, Mr. Wallace. The prisoner will be remanded to the King County jail, until such time as the New Mexico authorities send someone to escort her back."

"Your Honor?"

"Was there something else, Mr. Wallace?"

"We'd like to get her out of here tomorrow. We've been informed by New Mexico that they can't send a deputy until at least Tuesday of next week."

"Is that a particular problem?"

"It's a potential problem. Today is what? . . . Thursday. That means she'll be in our custody five days and nights. I know I don't have to remind Your Honor about potential problems with young female prisoners. We don't want another Bender case on our hands."

"Is there a special reason to think we might have such an incident?"

"I understand this prisoner has a history of suicide attempts."

"Is that true, Miss Rigby?"

"I wouldn't call it a history . . . I cut my wrist once."

"Your Honor—"

"I understand, Mr. Wallace. Nobody wants a replay of Bender. What do you suggest?"

"We have a man here to take her back."

"It's New Mexico's responsibility. Will Washington be reimbursed for the costs of such a trip?"

"It won't cost us anything."

"Tell me about it . . . gently, please."

"Shortly after the arrest of the prisoner and her transfer here from East King County, our office was contacted by a Mr. Cliff Janeway of Denver, Colorado, who was sent here to arrest the suspect and escort her back."

"Sent by whom?"

"An agent of the bail bondsman."

The judge closed her eyes. "Mr. Wallace, are you seriously asking me to release this young woman in the care of a bounty hunter?"

"He's not a bounty hunter, Your Honor."

"Please, then . . . what is he?"

"He's a rare-book dealer in Denver. More to the point, he's a former officer of the Denver Police Department with more than fifteen years experience."

"Is Mr. Janeway in this court?"

"Yes, ma'am."

She motioned with her hand. "Come."

I walked down into the arena.

"You are Mr. Cliff Janeway?"

"Yes, I am."

"And you were engaged, as Mr. Wallace said, to arrest the defendant and return her to New Mexico."

"Yes."

"Do you have papers? . . . Let me see them, please."

"We've checked him out thoroughly, Your Honor. We've talked with a Detective Hennessey at the Denver Police, who was his partner for several years, and to a Mr. Steed, who is chief of detectives. Both gentlemen spoke uncompromisingly of his dedication and character."

"All right, Mr. Wallace, I get the picture. Be quiet a minute and let me read this stuff, will you?"

Silence.

The judge cleared her throat. "Mr. Janeway?"

"Yes, ma'am."

"You were hired by a Mr. Slater of Denver, who was representing the Martin Bailbondsmen of Taos, is that correct?"

"Yes, it is."

She blinked and looked at me through her glasses. "I can't help wondering, sir, how a police detective becomes a dealer in rare books."

"He gets very lucky, Your Honor."

She smiled. "Have you ever done any bounty-hunter work?"

"No, ma'am."

"This is not something you do for a living?"

"Not at all."

"How did you come to accept this case?"

"It was offered to me. Mr. Slater didn't have time to come out of town, and he asked me to come in his place."

"How did you propose to escort Miss Rigby back to New Mexico?"

"By air."

She nodded her approval. Just to be sure, she said, "No three-day trips by automobile?"

"No, ma'am."

"What does New Mexico have to say, Mr. Wallace?"

"Well, naturally they'd love to come get her—you know how those sheriff's boys love to travel. But they understand our problem too."

"They have no objection to Mr. Janeway?"

"They're comfortable with him. One or two of them know him, as a matter of fact."

"What about you, Miss Rigby? Do you have any objection to being escorted by Mr. Janeway?"

"I don't care who takes me."

"We sure don't want to keep her any longer than we have to, Your Honor."

"All right. The prisoner is remanded to the custody of the jailer, who will release her to Mr. Janeway upon presentation of the papers *and* the airline tickets. I hope I'm making myself clear, Mr. Janeway. I'm holding you personally responsible for this prisoner's safe passage. I'm not interested in any deal you may have made with this . . . what's his name? . . . Slater, in Denver. You baby-sit this one all the way into Taos. Are we clear on that?"

"Yes, ma'am."

"Good. Next case."

11

The Rigbys sat in stony silence in the first row of Judge Marla McCoy's court. Archie Moon sat beside Crystal, directly behind the defendant's table. The room was nearly empty beyond the second row: there were a couple of legal eagles—people who drift from court to court, endlessly fascinated by the process—and across the aisle sat a young blond woman with a steno pad. I was surprised to find even that much Seattle interest in the plight of a defendant in a legal action thirteen hundred miles removed.

"I shouldn't even talk to you, you son of a bitch," Crystal said.

I had found them in the cafeteria, eating sandwiches out of a vending machine, and I sat with them and tried to explain how the deceit had begun, how the lie kept growing until the appearance of the cops put an end to it. We got past it quickly. It was my intent they now embraced, and they gripped my hand with the desperation of shipwreck survivors who come upon a lifeboat in choppy, hostile waters. I told them what was going to happen and what I was going to try to do. I would ferry Eleanor into Taos, meet with her lawyer, and see if any mitigating circumstances might be uncovered that would sway the court toward leniency. There had been a time, not too long ago, when I had done such work for a living, and I had been good at it. But I hadn't even heard Eleanor's side of things yet, so I didn't know what was possible.

"I've got to tell you," Crystal said, "we don't have any money to pay you. None at all."

"Call it one I owe you. If I can help in any way, it'll be my pleasure."

Crystal asked if she should try to come to New Mexico. I told her not yet: let me get my feet on the ground and see how the wind was blowing. Gaston Rigby watched us talk, his sad and weary eyes moving from her face to mine. "If it does become a question of money," he said, "you let us know, we'll get it somehow." Archie Moon said he had a little money put aside, enough to get him to Taos if I thought he could do any good. I told him to keep that thought on the back burner and I'd let him know.

Then there was nothing more for them to do but take the long ride home, face a house that would never again seem so empty, and wait out the days and weeks and months for the justice system to do what it would.

For me the case had taken on a kind of inevitable flow. Everything about it felt orchestrated, as if my part in it had been preordained. A woman named Joy

Bender had killed herself in the Seattle jailhouse and had named me her chief beneficiary. The Bender case was an ugly one, full of posthumous rape-and-abuse charges. A letter had been left with Bender's mother, who had released it to the press with a raging broadside at the system. In time the Bender letter had been discredited as the work of a sick and angry mind. The mother had written it herself, but the headlines were a cop's worst nightmare for a month. Even now there was widespread public belief that the true facts had been covered up and the mother was being framed to clear the real villains, the jailers and the cops. Things like that do happen, often enough that people retain their disbelief when a case against the cops collapses like a house of cards. So the DA was primed and ready when I walked in and made a case that sounded halfway legit. When I mentioned in passing my real concern that Rigby might harm herself, he was all ears. When I told him she had already tried it once, this hardened man who had seen everything shivered and drew in his wagons. And the overworked and bludgeoned system in Seattle had bent a rule or two and sent New Mexico's problem packing with the fastest reliable messenger—me.

I was still sitting at the table in the cafeteria when a shadow passed over my left shoulder, too close to be moving on by. I looked up and into the face of the young blond woman I had seen taking notes in the courtroom earlier.

"Mr. Janeway."

"Yes, ma'am."

"Trish Aandahl, *Seattle Times.*"

I gave her a long, wary look. "This must be a slow news day. I didn't think major metropolitan dailies bothered with simple extradition hearings."

"Nothing about this case is simple, and everything about it interests me. May I sit down?"

96

She did, without waiting for the invitation. The steno pad was still clutched tight in her left hand.

"Listen," I said. "Before you draw that Bic out of the holster, I don't want to be interviewed, I've got nothing to say."

"May I just ask a couple of questions?"

"You can ask anything you want, but I'm not going to let you put me in print saying something dumb. The fact is, I don't know anything about this case that could possibly be worth your time. And I learned a long time ago that when you don't know anything, the last guy, or gal, you want to see is a reporter."

"You've been burned."

"Basted, baked, and broiled. There was a time when Blackened Janeway was the main lunch course at the Denver Press Club."

She smiled, with just the right touch of regret. She was good, I thought, and that made her dangerous. She made you want to apologize for not being her sacrificial lamb.

"I'm not a hard-ass," I said by way of apology. "I like the press. Most of the reporters I know are fine people, great drinking buddies. I even read newspapers once in a while. But I've lived long enough to know how your game works."

"How does it work?"

"If you quote me accurately, your obligation ends right there, even if I don't know what the hell I'm talking about. My viewpoint gets run through your filter system and I wind up holding the bag."

She flashed a bitter little smile and I took a second, deeper look at her. She was one of those not-quite-rare but uncommon women, a brown-eyed blonde, like the wonderful Irene in Galsworthy's sadly neglected *Forsyte Saga*. Her hair was the color of wheat in September. Her face was pleasantly round without being cherubic: her mouth was full. She was in her thirties, about Rita's age, not beautiful but striking, a face carved by a craftsman who had his own ideas of what beauty was.

Belatedly I recognized her name. "You wrote the book: the Grayson biography."

"I wrote the book," she confessed.

"I should be asking you the questions. You probably know more than I do."

"That may be. That's what I'm trying to find out."

"I keep telling you, I don't know anything. I'm just a friend of the court, delivering a prisoner back to the bar."

"Right," she said with a tweak of sarcastic skepticism. She opened her purse and dropped the steno pad inside it. "Off the record."

"Everything I've got to say I said on the record in open court."

"You didn't say why you're really here and what you're doing."

"It's irrelevant. I'm irrelevant, that's what you need to understand."

"Who is Slater?"

"You're not listening to me."

"There's someone else involved in this. Slater's not just working for a Taos bonding company."

I shrugged and looked at a crack in the ceiling.

"I made some calls after the hearing. You left deep footprints in Denver."

"That's what they said about King Kong. On him it was a compliment. As a gorilla he was hard to beat."

I waited but she missed her cue.

"You were supposed to say, 'That gives you a goal to shoot for.' If we're going to play Wits, the new Parker Brothers game, you've got to be sharp."

She gave me a look of interested amusement.

"We'll put it down to midafternoon sag," I said.

"You are a handful, aren't you? My sources in Denver didn't exaggerate much."

"So who are these people and what are they saying about me?"

"Who they are isn't important. They told me what anybody could get with a few phone calls and a friend or two where it counts."

"Read it back to me. Let's see how good you are."

"You were with DPD almost fifteen years. Exemplary record, actually outstanding until that caper a while back. You have a fine-tuned but romantic sense of justice. It should always work, the good guys should always win. Then the end would never have to justify the means, a cop could always work within the rules and evil would always take the big fall. How am I doing so far?"

"You must be on the right track, you're starting to annoy me."

"You asked for it. Shall I go on?"

"You mean there's more?"

"You have an intense dislike of oppressive procedure. It galled you when the courts let creeps and thugs walk on technicalities. You nailed a guy one time on an end run that cops in Denver still talk about . . . probably illegal but they never stuck you with it. So the guy went up."

"He was a serial rapist, for Christ's sake. He got what he needed."

"You're getting annoyed all over again, aren't you? They told me you would. That case still bothers you, it's the one time you really stepped over the line and let the end justify the means. Your fellow cops remember it with a good deal of admiration, but it rankles you to this day, the way you had to get that guy."

"I sleep just fine. My only regret is that I didn't get

the son of a bitch a year earlier, before he started using the knife."

"You're a guy out of time, Janeway. You were a good cop, but you'd've been great fifty years ago, when there weren't any rules."

"There's probably a lot I'd appreciate about life fifty years ago."

"You don't like telephones, television, or computers. I'll bet Call Waiting drives you crazy."

"People who load up their lives with crap like that have an inflated sense of their own importance. You might not believe this, but I've never missed an important phone call."

"I do believe it. It's all in the eye of the beholder."

"If it's that important, they always call back." I looked at her hard. "You really are getting on my nerves."

"Good. If I can't get you to talk to me, at least I can ruin your day. If I tell you enough about yourself, maybe you'll understand something."

"And what is that?"

"If you don't talk to me, somebody else will."

"I can't help what other people tell you."

"They tell me you've got this code you live by and you've got it down pat. You see a lot of things in black and white: if you give your word, people can take it to the bank. The problem is, you expect the same thing out of others. You tend to be hard and unforgiving when someone breaks the code. When you come up against a brick wall, your tendency is to go right on through it. You had little finesse when it came to official policy and no patience with politics."

"I can't think of anything offhand that's as evil as politics. It turns good men into bad all the time."

"You spend a lot of your time alone. You trust no one in a pinch as much as you do your own self.

You've got such self-confidence that sometimes it strikes others as arrogance. Your reputation as a smart-ass is as high as the Rockies. Richly deserved would be my guess."

"I work on it every day. I hire four people to sit on a panel, test me once a week, and tell me how I'm doing. Lately I've been unable to afford the sex therapist, but you could probably tell that. I don't feel that my day's properly under way unless I've run three miles and verbally abused someone of far less mental dexterity than myself—preferably in public, where the scars of their humiliation will be shattering and damn near impossible to shake off."

She gave a little smile. "Actually, you're a champion of the underdog. The strong never abuse the weak in your presence."

"Now I'm a regular Robin Hood. You'll have to make up your mind."

"You've got quite a name as a fighter. People don't mess with you much."

"Some have."

"But they didn't come back for seconds."

"Not since I killed that blind crippled boy last summer."

She laughed. "You're an American original, aren't you? Listen to me, Janeway. I mean you no harm. I come in friendship and peace."

"That's what Custer said to the Indians."

"You and I are probably a lot alike."

"That's what Sitting Bull said back to Custer."

"And like the Indians and the cavalry, we'd probably end up killing each other. But I'll tell you this, it'll all be up front. I never break my word." She leaned forward and looked me straight in the eyes. Our faces were closer than strangers ought to be. "Who is Slater?"

I looked at her hard and gave her nothing.

"Maybe it would make a difference if I told you what else I know."

"What's that?"

"That Darryl and Richard Grayson were murdered."

Her sense of timing couldn't have been better: I felt the tingle of her words all the way to my toes. Without taking her eyes from mine, she reached into her bag and took out a card. "Both my numbers are here if you decide you'd like to talk. Anytime, all off the record. If not, have a nice flight to Taos."

She got up and walked out.

12

Who was Slater? The question lingered through the night.

Why was I here?

In my mind I saw him working his scam, dancing his way into my life with that cock-and-bull story about him and me and our brilliant future together. I watched again as he spread open that paper, where someone had written the particulars of Grayson's *Raven* so long ago that it was beginning to fall apart. It wasn't about me, it wasn't about a bounty fee on a skip, it might not even be about Eleanor except in an incidental way. The real stuff had happened long ago, probably before she was born.

But it didn't matter now, did it? I was under a court order, and I had to play according to Hoyle.

I sat up late reading a bad novel. I watched some bad TV. At three o'clock in the morning I sat at my window and looked down into the rainy Seattle street.

But I couldn't forget Trish Aandahl, or that parting shot she had given me.

I called the first travel agency that opened at seven-thirty and told them to get me to Taos with a fellow traveler ASAP. It was a heavy travel day. United had two flights that would put us in Albuquerque early and late that afternoon. From there I could rent a car or hook up with a local airline that would jump us into Taos. But both flights were packed. The agent could squeeze us in, but our seats would be separated by the length of the plane. The next viable flight was a red-eye special, leaving Sea-Tac at 11:18 P.M., arriving in Albuquerque at 2:51 A.M., mountain time. I took the red-eye, told the agent to deliver the tickets to the Hilton, and put the tariff on my charge card. The tickets were $800 each, typical airline piracy for last-minute bookings. I sucked it up and hoped to God I could get some of it back from the good people of New Mexico.

Then I called Slater and got my first surprise of a long and surprising day.

"Mr. Slater's not available," said his woman in Denver.

"When will he be available?"

"I'm not sure. He will be calling in. Who is this, please?"

"My name's Janeway. I've been working a case for him. Something's come up and I need to talk to him."

I heard her shuffling through some papers. "I'm afraid I don't know you."

"Then I must not exist. I'll bet if you tell him I'm here, though, he'll talk to me anyway."

I heard a spinning sound, like a roulette wheel in Vegas. "Everyone who works for us is in this Rolodex. Your name's not here."

"Then it's Slater's loss. Give him a message, tell him I tried."

"Wait a minute."

I heard her talking to someone, but her hand had covered the phone and I couldn't make out the words.

"I could maybe have him call you back."

"Won't work. I'm heading out in about five minutes."

"Hold, please." She punched the hold button: elevator music filled my ear.

There was a click. Another woman said, "Mr. Janeway? . . . I'm sorry for the hassle. It's just that we don't know you and Mr. Slater's out of town."

"How could he be out of town? He hired me because he didn't have time to go out of town. Where's he gone?"

"I'm not at liberty to discuss that. I guess I'll have to take a message."

"Tell him Janeway called, I've got the girl and I'm taking her on to Taos myself."

"Is that what he wanted you to do?"

"It doesn't matter what he wanted me to do. Tell him I'm not working for him anymore."

I sat on my bed feeling the first faint gnawing of a mighty hunch.

I placed another call to Denver.

"U.S. West."

"Howard Farrell, please."

I listened to the click of a connection, then a woman's voice said, "Mr. Farrell's office."

"Mr. Farrell, please."

"May I say who's calling?"

"Cliff Janeway."

Another click, followed by the familiar resonance of an old and confidential source.

"Hey, Cliff! Where the hell've you been?"

"Cruising down the river, you old son of a bitch."

"Jesus, I haven't heard your voice for what? . . . seems like a year now."

"More like two. So how're things at the good old phone company?"

"Same old shit."

"Howard, you need to start breaking in a new act. But then what would guys like me do when they need a favor out of old Ma Bell?"

"Uh-oh. You're not official anymore, are you?"

"Is that a problem?"

"Damn right it is. Just for old-time's sake, what do you want?"

"Clydell Slater."

"My favorite cop. He still playing smashmouth with Denver's finest?"

"He does it on his own now."

"What an asshole. Look, Cliff . . . this isn't likely to cause Mr. Slater any grief, is it?"

"It might pinch his balls a little."

"Then I'll do it. Same ground rules as always. Give me a number, I'll call you right back."

Five minutes later Farrell called and, for my ears only, gave me Slater's home number.

I placed the call.

It was answered by a recording, a woman's voice. "Hi, this's Tina. Me'n' Clyde are out now. We'll call ya back."

I hung up on the beep.

I lingered over breakfast in a downtown café. Read the high points in last night's *Times*. Looked for her byline but it wasn't there. Drank my third cup of coffee over the local homicide page.

Went back to the hotel. Took a shower and went upstairs to the lobby. My tickets had arrived. I slipped them into my inside jacket pocket with my court papers and went to the jail to see Eleanor.

It was still early, well before ten. They led her in and we sat with glass between us, talking through a bitch box.

"How're you doing?" I said.

"Just wonderful."

"I wanted to see you and say a few things."

"You don't have to."

"What are you now, a mind reader?"

"I know what you're gonna say, I can see it in your eyes. I know you're bothered by all this. Don't be . . . you don't owe me a thing."

"In a cold-blooded dog-eat-dog world, that would be one way to look at it."

"Well, isn't that what it is?"

"Only sometimes."

"I'll bet this was your big failing as a cop. People can look in your face and see what's in your heart."

"Would you believe nobody's ever said that to me? . . . Not once. In some circles I'm known as a helluva poker player, impossible to read."

"Amazing."

We looked at each other.

"If you're waiting for absolution, you already have it," she said. "You were doing a job. You've got a strange way of doing it, but I've got no kick coming. If it makes you feel better, you've got my unqualified permission to deliver me up and get on with your life, forget I ever existed."

"That's not going to happen, Eleanor. That's one promise I'm making you."

"What can you do, tell me that . . . what can you do?"

"I don't know. Did you do the burglary?"

"Yes, I did. So there you are."

"Why did you do it?"

"Personal reasons."

"Did you take a gun into the house?"

"Does it matter?"

"Does it matter? Hell, yes, it matters. It can be the difference between a first-time offender asking for probation and a gun moll doing heavy time."

She didn't say anything.

"You said something back in the restaurant when we were talking about your stalker. The subject of a gun came up. Do you remember what you said?"

She looked at me through the glass. "I've never fired a gun in my life."

"Did the cops do a gunshot residue test?"

"I don't even know what that is."

"So I'll ask you again. Did you take a gun into that house?"

"No. Believe it or not."

"Okay, I believe it. Did you get a gun while you were in the house, maybe from the guy's gun rack. Was it you that did the shooting?"

"I never shot at anyone. I was the one shot at. I'm lucky to be alive."

"If we can prove that, you've got a fighting chance. You were still wrong to be there. You broke in, they had every right to shoot at you. But almost any judge would wonder why they'd lie about it."

"I guess they want me to go to jail."

"For a long time, apparently." I leaned closer to the glass. "I'd still like to know why you broke in, what you were looking for."

"Maybe I'll tell you sometime. But not today; I don't think I know you well enough to get into the wired-up hell of my life with you. When do we leave?"

"Late tonight. I'll come for you around seven-thirty."

"Lots of dead time for you to fill. What'll you do, hit the bookstores?"

"Maybe."

"That's the only part of this that really surprises me. I never had a hint you were a book dealer. You played that card very well."

I tried to smile at her. "I'd better go." But something powerful held me there. Then, so quickly that I didn't know how it happened, I stepped off the straight and narrow for the first time that day. I stepped all the way off and said something that could never be unsaid.

"How'd you like to get out of here? . . . go with me? . . . be my guide through the Seattle book jungle?"

She looked like a person half-drowned who had suddenly been brought back to life. "Can you do that?"

"Probably not. The jailer will look at my tickets and wonder what the hell I'm doing taking you out ten hours early. The judge'll schedule a new hearing, I'll get drawn and quartered, and you'll end up riding back to Taos handcuffed to a deputy."

I shrugged. "We could try."

She reached out as if to touch my face. Her fingertips flattened against the glass.

"You've got to promise to behave." I felt a sudden desperation, as if I'd taken a long step into the dark. "I'm taking a big chance, Eleanor. It's my responsibility now. I'll take the chance because I like you. I owe you one for the big lie. And it just occurs to me that you'd probably rather spend the day in bookstores than chained by your neck to the wall of some crummy jail cell. But you've got to behave."

"Absolutely. Who wouldn't love a deal like that?"

The jailer gave our tickets a cursory glance. He looked at my papers, read the judge's order, and at half past ten Eleanor Rigby and I walked out into a drippy Seattle day.

13

It was a day of magic. The two of us were charmed: Seattle was our oyster and every stop coughed up a pearl. She took me to a place called Gregor Books on Southwest California Avenue. The books were crisp and fine and there were lots of high-end goodies. You don't steal books out of a store like that—the owner is far too savvy ever to get caught sleeping on a live one, but Rita McKinley's words echoed in my ear. *You can double the price on anything if it's fine enough.* Gregor had the finest copy of *Smoky* I had ever seen. Signed Will James material is becoming scarce, and James had not only signed it but had drawn an original sketch on the half title. Gregor was asking $600, $480 after my dealer's discount. I took it, figuring I could push it to $800 or more on the sketch and the world's-best-copy assertion. I figured James was a hotter property in the real West, Colorado, than here in Seattle, and when the day came for me to go in the ground, I could rest just fine if they threw this book in the hole with me. Speaking of dying, Gregor had a dandy copy of *If I Die in a Combat Zone*, Tim O'Brien's 1973 novel of the Vietnam War. He had marked it $450, but I was making his day and he bumped my discount to 25 percent for both items. I took it: the O'Brien is so damn scarce that I thought it was overdue for another price jump, and I left the store poorer but happier. Eleanor directed me downtown. We stopped at the Seattle Book Center, a lovely store on Second Avenue with half a dozen rooms on two floors. I bought a Zane Grey *Thundering Herd* in an immaculate 1919 dust jacket for $160. I was flying high now. There were books everywhere we looked, and even if the Seattle boys weren't giving them away, I saw decent margin in almost everything I touched. "This is one of those days, isn't it?" Eleanor said. "I'll bet if you went back there and flushed the toilet, books would come pouring out." We went to a mystery specialist called Spade and Archer. It was in a bank building downtown, in a fifth-floor office that old Sam Spade himself might have occupied in the thirties. The owner was a young blond woman whose credo seemed to be "keep 'em moving." She had two of the three Edgar Box mysteries at a hundred apiece, cost to me, and I took them, figuring they'd be good $200 items in the catalog I was planning. As mysteries they're just fair. But Gore Vidal had written them, hiding behind the Edgar Box moniker when he was starting out in the early fifties, and there's always somebody for a curiosity like that.

In another store I fingered a sharp copy of *White Fang,* amazed that the asking price was just $75. Eleanor warned me off with a look. In the car she said, "It was a second state, that's why it was so cheap." I felt like amateur night in Harlem, but I asked her anyway, what was the point of it, and this kid, this child, gave me another lesson in fly-by-your pants bookscouting.

"There was a mistake on the title page. Macmillan just sliced it out and glued a new one on the cancel stub. . . . You look perplexed, Mr. Janeway, like a man who's never heard the terminology. You don't know what a cancel stub is? . . . How long have you been in the business?"

"Long enough to know a lot about a few things and damn little about most of it."

"Well, this kind of thing happened a lot in the old days. The publisher would make a mistake in a line or word, but by the time they noticed it, ten thousand copies had been printed and maybe five thousand had been distributed. If it was an important author, like Jack London, they didn't want to release any more with the mistake, but they didn't want to redo all those books either. So Macmillan printed a new title page, in the case of *White Fang,* then they sliced out the old ones on all those flawed copies and just glued the new one right onto the stub."

"They just tipped it in."

"Sure. Labor was cheap then, and even those factory grunts could do a decent job of it. The average book collector won't even see it, but a bookman can't miss it unless it's done with real finesse. Just look down in the gutter and there it is, like a man who had an arm cut off and sewn back on again. Doran did the same thing with one of Winston Churchill's early books, *My African Journey.* They bought the remainder from the British publisher and just slashed out the title page and put in their own on the cancel stub. That's why the first American edition comes in a British casing, with Hodder and Stoughton on the spine and a tipped-in Doran title page. It was one of Doran's first books, and he was lowballing to save money."

"Oh," I said lamely.

We stopped for lunch. I wanted to talk about her case but she wouldn't get into it: it would only screw up an otherwise pleasant day, she said. We drifted back toward the Kingdome. Her car was gone: her father had picked it up for her and had it towed to a gas station a few blocks away. We drove past and saw it there in the lot. We were in the neighborhood anyway, so we stopped in the big Goodwill store on Dearborn. I don't do thrift stores much anymore— usually they are run by idiots who think they are book dealers, without a lick of experience or a grain of knowledge to back them up. In Denver the Goodwills have become laughingstocks among dealers and scouts. They have their silly little antique rooms where they put everything that looks old—every ratty, worn-out never-was that ever came out of the publishing industry. They mark their prices in ink, destroying any value the thing might have, and when you try to tell them that, they stare at you with dull eyes and say they've got to do it that way. The store in Seattle didn't ink its books to death, but it didn't matter—they had the same mentality when it came to pricing. The shelves were clogged with common, crummy books, some still available on Walden remainder tables for two dollars, marked six and seven in this so-called thrift store. Naturally, they missed the one good book. Eleanor found it as she browsed one side while I worked the other. She peeked around the corner with that sad-little-girl-oh-so-lost look on her face. "Scuse me, sir, could you loan me a dollar? . . . My family's destitute, my daddy broke his leg, my little brother's got muscular dystrophy, and my mamma's about to sell her virtue on First Avenue." I made a convulsive grab at my wallet. "Damn, you *are* good!" I said with forced admiration. "You're breaking my damn heart." She grinned with all her teeth and held up a fine first of Robert Traver's wonderful *Anatomy of a Murder*. It was a nice scarce little piece, worth at least $100 I guessed: a good sleeper because the Book of the Month edition is exactly the same size and shape and so prolific that even real bookpeople won't bother to pick it up and look. Goodwill wanted $4 for it. She paid with my dollar and her nickels and dimes, then haggled with me in the parking lot: "Gregor would give me at least forty for this, and I'm waiting breathlessly to see if you're inclined to do the honorable thing." I gave her forty-five, but made a point of getting my dollar back, and we both enjoyed my good-natured grumbling for the next half hour.

After wading through the dreck, it was good to be back in a real bookstore again. In a place downtown, she spent most of her money on a miniature book, a suede-leather copy of Shakespeare no larger than the tip of her thumb. "I'm really a sucker for these things," she said. "I'll buy them if there's the least bit of margin." I knew almost nothing about the miniature-book trade, only that, like every other specialty, it has its high spots that are coveted and cherished. Eleanor filled me in as we drove. "This was published by David Bryce in Glasgow around the turn of the century. Bryce did lots of miniatures, some of them quite special. I once had a Bryce's dictionary, which they called the smallest dictionary in the world. It was only about an inch square and it had about four hundred pages, with a little metal slipcase and a foldout magnifying glass. You could carry it on a key ring."

I held the Shakespeare between my thumb and forefinger. "You think there's any margin in this?"

"I don't care, I didn't buy it to get rich. Maybe I could double up wholesale, but I think I'll keep it for a while as a memento of this day. It'll be my good-luck piece. I think I'll need one, don't you?"

Bookscouting gives you the same kind of thrills as gambling. You flirt with the Lady in much the same way. You get hot and the books won't stop coming: you get cold and you might as well be playing pinochle with your mother-in-law. I was hot, and when Luck is running, she flaunts all the odds of circumstance and coincidence. I found two early-fifties Hopalong Cassidy books by a guy Eleanor had never heard of, some cowboy named Tex Burns. I savored the pleasure of telling her that Tex Burns was like Edgar Box, a moniker . . . in another lifetime he had been a young man named Louis L'Amour. Amazing to find two such in a single day, but I take Luck where I find her. These cost me $4 each and were worth around $250. I razzed Eleanor for not knowing. We headed north and I said, for at least the fifth time, "I thought *everybody* knew about Tex Burns." She crossed her eyes and looked down her nose at me, a perfect picture of rank stupidity.

It was the damnedest day, full of sorrow and joy and undercut with that sweet slice of tension. I'll blink and she'll be gone, I thought at least a dozen times: I'll turn my head for a second and when I look up, she'll be two blocks away, running like hell. But I had set my course and the day was waning, and still there had been nothing between us but the most cheerful camaraderie. Out of the blue, in midafternoon, she said, "I guess it's a good thing you turned into an asshole when you did: I may've been on the verge of falling in love with you and then where would we be?" Coming from nowhere like that, it put me on the floor. It also brought to a critical point a problem I had failed to consider—I had to pee in the worst possible way. I told her to stay put, disappeared into the rest room, and found her still there, working the shelves, when I came hustling out a minute later. I didn't worry much about her after that.

She took me to a place near the university called Half Price Books. It nestled modestly on a street named Roosevelt Way, a cornucopia of books on two

114

floors. There were no real high spots, but I could've spent two hundred on stock, it was that kind of place. I bought only what I couldn't leave and got out for less than eighty. We were going out the door when Eleanor spied a copy of Trish Aandahl's book on the Graysons. "You oughta buy this," she said. "It's a helluva read."

She was a little curious at how fast I did buy it. I still hadn't told her about my interest in Grayson and probably wouldn't now until we were on the airplane and well away from here. "You drive," I said, throwing her the keys. "I want to fondle my stuff." But all I did as she wove through the crowded, narrow streets was browse through Aandahl. The jacket was an art deco design, with elegant curlicues and old-style fringe decorations. It was dominated by black-and-white photographs of the Grayson brothers, a little out of focus and solving none of the mystery of the men. The art director had overlapped the pictures and then pulled them apart, leaving parts of each infringed upon the other, the ragged gulf between them suggesting disruption and conflict. The title, *Crossfire*, stood out in red: under it, in black, the subtitle, *The Tragedies and Triumphs of Darryl and Richard Grayson*. Richard's resemblance to Leslie Howard was more real than imagined: Darryl Grayson's image was darker, fuzzier, barely distinguishable. His was the face on the barroom floor, and not because it had been painted there. The jacket blurb on Trish Aandahl consisted of one line, that the author was a reporter for the *Seattle Times,* and there was no photograph. If the lady wasn't interested in personal glory, she'd be the first reporter I had ever known who felt that way. I thumbed the index: my eye caught the name of Allan Huggins, the Grayson bibliographer, mentioned half a dozen times in the text. Gaston Rigby made his appearance on page 535, and there were three mentions for Crystal Moon Rigby. Archie Moon was prominent, entering the Grayson saga on page 15 and appearing prolifically thereafter. A section of photographs showed some of Grayson's books, but, strangely, the only photographs of the subjects themselves were the same two of poor quality that had been used on the jacket. It was 735 pages thick, almost as big as the Huggins bibliography, and packed with what looked to be anecdotal writing at its best.

The only negative was that it was a remainder copy, savagely slashed across the top pages with a felt-tip marker. I hated that: it's a terrible way to remainder books, and Viking is the worst offender in the publishing industry. "Look at this," I griped. "These bastards must hire morons right off the street with a spray can. I can't believe they'd do that to a book."

"It's just merchandise to them," she said. "Nobody cares, only freaks like you and me. It is a fine-looking book, except for the remainder mark."

"I saw a woman once who would've been a beauty queen, if you could just forget the fact that somebody had shot her in the face with a .45."

We were stopped at a red light about a block from the freeway. She was looking at me in a different way now, as if I had suddenly revealed a facet of my character that she had been unable to guess before. "Are you interested in the Graysons? If you are, I know a guy who used to have the best collection of Grayson books in the universe. Maybe he's still got a few of them. His store's not far from here."

"I think we've got time for that. Lead on."

Otto Murdock was an old-time Seattle book dealer who had seen better days. Twenty years of hard drinking had reduced him to this—a shabby-looking storefront in a ramshackle building in a run-down section on the north side. "This man used to be Seattle's finest," Eleanor said, "till bad habits did him in. For a long time he was partners with Gregory Morrice. You ever hear of Morrice and Murdock?"

"Should I have?"

"If Seattle ever had an answer to Pepper and Stern, they were it. Only the best of the best, you know what I mean? But they had a falling-out years ago over Otto's drinking. Morrice does it alone now—he's got a book showplace down in Pioneer Square, and Otto wound up here. I hear he ekes out a living, but it can't be much . . . he wholesales all his good stuff. They call him In-and-Out Murdock now. A good book means nothing but another bottle to him."

She pulled to the curb at the door of the grimiest bookstore I had seen in a long time. The windows were caked with dirt. Inside, I could see the ghostly outlines of hundreds of books, stacked ends-out against the glass. The lettering on the hand-painted sign had begun to flake, leaving what had once said BOOKS now reading BOO. The interior was dark and getting darker by the moment. It was a quarter to five, and already night was coming. A block away, a streetlight flicked on.

"He looks closed for the night," I said.

"He's still got his OPEN sign out."

I knew that didn't mean much, especially with an alcoholic who might not know at any given time what year it was. We sat at the curb and the rain was a steady hum.

"I'll check him out," Eleanor said. "No sense both of us getting wet."

She jumped out and ran to the door. It pushed open at her touch and she waved to me as she went inside. I came along behind her, walking into a veritable cave of books. There were no lights: it was even darker inside than it had looked from the street, and for a moment I couldn't see Eleanor at all. Then I heard her voice: "Mr. Murdock . . . Mr. Murdock . . . hey, Otto, you've got customers out here." She opened a door and a dim beam of light fell out of a back room. "Mr. Murdock?" she said softly.

I saw her in silhouette, moving toward me. "That's funny," she said. "Looks like he went away and left the store wide open."

I groped along the wall and found a switch. It was dim even with the lights on. I took my first long look at how the mighty could fall. Murdock had tumbled all the way down, hitting rock bottom in a rat's nest of cheap, worn, and tattered books. His bookshelves had long since filled to overflowing, and the floor was his catchall. Books were piled everywhere. The piles grew until they collapsed, leaving the books scattered where they fell, with new piles to grow from the rubble like a forest after a fire. I walked along the back wall, looking for anything of value. It was tough work—the fiction section was almost uniformly book-club editions of authors who aren't collected anyway: Sidney Sheldon, Robert Wilder, Arthur Hailey. A sign thumbtacked to the wall said BOOKS FOR A BUCK. Cheap at half the price, I thought.

"You see anything?" Eleanor asked from the far corner.

"Four computer books, two copies of *The Joy of Sex,* and five million Stephen King derivatives."

She sighed. "Put 'em all together and what've you got?"

"Desk-top breeding by vampires."

She gave a sharp laugh, tinged with sadness. "This place gets worse every time I come here. I'm afraid

I'm wasting your time; it looks like Otto hasn't had a good book in at least a year."

You never knew, though. This was the great thing about books, that in any pile of dreck a rose might hide, and we were drawn on through the junk in the search for the one good piece. I had worked my way around the edge of the front room and had reached the door to the back when I heard Eleanor say, "Good grief, look at this." She had dropped to her hands and knees, out of sight from where I stood. I asked what she had and she said, "You'll have to come look, you'll never believe it." I found her near the door, holding a near-perfect copy of *The Fountainhead.*

"It's a whole bag of stuff," she said. "All Ayn Rand, all in this condition."

There were two *Fountainhead* firsts, both binding states, red and green, in those lovely crisp red jackets. There was an *Atlas Shrugged,* signed *Ayn* in old ink and inscribed with endearment as if to an old friend. Finally there was the freshest copy of *We the Living* that I ever hoped to see in this lifetime. A Rand specialist had once told me that there were probably only a few hundred jacketed copies of *We the Living* in existence.

Six, seven grand retail, I thought. Sitting by the door in an open bag, in an unattended store.

"It doesn't make much sense, does it?" Eleanor said.

I shook my head.

"If the door blew open, they'd get screwed by the rain in a minute," she said. "Jesus, Otto must've really lost it."

"Look, you know this guy—do you think he's so far gone that he wouldn't know what he could get for these?"

"I doubt that. Otto might not know about the new

guys—the Graftons, Paretskys, Burkes—but he'd sure as hell know about Ayn Rand."

We stood there for a minute and touched them.

"What're you gonna do?" Eleanor said.

"Damned if I know. I'm dying to buy these from him."

"What would you offer him?"

I pondered it. "Three grand. Thirty-five hundred if I had to."

"You could get them for less than that. There are some guys in this town who'd pay him that kind of money, but Otto's burned his bridges here. I'll bet you could get 'em for two."

"I'd give him three in a heartbeat."

"Take 'em, then. Leave him a note, make him an offer like that, and you'll be doing him the biggest favor of the year. Tell him you'll send the books back if he doesn't like it. I guarantee you you're doing him a favor, because nine out of ten people would come in here and see those books and take 'em and run like hell. You know that's true. Take 'em and leave him a note."

"That's probably against the law," I said, but I knew it probably wasn't. In most states, theft requires evil intent.

I put the books back in the bag, folded the top over carefully, and tucked it under my arm. "What's in the back room?"

"Just more of the same," she said.

We went on back. The room was cluttered with books and trash. In a corner was an ancient rolltop desk half-buried in junk books and old magazines

"I see he still reads the *AB*," I said.

"That's probably how he sells most of his books." Eleanor looked along the shelves behind the desk. She held up a thin canvas bag. "Here's his briefcase. He never goes anywhere without this. In the old days, when he and Morrice were top dogs, you'd see him at book fairs and stuff, and he'd always have his two or three best pieces in this book bag. It was his trademark: if he liked you, you'd get to look in the bag; if he didn't, you wouldn't."

She fiddled with the straps. "Wanna look?"

"I wouldn't do that."

Reluctantly, she pushed the bag back to the corner of the desk. "He probably hasn't used it in ten years, except to carry a bottle around." She sighed. "Not a Grayson book in sight. So much for my good intentions."

"That looks like another door over there." I walked across the room and opened it.

A set of steps disappeared into the dark upper floor.

"Try calling him again," Eleanor said.

I cupped my hands to my mouth and shouted Murdock's name up the stairwell.

"He's just not here," she said.

"I don't know. Something's not right." I moved into the stairwell.

"Don't go up there. That's how people get blown away."

I turned and looked at her.

"Otto's got a gun. I saw it once when I was here last year."

"Good argument." I backed away from the stairs.

"He's gotta be up there sleeping one off. He'll wake up in a panic over those books, come running down the stairs, and when he finds your note, he'll be so relieved he'll drop dead right there on the spot."

I wavered.

"Goddammit, take the books," she said. "Don't be a fool."

She's right, I thought. I went back and sat at Otto's

121

desk, pulled out a sheet of paper, and wrote out my offer. I made it three thousand and signed it with both my Denver phone numbers, then taped it to his canvas bag where he'd be sure to find it.

In the car we sat fondling the merchandise, lost in that rapture that comes too seldom these days, even in the book business.

It was just six o'clock when I happened to glance in the mirror and saw Pruitt watching from the far corner.

14

He appeared like a single frame in a set of flash cards. You blink and he's gone, and you're not quite sure he was ever there at all. I was as sure as I needed to be: I was suddenly tense, keyed up and ready to fight. We headed down to the Hilton. I was driving now, handling the freeway traffic with one eye on my mirror. If he was on my tail as I swung into town, I didn't see him. He was a magician, good enough to make you doubt your eyes. The invisible man, Slater had called him, the best tail in the business, and he wasn't keeping after me because he liked my looks. *Who is Slater?* The voice of Trish Aandahl played in my head. I had a hunch I was about to find out who Slater was and what he wanted. He had just five hours to break the stalemate: if Pruitt didn't play Slater's hand by then, we'd be in the air and it would all be academic.

I parked in the hotel garage and took Eleanor to my room. I poured us drinks, cutting hers slightly with water. She asked if she could use the shower and I said sure. I sat on the bed at the telephone, happy for a few minutes alone.

I punched up Slater's number in Denver.

A woman answered. "Yeah?"

The lovely Tina, no doubt.

I tried to sound like someone from their social set, a cross between George Foreman and Bugs Moran: "I need Slater."

"So who're you?"

"I'm the man with the money."

"I'm not followin' ya, Jack."

"Just put Slater on the phone, he'll be glad you did. Tell him it's the man with the money."

"Clyde's not here."

"So where's he at?"

"What's it about?"

"It's about a bagful of money, sweetheart, and I'll tell ya what, if I don't get to give it to him pretty damn quick, I'm out of here. Slater can fly to Jacksonville and pick it up himself."

"I don't know anything about this."

"That's how you want to keep it, hon. Let's just say Slater did a little job for me and this is the bonus I promised him."

"Well, damn."

"Oh, let's not agonize over it. If you don't wanna tell me where the man is, it's no skin off my nose."

She was breathing in my ear. "Is it . . ."

I waited.

". . . is it a *lot* of money?"

I couldn't help laughing: I had played her just right. "Let's say there's a good reason he wanted it in cash."

"Wait a minute, I'll give ya a number."

I could hear her fumbling around. "Call him at area

123

code two oh six. It's six two four, oh five hundred. Ask for seventeen twelve."

I sat staring at the phone. Slowly I straightened up and looked at the far wall.

Slater was in the room next door.

And I knew I might as well have him in my lap.

Eleanor came out of the bathroom in a swirl of steam. She sat at the mirror sipping her drink and combing out her incredible hair. I thought she was lovely, alive with the sparkle of youth in spite of her trouble. She wanted to talk. Our short mutual history was the topic of the moment, to which was added her general assessment that we were a damned exceptional book-hunting team. "Today was special," she said, "a real toot." I looked at the far wall, where Slater was, and told her the pleasure was all mine. To her way of thinking, it was the perfect day, one she'd remember: "This is how I'd live my life, every day of the year, if I had my way. A loaf of bread, a jug of wine, some good books . . ."

She looked at me with open affection in the glass. "And you."

She tugged at a place where her hair had knotted up. "We wouldn't even need much money," she said. "Money just takes the edge off. You need to be a little hungry to get that rush that comes with finding a really good one."

Again she amazed me, this kid barely out of her teens.

"It's not-having money that keeps you on your toes," she said, meeting my eyes in the mirror.

I told her we were probably the most on-our-toes pair since Ginger Rogers and Fred Astaire, and she laughed. "Why couldn't I've found you a year ago," she mused. "Why-o-why-o-why?"

"It wouldn't've done much good," I said absently, "since we've already got it well established that I'm old enough to be your father."

She scoffed at this. "Yeah, if you'd started hiking up skirts when you were thirteen, maybe." She looked at me in the mirror and said, blushing fiercely, "You're probably not up to a little seduction right now, I'll bet."

I thought long and hard about how to respond, the words to use. The ones I picked were clumsy and inadequate. "Under the circumstances, you know, this is not the best idea you've had all day."

"Well, it was just a thought."

I told her it was a lovely thought, I was flattered. In another time, maybe . . . in another place . . .

"In another life," she said, closing the book on it.

I decided to hang out here until just before our flight left. The certainty of Slater's listening in on us I accepted as the lesser of two evils: here I could keep my back to the wall until the last possible moment. I looked at the wall but it told me nothing. I knew what I needed to know. Detectives today can punch a hole the size of a pin through a concrete wall, run a wire into bed with a cheating housewife, record her ecstasy with the other guy in eight-track stereo, and add a Michael Jackson sound track for the entertainment of the office staff. I told Eleanor none of this: no sense waving a red flag just yet. I called out and ordered a pizza delivered. She kept up a running chatter while we ate—her way, I guessed, of relieving her own building tension. She talked about all the great books she had found that had been screwed up by one anal-obsessive chucklehead or another. I laughed as only a fellow traveler can: I too knew that peculiar heartache. You find a grand copy of an old Ross Macdonald and open it to see that some fool has written all over

125

it, destroying half its value and all of its factory-fresh desirability. Why is a book the only gift that the giver feels free and often compelled to deface before giving? Who would give a shirt or a blouse and write, in ink, *Happy birthday from Bozo* all over the front of it? Even worse than the scribblers, Eleanor said, were the name embossers. "When I become the queen of hell, I'm going to parade all those embosser freaks past me in a long naked line. I'll have an embosser with the word IDIOT on it, smothered in hot coals, and I'll emboss *them,* sir, in the tenderest place that *you* can imagine." That punishment sounded pretty sexist to me, which was exactly her point. "Have you ever seen an embossermark with a woman's name on it . . . ever?" I had, but only once and it probably didn't count—a sadistic dominatrix whose murder I had investigated long ago. "Women write in the spirit of giving," Eleanor said. "Men emboss like they're branding cattle, to possess." For the books, we sadly agreed, the result was the same.

I hoped Slater was getting an earful. I looked at the clock: the plane took off in three hours, I was almost home free. The day was ending on a wave of nickel-and-dime bookstuff. I asked her to define anal-obsessive chucklehead, please, and tell me how that particular characteristic expresses itself. She laughed and slapped my hand and said, "Get out of here, you damn fool," and the night wound down. We drank a toast to the defilers of good books—scribblers, embossers, and the remainder goons at the Viking Press—may their conversion to the cause be swift and permanent. At eight-thirty she asked if she could mail a letter. She sat at the table and scratched out a few lines on hotel stationery: then she turned away, shielding the letter with her body so I couldn't see it. I knew she had taken something out of her purse and dropped it in the envelope with the letter. I was riddled with second thoughts, but there wasn't anything to be done about it: I could either be her jailer or her friend. She licked the envelope, sealed it, and called for a bellhop to mail it. And I sat mute, her friend, and watched it disappear.

I was a bit curt with her after that. She asked when we should leave and I told her not to worry about it, I'd let her know. I had decided to linger here until exactly seventy minutes before takeoff, then haul ass for Sea-Tac in a cloud of smoke. I hoped the TV would cover our sudden retreat. I'd let Slater listen to the *Tonight Show* until reality began to dawn: if I was lucky, we'd be halfway to the airport before he knew it. Out on the street I'd have only Pruitt to deal with.

Duck soup, I thought, an even-money standoff.

I always bet on me with odds like that. I had forgotten that line from Burns about the best-laid schemes of mice and men. I should read more poetry.

15

At 9:35 the telephone rang. We looked at each other and neither of us moved. I let it ring and after a while it stopped. Now we'd see, I thought: if it had been a test, somebody would be over to see if we were still here.

At 9:43 it rang again. By then I had rethought the strategy of silence, and I picked it up.

"It's me." Slater's voice sounded puffy, distant.

"So it is," I said flatly, with a faint W. C. Fields undertone.

"We need to talk."

"Send me a telegram."

"Don't get cute, Janeway, your time's running out."

I gave a doubtful grunt.

"We need to talk now. I'm doing you a favor if you've got the sense to listen."

I listened.

"Come out in the hall."

"Yeah, right."

"I'm in the room next door." His voice was raspy, urgent. "I need you to come out in the hall so we can talk."

Then I got a break I couldn't have bought. Eleanor got up and went to the bathroom.

"You must think I was born yesterday," I said as soon as she closed the door.

"This is on the level. I know you're on the eleven-eighteen. I'm giving you fair warning, you're never gonna make it."

"Try and stop me and you're a dead man, Slater. That's fair warning for both of you."

"It's not me that's gonna stop you, stupid. Goddammit, are you coming out or not?"

I thought about it for five seconds. "Yeah." I hung up.

I opened my bag and got out my gun. Strapped it on under my coat and waited till Eleanor came out of the bathroom.

"Just a little problem with my bill, no big deal," I told her. "I've got to go upstairs and straighten it out. You sit right there, we'll leave as soon as I get back."

She didn't say anything but I could see she wasn't buying it. She sat where I told her and clasped her hands primly in her lap, her face a mask of sudden tension.

I opened the door and eased my way out into the hall. I had my thumb hooked over my belt, two inches from the gun.

Slater was down at the end of the hall, looking at the wall. I pulled the door shut and he turned. I think I was ready for anything but what I saw. His face had been beaten into watermelon. His left eye was battered shut, his nose pounded flat against his face. His right eye was open wide, a grotesque effect like something from an old Lon Chaney film.

"What happened to you?"

I had flattened against the wall so I could see both ways. Slater came toward me, shuffling in pain. His leg was stiff and he held his arm in a frozen crook, suspended as if by an invisible sling.

"Pruitt," he rasped, livid. "Fucking bastard Pruitt."

I just looked at him, unable to imagine what might have gone down between them. He came closer and I saw what had caused that puffiness in his voice. His dentures were gone—smashed, I guessed, along with the rest of him—and he talked like a toothless old man.

"Goddammit, I'll rip that fucker's guts out."

"What happened?" I said again.

"Bastard son of a bitch sapped me, damn near took my head off. I went down and he did the rest of it with his feet."

He did it well, I thought.

"He'll pay, though, he'll pay for this in ways I haven't even thought up yet. Even if he doesn't know it was me, I'll know, and that'll be enough." He took a little step to the side and held on to the wall for support. "And it starts today. I'm gonna tell you something, Janeway, and then it's your baby. Pruitt will kill you if he has to."

129

"He should play the lottery, his odds are better."

"Don't you underestimate that fucker, that's what I'm telling you."

"I'm reading that. Now why don't you tell me what he wants."

"The book, stupid, haven't you figured that out yet? He's been after it for years."

"Tell me something real. Grayson couldn't make a book worth this much trouble if he used uncut sheets of thousand-dollar bills for endpapers."

"That's what you think. Forget what you thought you knew and maybe you'll learn something. Your little friend in there's got the answer, and Pruitt's gonna take her away from you and get it out of her if he's got to tear out her fingernails."

"Say something that makes sense. Pruitt had her and you two handed her to me. Now he's ready to kill me to get her back?"

He started to say something but a click in the hall brought him up short. We both tensed. I gripped the gun under my coat.

The door swung in and Eleanor peeped into the hall.

She didn't say anything. She was looking past me, at Slater, and he was looking at her. Her face was ashen, her eyes wide with fright.

"Eleanor," I said, "go back in the room and sit down."

She backed away and closed the door.

"She knows you," I said to Slater. "She recognized you just then."

He tried to move past me. I stepped out and blocked his way.

"What do you want from me, Janeway? I'm doing you a favor here, maybe you should remember that. I didn't have to tell you anything."

"You haven't told me anything yet. Pick up where you left off. Make it make sense."

"Goddammit, I'm hurting, I need to lie down."

"Talk to me. Give me the short version, then you can lie down."

He grimaced and held his side. But I wasn't going to let him pass until he told me what I wanted to know.

"Me and Pruitt grew up together. Southside Chicago, early fifties. You want my life story?"

"The short version, Slater. We haven't got all night here, I've got a plane to catch."

They were kids together, birds of a feather. Nobody could stand either of them, I thought, so they hung together.

"He called me for a few favors when I was a cop. We'd have a beer or two whenever he passed through Denver. Four years ago, on one of his trips through, he told me about this book."

He coughed. "He'd been chasing it for a long time even then. He was trying to track down a woman he was sure had taken it, but he never could find her. He'd run every lead up a blind alley."

"What's the big attraction?"

"Pruitt knows where he can sell it. For more money than any of us ever saw."

"I don't believe it."

"Then fuck you. Do you want to hear this or not? . . . I can't stand up in this hall forever. I'll tell you this, he convinced the hell out of me. That night I wrote out the stuff he told me on that paper you read, but nothing ever came of it . . . until last month. Then I get a call from Seattle and it's Pruitt. It's all hitting the fan over this book he's after. There's a woman named Rigby in the Taos jail and Pruitt thinks she's got it."

"Why didn't he go down himself?"

131

"Later on he did: he had some Seattle angles to work out first. He thought the girl's parents might know about it, might even know where she'd hidden it; maybe she'd even mailed it to 'em. So he sent me to Taos to nose around, see what was what. I'd barely got there when she came up for bail. Pruitt came in the next day."

"And did what?"

"Made her wish she'd never been born. That was just the beginning of what he had up his sleeve for her. The book's been like a monkey on his back, I could see it driving him closer to the edge every day. I started thinking he might even kill her for it. But she wouldn't give it up."

"Probably because she didn't have it."

"But she went back to get it, didn't she?"

"She went back for something. Weren't you boys on her tail?"

"You're not gonna believe this, Janeway. She slipped us."

I just stared at him.

"She's cute, all right, a little too cute for her own damn good. The next thing we knew she'd skipped the state. Pruitt went nuclear."

"This must be when you got the bright idea of dragging me into it."

"Our time was running out. She could be picked up by the cops anywhere and we'd be up the creek. Pruitt thought she'd head for Seattle: he put out some people he knew to watch her haunts. And it didn't take long to spot her: she turned up in North Bend a few days later. I didn't know what to do. I sure didn't want to let it go. Pruitt had promised me a piece of it, if I helped him reel it in. I'm talking about more money than you'll believe, so don't even ask."

"I thought money didn't matter to you, Clydell.

What about the radio job? What about *Denver* magazine?"

"All bullshit. I owe more federal income tax than I've got coming in. I do a weekend gig on radio, not enough to pay my water bill. The magazine piece'll be lining birdcages before the ink's even dry. Business sucks; I'm almost broke. What more do you need to know? And besides all that, I really was afraid of what he'd do to that kid."

He took a long, painful breath. "So if you're looking for a good guy in this, it's probably me. That same night I told Pruitt about you. I thought I could tempt you with the bail money, it was easy to get the papers from the bondsman; hell, he doesn't care who brings her in. But the bail was just bait. I knew you'd never bust Rigby for that bail money, not once you had that book in your mind."

He touched his face. "I really thought you might get the book from her. You might have, too, if the cops hadn't busted her and messed everything up. I sold you to Pruitt as a bookhunter. He didn't like it but I talked hard and late that night he decided to try it."

"And that's what finally got your face kicked in. Pruitt didn't like the way it turned out."

"I had to try something. She knows us both on sight, and Pruitt's her worst nightmare. She's right to be scared of him: he's over the edge now. He's your problem, you and that poor kid in there. Me, I'm out of it, I've had enough. I'm goin' back to Denver."

He pushed his way past. Stopped at his door; looked back at me. "I'll give you two free pieces of advice. Pruitt didn't get to be called the invisible man for nothing. He can fade into a crowd and you can't see him even when you know he's there. He's great with makeup—wigs, beards, glasses—he can make himself over while you're scratching your ass wonder-

ing where he went. And he's always got people around
him, scumbags who owe him favors. One of 'em's a fat
man, but there may be others. Don't trust anybody.
Don't let 'em get close and sucker punch you."

He opened his door. "You didn't hear any of this
from me, okay? I'll figure out my own ways of paying
Pruitt back, and I don't want him sticking a knife in
my ass before I've got it worked out. So here's your
second hot tip. Pruitt fucked up your car. If you're
counting on that to get you to the airport, think
again."

He looked at his watch. "You cut it pretty short, old
buddy. You got one hour to get her there. Stay clear of
old ladies and fat men, Janeway. If you ever get back
to Denver, call me, we'll have lunch. Maybe I'll have a
job for you."

16

My brain kicked up in the cop mode. From then
on I was running on overdrive.

My goals had narrowed to one. Nothing else
mattered—not money or pain, not even the books I
had foolishly taken from Otto Murdock.

We were going on the run. That meant travel light,
travel fast: leave the books, leave the clothes, call the
Rigbys from New Mexico, hope Crystal could come
pick up my stuff. Not a perfect answer, but when
you've got a woman to guard, eight grand worth of
books in a cardboard box, and a man on your tail who

might be seriously unhinged, perfection is a little too much to ask for.

We were going to Taos, over Pruitt's dead body if that's how he had to have it.

No time for cops: no help there. By the time Seattle checked me out, my flight would be somewhere over Wyoming.

Move.

Move now and move fast.

I called out for a cab. The dispatcher said she had drivers in the neighborhood. The wait would be five minutes, ten tops.

Cover your ass.

I called the desk. Yes, the Hilton ran a shuttle service to the airport. It ran twice each hour, at seven minutes past the half hour.

It was now 9:55.

The key.

Crystal would need my room key to get in here and take out my stuff. Had to hide it somewhere so she could find it.

In the car.

Out there in the garage, all logic dictated, Pruitt would be waiting.

Good. Face the bastard head-on.

Eleanor sat rigidly in the chair. She looked terrified, her knuckles white as she gripped the armrests.

"Wh-why're you . . . d-do-ing this?"

I reached out to her but she recoiled. "I'm on your side, kid," I told her, but it didn't help.

"Th-at m-man in the hall . . ."

"His name is Slater. He's gone now."

"He's with the d-darkman."

"He's nothing. He's out of here."

"Darkm-man."

I squeezed her shoulder. "Cheer up now, you're in good hands."

I turned off the light, flipped off the TV. Nobody was fooling anybody anymore.

"Let's go," I said.

We went with the clothes on our backs. I hung a DO NOT DISTURB sign on the door.

"Stay close," I said as we came into the garage.

She was shivering so violently she could barely walk. Our footsteps echoed as we crossed to the far wall where I had left my car.

He was with us all the way, I could feel him out there in the dark. "Oh, please." Eleanor's voice quaked with fear. She too had sensed him there, and Slater had it right, he was her bogeyman: just the thought of him made her incoherent and numb.

"Darkman," she whispered. "D-d . . . kman."

I put an arm over her shoulder. "Everything's cool. We'll laugh about it on the plane."

"Darkm-m-an's s-here."

"Hush now. We're heading for the land of sunshine."

I jerked open the door and hustled her into the car. I looked over the roof, my eyes sweeping down the ramp and across the garage to the door. Just for show, I moved around the car, opened the driver's door, and slid under the wheel.

I kept watching through the mirrors. I put the key in the ignition and turned it. It did nothing but click.

Eleanor whimpered faintly in the seat beside me.

"It's okay, I expected that," I said calmly. "Just sit tight, we'll be out of here in a minute."

I got out of the car, locking the doors.

Went through some motions, with peripheral vision working like sonar.

Raised the hood.

Scanned the garage.

Looked at my watch while pretending to look at the engine.

Ten oh one. The shuttle took off in six minutes.

Got down on the garage floor. Pretended to look under the car. Palmed the key to my room and slipped it behind the front bumper.

Scanned the garage from there. With my back to the wall, I could see everything under the wheels of fifty automobiles.

Two pairs of feet . . . two men, coming my way.

I came up slowly, an Oscar-winning performance. It was a fat man with dark hair, flanked by a young, muscular guy in jeans. The fat man wore a business suit and waddled my way with an air of sweet benevolence.

I slammed the hood and wondered why I wasn't surprised when they came to the car in the slot next to mine.

"Hey, buddy," the fat man said. "You know how to get to Queen Anne Hill?"

"I think it's on the west side, just north of town. I'm a stranger here myself."

He looked at me over the roof of his car. "Got trouble?"

"Yeah. Damn thing won't start."

"I'll have the guy downstairs call you a tow truck if you want."

"Won't do much good. I'm in kind of a hurry."

"Might be something simple. Bobby here's good with cars. Why don't you just let him take a peek under your hood?"

"That can't cost me much."

I raised the hood and the three of us crowded into the space between the car and the wall. Here they were, close enough to kiss. I could see a fresh scrape on the fat man's neck where he'd cut himself shaving.

The meat quivered around his ears like vanilla pudding. The kid was carrying his right hand in a fetal position, curled inward toward his belt. He was cradling a roll of quarters, I thought—almost as effective as a set of brass knucks if he got his weight behind it.

Here I am, I thought, take your best shot. When the kid moved, I took a fast step to one side. His closed fist smacked against the car, the roll broke open, and the coins clattered across the floor. I hit him a hard right to the jaw and he went down like a sack of laundry. I could sense the fat man groping for something under his coat, but I was faster and I had the same thing under mine. I whirled around and kneed him in the groin. I punched his wind out, and the next time he blinked I had my gun in his jowls, half-buried in fat.

He was breathing hard through his nose, his eyes wide with fear and surprise. I slapped him across the mouth and spun him around, slamming him against the wall. I took a .38 snub-nose out of his belt and put it in mine. The kid was still cold. I knelt down, frisked him, and got another gun for my arsenal.

I manhandled the fat man back around the car. "Where's Pruitt?"

"I don't know any Pruitt."

I grabbed his necktie and jerked him silly. He tried to roll away: I hammered him under the ribs and he doubled over, wheezing at the floor. I grabbed his hair and smashed his head hard against the car, got down there with him between the cars, and said, through gritted teeth, "You wanna die in this garage, fat man? You wanna die right now, here on this floor?" I had the gun jammed between his jawbone and his eardrum, and I had his attention.

He rolled his eyes down the ramp, into the spiraling darkness.

"That's better. Lie to me again and you're dog food. Tell me now, are there any more rats down there with him?"

He shook his head none.

"Gimme your keys."

He fished them out of his pocket.

"Which one's for the trunk?"

He held it up. I took the ring and opened the trunk.

"Get in and lie down."

He looked at me with pleading eyes. I grabbed him by the scruff of the neck and spun him around and sat him down hard in the trunk. I motioned with the gun and he swung his legs over the rim, curling his butterball body around the spare tire.

I slammed the trunk. It was 10:08, and the enemy himself had delivered us from evil.

I got Eleanor moved over and threw the guns on the seat between us. We careened down the ramp in the fat man's car. Eleanor sat frozen, gripping her knees like a kid on her first roller-coaster ride. I reached the street just as the shuttle pulled out. I pealed rubber turning north into Sixth Avenue. I was soaring, I was high enough to hit the moon. I had to rein myself in, force myself to stop for a red light. The last thing I needed, now that I had the game all but won, was to get stopped by a traffic cop, and me with a car full of guns.

I was trolling the side streets looking for an on-ramp. I stopped for another light. "Darkman," Eleanor said, but I looked and the street was empty.

"He's gone. We kicked his ass, Rigby. It's time to start thinking about what you'll do when you get to New Mexico."

I leaned over the wheel and looked at her. She looked like a stranger, mind-fried with fear.

"We won," I said.

She looked like anything but a winner. She looked

like the thousand and one women a cop meets in a long and violent career. A victim.

"Darkman . . ."

"Is he your stalker?"

She looked at me. "He's everywhere. I can't turn around . . ."

"He's a wrong number, honey, a guy in a gorilla suit. He's only scary if you let him be."

"He was in New Mexico." She closed her eyes and quaked at some private demon. "No matter where I go he finds me. I pick up the phone and he's there, playing that song."

The guy behind us blew his horn. The light was green. I moved out, giving her shoulder a little rub, but she seemed not to notice.

"He's there," she said. "I saw him."

I scanned the street in my mirrors and saw nothing.

"Oh, God," she said. "Oh God oh God oh God . . ."

"We beat him. We're gettin' out of here."

"Take me back to jail."

"We're going to New Mexico."

"No! . . . No . . . take me back to jail . . ."

"I want you to listen to me."

"Take me back to jail . . . take me . . . take me . . ."

No more talk, I thought: the less said at this point the better. I thought if I could get her on the plane, I could win her back: then we'd have the whole ride into Albuquerque to calm down and start digging the truth out. I gave her a long sad look. She had covered her face with her hands, but I could see her eyes looking at me through her fingers.

I gunned the car and banked south into the freeway. I was almost up to thirty when she wrenched open the door and, with a shriek of madness, jumped.

17

I hit the brakes and the car spun across the wet
pavement and slammed into the guardrail. I
leaped out on the rim, running along the edge of a
dark gulf. She was somewhere down in the street: I
couldn't see her, but I heard her scream as I skidded
down the slope. I had a long clear look at the street
running back downtown: she hadn't gone that way, so
she had to have ducked under the freeway to the east.
This led me into a dreary neighborhood of shabby
storefronts and dark flophouses. The rain had kept
people off the street and the hour was late . . . the
block was as dead as an old graveyard. The wet clop of
my feet punctured the steady hiss of the rain, but I
was chasing a ghost. She was gone.

I reached a cross street still clinging to a shred of
hope. She could be blocks away by now, going in any
direction. Guess wrong and kiss her good-bye: the
next time she stuck her head up, she'd be scouting
books in Florida. She could make a pauper's living
forever in that anonymous subculture, never pay
taxes, never have her name recorded on any official
docket, never be seen again by friend or foe. I pushed
on into the rain, as if she had suddenly materialized
in the block ahead. But the street was as empty as
ever. I came to another intersection and stopped to
look. No use running anymore, I could just as likely

be running away from her. I walked along a dim wet block looking in cracks and crevices. Gone with the goddamn wind, son of a bitch. I passed the flickering light of a neighborhood bar and looked at my watch: 10:23. It was still possible to make the plane, if she came to her senses this very minute, if we stumbled into each other in the murk, if the car was still on the ramp where I'd left it, if I was all paid up with the man upstairs, if pigs could fly and I could break every speed limit going to Sea-Tac and get away with it. I stopped and leaned against a mailbox and longed for a break, but Luck had gone her fickle way.

I looked into the bar on a hunch. Nobody there but the neighborhood drunk, who'd been holding up his end of the bar since Prohibition ended. I walked up the street in the rain, unwilling to admit that the fat lady had sung her song. Something could still happen. Something can still happen, I thought again, but my watch was pushing ten-thirty, and it had to happen now.

What happened wasn't quite what I had in mind. A car turned into the street and I knew it was Pruitt half a block away; I had the color and shape of that Pontiac cut into my heart forever. I stepped into the shadows and watched him roll past me. Apparently he hadn't seen me: he cruised by slowly; I stood still and watched him go the length of the block. He was hunting, same as me: he would drive a bit, slow, occasionally stop and look something over. It seemed she had given us all the royal slip. Pruitt stopped at the corner and turned. I broke into a full run, reaching the cross street well before he had turned out of the next block. He was taking it easy, trying to miss nothing as he worked around one block and into another. The block was dark: a streetlight was out, and I thought I could run along the edge of the buildings without being seen. Something might still be salvaged from this rotten night, if I could get close enough to pull that door open and jerk Pruitt's ass out of that car.

A pair of headlights swung toward me two blocks away. I flattened into a doorway as the two cars flicked their brights on and off. It was the fat man's car—I could see the crushed fender where it had hit the guardrail. I patted my pocket and knew I had left them the keys, a stupid mistake, and I'd left their guns there on the seat as well. The two cars pulled abreast for a confab. Then Pruitt turned right, went on around the block, and the fat man was coming my way. He passed and I could see there were two of them in the car—the kid, riding shotgun, was slumped in the seat as if he hadn't yet come back to the living. Lacking Pruitt, I'd be thrilled with another shot at these two. I wanted to put somebody in the hospital, and any of the three were okay with me.

I let the fat man go on into the next block. I moved out in the rain and ran after Pruitt. He was still the grand prize in this clambake, but by the time I reached the next corner he was gone. Again, I could go off in any direction and be right or wrong, or wait right here while the wheel took another spin. When nothing happened, I crossed to the dark side of the street and walked along slowly, hoping they'd all catch up. For a time it seemed that the action had moved on to another stage. No one came or went. I worried about it, and I was worrying three blocks later when Eleanor turned a corner far ahead and walked briskly up the street toward me.

She was two blocks away but coming steadily. I stood flat in a shallow doorway and egged her on in my mind. I peeped out and she was still there. She passed a light in the next block and I could see her clearly now, looking none the worse for her tumble down the slope. Her hair had come down but that was good: I could get a grip on it and hold her that way if I had to. She was close enough now that I could catch her, but I let her keep coming, each step a little added insurance. If she kept on, she'd pass so close I could grab her without a chase. I had pushed myself as far back in the doorway as I could get: I didn't dare even a peep as she came closer. I thought sure I'd have her, then everything seemed to stop. I had lost the sense of her, I had to look. She was still a block away, stopped there as if warned off by intuition. I waited some more. With a long head start and terror in her heart, she could still make it though.

She crossed the street. Something about the terrain was bothering her: an alarm had gone off in her head and she was like a quail about to be flushed. I buried my face in the crack and held myself still as death. But when I looked again, she was walking in the opposite direction, back up the street the way she had come.

I leaped out of the doorway and ran on the balls of my feet. I stretched myself out and ate up the block, trying to make up lost ground before she turned and saw me. She ducked into an alley. I clopped up and looked down a dark, narrow place. Something moved a block away, a fluttery blur in the rain. She was spooked now, going at a full run: I gave up stealth and chased her through the dark. I hit a row of garbage cans and went down in a hellish clatter, rolled with the momentum, came up running. But I didn't see her anymore, didn't see anything in the murk ahead.

I came out into a street lit only by a distant lamp. It was high noon on Pluto, a world bristling with evil. She screamed, a shriek of such ungodly terror that it smacked me back in my tracks and damn near stopped the rain. Far down the block I saw Pruitt's kid manhandling her into the car. The fat man stood by the driver's door, smoking a cigarette down to his knuckles. I had no chance to catch them. The fat man gave me the long look as I ran up the block. He flipped his smoke, flipped me off, got in the car, and drove away in a swirl of mist.

18

I walked under the freeway and up toward Sixth Avenue. I no longer felt the rain. The specter of Pruitt dogged my steps, spurring me along the deserted street. I saw his face on storefront mannequins and felt his eyes watching me from doorways. I heard his voice coming up from the drains where the water ran down off the street. Then the heat passed and I felt curiously calm. I had remembered something that might be his undoing: I had a sense of urgency but none of defeat. The night was young, the game wasn't over yet, I was more focused with each passing block. I wasn't going to sit in my room all night knitting an afghan.

I had a pretty good idea what Pruitt would be thinking. In the morning I would call the court, file a complaint, and put the cops after him. This meant he'd be on the move tomorrow but perhaps holed up tonight. As far as they knew, I was a Denver knuckle-dragger who couldn't find my way around Seattle at midnight if the mayor suddenly showed up and gave me his chauffeured limo. This was good: this was what I wanted them to think.

By the time I was halfway up Sixth my juice was pumping. I stopped at the Hilton, fetched my key, and let myself into my room. I didn't bother changing clothes—this was just a pit stop, I'd be going out again, I'd be on foot, and I was going to get wet. I sat on the bed with the Seattle phone book and did the obvious stuff first. There was no listing for a Ruel Pruitt or an R. Pruitt in the white pages: nothing under his name under *Detective Agencies* or *Investigators* in the yellow. In a strange way, this too was good: it contributed to that sense of security that I hoped Pruitt was counting on for tonight.

Now to find him.

I dug through my dirty clothes, and in the pocket of the shirt I'd worn that first day, I found the scrap of paper I had used to jot down his license number.

I called Denver.

A sleepy voice answered the phone. " 'Lo?"

"Neal?"

"Yeah . . . who's this?"

"Cliff Janeway."

"Cliff . . . Jesus, what time is it?"

I looked at my watch. It was exactly 11:18. My plane for Albuquerque was taking off even as we spoke.

"It's after midnight back there. Listen, I'm sorry, I know how hard you sleep. But I'm lost in Seattle and I need one helluva big favor from an old pal."

I heard him stirring on the bed thirteen hundred miles away. His wife asked who it was and he told her. She gave a long-suffering sigh and I told him to give her my regrets.

"Lemme move to the other phone," he said.

I waited, hoping that loyalty between old partners was still alive and well in Denver.

"Yeah, Cliff? . . . What the hell's goin' on?"

"I need a big one, Neal." I slipped into the lie with a

146

little dig from my conscience. Hennessey was too straitlaced to hear the truth, and I'd make sure that none of it ever came back to bite him. "I'm supposed to meet a guy and we missed each other in the night. All I've got is his plate number and I need an address."

There was silence on the line.

"This is important, Neal . . . I can't tell you how badly I need this. I thought there might be something on NCIC . . . you could tap into that in twenty seconds."

"You got reason to suspect the guy's car is hot?"

"No, but those goddamn computers tell you everything. If the guy's even been late paying his traffic tickets . . ."

"Cliff," Hennessey said in that measured tone I knew so well, "sometimes you're a hard guy to be friends with."

"I'll be singing your praises with my dying breath."

"Dammit, this information is not intended for this kind of use."

We both knew that. As always, I waited him out.

"I'll make a call, but I'm promising you nothing. Call me back in half an hour, forty minutes."

I knew it wouldn't take that long: Hennessey would have the information almost instantly, such was the power of a cop in the age of computers. He would get the dope through the DPD dispatcher, who would tap into the national system, and then he'd brood for half an hour before he decided to let me have it.

Meanwhile, I had some time on my hands.

I was walking again, on through the rain into the night. I needed wheels, so I went to the gas station where Rigby had had Eleanor's car towed. It was still there, in a fenced yard behind the rest rooms. I told the attendant I was her brother and they had sent me over to fetch it for her. He didn't worry much: we weren't exactly dealing with a Lexus here, and he was anxious to get it off his lot. "I rustled up four pretty fair used tires with another eight, ten thousand in 'em. Tab comes to eighty-six dollars and ten cents. You wanna pay that now?"

I said sure: I was well past the point of brooding over money, so I handed him my sagging MasterCard. "She's all yours," he said, slotting my card through his machine. "Keys're over the visor." I went back to the yard and opened the car door. It squeaked on rusty hinges. The seats had worn through, the windshield was cracked and a cold draft wafted up from below. The odometer was playing it for laughs—it showed 34,512, which could only be serious if the meter was on its third trip around. I opened the glove compartment. A small light came on, a pleasant surprise. I saw some papers—registration, proof of insurance, and a sheath of notes that looked to be tables of current book valuations, handwritten on ledger paper in ink. They were all Grayson Press books.

There were separate pages for each title. They were fully described, with many variants noted, with prices and the names of dealers who had sold them. These had been taken from *Bookman's Price Index,* with the volume numbers in the margins. She had sifted the material as professionally as any book dealer, noting the year of sale and the condition, along with her own impression of whether the dealers tended to be high or low. It was a ready reference on Grayson's entire output. The final sheet was marked *Poe/The Raven, 1949 edition.* Only three copies were listed for the past ten years. In pencil she had noted that Russ Todd down in Arizona had sold an uncataloged copy for $600. I knew Russ well enough to call and ask if I needed to. Most interesting, I thought, was the word *edition,* which appeared for this book only. It seemed to indicate what I already knew—that some people believed there had been another edition and Eleanor may have been one of them.

I tucked everything back as it was. In a slipcase at the side of the glove compartment I found her address book. It fell open to the letter *G,* so often had that page been used. She had written some names under the general heading *Grayson.* There were book dealers from coast to coast, several of them known to me as specialists in fine-press books. There was a local number for Allan Huggins, the Grayson bibliographer, and at the bottom of the page were three names in bold, fresh-looking ink.

Nola Jean Ryder.
Jonelle Jeffords.
Rodney Scofield.

Jonelle Jeffords I remembered as the name of the woman in Taos whose house Eleanor had burglarized. There was a phone number beginning with a 505 area code. The number for Rodney Scofield was a 213 exchange, which I recognized as Los Angeles. The space beside Nola Jean Ryder was blank.

I sat behind the wheel, crossed my fingers, and turned the ignition.

Yea, verily, it started.

I was back in business. I had wheels.

I stopped at the Hilton and called Hennessey. I knew by the cautious sound of his voice that he had what I wanted.

"I've got bad vibes about this."

"Neal, it's your nature to have bad vibes. The time for you to really start worrying is when you don't have bad vibes."

"Very funny. Someday you'll get me fired, I've got no doubt of that at all. No, don't tell me about it, please . . . you're not gonna kill this guy, are you?"

"Now why would you ask a thing like that?"

"I don't know. I just had a vision of the beaches up there littered with cadavers, all of 'em named Pruitt. It doesn't sit well at one o'clock in the morning."

"I'm just gonna pay him a friendly little visit."

"Like the Godfather, huh? You've got that edge in your voice."

There was nothing else to say: he'd either give or he wouldn't.

"Your plate's registered to a Kelvin Ruel Pruitt. He's got half a dozen old unresolved legal problems, all in Illinois. Careless driving, failure to appear, a bad check never made good, stuff like that. They're not about to go after him in another state, but if he ever gets stopped in Chicago, it'll be an expensive trip."

He sighed and gave me Pruitt's address.

"Bless you, Mr. Hennessey, you lovely old man. Now go back to bed and make your wife happy."

"She should be so lucky."

I sat at the table and unfolded a Seattle street map. Pruitt lived in a place called Lake City, north of town. I marked the map, but I already had the routes memorized. As a courtesy I called Taos and told them Rigby had escaped. The lonely-sounding dispatcher took my message and managed to convey his contempt across the vast expanse of mountains and plains. I didn't bother telling him that I was going to find Rigby and bring her back to him. I didn't think he'd believe that anyway.

19

It was a fifteen-minute drive at that time of night. The draft from the floorboards became a freezing gale, numbing me in my wet clothes. The heater was only partly effective, just beginning to get warm as I reached the Lake City turnoff. I went east on 125th Street, zigzagging through dark and narrow residential lanes until I found the street where Pruitt lived. It was wrapped in wet murk, the sparse streetlights as ineffective as candles. The rain kept coming, beating down like a draconian water cure. The first thing I saw as I turned into the block was the fat man's car, parked under a tree at Pruitt's address. I whipped around and pulled in behind him, then sat for a few minutes with the heater running, recovering from the cold drive. The house was draped by trees and flanked by thick underbrush. None of it could be seen from the street. There was also no sign of Pruitt's Pontiac, which was troubling but might be explained by a garage out back. It was now 1:18 by my watch: almost three hours since they'd snatched her off the street. I had to assume the worst and go from here. Assume all three men were in the house. Figure one of them would be posted as a lookout. The fat man and the kid didn't scare me much: I had dealt with goons many times, and they always fold when the game gets rough. Pruitt was the X-factor, the unknown. You never know what a psycho will do, or what you'll have to do if you get him started.

I pulled my gun around to the front of my belt. Still I sat, bothered by something I couldn't pin down. Then I saw that the fat man's car door was open in the rain, cracked about six inches. The interior light had come on: this had run the battery down and cast the car in a dim, unnatural glow. He took her in the house, I thought: he had to carry her and never got his door closed, then he forgot to come back out and shut it. I thought of Otto Murdock's store, pulling that connection out of the rain, from God knew where. Things were left empty, open, unattended. People went away and didn't come back. Nothing sinister about that, except my own nagging feeling that somehow it shouldn't be that way.

I'd have to move Eleanor's car, I knew that. Pruitt would know it on sight, and if he happened to drive up, I'd lose my biggest advantage, surprise. I drove around the block and parked in the dark behind a pickup truck. Again I was walking in the rain. I approached the fat man's car cautiously. Walked around to the driver's side and looked in. His wallet lay open on the seat. It was stuffed with money . . . five, six hundred dollars. I fished out his driver's license and stared at his picture. William James Carmichael, it said. I wrote down his name and address. I looked in the glove compartment and found several letters addressed to Willie Carmichael. I put them back, got out of the car, and walked to the driveway that led back to the house.

It was heavily draped with trees. I could see lights off in the distance, and a walk that skirted the drive. The walk was shrubbed but too visible, I thought, from the house. I came up the drive, dark as a load of coal, planting each step firmly. It converged with the walk near a flagstone approach to the front door. The only light came from the front windows, dimmed by curtains and reflecting off the slick stones of the walkway.

Three long strides brought me flat against the house. I moved to the door, looking and listening. There was nothing doing anywhere. The door was locked, hardly a surprise. I put my head against it, listening for footsteps, movement, anything that betrayed some living presence. There was nothing.

Just . . . a faint strain of music.

I took my head away and the music stopped. I listened again. The beat sounded tauntingly familiar, like something I knew but couldn't quite call up. The steady hiss of the rain all but drowned it out. It quivered just outside my senses, one of those half-remembered bits of business that drives you crazy at two o'clock in the morning. Other than that, the house was still, so quiet it gave me a queasy feeling. I eased back into the brush and around to the side. I saw a light in a window, dim and distant, escaping from another room well back in the house. I pushed through the undergrowth and looked through a small crack in the curtain. I could see a piece of a drawing room, neat and well-furnished with what looked to be antique chairs. Somehow it didn't fit what I knew about Pruitt, but you never can tell about people: I really didn't know the man. I squinted through the crack and saw a doorway that led off to a hall. The light came through from the front, and nothing was going on back here.

I touched the glass and there it was again, that rhythmic vibration, as much feeling as sound. I put my ear against it, and on came that faraway melody, that staccato tune that was right on the tip of my . . .

I froze, unable to believe what had just gone through my head.

"Eleanor Rigby."

Somewhere inside, someone was playing that song.
Over and over.
Loud enough to shake the walls.
At two o'clock in the morning.
I kept moving. Everything was the color of ink. I
came into the backyard, taking a step at a time.
Around the edge of a porch, groping, groping. I
touched a screened door and saw a long, dim, narrow
crack of light. I pulled open the door and moved
toward it. It was the back door of the house itself,
cracked open like the fat man's car. The music seeped
through it like some dammed-up thing that couldn't
get through the crack fast enough. I had my gun in my
hand as I nudged the door with my shoulder. It swung
open and the music gushed out.

I was in a black kitchen, lit only by the glow from
another room. I could see the dim outlines of a range
and refrigerator, nothing more . . . then, straight
ahead, a table with chairs around it. I crossed the
room, feeling my way. The music was loud now: I had
come into a hallway that led to the front. I walked to
the end, to the edge of the parlor. It looked like some
proper sitting room from Victorian days. The light
came down from above, where the music was playing.
I reached the stairs and started up. There was a blip
that sounded like a bomb, and the music started
again, a shock wave of sound.

I saw a smudge on the stair, a red smear ground into
the carpet . . .

Another one . . .

. . . and another one.

More at the top.

I heard a soft sigh. It was my own. The overhead
light at the top revealed a dark hallway. I could see a
room at the end of it, dimly lit as if by a night-light. I
saw more red marks on the carpet coming out of the

hall. I moved that way, the hall closing me in like a
tunnel. There was a door on each side halfway down,
the one on the left open, the room there dark. I kept
flat against the wall, breathing deeply, aware of the
sudden silence again as the record ended. The room
smelled strongly of ashes. My mind caught the smell
but it didn't hold: there was too much going on. I
reached inside and felt along the wall with the palm of
my hand, found the light, flipped it up, and the flash
turned the room the color of white gold. I could see
my reflection in a mirror across the room: I was
standing in a half-crouch with the gun in my hand,
moving it slowly from side to side. It was some kind
of office. There was a desk and a filing cabinet, with
one drawer hanging open and several files strewn
across the floor. The walls were painted a cream color:
the only window was covered by a dark curtain.

I turned and faced the room across the way. I could
see the thin line of light at the bottom of the door, and
in the light cast out from the office, more crusty red
smears on the floor. There, I thought: that's where all
the blood's coming from. I pivoted back on my heel
and flattened against the wall. Turned the knob,
pushing the door wide. And there he was, Fat Willie
Carmichael, and I didn't need a medical degree to
know he had done Pruitt his last favor. The room
looked like a slaughterhouse, with blood on the bed
and the floor and the walls: splotches of it spewed as if
by a high-pressure pump. The fat man had fallen on
his back and died there. His head was wrenched back
and I could see that his throat had been cut. His
fingers were rigid and clawlike, clutching at nothing. I
stood in the doorway, heartsick with fear for Eleanor.
My hand was trembling, I felt like a rookie cop at his
first bad murder scene. I had looked upon more
rooms like this one, streaked with red violence, than I

could ever add up and count, and now I shook like a kid. There was still one room to check—the open door at the end of the hall.

I reached the dim circle of light and the music came up full as I peeped in. I almost laughed with relief—nobody there! The record player squatted on a table near the window, one of those old portables from the days before stereo. A 45-rpm disc spun wildly. The set was fixed to the automatic mode: the record would play like that forever, till the power failed or the needle wore the grooves off. It was starting again now, a concert from hell.

It was so loud I felt shattered by it. I had an urge, almost a need, to rip out the plug. The night-light flickered precariously, the bulb on its last legs. I found the switch and turned on the overhead, washing the room in light. It looked like a guest room: there was a single bed in a corner facing a portable TV set, a telephone on a table near the record player, a digital alarm clock. The bed had been rumpled but not slept in. Someone had lain or sat on top of the covering.

Handcuffed to the bed.

The cuffs were still there, one bracelet snapped tight to the bedpost, the other lying open on the pillow. The key had been left in the slot where it had been used to release the prisoner from the bed. The cuffs were the same make and style as the set Slater had given me. I came closer and examined the bed, turning back the rumpled folds of the blanket. There I found the book, no larger than a thumb joint, Eleanor's miniature Shakespeare, her good-luck piece.

I fingered the soft suede leather, opened the cover, and looked at the publisher's name. *David Bryce and Son/Glasgow.*

I put it in my pocket and came back up the hall. Last chance at the death scene, I thought. I was thinking like a cop, and I was not a cop, this was not my town. In an hour the room would be full of real cops. I stepped inside, giving the body a wide berth. I looked at Fat Willie Carmichael and thought, *Talk to me, baby,* but the fat man was keeping his last awful secret to himself. He had been taken from the front, stuck in the sternum with a weapon that was wicked and sharp, then slashed deep across the neck. Either wound was probably fatal, but the killer had hacked him up in other ways, as if venting some raging fury or settling an old score. His clothes were ripped apart: pocket change was scattered around, and his keys were thrown against the wall. The killer had been looking for the one key, I guessed, to unshackle his prisoner in the next room. I looked around the edges of the body: I could see his gun—he had retrieved it from the car and it lay under his hip, still in its holster. This indicated an attack of surprise: taken from the front, but too quickly to react. Or done unexpectedly, by someone he knew.

Time to call the cops, I thought. Out in the hallway, I smelled again that faint whiff of ashes. The office across the hall was thick with it. I looked into the room and saw where it came from—a wastebasket, half-filled with some burned thing, a bucket of ashes. I got down on the floor and touched the can with the back of my hand. It was still warm. I probed into it with my knife, carefully . . . carefully, lifting one layer away from another. Whatever it was, it had been thoroughly burned, with only a few solid remnants left to show that it had once been sheets of paper. Maybe a police lab could make something out of it; I couldn't. Then I saw a flash of white—two pages fused together in heat, with small fragments un-burned. And as I leaned over it, I smelled another odor, half-hidden under the ash but unmistakable if you knew it. Ronsonol. The can and its contents had been doused with lighter fluid to make sure the papers would burn. Some of the fluid had soaked into the carpet but had not burned because the fire had been confined to the inside of the can. Lighter fluid was a smell I knew well. It is one of the bookscout's major tools, used for removing stickers from book jackets safely and without a trace. Paper can be soaked in it without getting stained, wrinkled, or otherwise damaged, unless someone remembers what lighter fluid's really for and sets it on fire.

I sniffed around the can and again probed it with the knife. I worked the point between the two pages and jiggled them apart. The words *still* and *whisp* stood out on the unburned fragment, the two words arranged one over the other, at a slight angle, with the paper charred close around them. The lettering was striking and quaint: the typeface lovely. Here was the *Raven,* I thought. It might not make sense, but it looked as if Pruitt had it all along, lost his mind, whacked Willie Carmichael, and burned the damn thing. It didn't make sense, I thought again. I parted the ashes and went deeper. There was only one other scrap with unburned letters: *ange,* it said. I took this piece, to have a sample of the typeface, and left the other segment for the cops.

I nudged off the light with my elbow and left the room as I'd found it. I stood for a moment in the hall, listening. But the record had numbed my senses, and now I had to concentrate just to hear the song.

I moved through the hall to the stairs. Looked down into the drawing room.

Something was different. I waited and listened and waited some more, but I saw and heard nothing.

It was my life that had changed. My dilemma. The universe.

I took a solid grip on the gun and went down quickly. Everything was turned around, like a house of mirrors at a carnival. There were two doors: I looked through the other rooms with that same sense of dread and found nothing: then went back through the hall the way I had come. I didn't know what was eating me until I got to the kitchen. There's more, I thought: I've missed something, I haven't seen it all yet. I nudged open the swinging door, groped for a light, found it, flipped it, and saw what it was that I had missed.

The woman was sprawled in a lake of blood by the table. I had walked past her in the dark, so close I might've stepped on her hand. Like Fat Willie Carmichael, she had died by the knife—throat cut, body ripped and torn. I moved closer and looked at her platinum blond hair. I didn't want to look at her face, but I did. It was Pruitt's girlfriend, Olga.

Then I saw the footprints, my own, and, oh, Christ, I had walked through her blood coming in. It was like looking down and seeing your crotch covered with leeches: your skin shimmies up your tailbone and your gut knots up and you just want them gone. I didn't even stop to think about it—the whole fifteen years I'd spent with DPD was so much jackshit, and I went to the roll of paper towels near the range and ripped some off, wet them in hot water at the tap, and washed out the prints. And in that moment, while I played footsie with the killer, I became part of his crime.

Call the cops, I thought: call them now, before you're in this any deeper.

I rolled the bloody wet towels into a tight ball, wrapped it in two fresh ones, and stuffed it in my pocket. Everything till then had been blind reflex. Again I thought about the cops, but even then I was smearing the water tap with my handkerchief, where I'd touched it wetting the towels.

Stupid, stupid . . .

I left the record playing: give the cops that much, I owed it to Eleanor, even if I had to pay the price.

I was lucky on one count—the heavy underbrush made it unlikely that neighbors would see me coming or going. Almost too late, I remembered that I had gone through Fat Willie's wallet: I went back to his car and smeared it with my handkerchief. I walked around the block and sat in Eleanor's car with my feet dangling in the rain. I took off my shoes, knowing that human blood can linger in cracks longer than most killers could imagine, and I turned them bottoms-up on the floor.

I drifted downtown, my conscience heavy and troubled.

I was at least five miles away when I called them. I stood in a doorless phone booth outside an all-night gas station and talked to a dispatcher through my handkerchief. Told her there were two dead people, gave her the address.

I knew I was being taped, that police calls today can be traced almost instantly. When the dispatcher asked my name, I hung up.

I stopped at Denny's, put on my shoes, and went inside for a shot of coffee. It was 3:05 A.M. I sat at the fountain and had a second cup. I thought of Eleanor and that record blaring, of Slater and Pruitt, of Crystal and Rigby and the Grayson boys. I wished for two things—a shot of bourbon and the wisdom to have done it differently. But I was in the wrong place for the one and it was too late for the other.

BOOK II

TRISH

20

I found what I needed over my third coffee. It always happens, I don't know how. When life goes in the tank, I bottom out in the ruins and come up with purpose, direction, strength.

I knew what I had to do. It was too late now to do it the right way, so the same thing had to happen from a different starting point.

I sat at the counter looking at her card.

I made the call.

She caught it on the first ring, as if she'd been sitting there all night waiting for me.

"Hello."

"Trish?"

"Yup."

"Janeway."

"Hi."

She didn't sound surprised: she didn't sound thrilled. She sounded wide-awake at four o'clock in the morning.

"You said if I'd like to talk . . . well, I'd like to talk."

"When and where?"

"As soon as possible. You say where."

"My office, half an hour. Do you know where the *Seattle Times* is?"

"I'll find it."

163

"I'll tell you, it'll save time. Go to the corner of Fairview and John. You'll see a big square building that looks like all newspaper buildings everywhere. You'll know you're there by the clock on the Fairview side—the time on it's always wrong. Turn into John, park in the fenced lot on the left, come across the street and in through the John Street door. The guard will call me and I'll come down and get you."

The clock on the building said 11:23, but it was an hour before dawn when I got there. The rain was coming down in sheets. I parked in a visitor's slot and made the sixty-yard dash in eight seconds, still not fast enough to keep from getting soaked again. I pushed into the little vestibule and faced a middle-aged man in a guard's uniform. I asked for Miss Aandahl: he didn't think Miss Aandahl was in. He made a call, shook his head, and I sat on a bench to wait. Water trickled down my crotch and I felt the first raw tingle of what would probably be a raging case of red-ass. I squirmed in my wet pants and thought, I *hate* this goddamn town.

She came in about ten minutes later. She was wearing a red raincoat and hood. She was brisk, getting me quickly past the formalities with the guard. He looked at me suspiciously as I disappeared with her into the building. We went past a receptionist's booth, empty now, then through a door to the right and up a set of stairs. We came out on the second floor, in a corridor that led past a string of offices. There was a bookcase filled with review copies, over-flow from the book editor, with a sign to the effect that the staff could buy them (the money to go to charity) at $3 a copy. In a quick flyby, I saw some hot young authors—David Brin, Dan Simmons, Sharyn McCrumb—whose newest books, with author photos and publicity pap laid in, could already command cover price plus 50 percent in a catalog. That's the trouble with review books; they tend to be wasted on book editors. I wanted to clear out the case, buy them all.

She was standing about thirty feet away, waiting. I joined her at the edge of the newsroom, a huge chamber quiet in the off-hours. It gave the impression that news happened on its timetable, at its command. *Let there be news,* the keeper of the key would shout at eight o'clock, and fifty reporters would materialize at their computers, clicking furiously. On the far wall was a full-length mural of the world, with clocks showing times in various places. The world looked as peaceful as the newsroom, which only proved how little the world knew.

She hung up her raincoat, then led me into a narrow place defined on both sides by tall filing cabinets. It was crowded with desks, maybe a dozen of them packed into a space the size of a medium-sized living room. It was like walking into a canyon: it was part of the newsroom yet it wasn't, because an editor couldn't see in there without getting up and making the grand effort. I didn't have to be a reporter to know what a coveted spot it was . . . out of sight, out of mind. Her desk was far back in the corner, as secluded as you could get without moving up in management, getting yourself glassed in and becoming a different breed of cat.

She sat and motioned me to a chair. She looked different somehow from the image I had retained from our one meeting in the courthouse cafeteria. She looked harder and tougher, more of the world. Then she smiled, like the child looking up at Frankenstein's monster, and I felt good again.

"Nice racket you've got," I said. "You people must get some great poker games going back here."

"We call it the Dead Zone. They'll have to kill me to get this desk."

JOHN DUNNING

"Are they trying?"

"So they say."

She didn't push me. If I wanted to small-talk and break the ice, she could do that. She was looking straight in my eyes.

"You look miserable . . . tired, wet, and hungry."

I nodded. "Your city has not treated me well."

"I'm sorry," she said, and managed to look it. "You've come in the rainy season."

"Oh. How long does that last?"

"Almost all year."

She offered coffee but I had had enough. We looked at each other across her desk.

"I came here from Miami," she said. "My first month was a killer. It rained twenty-eight out of thirty days. I was a basket case. I was ready to go anywhere. If the newspaper in Grand Island, Nebraska, had offered me a job covering the grasshopper beat, I'd've been on the next bus out of here. Then it cleared up and I learned what a sensational place this is."

"I guess I'll have to take your word for that."

"There're two secrets to living here. You've got to dress for weather and you can't let it get you down."

"That's two for two I missed."

"Now the only thing that bothers me is the traffic. This town has got to be the worst bottleneck in the United States. It's great as long as you don't need to drive, or if you do need to drive, you don't need to park."

"It sounds better by the minute."

"I guess I'm here for the long haul. I can't imagine going anywhere else. What's Denver like?"

"I had forgotten what rain looks like till I came here."

"Sun city, huh?"

"Somebody once said that Denver has more sun

166

and sons of bitches than any other city in the country."

She smiled and said, "I'll stay with the rain. I bought a boat last year, I'm a pretty fair sailor now. Sometimes I just take off on Friday and drift up the coast. I put in at some warm-looking marina and spend the weekend exploring. If I've got a difficult piece to write, I do it there, out on deck if the weather's nice."

"Is that where you wrote your book?"

"Would have, if I'd had it then. Have you read it?"

"Not yet, but it's high on my list. I just picked up a copy."

"Yeah, well, don't believe everything you read."

I thought that was the strangest thing I had ever heard a reporter say. She shrugged and said, "It's a good book, I'm not apologizing for it; if I had it to do over again, I'm sure it'd come out mostly the same. A little better, maybe. That's the curse of being a writer, you never want to look back at what you did last year because the trip's too painful. You see stuff you should've done better, but now it's set in stone."

"What would you change?"

"A thousand little things . . . and of course I'd write a new ending."

"Of course?"

"The ending leaves the impression that the Graysons died in an accident. Just some tragic twist of fate."

"Which is . . . ?"

"Not true."

"They were murdered, you said."

"Read the book, then talk to me again. Just keep in mind that the last chapter wasn't what I would've done, then or now."

"If you didn't do it, who did?"

"It was sanitized by an editor in New York. The problem was, I had produced this monster-sized book and it was ending with more questions than it answered. They didn't like that, they felt it would not be satisfying for a reader to go through seven hundred and fifty pages and come out with the kind of questions I was asking. Especially when the experts seemed to agree that it was an accident and I couldn't prove it wasn't. The book really didn't need to end with any unanswered questions at all. They died. That was the end of it."

"But not for you."

"I still keep my finger in it. As you can see."

"You must have something in mind."

She smiled into the sudden pause that stretched between us. "I've been doing some fiction lately. I'm finding a voice, as the literati say. I've had three or four pieces in the literary reviews and I'm working on a novel. Maybe that's how I'll finally get rid of the Graysons. I read somewhere that fiction's the only way you can really tell the truth. I never even understood that when I was learning the ropes, but I sure believe it now."

She gave me a look that said, *Hey, I'm not pushing you, but why the hell are we here?*

I said, "I've got a deal for you."

"I already own the Space Needle, I bought it last year. I never could resist a deal." She got up and came around the desk, patting me on the shoulder. "Let's go get some breakfast. I don't think I want to hear this on an empty stomach."

21

It was a lick and a promise, all I had time for. My reading on her would have to be the abridged version, once over lightly. This is your life, Trish Aandahl, a tour of the high spots. From that I'd decide: move on alone or bring her to the party.

Conventions and courtesies, five minutes. She had grown up in Ohio, her parents simple people who lived for the moment. Life was what it was: you worked at it every day and got up the next day and did it again. Her father had worked for wages in Cincinnati; her mom found jobs in restaurants, dime stores, car washes, wherever there was women's work that demanded no special skills. They had produced a child unlike either of them, a daughter who didn't believe in women's work and grew up thinking she could do most anything. At least the parents had had the wisdom to indulge her differences.

She beat the clock with a minute to spare. She knew I was fishing, but she had tapped into my growing sense of urgency and was willing to give me some rope.

Personal color, three minutes. Trish was her real name, listed that way on her birth certificate. Her mother had named her after a best friend and had never known that the name was a diminutive of Patricia.

She was alone in the world. Her parents were dead

169

and there were no other children. If there was a man in her life, it wasn't readily apparent. She wore no rings, but that doesn't mean as much as it once did.

She was amused now, wondering how far I'd go into this Dick-and-Jane style personal Baedeker. I wondered about her gripes and dislikes and gave her one minute for that.

She didn't need it. Phonies, stuffed shirts, chiselers, and liars. Her code was much like mine, her hate list virtually identical.

Extra bit of business, thirty seconds. She was a chronic insomniac, able to sleep undisturbed only about one night in four. That's why she had been sitting there by the telephone, reading a novel, when I called.

I knew everything about her by the time the waitress brought our breakfasts. What more do you need to know about anyone, until the chips are down and you discover that you never knew anything at all?

"I'm ready to tell you about Slater," I said.

"Why the change of heart?"

"Because the circumstances have changed and I want something back from you. Isn't that how life works?"

"If it's an even trade, sure. Is the Slater story worth anything?"

"I think you'll find it interesting. The entertaining part is trying to figure out where it's heading. It's still unfolding, as you newsies might put it."

"The terminology is *breaking*. I don't do breaking stories anymore."

"I think you'll do this one."

"So what do you want for it?"

"A lot less than you paid for the Space Needle. Are we off the record yet?"

"If that's how you want it."

I threw in a zinger, to test her dedication to the code. "Don't take offense at this, but how do I know your word is good?"

She did take offense: she bristled in her chair, and for a moment I thought she might pick up and walk out. "I'll tell you the answer to that, but you're only allowed to ask it once. You can check me out with a phone call. I worked in Miami for four years. I went to jail down there over just this kind of stuff."

"Really?" I said in my most-interested voice. "How long were you in?"

"It was only ten days. My paper made it a front-page embarrassment for them and they were glad enough to see me go. I might still be there, though, if they hadn't gotten their information from someone else."

"That's okay, ten days is long enough. At least you know the taste of it."

"The taste, the smell, the color. It colors your whole life. But I'll go back again before I let them make me betray . . . even you."

"Hey, I believe you. In a funny way, though, it makes what I'm trying to do more difficult."

"I don't understand."

"I'm not quite ready to go on the record yet. But I can't even explain the situation to you off the record without handing you a piece of my legal jam."

"What kind of legal jam?"

"There was a crime done tonight. A bad one."

"Did you do it?"

"No, ma'am, I did not."

"Then . . ."

"I did some other stuff, stupid stuff that will not make them love me. If the cops don't love you, you need something in your corner besides a motive, the means, and no alibi. You'd look good in my corner. But you need to know the risks."

Warily, she said, "Can you tell me in general terms what happened?"

"Generally speaking, two people got killed. I've been busy all night destroying evidence and obstructing justice. They'll almost certainly charge me with that, but at least I can bail out on it. That's my magic word right now, *bail*. I have this compelling need to be out. I've got to be out." I let a long pause emphasize that point for me, then I said, "But over the last two hours I've come to realize that the magnitude of my fuckup may make that impossible. I've got a growing hunch they might start taking my measurement for the murder rap."

She let out her breath slowly, through her nose. I saw a slight shiver work its way across her shoulders.

"That's it in a nutshell," I said. "I'm still trying to figure out how to handle it. I need to do that before I can get into the story or tell you what I want from you."

"I don't think it's a problem. I'm not legally obligated to tell the police what you tell me."

"I can see a situation, though, where they'd call you in and ask some questions you'd rather not answer."

"I'll claim privilege."

"And end up in jail again."

"Maybe I'll take that chance, if the story's worth it."

"The story's worth it. But between the two of us, we may still have to dig for the end of it."

She looked out into the rainy street, just now awash with the palest light of morning. I floated a hint of what I hoped she could do for me.

"I'm hoping you know a great cop in this town, or a DA with a real head on his shoulders. The closer you'd be to such an animal the better."

172

"I'm not sleeping with anybody right now," she snapped. "If I was, I sure wouldn't use him that way."

"You're touchy as hell at five o'clock in the morning, aren't you? You should learn to sleep better."

"Janeway, listen to me. You and I may become the best of pals, but we won't get to first base if you keep dropping insults on my head."

"And we'll never get anywhere if you're one of those politically correct types who takes offense at everything. I'm no good at walking on eggs. Do you want to hear what I meant or sit there and be pissed off?"

"Tell me what you meant, maybe I'll apologize later."

"I may need to turn myself in. If I do, all this is a moot point, you can do anything you want with it. But I'd at least like to be talking to my kind of cop, not one of those tight-asses who thinks the first mistake I made happened way back in Denver, when I quit the brotherhood."

She didn't say anything.

"The Rigby girl's gone. I have good reason to believe that the killer may have taken her. I want to be out looking for her: I *need* to be looking, I really can't overstate that. I will come totally unzipped sitting in a jail cell. All humility aside, I'm still the best cop I know. I'm not saying Seattle will give her a fast shuffle, but I know how it is in these big departments, I know how many cases those boys have to clear. I'm here, I'm focused, I'm looking for Eleanor, and I'll open all the doors."

I took a deep breath, which became a sigh. "But I'm far from home, I'm being slowly driven crazy by this rain, and I know nobody here but you. The cop in me wants to tear up this town looking for her, but I'm not even sure yet where the doors are. And if that kid winds up dead and the real cops could've prevented it while I'm out playing policeman . . ."

We looked at each other.

"I'll tell ya, Trish, I'd find that damn near impossible to live with."

She answered my sigh with one of her own, but it was a long time coming. "You want it both ways. It can't be done."

"If it can't be done, I go in—no arguments, no questions. Her welfare is the first priority."

"Maybe you should go in. Can you really do her any good out here by yourself?"

"I might surprise you. I really was a decent cop. With me looking too, her chances would have to go up. I don't know, I've got to try. But there isn't much time."

I droned on, summarizing the immediate problem. The cops had to be told about Rigby now, this morning, before they closed down the scene. In a homicide investigation, every minute wasted on the front end is critical. I looked at my watch: I had already blown three hours.

"Let's make it very clear, then, what you want from me and what kind of restraints I'm under," she said. "As it stands now, I can't even ask the cops an intelligent question."

"That's why I was hoping you knew somebody."

"That I was sleeping with the chief of police, you mean. Sorry, Janeway, no such luck. I don't drink with them or eat lunch with them, I don't backslap or schmooze or let them tell me dirty jokes. My relationship with these guys is respectable but distant. It's extremely professional and I've taken some pains to keep it that way."

"Do you know anybody on the paper who does schmooze with them?"

"Nobody I'd trust, and I'd be wary of any cop such

a guy might bring me. I don't like reporters who party with people they write about."

We thought it through another stretch of quiet.

She said, "I feel like I'm playing pin the tail on the donkey, or a card game with half a deck."

"You want to hear the story, I'll tell you the story."

"Sure I want to hear it, isn't that why we're here? I'll take it any way you want to tell it, on the record or off."

I told it to her with no more clarification than that. I took her from Slater's arrival in my bookstore through my hasty retreat from Pruitt's house three hours ago. She asked nothing and made no judgments until it was finished. Her eyes darted back and forth as if she'd been replaying parts of it in her head.

"God, I've got more questions now than I had at the beginning. I know who Slater is, but who is Pruitt? Is this really about a Grayson book or is something else at the bottom of it? What happened to the kid who was tagging along with the fat man? And you . . . oh, Janeway, what on earth possessed you and what're you thinking now? Do you think Pruitt lost his mind, killed his friends, and took off with Rigby? Does that make sense to you?"

"All I know for sure is there were five people, counting Eleanor. Only two are accounted for and they're dead."

"And what about that record playing? What do you make of that?"

"She was being stalked and harassed on the phone. It had to've been Pruitt, that's obvious now. He was her darkman, her worst nightmare."

"But why leave the record playing, at home, with a dead man there?"

The check came. I made a stab at it but she was quicker. She looked through her purse and fished out a twenty.

"I'm going on up to the scene," she said. "At least then we'll know what cops are working it. Maybe I can take them off the record and get them to tell me something."

We walked out in the rain. I stood beside her car, getting wet again, and talked to her through the narrow crack at the top of her window.

"I'll be holed up in my room at the Hilton. You call me."

"As soon as I can."

"Sooner than that. Remember, I am not calm, I'm not taking this in my stride. I am very nervous."

"I hear you."

"You call me, Trish. The minute you can get the smell of it and break away, you get on that phone."

"I'll call, but don't get your hopes up. I think you're gonna have to go in to get what you want. And the cops won't be naming you citizen of the year."

22

I stood under a hot shower, put on dry clothes, lay on the bed with the TV low, and waited uneasily.

She called just before eight.

"The cops on the case, Quintana and Mallory . . . I know them both, not well, but maybe enough to give you a reading. It's not good news."

"Of course not," I said, sitting up on the bed.

"You might be able to talk to Mallory if you could

get him alone. But it wouldn't do much good, he'd take it all to Quintana anyway."

"It's pretty hard to hold out on your partner."

"And then Quintana would be running it, and your troubles would just begin. Mallory's the weak sister in this Mutt-and-Jeff show: you can't ask him about the weather with Quintana in the same room—you ask him a question and Quintana answers it. Quintana's an overriding presence, extremely inhibiting. He is tough, intelligent to the point of being cunning, and damned condescending to women and other small animals. I don't think he'd look at a former cop with much sympathy. People call him supercop, and not all of them mean it the way he'd like to think."

There's one in every department, I thought. I'd had one for a partner myself, before Hennessey. It didn't last long. Steed had had to split us up to keep us from killing each other.

The prognosis was obvious. Grimly I moved on to the next round of questions. Had the cops been able to make the Rigby connection from the "Rigby" record?

"I haven't been able to get into that with them. They're just not open with stuff like that, and everybody's wondering what I'm doing here anyway. I told you I don't do breaking stories. We've got other people covering this, and I'm bumping into them every time I turn around."

"What's your best guess?"

"About the record? . . . I can't see them linking it."

I lost my temper, probably because I couldn't see them linking it either. "Goddammit, who does Seattle put on these homicide jobs, Peter Sellers? What's the matter with these fucking cops, what does it take to get their attention?"

"You asked me what I think and I told you. I could

be wrong. But I think they'll figure the record as noise, to cover up what was happening in that house. The music will go right past them. A million people in this town like Beatles music—it might as well have been the Judds on that deck, or the Boston Pops. Why would the police think twice about 'Eleanor Rigby'?"

"Because a woman by that name just went through their stupid nitwit court system!"

"You're assuming the right hand knows what the left hand's doing. In a system this big, you should know better. Anything's possible: I just think it would take one brilliant cop or a stroke of luck for that to happen."

I heard an emergency vehicle pass in her background, the siren fading as it went by on the way somewhere else.

"They'll be putting a wrap on it soon," she said. "Are you coming in?"

I thought of supercop. It was almost more than I could bear.

"Janeway . . ."

"I hear you. I'm just having a lot of trouble with it."

"It's the right thing to do."

"What if I didn't come in?"

"I think that would be a mistake."

"What have I got to lose at this point, supercop's gonna have my ass for breakfast anyway. They don't need me, they've got you."

"I think I'm still off the record. Did we ever get that straight?"

"If we did, consider it inoperative."

"What do you want me to tell them?"

"Everything. Anything that helps them find Rigby. Tell them if they waste manpower looking for me, they're a bunch of losers."

"What are you going to do?"

"Start from ground zero, go till I drop."

"Listen," she said as if she had just made up her mind about something. "We need to talk some more. Don't just disappear on me. Call me tonight."

"I'll see where I am then."

"I know some stuff I didn't tell you yet . . . things you need to hear. Will you call me?"

"I'll try."

"It's important."

We seemed to have reached the end. But she was reluctant to let me go.

"Cliff, is this really what you want?"

"No. But it's what I'm going to do."

23

How do you disappear in the other man's town? I went about it step by step, covering my tracks, playing the odds, counting on what I knew of the supercop mentality to help me along. Aandahl would be getting back to the scene right about now, just as I was packing my stuff out of the Hilton and loading up in Eleanor's trunk. She'd be starting to tell them now, as I turned into University and hit the freeway. She'd probably start out talking to the quiet one, Mallory: that was her nature, avoid the supercops of the world as long as possible. It wouldn't be possible for long: Mallory would call in supercop as soon as he realized what he had . . . just about now, I thought. She'd be segregated in one of the rooms away from the investigation and they'd start on her slowly and work their way up to heat. She'd have to repeat it all, everything she'd told Mallory: supercop never settled for hearsay, even from a partner. Again Mallory would ask the questions and she would answer, and when it was time for the heat to come down, supercop would take over and see if she scared. Maybe she'd tell him where to shove it. I thought about her and decided she just might. It would take an hour off the clock for them to get to that point.

I found a bank that was open on Saturday, half-day walkup-window service. My paper trail would end here, it was cash-and-carry from now on. The paper I had already left would soon take them through Slater to the Hilton. Supercop would also know that I'd been driving an Alamo rental, but he'd be annoyed to find it disabled in the Hilton garage. How long a leap would it be until he had me driving Rigby's car? It could be half a day or it might be done with two two-minute phone calls. A lot depended on luck—his and mine—and on how super the asshole really was.

I drew a $3,000 cash advance on my MasterCard. There was more where that came from, an untapped balance maybe half again as much. In the other pocket of my wallet I had a Visa, which I seldom used: the line of credit on that was $2,000. I never maxed out on these cards: I always paid it off and the jackals kept bumping my line upward, hoping I'd have a stroke of bad luck and they could suck me into slavery at 18 percent along with the rest of the world's chumps. It was good strategy, finally about to pay off for them.

I took the cash in hundreds, two hundred in twenties. It made a fat wad in my wallet.

I stopped in a store and bought some hair dye, senior-citizen variety, guaranteed to turn me into a silver panther. I'd have to do it in two stages, bleach my dark hair white and then dye it gray with an ash toner. I'd be an old man till I dyed it back or it grew out. I bought a good grease pencil with a fine point and a hat that came down to my ears. I bought some sealing tape, shipping cartons, a marking pen, and a roll of bubblewrap. I doubled back toward town. In the Goodwill on Dearborn I bought a cane and an old raincoat. For once in my life I left a thrift store without looking at the books.

I sat in the car with the windows frosting up and did my face. I gave myself a skin blemish under my right eye, added some dirty-looking crow's-feet to the real ones I was getting through hard living, and headed out again. I looked at myself in the glass. It wasn't very good, but maybe it didn't have to be. All I needed now was to pass in a rush for an old duffer with the hurts, when I talked to the man at the check-in counter.

I chose a motel not far from the Hilton, the Ramada on Fifth just off Bell Street. I pulled my hat down and leaned into the cane as I walked into the lobby. For now I would be Mr. Raymond Hodges, a name I pulled out of thin air. I also pulled off a pretty good limp, painful without overdoing it. I gave a half-sigh, just audible with each step down on my right foot. The guy behind the desk didn't seem to notice me beyond the bare fact of my presence, a sure sign that he had taken me at face value. *There's nobody in that room but an old guy who can barely walk,* he'd tell anybody who wanted to know. It wouldn't fool supercop if he got this far, but if they were checking around by phone, it might discourage them from coming out for the personal look.

It was still only midmorning: registration for the night wouldn't be opening for another four or five hours, but the man let me in when I told him I was tired. The only thing that seemed to throw him momentarily was the sight of cash. In the age of plastic, a man with cash is almost as suspicious as a man with a gun.

For my own peace of mind, I had to get rid of Otto Murdock's books, and it was Saturday and the post office was on a banker's schedule. In my room I sealed the books in the bubblewrap and packed them tight, with the other books I'd bought all around them. I sealed the boxes and addressed them to myself in Denver. I called the desk for directions and he sent me to the main post office at Third and Union. I insured the boxes to the limit—not nearly enough— and felt a thousand pounds lighter when they disappeared into the postal system.

The library was just a few blocks away, and I stopped there to look at a copy of *The Raven*. The most accessible Poe was the Modern Library edition, on an open shelf in the fiction section. I sat at a table and browsed it, looking for the words *still* and *whisp*, printed diagonally one above the other. I found them in the fifth stanza, partial words but strong as a fingerprint.

> *Deep into that darkness peering, long I stood*
> * there, wondering, fearing,*
> *Doubting, dreaming dreams no mortal ever dared*
> * to dream before;*
> *But the silence was unbroken, and the stillness*
> * gave no token,*
> *And the only word there spoken was the whispered*
> * word, "Lenore?"*
> *This I whispered, and an echo murmured back the*
> * word, "Lenore!"*
> *   Merely this and nothing more.*

I took the charred scrap from my wallet and looked for the letters *ange*. It was there, twice, in the sixteenth stanza, reference to the sainted, radiant maiden Lenore, who had been named by the angels.

I made photocopies of the three pages and headed back to the Ramada.

In my room I did my hair, watching with some amazement as the black became white and then gray and by degrees I took on the appearance of my father. I quit when it seemed right. When it dried, I hit it with the grease pencil, giving myself a slightly speckled look.

I redid my face and made a better job of it.

There was a kind of fatalistic rhythm to my movements. I was doing what I had to do and time no longer mattered. Eleanor was either dead or alive: if she still lived, I rather liked her chances for the immediate future. He wasn't about to kill her, not after all this grief, till he had what he wanted. Never mind the ashes: appearances could be deceiving, and the feeling persisted that what I wanted was still out there somewhere, alive and well. If I could find it first, I'd have a strong bargaining chip, and there was a fair chance we'd even converge in the hunt. I didn't know Seattle, I had no idea where Pruitt or the fat man's kid might do their drinking, but I did know books. I'd let the cops do the legwork—the job I'd set them on at no small personal risk to myself, the work they had the manpower and the skill to pull off—and I'd go after the book.

It was now after ten-thirty. Supercop would be finished with Trish, at least for the moment, and he'd be on the phone to Denver, going after my mug shot and stats. I pictured the looks on Hennessey and Steed and almost laughed at the thought. It would go against Steed's grain, but he'd have to honor supercop's request and wonder to himself if I had finally popped my buttons and started cutting out paper dolls. As for Hennessey, I'd have some serious fences to mend there, but what else was new?

I knew I was tired—the last real sleep I could remember was the Rigby loft, more than forty-eight hours ago—but I didn't want to stop. I sat on the bed and began working the phone. I opened Eleanor's little address book to the Grayson page and decided to start with Allan Huggins, the man who knew more about the Graysons than they had known about each other. I punched in the number, but there was no answer.

I kept going. I called Jonelle Jeffords in Taos. A machine answered. "Hi, this's where Charlie and Jo live. If you've got something to say that I might want to hear, leave a number, maybe I'll call you back."

No bullshit there: old Charlie cut right to the short strokes. I hung up on the beep.

I sat for a while looking at the name Rodney Scofield. It seemed vaguely familiar, like something I'd heard once and should've remembered. Finally I called his number cold, a Los Angeles exchange.

A recording came on. I wondered if it's possible in this day and age to punch out a phone number and actually speak to a living human being.

I hung on through the entire recording, hoping for some hint of what Scofield was about. A female voice began by telling me I had reached the business offices of Scofield Plastics on Melrose Avenue. Their hours were nine A.M. to five P.M., Monday through Friday. At the end was a menu of punch codes: if I wanted to reach the voice mail of various department heads, I should punch one, two, three, and so on. Finally, there was this:

"If you have business pertaining to the Grayson Press, please press number eight, now."

I punched it.

The phone rang.

A recording began on the other end.

"This is Leith Kenney. I'm not here but I do want to talk to you. If you have Grayson books for sale, or information about single books or collections, please call me back or leave a number where you may be reached. You may also reach me at home, at any hour of the day or night. We are interested in any primary Grayson material, including letters, photographs, business records, broadsides, and even incomplete projects and partial layouts. We pay top cash money, well above auction rates. We will match any offer for important material, and we pay equally well for information that results in major acquisitions."

He gave a home number and I called it. Again came that scratchy, unmistakable sound of a recording machine. There again was Kenney's voice, apologizing. He had stepped out but would return soon. Would I please leave a number?

No, I would not.

I had a hunch I had found Pruitt's moneyman, and I wanted to catch him cold.

I slept five hours. No apologies, no bouts with conscience. My tank was empty: I needed it.

I awoke at four o'clock in a state of anxiety. I had heard a bump somewhere and had come to life thinking of supercop. Dark shadows passed outside, beyond my window, probably a SWAT team getting ready to crash the door.

But when I parted the curtains, it was just a family checking in. The rain had stopped for the moment, but a heavy cloud cover hung over the city, and the streets were wet from a recent drenching. I took a hot shower and dressed, thinking of my immediate future in terms of moves.

My first move had to be to ditch Eleanor's car. I walked over to the lobby, giving the clerk a good look at me in my old-man role. I used the cane well and was satisfied when he gave me nothing more than a smile and a passing glance.

I bought a *Seattle Times* from a box and sat in my room browsing the classifieds. I found the car I wanted in less than a minute, but when I called, the party had sold it. I tried again: there were plenty more like that. All I wanted was something cheap that would run for a week.

The one I found was twenty minutes away, in a ramshackle garage behind a tenement house. It was a Nash from the fifties, the oldest car I would ever own. The body was consumed by rust but the engine sounded decent, rebuilt, said the young man selling it, just three or four years ago. He wanted four hundred: it was a classic, he said, selling hard. I told him everything today was a classic and offered him three. "This is a great make-out car," he said. "The seats fold back into a full bed, with five different positions." I gave him a long gray stare and asked if I looked like a guy who needed five different positions. He grinned and said, "Just need wheels to get you to the VA, huh, pops?" We settled on three-fifty with no further commentary.

The whole business took less than half an hour. He brought out some papers and signed them over to my Raymond Hodges alias and had one last-minute doubt about the license plates. "I think you're supposed to pull those plates and go down to motor vehicles and get a temporary." I told him I'd take care of it and he accepted this cheerfully. I left Eleanor's car on the street a block away, noting the address so I could call the Rigbys to come pick it up. It was a quiet residential neighborhood and I thought the car would be safe there for a few days before somebody called in and reported it to the city as abandoned.

Back in the motel, I made my phone checks again. Neither Leith Kenney in L.A. or Charles and Jonelle Jeffords in Taos were yet answering the telephone, but I reached Allan Huggins on the sixth ring.

"Mr. Huggins?"

"Speaking." He sounded out of breath, as if he'd run some distance to catch the phone.

"My name's Hodges, you don't know me, I'm a book dealer from Philadelphia. I've been hired by a private investigator to track down a book and I'm hoping it's something you might be able to help me with."

His laughter was sudden and booming. "You're a card, aren't you, sir? . . . A book dealer who's also a detective, you say? What'll they think of next?"

"I guess it's that combination of skills that makes me as good a bet as anybody to find a book that nobody thinks is real."

"Aha, you must be looking for the Grayson *Raven* . . . Darryl Grayson's lost masterpiece."

"How'd you know that?"

"It's what everyone's looking for. I must get half a dozen calls a year on it, maybe more. It's one of those urban myths that got started just after the Graysons died. It just won't go away, and it's all preposterous, just total nonsense. Read my bibliography."

"I've done that."

"Well, then . . ."

"It's a great piece of work, but it won't answer the one question that keeps coming up."

"Which is . . . ?"

"If there's nothing to it, why do so many people keep chasing it?"

"Now you're asking me to be a psychologist, and all I ever was, was a poor bibliographer. This is the reason I stick to books. No matter how complicated they become, bibliographically, their mysteries can always be solved. With people, who knows? Have you ever solved the mystery of anyone, sir—your brother, your son, the woman you love?"

"Probably not. Maybe I could come see you, we could put our heads together and solve the riddle of the Graysons."

"Not very damned likely."

"I won't take much of your time."

"If you think it'll help, come ahead. But I can tell you right now, you won't get any encouragement from me in this Grayson *Raven* business. If you ask me was Grayson planning another *Raven,* my answer would have to be yes. I've alluded to that much in my bibliography. But there've been no major changes in the Grayson Press bibliography since my book was published. Some poems by Richard have turned up, and maybe fifty significant broadsides. But in my humble opinion, the *Raven* project never got off the ground. If you want to ask me why foolish people keep chasing that myth, I have no idea."

"Maybe you could show me some of their books. I've heard you have the biggest collection in the world."

My compliment fell strangely flat: he didn't seem unusually proud of the fact, if it was a fact. But he said, "When will you come? I'm not doing anything wonderful right now."

"Now is fine."

I took down his address. He lived on the sound, in Richmond Beach. Five minutes later, I banked the Nash into I-5, heading north.

24

Huggins lived in a two-story brick house on a large wooded lot facing the water. It was well back from the street, hidden from the world. In the last light of the day I could see the water gleaming off in the distance as I drove into his yard. I saw a curtain flutter: a door opened and he came out on an upper deck.

He had a shock of white hair and a curly white beard, a big belly, and burly, powerful arms. Santa Claus in coveralls and a flannel shirt, I thought as I came toward him. His sleeves were rolled up to the elbows: he looked like a working man waiting for some wood to chop. We shook hands and he welcomed me to his home. There was a spate of polite talk as we went inside. I asked if he'd been here long and he said yes, twenty-six years in this house this coming November. His wife had died a few years ago and for a while he had considered selling it—lots of old memories, you know, lots of ghosts—but he had kept it and now he was glad he had. It was home, after all: everything he had was here, and the thought of moving it all, of winnowing down, was . . . well, it was just too much. Then about a year ago all the pain had begun melting away. He had begun taking comfort in these nooks and crannies and in all the thousands of days and nights he had lived here.

We went through the living area and into his

kitchen, where he had just brewed a pot of coffee. The window looked down a rocky hillside to Puget Sound, which stretched away like an ocean into a wall of coming darkness.

"You'll have to forgive me," he said, "I'm terrible with names."

I fed him my alias again and he repeated it in an effort to remember. The coffeepot gushed its last orgasmic perks and he poured two huge mugs without waiting for it to end. "I like it strong," he said, and I nodded agreeably, waving off the sugar and cream. "So," he said, getting down to cases, "you want to know about the Graysons. Where do you want to start? I'm afraid you must be the guide here, sir—I don't mean to brag, but my knowledge of the Grayson Press is so extensive that we could be here for days." He gave a helpless-looking shrug.

"I'm not sure where to start either. I said I wouldn't take up much of your time, but I'm just beginning to realize what a deep subject this is."

"Oh, my dear," he said, rolling his eyes.

"Even the Aandahl biography is a monster. It'll take me a week to read it."

He made a derisive motion with his hand. Santa was suddenly cross. "The woman's a maniac."

"Who, Aandahl?"

"Journalists," he sneered. "All they ever want is the garbage in a man's life. Gossip. Bedroom stories. Lurid sex. But what can you expect from a newspaper reporter?"

"I guess I won't know that till I've read it."

"Don't waste your time, you won't learn anything about the books, Mr. Hodges, and isn't that what we're here to discuss? Listen, if Darryl Grayson himself were sitting with us at this table, he'd tell you the same thing. A man is nothing. All that matters is his work."

190

I had never been able to swallow that notion, but I didn't want to push him on it. It seemed to be a sore spot that he had nurtured for a long time.

"I don't mean to be harsh," he said in a kinder tone. "It's easy to like Trish: she's witty and quick and God knows she does turn a phrase. I'm sure she can be delightful when she's not chasing off to Venus or obsessing over the Grayson brothers. But get her on that subject and she's crazy. I don't know how else to put it."

He gulped his coffee hot. "I'll tell you how crazy Trish Aandahl is. She thinks Darryl and Richard Grayson were murdered."

I stared at him as if I had not heard the same words from Trish herself. "Is she serious?"

"Damn right she is. She gets her teeth into something and never lets go of it. She's like a bulldog."

"I guess I'm at a disadvantage here. I just got her book and I've barely had time to look at it."

"You won't find any of this in there. The publisher made her take it out."

"Why?"

"The obvious reason—she couldn't prove any of it. It was all conjecture. As a reporter you'd think she'd know better. But I hear she fought with her editor tooth and nail, really took it to the wall. It almost jeopardized the book's publication. If she hadn't listened to her agent's advice, the whole deal might've fallen through."

"What advice?"

"To take what she could get now—publish the biography without all the trumped-up mystery. To keep working the other angle if she believed it that strongly. If she could ever prove it, it might make a book in itself, but as it was, it just undercut the credibility of the book she'd written."

"That sounds reasonable."

JOHN DUNNING

"Of course it's reasonable. But a reasonable person also knows when to stop. What's it been now, three or four years since her book was published? Four years, and I don't think she knows anything more today than she did then. But she's still out there digging. Or so I hear."

"I take it you and she are not bosom buddies."

He smiled, struggling to mellow. "We're certainly not enemies. It's just her book I don't like: I don't like it even without the epilogue, or whatever she called the murder chapter. Who *cares* how many prostitutes Richard Grayson knew in Seattle, or that even poor Darryl never could keep his own pants zipped? I just don't like that kind of business. I'm not a prude, I'm just suspicious of it. Trish will tell you she did more than three hundred interviews for her book. I say so what. How can we be certain that even Archie Moon, who was Darryl Grayson's friend for life, was telling her the truth?"

"People usually tell the truth when they know they're being quoted in a published record of their best friend's life."

"That's what you think. You'll pardon me if I remain a skeptic. I'm not saying Moon would lie—I just know that people do put their own spin on things. It's human nature. How can anyone know what really went on between Grayson and Moon over a forty-year friendship, when one of them's dead and the other might have an ax to grind? Moon's agenda might be nothing more devious than to have Grayson viewed well by posterity. So he might not tell you something that would undercut that, even though it might well contribute to a better understanding of Grayson's genius and how he made his books."

"It sounds like you're saying that Grayson's genius had a dark side."

"Can you imagine any genius that doesn't? It comes with the territory, as people say these days. You'll hardly ever find a truly brilliant man who isn't a little sick in some way. But what difference does it make? The Graysons are of general interest only because of the books they produced. If they hadn't done the books, they'd be nothing but a pair of swaggering cocksmen, forgotten by everybody including Ms. Trish Aandahl. Anyone can lie down with whores, but only one man could have done the Thomas Hart Benton *Christmas Carol*. Only one. That book was a *creation*, you see, and that's what I choose to focus on. I don't do interviews for my work, I'm not interested in what people *say* about the Graysons, all I want to know is what really happened. My disciplines are rigid, precise, verifiable, true. If that sounds like bragging, so be it. I don't report rumors or pillow talk."

He held my eyes for a long moment, then said, "You look like you disagree with everything I've just said."

"I'm absorbing it."

He poured me another cup, got a third for himself, and sat down again. "Very diplomatic, sir. But look, tell the truth—as a bookman—do you actually *like* biography?"

"It's like anything else, a lot of it's slipshod and crummy. I don't like the *Mommie Dearest* crap. But I guess I believe there's a need for biographies of people like the Graysons, done by a writer who's a real writer, if you know what I mean. No offense to you— what you do is indispensable, but . . ."

"But I'm not a writer and Trish is. You won't get any argument from me on that point. The woman is just a sorceress when it comes to words. There's a seductive quality to her writing that hooks you by the

193

neck and just drags you through it. Just wait till you get started reading her book—you won't be able to leave it alone. You'll wake up in the night thinking about Darryl and Richard Grayson, their times and the lives they led. Trish is just brilliant when it comes to conveying emotions with images and words. She could've been a great fiction writer, done the world a favor and left the Graysons alone."

"What about you? Did Aandahl interview you?"

"Several times. I had to overcome a good deal of reluctance to sit still for it. In the end, I'm no better than anyone else, which only proves my point all the more. I'm a ham, Mr. Hodges. I was fascinated with her subject, with the things she was finding out, and I was flattered that she considered me an indispensable source. There's no getting around it, I did want to know what she was doing."

"Did she quote you accurately?"

"I didn't give her much choice. I insisted on reviewing her material—at least the parts where I was mentioned."

"Did you find any errors when you read it?"

"No."

I raised an eyebrow and cocked my head slightly.

"She had a *tape* recorder, sir, how can you misquote someone when you record every syllable and grunt? Look, I'm not saying she isn't a good reporter—she may very well be the greatest newspaperwoman since Nellie Bly. And if she keeps digging at it, who knows what she might uncover? Maybe she'll prove that Richard Grayson was in league with Lee Harvey Oswald and her work will go down in history. Pardon me in the meantime if I doubt it. We're going around in circles—I have my opinion, Trish has hers, and I'm sure you have yours. Where do you want to start?"

I didn't know. "It's a little like jumping into a sea.

All I know about the Graysons so far is what I got from that capsule biography in your book."

He fidgeted. "I hated to do even that much. But the requirements of the book . . . the publisher demanded it, it was felt that readers would want at least the essentials of their lives. So I did it, but I kept it short—only what could be absolutely verified. It's still the part of the book that I'm least proud of."

"That doesn't mean you didn't know the lurid details."

"I know *all* the lurid details. I've read everything that's ever been published on the Graysons. I can touch the paper a Grayson book is printed on and tell you whether it's the regular run or one of his variants. In a sense, every book he made was a variant. Did you know that?"

I shook my head no.

"It was one of his trademarks, one of his eccentricities. That's what makes the man so endlessly interesting. Try to get a grip on him by looking at his work— you'll end up in a rubber room talking to men in white coats. I can spend days with his books, and I'm talking about different copies of the same title, and I'll find some little variation in every one of them. Every time I look! *I'm* supposed to be the Grayson expert, I'm supposed to know everything there is to know about these things, and I can still sit down with five copies of his *Christmas Carol* and find new things in every one of them. Sometimes they're subtle little things in the inks or the spacing of words. Can you imagine such a thing in this day of mass production? —Grayson made every copy in some way unique. It was a trademark, like Alfred Hitchcock appearing somewhere in all his films. Only what Grayson did was far more difficult than anything Hitchcock ever dreamed of. Try to imagine it—the chore of produc-

JOHN DUNNING

ing an exquisite book in a run of five hundred copies,
and making many copies different from the others
without messing anything up. It would drive a normal
man nuts. He must've worked around the clock when
he had a book coming out. The binding alone
would've taken anyone else six months to a year, full-
time. Grayson did it in a gush."

"He had Rigby to help him."

"But not until 1963."

"Before that there was Richard."

"Who was a pretty fair binder, as it turned out. I'm
sure these people helped out, but I don't think anything ever went out of that shop that Grayson himself
didn't do. This is partly where the mystique comes
from. Grayson did things that to other printers look
superhuman, and once he decided *what* he was going
to do, he did it with a speed that defies belief. He'd
fiddle and change things in the process: then, for
reasons no one understands, he'd toss in a real
variant. It's as if he suddenly got a notion in the
middle of the night, and he'd change the paper or the
binding, for that one book only. If the book passed
muster when he'd finished it, he'd go ahead and ship
it. People on his subscription list were always thrilled
when they discovered they had a variant—though it
was sometimes years later that they found out."

"Some of them probably never found out."

"That's an excellent assumption. You can bet there
are still many Grayson books sitting on the shelves of
people who have no idea what they've got."

"The original owner dies, leaves them to his
children . . ."

"Who don't understand or care."

"Is there any way of tracing these books?"

"Don't think that hasn't occurred to me . . . and to
one or two other people. You'd think it would be

196

simple—Grayson must've kept a master list of his subscribers, but it's never been found. Some of the books have come to light on their own. They'll pop up in the damnedest places . . . last year I got a card from a woman in Mexico City. Her husband had been a subscriber. He had just died and she had all the books, still in their shipping boxes."

"What did you do?"

"I flew down and bought them. On the first available plane. That's one of the perks that comes with being an expert. Everything gets funneled your way."

"I wonder if Aandahl gets any of that."

"I wouldn't be surprised. When you've published a book on something, people do tend to think you know what you're talking about, whether you do or not. And they'll call you when they think they've got something you'd buy for a price. Trish has a certain advantage in that her book will be read by many thousands more people; mine is so narrow and specialized. But I really doubt if she'd know the differences between the Benton standard issue and the Broder variant"—he grinned widely—"without consulting my book first."

I didn't say it, but it seemed to me that Huggins had been reading Aandahl at least as much as Aandahl had been reading Huggins. He caught my drift at once.

"I've read that goddamn book cover to cover ten times. That doesn't count endless browsings. Sometimes I dip into it when I'm at loose ends. I've got two copies back there, one for the shelf and the other for the workroom. The working copy's so marked up you can barely read it anymore. I argue with her in the margins, I rail at the liberties she takes. The book is bashed and battered where I threw it against the wall when I first read it. So, yes, I do know it well. I can quote passages from it the way some people quote Shakespeare. And if we're going to be totally honest, I've got to tell you this: the goddamn thing can move me to tears in places. It has a brilliance that I . . . I don't know how to describe it. At its best it rings so true that you just *know* . . . you find yourself pulling for Trish to be right. But her book is fatally flawed because there are many other places where you know she's stretching it. I can tell the minute she starts that horseshit, sometimes right in the middle of a sentence. And in the end the whole book's meaningless: it's a fascinating piece of pop culture. Trish can talk to a million people, and even if they all slept with Grayson, they still won't be able to tell her what she really wants to know."

"Which is what?"

"For starters, *what* drove the man, *what* made him do things, *why* he did them the way no one before or since has come close to doing, and *where* did the genius come from. I can't remember who said this, but it's got the stamp of truth all over it. James Joyce could spend a lifetime trying to teach his son to write, but the son could never write a page of *Ulysses.*"

"Grayson sounds like a pure romantic."

"Trish seems to think they both were—that's one of the many flaws in her book. Take the term *romance* strictly in its sexual context and you'll see right away how silly her thinking is. Darryl Grayson couldn't have been more his brother's opposite in his relations with the opposite sex, even if encounters with women invariably ended up in the same place. In bed, I'm saying—they both had enormous sexual appetites. But women to Richard were just objects. Richard sometimes said that he had slept with more than twelve *hundred* women, Mr. Hodges, can you even begin to imagine such a thing? Trish Aandahl must've been in hog heaven when she uncovered that juicy little tidbit. But the point is this—Richard hated women; Darryl loved them. That's the difference. Darryl Grayson never met a woman he couldn't just love to death. And it didn't matter what they looked like: he loved the homely ones the same as the beauties. I've known a few of Grayson's ladies and they all say the same thing. He had a way of making them feel cherished, even when they knew he'd be with someone else tomorrow."

"The most difficult kind of man there is, from a woman's viewpoint."

"Absolutely. Richard had the reputation of being the ladies' man, because he conquered so many and they fell so fast. But it was Grayson who broke their hearts. His printshop fascinated them—they'd go in there and it was like stepping into a world they'd never dreamed of. Then they'd see what he was *doing,* and what he had *done,* with all those Grayson Press books lined up on a shelf above his matrix, and even a whore would know that something great had touched her life."

"Did he ever show them work in progress?"

"All the time. Grayson was completely secure in himself. I don't think the notion that anybody might steal his work ever crossed his mind. How could you steal it?—he created it all, from the alphabets to the designs. He took special delight in seeing the uninitiated light up at their first encounter with his art. In the last five years of his life, Darryl Grayson enjoyed his celebrity, as restricted as it was. He loved his uniqueness. He didn't brag, but he'd spend hours talking to you, explaining the process, if you were interested."

"Would you mind telling me a little about his process?"

"He was like great artists in every field, from literature to grand opera. Ninety percent of his time on a given project was spent in development, in planning, in trial and error. He created and threw away a lot of books. Sometimes he made a dozen copies, using various papers and inks, before he decided what was what. On the *Christmas Carol,* for example, he spent a year comparing the color reproductions on various papers. It wasn't every day you got Thomas Hart Benton to illustrate one of your books, and it was damn well going to be perfect. And it was! What he finally chose was a fifty-year-old stock that he bought from a bank, which had taken over a publishing house and was disposing of the assets. The paper had been in a warehouse, sealed in boxes since 1905. It was very good stuff, intended for the fine-press books of that day but never used. It took the colors perfectly, the registers are just gorgeous."

"What did he do with the dummy books?"

"Destroyed them. They were just for experimental purposes, and the last thing he wanted was for some flawed copy to turn up later, in the event of his unexpected death. Grayson was extremely aware of his place in publishing history. Rightly so, I might add. A hundred years from now his books will be as prized as anything you can name."

"And he knew that."

"Oh, yes. Oooooh, yes, my friend, no doubt of that at all. Grayson gave the impression of being a humble man, and in some ways he was. But don't let anyone tell you that he ever sold his art short, or that he wasn't acutely aware of his own importance."

A thought crossed my mind and I shivered slightly. Huggins asked if I was cold and I said no, I was just thinking of Grayson's dummy books. "Imagine turning one of those up. What do you suppose it would bring if a thing like that just turned up suddenly at auction?"

He rolled his eyes.

"What if a whole set survived?"

He was too much a gentleman to say it, but the look he gave me said it well. *You've been out in the rain too long, mister, it's starting to make your brain soggy.*

"So what about *The Raven?*" I said.

He gave a laugh and rolled his eyes, a vision of Looney Tunes.

"You did know he was working on it—that much is in your book."

"Obviously he died before the project was finished."

"Do you know how long he'd been working on it when he died?"

"In a sense you could say he'd been working on it since 1949. That's where it started, you know, that obsession with Poe. It began in Grayson's nagging dissatisfaction with his first *Raven*. Personally, I love the book. I'll show it to you when we're through here, you can see for yourself. It's simple and lean, but what's wrong with that? It was done on a shoestring budget, that's all. It wasn't the lack of money that kept *The Raven* from being a great Grayson—Grayson would never let money stand in his way. If the money wasn't there to commission an artist like Benton, he'd get someone else to do the art. That someone might be a total unknown, but he'd be good, you could bet on it, and the book would still be a Grayson. The trouble with *The Raven* was with Grayson himself. He was just too young, he didn't know enough yet. His alphabet was wrong: he was trying for an effect he couldn't yet achieve—letters that combined the modern and the Gothic in a way that had never been done, that would draw out Poe in the context of *his* time and still keep him relevant to a modern reader. It was too ambitious for a boy, even a genius, not yet out of his twenties. His vowels in particular were too modern for the rest of it—the *A*'s and the *O*'s, but even the bowls of the *D*'s and *B*'s too sleek-looking to give him the effect that the other letters were working for."

"Damn, it sounds complicated."

"You can't begin to imagine. At Grayson's level it can't even be adequately explained to a layman. But look, let's try. You have twenty-six letters. Your goal is to have them mesh perfectly, each with the others in every possible sequence, and in absolute harmony. So you tinker around with your *E*. At last it seems perfect, it looks great, until you discover—*after* the goddamn book has been bound and shipped—that when you put it between an uppercase *L* and a lowercase *n,* as in the name *Lenore,* it looks just like dogshit. You can't do this mathematically and you can't do it with computers: you just have to slug it out in the trenches and hope you don't overlook some silly thing that makes your work look to all the other printers in the world like it was done by a kid in kindergarten. Sure, the average guy won't know the difference—even a collector or a bookman like yourself wouldn't know. Any of you would look at the Grayson dummies and think they were perfect. But a printer like Frederic Goudy could tell right away, because he was also a master designer. Goudy was dead by then, but Bruce Rogers was asked about Grayson and he said what Goudy probably would've said—'This is very good, but it was done by a young man who will get nothing but better.' The remark got into print and Grayson read it. Rogers meant it as a compliment, but it stung him, and the book always haunted him. He wouldn't discuss it, and he went through a time when he considered denying that he'd ever done it. Good sense prevailed and he soon got off that silly kick. Grayson in the end was like most great artists, he could never reach his idea of perfection, and he was always too hard on himself. He didn't understand that the charm of his *Raven* lay in the very flaws that always tormented him. They show the budding genius at work. The flaws illuminate the brilliance of the other parts, and they do what none of Grayson's other works can begin to do. They show him as human after all. Especially the mistake."

"What mistake?"

"There was a spelling error in the poem 'Annabel Lee.' He never forgave himself for that."

"What did he do?"

"He spelled the word *sepulchre* wrong—with an *re* in one place, and an *er* in the other."

"That's an easy mistake to make."

"Of course it is. But gods don't make mistakes."

"Actually, I think you can spell it both ways."

"It had to be spelled the way Poe spelled it. To've messed that up was to a man like Grayson the height of incompetence. But it proves what old-time printers all knew—there's no such thing as a perfect book."

"Damn. Then what did he do?"

"After the denial stage, he went through another silly time—he decided to round up all the surviving copies and destroy them. Trish has this wonderful scene in her book, and who knows, maybe it even happened that way. Grayson had retrieved five copies and was about to set them on fire in the dump behind his house. But he couldn't do it—thank *God* he couldn't light that fire. I think it was then, that night, when he decided he'd do another *Raven* someday, in the distant future, when he had the money and the skills to do it right. He saw his career enclosed by those two *Ravens,* like definitive parenthetical statements."

Huggins let a long, dramatic moment pass. Then he

said, "Isn't it too bad he never got a chance to do that second one?"

The clock ticked and the question hung in the air. A long silence fell over the room. I knew we were thinking the same thing, but Huggins would never admit it. Once or twice he looked to be on the verge of something: then he'd look away and hold his peace. I still had a million questions and the sinking hunch that even then it would come to nothing.

A simple question could tie us up for an hour. Huggins was expansive: a gesturing, conjecturing, extrapolating encyclopedia on the Graysons, and I didn't know enough to be able to decide what of all he was telling me was relevant. Then I thought of the one thing that might boot us up to another level—that scrap of charred paper in my wallet.

"Could I ask you something . . . in confidence?"

"Certainly."

I took the paper out and put it on the counter between us.

"What's your opinion of that?"

He squinted at it, then got out his glasses. I heard him take in his breath as if an old lover, still young and beautiful, had just walked into the room. He looked up: our eyes met over the tops of his glasses, and I could see that my hunch was right. I had shaken him up.

"Where'd you get this?"

"I can't say. That's part of what has to be kept confidential."

"What do *you* think it is?" he said, suddenly coy.

"You're the expert."

He gave a mirthless grin. "You're trying to tell me that this little fragment is part of something that I'm an expert in. But what can you expect from me, with such a small piece? There are only four letters. How can I tell?"

"The word *angel* appears in *The Raven*."

"I know that. But what's it prove? You think this is part of Grayson's *Raven?* It isn't."

"How can you tell?"

He picked up the fragment and held it up to the light. He looked at it through a jeweler's eyepiece, then put it back on the counter.

"The paper, for one thing. Grayson would've used a much finer stock than this. Probably an old stock. And he'd have printed it damp. You follow what I'm saying—he'd dampen the paper slightly, so the press could get a real bite into it, so the ink would go deep and become part of the page. Look at this and you'll see the ink's sitting right on top of the paper, which is a common and I'll bet cheap brand of copy paper."

I felt a surge of relief. It was a photocopy, my hunch was right, the real book was still out there, somewhere.

I picked up the paper chip and put it in my wallet. Huggins followed it with his eyes. He seemed irritated when I put the wallet away in my pocket.

He looked at the clock. "It's getting late."

I apologized for eating up his evening.

"A few more questions?"

He nodded. "Make it quick, though. I've got a headache coming on."

I took Eleanor's address book out of my pocket and opened it to the Grayson page.

"Does the name Nola Jean Ryder mean anything to you?"

He took off his glasses and squinted at the book, then at me.

"Where'd you hear that?"

"It just came up," I said, not wanting to tell him. "It's probably not important."

"She was one of Richard's . . . girls."

"Is she still around?"

He gave a faint smile. "Thinking of talking to her?"

"Sure, if I can."

"What could you possibly hope to gain by talking to one of Richard's old whores?"

"Is that what she was?".

He shrugged.

"It's like you said yourself," I said. "With a man like Grayson, who knows where the answers are?"

He grunted. "You think she's got your *Raven?*"

Before I could answer, he said, "You'll find everything that's known about Nola Jean Ryder in Trish's book."

"You sure make her sound mysterious."

"Do I? I don't mean to, though she's certainly mysterious enough. She disappeared after the fire and she hasn't been seen since."

We looked at each other and the questions rose in my throat. He cut them off unasked. "Look, I don't know a damn thing about that. I told you before, this is not my thing. If you want to talk about Grayson's *books,* then I'm your man. But if you're interested in people, especially the whores in their lives, then you'll have to ask Trish. Or read her book."

I started to put the address book away.

"What other names do you have in there?" He was suspicious now, his tone accusing.

I looked at the page. "Jonelle Jeffords."

He shrugged.

"Rodney Scofield."

He sat up with a start. "What about Scofield?"

"That's what I was going to ask you."

"Did Scofield send you here?"

"I don't even know the man."

He looked dubious.

"Really."

"Then where'd you get his name?"

"It's just something I picked up."

"Of course it is." His tone was suddenly mocking, almost hostile. "Really, sir, I think you've been taking advantage of me."

"I can't imagine how."

"Can't you really? Do you think I'm a complete idiot? You come in here and I don't know you from Solomon Grundy. How do I know who you are or what you really want? You'll have to leave now. I'm tired."

Just that quickly, I was hustled to the door.

I took a chance, told him to call me at the Ramada if he had second thoughts, but I probably wouldn't be there beyond tonight. I sat in the car and looked at his house. The questions had only begun. I still didn't know why Trish Aandahl thought the Graysons had been murdered, and I never did get to see Huggins's books.

25

On the way downtown I stopped at a Chinese joint. I ate some great moo-shoo and arrived back at the Ramada at eight o'clock. I sat on the bed and made my phone checks. Leith Kenney was still incommunicado: in Taos, the recorded welcome mat continued on the Jeffordses' phone. By nine o'clock I was tight in the grip of cabin fever. I tried Trish Aandahl, but there was no answer. Outside, the rain had resumed its hellish patter.

Nothing to do at this time of night but wait it out.

At quarter after nine a knock at the door made me jerk to my feet, knocking the phone to the floor. I stood for a moment, that line from Poe running through my head . . .

> *"'Tis some visitor," I muttered, "tapping at my chamber door—*
> *Only this and nothing more."*

. . . and slowly I moved to the window and parted the curtains. I could see the dark outline of a man, his shoulders and legs and the back of his head. He knocked again: he meant business. He had probably heard the phone falling and knew I was here, and he didn't seem interested in helping me by moving back out in the light so I could see his face. I bit the bullet: went to the door and opened it.

It was the deskman. "Sorry to disturb you, I just wanted to check and see if that's your car. I didn't recognize it from anybody who checked in today."

I assured him it was mine: the other car had belonged to a friend. He apologized and went away. But he stopped in the courtyard and looked back at the Nash, just long enough to give me the jitters. He didn't write the plate number down, and I watched him through the curtain until he disappeared into the office.

If I had any thought about staying here past tonight, that ended it. I'd be gone with the dawn, looking for a new place and a new name. I sat on the bed and tried the phone again, but the world was still away from its desk. Kenney and Jeffords I could understand, but Trish had asked me to call, you'd think she'd be there. I would try her each half hour until she came in. I was reaching over to make the ten-o'clock call when it rang almost under my hand. It caught me in that same tense expectancy, and again I knocked it clattering down the table to the floor. I gripped the coiled wire and the receiver bumped its way back up the nightstand into my hands.

"Hello."

"Mr. Hodges?"

"Yes . . . yeah, sorry about the racket."

"It's okay, I've done that a few times myself." There was an awkward pause. "It's Allan Huggins."

"Ah."

"I've been thinking about that chip of paper you showed me."

I waited, letting him get to it in his own way.

"Actually, I haven't thought about anything else since you left."

"Have you changed your mind about it?"

"No . . . no." I heard him breathe . . . in, out . . . in, out. "No, I feel sure it's a photocopy. The question I can't get out of my mind is, what's it a photocopy of? . . . And where's the original? . . . And how and when was it made?"

"Interesting questions."

"I'm wondering if I could see it again. I know I wasn't too hospitable when you were over earlier. I apologize for that."

"It's no problem."

"Would it be asking too much . . . Could I perhaps make my own photocopy from your sample? I'd like to study it at greater length."

"I don't think I want to do that just now. You can see it again, if you'd like."

"I would like, yes . . . very much. The lettering's what's getting to me. The more I think of it . . . I've never seen that exact typeface, and yet . . ."

He didn't have to elaborate: I knew what was going through his head.

"Tomorrow, perhaps," he suggested hopefully.

"I'll give you a call if I can."

"Please do . . . please."

"You could do something for me while we're at it. Call it a trade-off."

"Surely," he said, but his voice was wary.

"Tell me why the name Rodney Scofield set you off like a fire."

"Don't you really know?"

"No," I said with a little laugh. "I keep telling you, I never heard of the guy."

He grunted a kind of reluctant acceptance. "Tomorrow, then. We'll talk about it then."

He hung up. I made my phone checks yet again, to no avail. Outside, the rain fell harder, bringing my spirits down with it.

In this mood of desolate pessimism, having exhausted for the moment my last best hopes by telephone, I lay back on the bed and started reading Trish Aandahl's book on Darryl and Richard Grayson.

26

The earliest Grayson alphabets were etched in the cool, hard sand of Hilton Head Island in the fall of 1937. It was a wild beach then: there were no luxury hotels or golf courses, and the beach was fringed by strips of jungle. On Sunday mornings Grayson would crank up his '29 International pickup and clatter out on the oyster-shell road from Beaufort. *Never again have I known such a sense of freedom and raw potential,* he wrote, years later, to a friend in Atlanta. *Never have I had such a clear vision of the road ahead.* He was seventeen and on fire with life. He walked the beach alone, glorying in the solitude and in the wonder of his emerging wisdom. His cutting tool was a mason's trowel. He covered the beach with alphabet, running with the sunrise and racing the tide. He knew all the classic typefaces: he could freehand a Roman face that was startling, and when the tide came up and washed it all away, it left him with a feeling of accomplishment, never loss. It was all temporary, but so necessary—the sweet bewilderment, the sudden clarity, the furious bursts of energy that sometimes produced nothing more than a sense that in his failure he had taken another vital step. It would come, oh, it would come! He could do things at seventeen that he could not have dreamt at sixteen. His youth was his greatest ally, as fine an asset as experience would be when he was forty. A photograph exists—two photographs, reproduced back-to-back in Trish's book. The young Grayson stands on the beach, his face in shadow, the sand behind him etched with letters. The same scene on the verso, a young woman standing where Grayson had been. The capsule identifies her as Cecile Thomas, the day, September 15, 1937. *He was my first love, the dearest, most desperate, most painful. I was eighteen, a year older than he was, but he was in all ways my teacher.* On that moonlit night, warm for early autumn, they had become lovers on the sand, obliterating the writing he had done by firelight. *Never mind,* he said, *I'll make you another one,* and he did, running blind in the dark with the tide going out, and when they came back in the morning, the incoming tide had not yet reached it.

Oh, it's perfect, she had said: *when the tide finally did come up and wash it away, I cried, and he laughed and said it was nothing.* Someday, Grayson told her, he would create something that couldn't be washed away, so why cry now for trifles such as this? *God, I loved him . . . still do in a way. I couldn't believe how it affected me when I read of his death, and I hadn't seen him in more than twenty-five years.* The world was a poorer place when he died. He cared nothing for money or roles or the things that drove others. He learned his art the only way an artist ever learns, by probing the secrets of his own vast heart. He always took the road less traveled, always: he rose up on the page and strode across it, an unspent force even in death. Here he comes now, walking up Hilton Head alone. He carves up the sand with his trowel, running an alphabet of his own creation, knocked off on the spot. The tide licks away the *A* even as he touches off the small *z,* and he stands ankle-deep in the surf, breathing the pure Carolina air and tasting his coming victories. Only the spirit of Trish Aandahl is there to keep him company, this woman yet unborn, a kindred essence wafting in the wind. Somewhere in the cosmos they connect, inspiring her to better prose, perhaps, than she can ever do. And slowly as she writes of Grayson, a dim picture emerges of herself. She's there beside him, coaxing him along the sandy shore. She tells me things about Grayson that would leave a photographer baffled. The camera would miss it all. A magnificent picture is never worth a thousand perfect words. Ansel Adams can be a great artist, but he can never be Shakespeare. His tools are too literal.

27

I finally reached Leith Kenney at midnight. The conversation was short but potent.

"Mr. Kenney?"

"Yes."

"I'm calling from Seattle." I didn't tell him who I was. I was more interested at this stage in finding out who he was. I played my trump card right out of the gate. "I'm calling about Grayson's *Raven*. The 1969 edition."

I heard him catch his breath, as Lewis and Clark might've done at their first glimpse of the Pacific Ocean. I knew one thing right away: I had dealt myself a strong hand, even if I couldn't see all the cards.

I let his pause become my own. Then I said, "Are you interested in talking about it?"

"Oh, yes." His voice quivered at the prospect. "Yes, sir," he said, underlining the *sir* part.

His eagerness was so palpable that I knew I could run the show. "Tell me about Rodney Scofield."

"What do you want to know?"

"Look, I'm just a guy who's stumbled into something. I was tipped to you people by somebody who might know a lot more than I do. But right now I don't know you boys from far left field."

"Mr. Scofield is a businessman . . ."

"And?"

"He collects books."

"Grayson books."

"Yes."

"And it's fair to say that Mr. Scofield is a pretty substantial man."

"You can check him out. You'll find him in most of the financial reports that are available in the library."

"And who are you?"

"Well," he said as if it should be obvious, "I work for Mr. Scofield."

"Doing what, besides taking questions about Grayson?"

"That's my full-time job."

I thought my way through a stretch of silence. "Would it be fair to say that Scofield would pay a small fortune if a Grayson *Raven* were to fall into his hands?"

The silence was eloquent. Mr. Scofield would pay more than that. Mr. Scofield was that most dangerous of book animals, the man with the unquenchable passion and the inexhaustible bank account.

"I'll get back to you," I said.

I hung up before he could protest. I wouldn't worry anymore about Leith Kenney or Rodney Scofield. I had their number, I knew where they were, and they'd be there when I wanted them.

Trish was another matter. I let her phone ring ten times before giving her up. I tried her desk at the *Times,* but she wasn't there either.

Jonelle Jeffords continued keeping the world at bay with her husband's answering machine.

At half past midnight, I shut down for the night.

I would sleep six hours. If supercop didn't come in the night, I'd be well out of here in the morning.

I had a plan now, a destination that I hoped would

take care of the lodging problem. It was a gamble, gutsy as hell. For that reason alone I thought it was probably the safest hotel in town.

In the morning I would become Mr. Malcolm Roberts of Birmingham. I was going back to the Hilton.

I let Trish put me to sleep with her lovely prose.

In the first hour of the new day, I walked in Grayson's shoes.

28

The Grayson odyssey twisted its way through Georgia half a century ago. The forces that shaped them were already centuries old when they were born. Their grandfather was still alive and whoring when they were boys in grade school, the gnarled old buzzard a whorehouse regular well into his eighties. The old man never stopped fighting the Civil War. The big regret of his life was not being born in time to be killed at Fredericksburg, where his father had died in 1862.

A plantation mentality ran the house of Grayson. The father ruled and allowed no dissent. His politics were boll-weevil Democrat and his neck was the color of the clay hills that stretched around Atlanta. Women were placed on pedestals and worshiped, but they quickly lost their sex appeal if they wanted anything more out of life than that. It was Darryl senior's profound misfortune to marry Claudette Reller, a free spirit who could never quite see the charm of life in a cage. She abandoned her family on a sunny day in 1932, walking off in the middle of her garden-club luncheon without notice or fanfare. Her sons, ages eight and twelve, never saw her again. She was said to have died three years later in Paris. The old man announced it at supper one night and forbade her name to be uttered again under his roof.

The young, fair-haired son obeyed his father well. A psychologist would say, years later, that he never forgave his mother and that every experience with sex was a slap at her memory.

The older son remembered her less harshly. He knew why she'd done what she'd done, and he wished she would write him from wherever she'd gone so that he might answer her and tell her he understood. He and his father were locked in their own battle of wills, and when he thought of his mother, there was sympathy in his heart.

In the summer of his seventeenth year, young Grayson escaped to the Carolina coast. There he lived on a sea island, thinking about life and supporting himself by working in a Beaufort garage. But in the fall he was back in Georgia, doing battle with his father in the determined effort to become his own man. Women became an ever-larger part of his life. Cecile Thomas had been lovely but temporary: now there was Laura Warner, older and more experienced, twice married, widowed and divorced, cerebral, money-eyed, and addicted to genius. She saw herself as Mrs. von Meck to Grayson's Tchaikovsky, one of their literary friends suggested, but Grayson was having none of that. They parted amicably after a short but intense friendship. She moved to Birmingham and, in 1939, sailed from Miami to London, where her trail petered out.

But Grayson's life was rich with women like that. A biographer trying to dig up his footprints forty years later could still find some of them eager to talk and have their memories mined. Others had been swallowed by time. A line had to be drawn on the hunt for old girlfriends and the book brought back to its dual focus. So Trish Aandahl let Laura Warner slip away into wartime London while she worked her narrative around and brought Richard again into the picture.

There are people in Atlanta today who remember Darryl and Richard Grayson and believe that a strong streak of real hatred existed between them. But there are others who tell a different story. They remember the hazing Richard took from a pack of bullies when he first started high school. The leader of the gang was one Jock Wheeler, a mean little bastard as remembered by the Marietta shipping clerk who had known them all. Today Jock Wheeler is an elderly mechanic in an Atlanta garage. He's a quiet man who lives alone and bothers no one. Ask Jock Wheeler about the Grayson boys, said the shipping clerk to Trish Aandahl. Ask him about that night in the midthirties, when he was ambushed on a dark country road by two men he couldn't, or wouldn't, identify and beaten so badly he almost died. Wheeler had nothing to say, but the rumor mill persisted that one of the assailants was little more than a boy, twelve or fourteen years old. The sheriff floated the Grayson boys as the leading candidates, but Wheelers said no, t'wasn't them. The rumor mill churned. The more thoughtful of their contemporaries pointed to it as a strange quirk of human nature. Probably on some level the Graysons truly did hate each other, but blood is thicker than water. That's the thing about clichés, you know. They are usually true.

29

I woke to a gray dawn, certain I'd heard a noise off my left elbow. It went click-click, like the sound a lockpick makes when someone is trying to open a door. But I had been dreaming about a raven, its talons clicking as it walked across the table to peck my eyes out.

Both sounds stopped as I came awake and sat up in the bed.

It was Sunday, the day of rest.

Television promised more rain, followed by bad weather. The weather clown played with his million-dollar toys, swirling clouds over a map and grinning with all thirty-two as he did his dance. But this was a floor show next to the competition. Evil, two-faced evangelists pranced about, talked of Jesus and money in the same foul breath, and sheared their glass-eyed flock. Praise the lord, suckers.

The radio was fixed to an oldies station, with something called a salute to the British Invasion already in progress. I got "Eleanor Rigby" as a curtain call to my shave-and-shower, and I stood in the buff anticipating every beat and lyric, for all the good it did me.

The clock was pushing nine, and my departure seemed somehow less urgent than it had at midnight. Nothing was open yet. Check-in at the Hilton wasn't

till three o'clock. The library, another of my scheduled stops, informed by recorded message that its
Sunday hours were one to five P.M. I had time on my
hands.

I sat on the bed and started my phone checks. It was
ten o'clock in Taos.

I punched out the number and heard it ring.

"Hello?"

"Jonelle Jeffords?"

"Who are you?"

It didn't seem to matter so I told her my real name,
then began to improvise. "I'm a friend of the court.
The judge in Seattle gave me the job of getting Miss
Rigby back to New Mexico in the burglary of your
house. I need to ask you a few questions."

She expelled her breath like a hot radiator.
"Goddammit, can't you people leave us alone?"

This was a strange attitude for a victim, but I
already knew she was not the run of the mill victim. I
put an official tone in my voice and said, "Most
people who've been burglarized cooperate. I find your
attitude a little unusual. Is there a reason for that?"

She hung there a moment, surprised, then said,
"My husband is very upset by all this. It's going to be
bad enough having to go to court when they finally do
bring that crazy girl back here. What can I tell you
that hasn't already been asked and answered fifty
times?"

"I'm sure you're tired of answering questions. But
I'm in Seattle, I don't have access to the files they've
built in Taos, and I need to know more about what
she stole from you. Otherwise I don't know how you
expect to get your property back."

"I don't want it back. I should've burned it years
ago."

"Burned what?"

"That book."

"It was mainly a book, then, that she took from you?"

"If I'd just given it to her when she first came here, maybe she'd've just gone away. Then none of this would've happened."

"Where did you get the book?"

"I don't see what that has to do with anything. It's personal business, very old business. It doesn't have any bearing on this."

"It might, if we have to determine who owns it."

"What are you saying, that *I* stole the book?"

"I'm just asking a few questions, Mrs. Jeffords. If I seem to be going in a way you don't like, it's your attitude that's leading me there. You're going to have to answer these questions, you know, sooner or later."

"Listen to me, sir, and understand what I'm telling you. My husband is extremely upset by all this. He's outside now on the deck, he'll be in here any minute, and the last thing I need is for him to find me talking to you about that crazy girl. It hasn't been easy coping with this. She could've killed us. Charlie gets a little crazy himself just thinking about it. If you call here again, you'll cause me a lot of trouble."

"Can you describe the book?"

"No! Can't I make you understand English? I haven't even looked at it in twenty years."

"Are you familiar with the names Slater or Pruitt?"

"No. Should I be?"

"Slater says you hired him to find your book."

"He's lying. I never heard of the man."

"What about Pruitt?"

Her voice dropped off to a whisper. "Charlie's coming. Charlie's here. Go away, don't call me again."

She banged the phone down.

What a strange woman. I could just see her, scurrying across the room to distance herself from the telephone. Smoothing her dress, sitting primly, trying to look like a poster from *Fascinating Womanhood* as her big old bear came home from the hill.

Trying her damnedest to give away a book others would kill for.

I hadn't gotten to the hard questions yet. Who really fired that gun, Mrs. Jeffords? What's the link between you and the Rigby girl, and why do I get the feeling that it's personal?

I knew, though, that I'd had my one shot at her. She was far away and she wouldn't be picking up the telephone again without letting that recording screen it first.

I tried Trish and got nothing.

Decided to put Allan Huggins on hold for the moment.

Checked out of the motel and went looking for breakfast.

At eleven o'clock, I parked on the street outside the library and passed the time reading.

30

Suddenly it's 1963. Gaston Rigby stands in North Bend at the dawn of his life, ready and waiting to be molded by the genius Darryl Grayson. Who would think that Grayson might hire him, even to sweep out the shop? Now there are days when every green kid

221

JOHN DUNNING

with a yen to publish turns up on Grayson's doorstep, hat in hand, begging for a chance to work for nothing. The mystique is in full bloom, and Grayson is still well on the sunny side of fifty. What is it that separates Rigby from the others? . . . How does he get to Grayson on that primal level, that place where the genius lives? Grayson leaves no clue. He is not one to talk of such things. The hunt for verbal profundity makes him uneasy and, if he's pushed too hard, cross. Speaking of Rigby, Grayson will say only that he's a good one. He's willing to let it go at that, as if trying to isolate and define everything that goes into making a good one is beyond him. And this is Archie he's talking to, and Archie knows a good one as well as he does.

Moon looks back at it many years later. At times he thinks Rigby took the place of the younger brother—almost but not quite. He thinks Grayson and Rigby were, almost but not quite, like father and son. That spiritual bond can be difficult to understand when you stand outside it: it goes deeper than anything Moon has ever seen between men of solidly heterosexual persuasion. He insists he felt no jealousy: he is secure in his own importance to Grayson, and if Rigby mattered as much on another level, why should it worry him? He was still Grayson's best friend in life. They grew up together, they swam buck naked as kids, tramped woods and fields, hunted deer and birds, chased women as young hell-raisers, drank, dreamed and shared the same calling. When Grayson left the South after the war and wrote that he had found a promised land, Moon came along to see for himself. Moon still remembers the first words he spoke as he got off the train in Snoqualmie. *What the hell is this little burg gonna do with two goddamn printers, for Christ's sake?*

But Moon is a mechanic and Grayson is an artist.

They coexist perfectly, perhaps the only friends in history—to hear Moon tell it—who never had a disparaging word between them. Moon does worry, especially in the beginning, that Grayson is chasing an impossible dream. Nobody ever made money doing small-press books. Put that in caps and say it again. NO-body. If you can do it for twenty-five years and not lose your pants, you can call yourself blessed. Grayson never made a dime. His entire operation was bankrolled with family money. Eventually the boys came into hundreds of acres of prime Georgia planting land—peaches, corn, just about anything a man wanted to grow. But Darryl and Richard Grayson were not farmers. They sold the land and Grayson took his half and did what he did with it. His books made enough to keep most of his principal intact, and that's all they ever made in his lifetime.

What is it about the book business anyway, Moon wonders. Sometimes it seems like nobody on any level of it makes any money. Maybe if you're Random House and you can figure out how to publish nobody but James A. Michener, you can make a little money. Everybody else picks up peanuts.

Why do they do it? he wonders. But he knows why.

Now it's 1963 and Rigby arrives, joining Grayson in the quest for the perfect book. *Look at you, Darryl,* Moon says over beer in the town bar, *you're launching a life.* Grayson just nods in his cups. What has never been said—what Moon tells Trish Aandahl years after Grayson's death—is how much influence Rigby had on Grayson. Rigby was truly remarkable for a kid: *damn, he had the greatest hands,* Moon says, *he'da been a great doctor, delivering babies, coaxing 'em into the world . . . he could coax butter out of a witch's heart* and his instincts for binding and design were almost as fine and fully formed as Grayson's. Rigby offers his opinions timidly at first—a kid does not come in and tell a genius how to run his business—but he soon learns that Grayson has no ego in the heat of the work. Grayson will listen to the man in the moon if the guy can give him an idea, and Gaston Rigby is a fountain of ideas. *Do you think, Darryl, that the center of the page is too dense? . . . Not by much, maybe, but listen to what the words are saying and look at it again.* Grayson studies it. He walks away and looks from afar. More often than not, he decides that Rigby is right. Their talk runs nonstop through the day, every word germane to the work at hand. There is never a joke between them or a comment on the outside world or a reflection on womanhood. There are no calendar-girl pinups, no radios or newspapers, nothing that would take away Grayson's concentration even for a moment. There are no clocks. Grayson comes down to the shop in the morning and Rigby is already there. They work until some inner clock tells Grayson that the day is done. In Grayson's shop, time stands still. He alone knows when the work is through and he walks away, leaving Rigby to wash the press and tidy up the workbench and put everything back where it goes.

Rigby's responsibilities grow along with his salary. By his second year he seems indispensable. His eye is uncanny: he catches things that might even escape the master in various stages of trial and error. Broken serifs, hairline cracks, typos: he spots them instantly. He checks each impression for indentation, uniformity of punch, blackness of ink ("needs a little more color here, Darryl"). His eye is so good that Grayson comes to depend on him in those final stages when the books are inspected and shipped. This gives him a sense of family, something he's never known. Rigby lives upstairs, in the loft over the shop. He stands in darkness now, staring off through the black woods at the lights of the big house. He knows that sometimes the brother brings whores over from Seattle, but this too he sees as part of the process. If Grayson can be relaxed and made ready for tomorrow by the services of a whore, let him do it. They come and go, harmless fluff. Only near the end does the one called Nola Jean take on a major negative importance. She screws with Grayson's head and is not good.

It is now 1968. Rigby is twenty-two. He has been with Grayson five years and life is sweet. He has a woman of his own, a relationship nurtured slowly like a courtship from another time. This is Crystal, Moon's teenage niece, who ran away from her home in Georgia and now finds work in the North Bend bakery. Crystal loves Rigby's shyness, his brilliance, his teddy-bear presence. He is the first solid man in her life, always the young gentleman. Rigby has none of the stormy impatience that runs rampant through his generation. Politics bores him: even the Kennedy assassination, he tells her, struck him as little more than another TV show. Crystal marvels at this. She is seventeen, and in love.

31

I reread the last chapter, which told of the fire. The facts rolled out like an epilogue. On the night of October 14, 1969, the shop had caught fire and gone up like a torch. A fire investigator had come out from Seattle, poking through the ashes for days before calling it, officially, an accident. But I knew from my own experience that these things are often vague. At least one hundred thousand fires a year are written off to unknown causes, Aandahl pointed out, and the presumption in law is that these are accidents. Arson must be proved beyond a reasonable doubt: a fireman's suspicion, however strong, doesn't cut it. An old-fashioned printshop like Grayson's was a fire-bomb waiting to go off.

In the first place, there is paper everywhere. There are rags, often soaked with solvents or ink. The printer must work with fine papers and keep them in pristine condition, but he also works with ink, which gets on his hands, under his fingernails, and on his tools. Everything must be washed, many times a day. A working printer might go through 150 gallons of solvents a year. Kerosene was the stuff of choice for many shops. Grayson liked gasoline because it was harder and faster. He kept it in a fifty-gallon drum behind the shop. The drum sat upright in a wooden frame, with a spigot at the bottom where the squirt guns could be filled.

The fire broke out in the main part of the shop—the fire investigator was able to figure that out by the pattern of the wood charring. It had quickly consumed that room, spread up to the loft, then to the little storeroom in back. By the time it was seen from the road, flames had broken through the ceiling and back wall. The gas drum caught on fire and exploded, sending a fireball a hundred feet in the air. The remains of Richard Grayson were found in the shop: he had been drinking and had apparently passed out in a chair. His brother was in the back room. He too was drunk, and the fireman theorized that he had gone back to lie down on a cot that was kept there for just that purpose, when he'd had too much booze to walk himself back up the dark path to the main house.

Gaston Rigby had gone to town. It was for him a

rare night out. He had taken his girl, Crystal, to dinner in Seattle and arrived home at midnight to find his world in ruins.

I was standing at the door when the library opened. It didn't take long to dope out Rodney Scofield. I looked through periodical and newspaper indexes, and in half an hour I had come up with all the applicable buzzwords.

Oilman . . . manufacturer . . . eccentric . . .

Billionaire, with a *b*.

Recluse. Twenty years ago, when Scofield was in his late forties, he had taken a page from Howard Hughes and disappeared from the public eye. He had been written about but seldom seen since 1970. His business deals were conducted and closed by the battalion of toadies and grunts who worked for him. Nowhere in the general press was his hobby, books, given a line.

I went to *AB/Bookman's Weekly,* which publishes its own yearly index.

I found nothing on Scofield, but Leith Kenney was prominent in the magazine's index of advertisers. He had been a bookseller, with a store in San Francisco.

He had been a notable bookseller, with membership in the Antiquarian Booksellers Association of America. This is not an easy group for flakes and fly-by-nights to get into. They nose around in your credit, they check your bank references and take a long look at your stock before admitting you to the club. People who bounce checks and cheat little old ladies get a quick brush-off from ABAA.

Kenney was a past president. His field was fine-press books.

But he had not run an ad in the magazine since 1986. I found out why in that year's December issue, in a news column headlined "Kenney to Close S.F. Bookstore." No, he laughed, he was not going broke.

He had been offered a job that was simply too lucrative and challenging to pass up. He was going to create a world-class library on the career of Darryl Grayson. He would be looking for anything that pertained to the man's life or work—ephemera, photographs, correspondence, business records, and, of course, the books, in any quantity. Multiple copies were eagerly sought. The work of Richard Grayson was also of interest, Kenney said, but it was clear from the tone that he was considered an association figure. As far as posterity was concerned, there was only one Grayson.

I didn't want to park in the Hilton garage: my rust bucket was a little too prominent for a class hotel like that. I put on my raincoat and carried my bag, leaving the car parked on the street.

I rode up the elevator to the lobby on the ninth floor. Paid cash for two nights and told them I might be longer. I asked for a quiet room on a high floor, where I could see the city.

The clerk had rooms on fifteen, seventeen, and twenty.

Seventeen would be fine, I said. I was given a key to 1715.

I rode the elevator up and walked along the hall. The door to my old room was open. I walked past and looked in.

Two men were there, going through the wastebasket. The big one with the pale olive skin stood up and turned as I came by. I turned as he did, letting him see the back of my tired gray head.

I opened the door and went into my new room. Couldn't help gloating just a little as my door clicked shut.

Score one for old dad in the game of guts football.

Up yours, supercop.

32

I sat on the bed and called Leith Kenney in Los Angeles. This time I had no trouble getting through to him.

He had had a dozen hours to think about it and decide how he wanted to handle it. He gave me the direct frontal approach, which I liked. We were two bookmen talking the same language, even if only one of us knew it.

If the material was genuine, he wanted it. If there were questions of ownership or provenance, he would still pay top money for possession and would hash out the legality when the thing went to court. This to him was a foregone conclusion. We were talking about a substantial sum of money, and people tend to bicker when money arises. At the same time, Kenney had no doubt where *The Raven* would end up, where it *should* end up. He was prepared to top any offer, many times over. He was prepared to fly to Seattle at a moment's notice or fly me to Los Angeles in Scofield's private jet. He was prepared for just about anything.

"Let's put it this way," he said. "If you've got something you even *think* might be the genuine article, we want to see it and we'll pay you for that privilege no matter how it turns out. We've been looking for this item for a very long time."

"That's pretty good, for a book the bibliographer swears was never made."

"We know it was made. Mr. Scofield has seen it. He's held it in his hands. Maybe Allan Huggins wouldn't be quite so smug if he had done that."

Before I could ask, he said, "It was a long time ago, and that's all I want to say about it until I know more about you. You've got to appreciate my position, sir. I don't even know your name. Mr. Scofield may be the only man alive who has actually touched this book, and we don't want to be put in the position of giving away what we know about it."

That was fair enough. I didn't like it, but I had to live with it.

"Remember one thing," Kenney said. "If you do turn it up, people like Huggins will be all over you. Don't make any deals on it without giving us a chance to top their bids. We *will* top them, you'll be shocked at how much. And you'll be doing yourself or your client a terrible disservice if you sell it anywhere else."

At last we were down to bedrock. The big question.

"How much money are we really talking about here, Mr. Kenney?"

"Whatever you'd like."

33

I didn't move for a while: just sat on the bed listening to my inner voice. It drew my mind back across the hall to the room where Eleanor and I had spent our last few hours together.

Homework's finished, said the muse. One more phone call, maybe two, and you can hit the street.

In the room across the hall, Eleanor had mailed a letter. Against my better judgment, I had watched her write it and then I had let her send it off.

What was it, who got it, where had it gone?

Questions with no answers, but sometimes the muse will give you a hint. Her nearest and dearest was one obvious call, a risky one I'd rather not make on this telephone. Still the letter had to be chased—if it deadended, at least it would lead up an alley that had to be checked anyway.

And then there was Trish, a source of growing discontent. I seemed to have lost her in the heat of the moment. She faded to black while I scrambled around covering my tracks, and now, suddenly, my need to hear her voice was urgent.

The muse played it back to me.

Call me, she said. Don't disappear, I have some things to tell you.

Having said that, she herself had dropped off the earth.

So the nightwork was there. Chase the letter, track down Aandahl.

I called her home, wherever that was, but the telephone still played to an empty house. I tried her desk at the paper, without much hope. At the end of three rings there was a half-ring, indicating a shift to another line.

A recording came on, a woman's voice.

"Hi, this's Judy Maples, I'll be running interference for Trish Aandahl for a few days. If it's vital, you can reach me through the main switchboard, four six four, two one one one."

I called it. The operator wouldn't give me a number for Maples, but did offer to patch me through to her at home. The phone rang in some other place.

231

"Hello."

"Judy, please."

"This is she."

"I'm a friend of Trish."

"Aha. What friend would you be?"

"One who's a little worried about her."

"She's fine. Something came up suddenly and she had to go out of town."

"When will she be back?"

"Not sure, couple of days maybe." There was a kind of groping pause. "Trish left a package for a friend, if you happen to be the one."

"What's in it?"

"Can't tell, it's sealed up in a little Jiffy bag. Do you think it's for you?"

"Is there a name on it?"

"Initials."

I took a long breath. "How about C.J.?"

"You got it. Trish didn't know if you'd get this far or not. For the record, I have no idea what this is about. I'm just the messenger gal. She told me to say that. It's true. I left your package with the guard at the paper. If you want to go pick it up, I'll call him and tell him to release it to you."

I said okay, though nothing about it felt okay.

I walked out past my old room. The cops were gone and the place was closed tight. I rode the elevator down, drew my raincoat tight, pulled my hat down to my eyebrows. The day was going fast as I went out into the timeless, endless rain. Everything in the world was gray, black, or dark green.

I fetched my car, went to the *Times,* and got my package.

It was a cassette tape, wrapped in a single piece of copy paper. A cryptic four-line note was handwritten on the paper.

*If you'd like to stay at my house, consider it yours. I
have no reason to believe you'd be unsafe there. The
key's in the flowerpot. Don't mind the dogs, they're
both big babies.*

Trish

A postscript told her address, on Ninetieth Avenue
Southeast, Mercer Island.

I put it back in the bag and slipped it under my seat,
then moved on to the main business of the evening.

I wanted to be well out of the downtown area when
I made this call. I drove south, got off the freeway near
Boeing, and looked for a telephone. Phones are like
cops: there's never one when you need it.

At last I stood at a little lean-in booth and made the
call. It was a hard quarter to drop.

I heard it ring three times in North Bend.

"Hello."

"Crystal?"

"Yeah, who's this?"

"Janeway."

You could eat the silence, it was that heavy. I didn't
know how to begin, so I began by telling her that. But
she already knew.

"The police were here. They've been here off and
on since noon."

Good for the cops, I thought: good for them, not so
hot for me.

I was getting nervous. It already seemed I'd been on
that telephone a long time.

"Are the police there now?"

"No. They may come back tonight."

The funny thing was, she never once stated the
obvious: she never said, "They're looking for you, you
know," or anything like that. Still, she wasn't going to
give me what I needed unless I could move her that
way.

"I'm going to ask you for something. I wouldn't blame you if you told me to go to hell. I haven't done much right so far."

She was listening.

"I guess I'm asking you to trust me. I'd like you to believe that everything I've done, at least after that first night, I've done for Eleanor."

She punished me with silence. I endured it till I couldn't anymore.

"Crystal."

"Yeah, I hear you."

"I'm trying to find your daughter."

"I guess I knew that. And I don't know why, but I do believe it."

The wall between us crumbled. Whatever she'd been telling herself with the logical part of her brain gave way to instinct.

"Even when we were talking to the police, I kept thinking of you," she said. "Kind of like an ace in the hole."

"That's what I am. It may not be much . . ."

"I get feelings from people. Not psychic, nothing like that, but people hit me either warm or cold. When I hugged your neck on the porch that first night, I felt the warm between us. Sometimes people just connect, you know what I mean? I could see that between you and Ellie right from the start. It was warm, but not the kinda thing a mother needs to worry about . . . except maybe on her side."

She gave a little laugh. "That's why I never really gave up on it, even when it came out why you were really here."

"I'm going to find her if I can. I don't know how and I'm starting pretty far back. I need your help."

"Tell me what you want."

"Are the cops taping this call?"

"They talked about doing that. There was some

doubt about whether it'd be productive. Just a minute." She put the phone down and blew her nose. Then she said, "They're not exactly expecting a ransom demand."

"When will you know?"

"They may come back tonight and put it on. Or they may not."

"If they do and I call back, could you let me know?"

"How?"

"Clear your throat when you answer the phone. I'll try to find a way to let you know if I've got anything new."

"Or you could call Archie. He wants what we all want."

"A couple of questions. Do you know a guy named Pruitt?"

"He's the one the cops are looking for. They think he took Ellie with him."

"Had you ever had any contact or dealing with Pruitt before this came up?"

She paused as if groping for words. "I knew who he was."

"Tell me about it."

"A crazy man. He seemed to think we had something . . ."

"A book."

"Yeah, but I didn't know what he was talking about. He wouldn't go away, though, wouldn't leave me alone. I'd go to town and see him watching from a car. Then he started bothering us on the telephone. At night he'd call, play music. Just a few notes, but we knew it was him."

"He was stalking Eleanor too."

She expelled a shivery breath.

"Listen, did you get a letter from Eleanor in yesterday's mail? It would've probably been on Hilton Hotel stationery."

"It never came here."

"It may come tomorrow. What time is your mail delivered?"

"Whenever he gets here. Early afternoon as often as any."

"I'll try to call then."

"What's in the letter?"

"That's what I need to find out. It might be her laundry bill. For our purposes, think of it as some dark secret she'd rather not tell the world. Is there anybody else she might send something like that to?"

"Amy Harper," she said immediately. "Nobody but Amy."

I remembered the name. "Eleanor mentioned her once. Said she'd gone to see Amy but Amy wasn't there."

"Amy moved into Seattle, I coulda told her that. Her life out here'd turned to hell the last six months, especially after her mom died. I worry about that child, don't know what's gonna become of her. She's made some wrong choices in the last few years. But really a sweet kid. She and Ellie were like sisters all through school."

"I seem to remember there was some kind of rift between them."

"They had a falling-out over Coleman Willis. That's the fool Amy let knock her up when she was still at Mt. Si High. Then she made it worse: married the fool and quit school and had a second kid the next year. The trouble between them was simple. Ellie had no use for Coleman Willis, couldn't be in the same room with the man. Amy was still trying to make it work. You can see what happened."

"Sure."

"But Amy's no fool. There came a time when even she'd had enough of Coleman and his bullshit, and

236

she took her kids and left him. She and Ellie got together once or twice after that. I really think they'd fixed things up between 'em, I think they were good as new."

"Is there a phone number for Amy?"

"God, Amy can't afford a telephone, she's lucky she's got a roof over her head. I've got an address if you want it . . . it's a rooming house on Wall Street. Are you familiar with the section they call Belltown?"

I wasn't.

"It's easy, right off downtown. Just a minute, I'll get it for you."

34

It was just fifteen blocks from the Hilton, about as far as Oz is from Kansas. It made me remember myself as a kid, bouncing around for a year of my life in places not much better than this. Now I go through these neighborhoods and the memory of rank and scummy beds hits me like a shot of bad whiskey. It's a chilly reminder of what life hands out to those who slip and can't climb up again. The young seem unbothered by the lack of elegance: time, they believe, will see them through it, and time when you're twenty is a thing you'll never run out of. You can sleep anywhere when you're running on your rims, and you don't give too much thought to the dripping tap or the cracked and faded walls or the mice that come tearing across your landscape. The young endure and hope, until suddenly they're forty and time isn't what it once was. The old suffer and save their hopes for the real things in life—a high, dry present and a quiet place to die.

On the second floor of this environment, at the end of a long, dim corridor, lived Amy Harper. The floor creaked with every step and the walls were thin. I could hear people talking—in one room shouting—as I walked past the doors and stopped at 218.

Be there, I thought, and I knocked.

She was: I could hear her move inside. Soft footsteps came at me and a soft voice asked who I was. I said I was a friend of Eleanor's.

She opened the door and looked at me through a narrow crack. I could see a chain looped across the crack, a little piece of false security she had probably bought and installed herself. A man like me could break it with one kick, long before she had time to get the door closed.

"I'm sorry, who are you?"

"My name's Janeway, I'm a friend of Eleanor's."

For a moment she didn't know what to do. I got the feeling she'd have opened the door if she'd been there alone. But I could hear a baby crying and I knew she was thinking about her children.

"Crystal gave me your address," I said, and at that she decided to let me in.

It was just what I'd expected—a one-room crib with a battered couch that pulled out and became a bed; a table so scarred by old wars and sweating bottles that you couldn't tell what color it had been; two pallets for the children; a kitchenette with a gas stove and an old refrigerator; a bathroom the size of a telephone booth. There was one good chair: she had been sitting in it, reading a paperback. Stephen King, the grand entertainer of his time. God bless Stephen King when you couldn't afford a TV.

She had been nursing the baby: she still held it in the crook of her arm. Her left breast had soaked through the faded blouse she wore. She covered it, draping a towel over her shoulder, excusing herself to put the child in the pallet next to the other one. "So, hi," she said with a cheery smile as she stood and brushed back a wisp of red hair. Crystal had called her a sweet kid and the adjective seemed just right. Amy Harper had the sweetest face I'd ever seen on a girl. You looked at her and saw a young woman who wanted to love you.

She couldn't offer much—a cup of instant decaf or a diet Coke maybe—but her manners were alive and well. I let her fix me some coffee, mainly because she seemed to want to. She went into the kitchenette, stand-up room for only one, and turned on the gas. "So how is Eleanor?" she called back across the room. Apparently they had not been in touch.

"Actually she's not so good," I said, sitting on the chair where she had been. "She seems to've disappeared on us."

She looked out of the kitchen, her face drawn and suddenly pale.

"I'm trying to find her."

"What're you, some kind of detective?"

"Some kind of one. Crystal hoped you could help us."

"If I could, God, you know I would. I haven't got a clue where she might be. Just a minute, this water's boiling."

I heard the sounds of water pouring and the tinkle of a spoon stirring in the coffee crystals. She came out with two steaming cups, insisting that I stay in the chair. She sat on the floor against the wall and looked at me through the steam rising from her cup.

"I haven't got a clue," she said again.

"When was the last time you saw her, or heard from her?"

"Haven't seen her in . . . must be more than a month ago."

"Any mail from her . . . cards, letters . . . anything?"

"No, nothing."

"I'm looking for one letter in particular. I'm not sure if it's had time to be delivered yet. She may've mailed it Friday night."

"To me, you mean?"

"We don't know. Crystal thinks that's a possibility."

"Probably come tomorrow then."

"If it does, would you let me see it?"

"Yeah, sure, if it'll help; I'll do anything I can."

We sipped our coffee: I could see her running it all through her mind.

"If she mailed something to me, it probably wouldn't come here. I haven't seen her since I moved into town. She'd send it out to my mamma's place in Snoqualmie."

"Could we ride out there and see?"

"Yeah, sure. I'll have to take off from work . . . my boss is a little touchy about that . . . I'll just tell him I'm taking off. If he fires me, he fires me."

"I don't want you to get fired. Maybe I could go check the mail for you."

She shook her head. "No, I want to go too. You've got me worried. Jesus, I hope she didn't hurt herself again."

"Crystal said you were special friends."

I saw a tremor of feeling ripple through her. "Oh, yeah. She's like my soul mate. I don't mean . . ."

I knew what she didn't mean. She said, "We were just great together, all through grade school, then high school. We were inseparable. If I wasn't sleeping over there, she was over with my mamma and me. We'd sit in our rooms and talk about boys, and the drudgery of life at Mount Success."

She gave a sad little laugh. "That's what we used to call Mt. Si High—Mount Success—because so many of the people who went there seemed to go nowhere afterward. They just stayed in that little town forever. I never understood that, but now I do. Here I am in the big city and all I want is to get back home."

"Why don't you? It's only twenty-five miles."

"It's a lot farther than that." She shrugged. "I had to get out of there. My ex lives there and he's bad news. If I went back, he'd just hassle me."

"Crystal said you and Eleanor had drifted apart, then got together again."

"The drifting was my fault. I married a guy who was a jerk. Want some more coffee?"

"Sure."

She got up, poured, came back, sat. "That's the first time I ever said that. My husband was a jerk. There, maybe now I can get rid of it. He was a grade-A heel." She laughed. "Hey, it feels better all the time. Maybe if I call him what he really was, I'll be good as new. Wouldn't be very ladylike, though."

I let her talk.

"Ellie tried to tell me what he was like, that's why we almost lost it. I didn't want to hear that. But the whole time I was married to this fella, and carrying his children, he was trying to make it with my best friend. What do you do with a guy like that?"

"You leave him."

"Yeah. And here I am, bringing up my children in this palace. Working in a bar and giving most of my money to the day-care people. Wonderful, huh? But I'll get through it."

I leaned forward, the coffee cup clasped between

my hands, warming them. "Amy, I don't have any doubt of that at all."

She smiled that sweet smile. I thought of Rosie Driffield, the lighthearted heroine of *Cakes and Ale.* Maugham would've loved this one.

"The great thing about Ellie, though," she said, "is, she never let it bother her. The hard feelings were all on my side."

"But you got over it."

"Yes, thank God. Even an ignoramus sees the light if it's shined right in her face."

"And Crystal said you two got together again and patched it up."

"My mamma died. Ellie came to the funeral and we cried and hugged and it was all over, just like that. Then I found that stuff of hers . . ."

She looked away, as if she'd touched on something she shouldn't be talking about.

"What stuff?"

"Just some things my mamma had."

"Things . . . of Eleanor's?"

"Not exactly. Just . . . stuff. Papers in Mamma's stuff . . . it really isn't anything."

I felt a tingle along my backbone. "Tell me about it."

"I can't. I promised."

I looked straight into her eyes. "Amy, whatever you tell me, I'll try not to let it out. That's all I can promise you, but this may be important."

Her eyes were green: her face radiated hope, her eyes searched for trust. But she was also a child of this planet who had begun to learn that you can't trust everyone.

"I don't even know you."

"Sure you do."

She laughed at that and I laughed with her.

"You don't know, do you," I said, "about the trouble she got in, down in New Mexico."

Her eyes opened wide. No, she didn't know.

I told her.

Tears rolled down her cheeks. "I knew it, I knew it, I just knew something bad was gonna come of this. This is my fault, I should've burned it, I never should've shown it to her."

"Shown her what?"

"When Mamma died she left me some stuff. God, you never saw so much stuff. My mother was a pack rat, that house of hers is just full of stuff, it's packed to the rafters. You won't believe it when we go out there. I know I'm gonna have to start going through it, it's got to be done, but I just can't face it yet. I've got to soon, though . . . that house just has to be cleared out."

It seemed she had lost her drift in the maze of problems she had to deal with. She got it back, looked at me, and said, "There were some papers in Mamma's stuff . . . things I thought Ellie should see."

I nodded, urging her with body language.

She got up and went to a little end table half-hidden by the couch. I heard a drawer squeak open and saw her leafing through some papers. She pulled out a manila envelope, came over, and got down on one knee beside my chair. She opened the flap and handed me a photograph.

It was an eight-by-ten black and white. It was Eleanor in jeans and a sleeveless blouse, taken in the summertime in good light. She was leaning against the door of an old frame building, smoking a cigarette and smiling in a sly, sexy way. "Nice picture," I said.

But I looked again and in fact it wasn't a nice picture. It was her eyes, I thought, and that killer smile. She looked almost predatory.

"It's not her," Amy said.

I turned the picture over. On the bottom, handwritten in fading ink, was an inscription.

Darryl's printshop, May 1969.

35

Isn't that a kick in the head," Amy said, looking around my shoulder. "Imagine looking at a mirror image of yourself, in a picture taken the year you were born. I thought about it for weeks, you know, whether I should show it to her or not. I knew the minute I saw it that nothing good would come of it. I felt all along that I should've burned it."

"Why didn't you?"

"It didn't seem like I had the right. It wasn't my call to make."

"What did you do?"

"One day I just showed it to her. She had come out to Mamma's to help me get started on going through things. We putzed around all morning on the first floor—I didn't even want to go upstairs where all this stuff was—and we were sitting in the kitchen having lunch. It had been on my mind all morning, and I still didn't know what to do. Then she looked across the table at me and said, 'You're like the sister I never had, you're just so special, and I'm happier than you'll ever know that we're okay again.' I felt tears in my eyes and I knew then that I had to tell her, there was no stopping it, and the best I could do was put a happy face on it."

"How did she take it?"

"I couldn't tell at first. I was hoping she'd look up and shrug it off, say something like, 'Yeah, I never told you, I was adopted,' and that would be the end of it. Then we could laugh about it and let it blow away and I could rest in peace knowing I'd done right by her. But the longer she sat there, the worse it got, and I came around the table and took her hands, and I knew for sure then that it had just knocked her props out. Her whole world was scrambled, it was like she couldn't think straight for a long time, like she couldn't get a grip on what she was seeing. I put my hand on her shoulder and said something stupid about what a coincidence it was, but we both knew better. There's no way."

"Then what happened?"

"She said she had to go home, she wasn't feeling well. And she left."

"Did you see her again after that?"

"Yeah, she called the next day and asked if she could come out to the house again and look through the stuff in the attic. So we did that. I worked downstairs and she sat all day in that hot attic, going through papers and old letters."

"Did she tell you if she found anything?"

"All I know is, she didn't *take* anything . . . just the one picture of this woman. I think she made some notes though."

"Were there other pictures?"

"There was a whole roll taken at this same place. I think Mamma took them; it's her handwriting on the back and I know she was doing some photography then. There were maybe twenty shots of different people."

245

"Do you have the other pictures?"

"They'd still be out at the house, up in the attic."

"Were they people you knew?"

"Mostly, yeah: there were pictures of Gaston and Crystal and Archie. God, were they young!"

"What about Darryl and Richard Grayson?"

"I don't think so. But I wouldn't know them if I saw them. I think they were just friends of Mamma's, way back then."

"Do you know if Eleanor ever told Crystal about this?"

"No, and I wasn't going to. I felt like I'd done enough harm."

"Then it's possible they still don't know."

"Yeah, sure it is. But we can't tell them. The last thing Ellie said to me was not to tell anybody, especially not Crystal and Gaston. She made me promise I wouldn't."

"It takes courage to break a promise like that. Sometimes you have to, if the person's welfare is at stake."

"Is that what you think?"

"I don't know what I think. Has anybody else been up in that attic since your mother died?"

"There was a man who came, just after it happened."

"What man?"

"Just a minute, I'm trying to think, he gave me his name. He said he was an old friend of Mamma's who saw the item about her funeral in the newspaper."

"What'd he look like?"

"Old . . . older than Mamma, even. Kinda frail."

"What did he want?"

"He said she had promised to help him on something he was writing . . . some magazine article. She had some information he needed to make it work."

246

"Why didn't he get it from her while she was still alive?"

"He was going to. Her death was pretty sudden. She was in the kitchen, peeling potatoes for supper, when her heart gave out."

"So what did you do?"

"About this man, you mean? . . . I let him look through the attic. I didn't think there was anything special or valuable up there."

"This was even before Eleanor got up there, then?"

"Yes, at least two, three weeks before."

"And you don't remember this man's name?"

"It's right on my tongue, I'll think of it in a minute."

"Did he take anything out of there?"

"Not that I remember. He did have a big canvas briefcase with him. I suppose he could've put something in that. I don't know, maybe I shouldn't trust people so much. Do you think he took something?"

"If you remember his name, I'll see if I can find him and ask him."

She shrugged.

"You said your mother may have shot the picture herself. Did you ever ask her about her life when she was young—who her friends were, what they did, stuff like that?"

"I was a kid. You know how it is, all I ever thought about then was kid stuff. Now I wish I'd taken more time with her, but then we were all into boys and music and makeup. When you're a kid, your parents are probably the least exciting people in the universe. And you never want to learn too much about them, you're always afraid they'll just be human, have the same failings and hang-ups you've got."

"You said there was other stuff in the attic . . . besides the pictures?"

"Tons of stuff . . . boxes and boxes of records and papers and letters. It just fills up that attic."

"What was the purpose of it? Did she ever tell you?"

"She always said she was going to write a book about Mr. Grayson, who had been her friend for years."

"Did she tell you how they met?"

"No."

"What about your father?"

Her brow furrowed: dark clouds gathered behind her eyes. "What about him?"

"Who was he?"

"Just a man Mamma knew. He wasn't around long."

"Was his name Harper?"

"What's that got to do with Eleanor? My father's been nothing in my life."

"It's probably got nothing to do with anything. It's just a question a cop asks."

"My father's name was Paul Ricketts. I don't know whether he's dead or alive."

"Was he there then?"

"When?"

"The year we're talking about . . . 1969."

"He must've been, at least for twenty minutes." She blushed a little. "I was born that year."

"Where'd the name Harper come from?"

"It was Mamma's family name. She never married this man. I really don't see why you're asking me this."

I backed off. I didn't want to lose her. "I'm just trying to find out who was there, who's still around, and what they might know. What about this book your mother was writing?"

"She never wrote a word, never had the time. It was

248

always tomorrow. 'Tomorrow I'll get started.' But tomorrow came and guess what? . . . She didn't have the time. She always had to work two jobs to keep me in shoes and have good food for us to eat. And then that other Grayson book came out, you know, by that woman at the *Times*, and that put the kibosh on it. Mamma knew she'd never write anything after that."

"But she did keep the material?"

"She never threw away anything in her life."

The thought that had been building in my mind now occurred to her. "Are you thinking maybe Eleanor found something up there in Mamma's stuff that caused her to go to New Mexico and break into that house?"

"There's a fair chance of it. That does seem to be where everything started coming apart for her."

"Damn. Makes you want to go out there now and start looking through it, doesn't it?"

"If that's an invitation, I'd love it."

She shook her head. "The house is dark, there's no power, they turned off the lights three weeks ago. And I'll feel a lot better tomorrow without the kids. I can drop 'em in day care at seven-thirty and we can head out then."

"If that's what you want."

"I'm as anxious as you are. I'm just not crazy about having my kids spend the night in a dark house in the country . . . you know what I mean?"

"In the morning then."

But she was my one real link to the past and I hated to leave her there.

Then I realized I didn't have to.

36

I talked her into my room at the Hilton with little effort. I explained it away as a room I had rented but couldn't use, and she wasn't inclined to ask questions. To her it was a *Wheel of Fortune* vacation: two nights in Oz, with a color TV, a king-size bed, and room service. I told her to order whatever she wanted, it was already paid for; then I left another hundred on deposit at the desk to cover it. It was after nine when I got over to Mercer Island, a wooded, hilly residential neighborhood just across the bridge from the city. Mercer dominates the lower half of Lake Washington: you come off Interstate 90 and swing along a spectacular bluff that overlooks the highway; then you curl back inland on a street called Mercerwood Drive and up past some expensive-looking real estate. It was not a place I'd imagine a working reporter to live in. So she had a boat, pricey digs, and a job that let her write her own ticket: I still couldn't imagine the *Times* paying her more than fifty grand. As I backtracked west, the houses seemed more ordinary. I turned left, deadended into a high school, and eventually found my way around it and came into her block.

It was an older house with a well-lived look to it. It sat on a large lot surrounded by trees. I pulled into her driveway and fished out the package she had left me from under the seat. She had left the night-light on as

well as two lights inside the house. I got out and
walked up like I owned the place.

The key was in the flowerpot, just where she'd said.

I came into a dark hallway. A brief memory of
Pruitt's house flashed through my mind before the
place burst into life—two golden retrievers charged
from the rear in joyous welcome. I got down with
them and roughed them the way big dogs seem to like
it. Mitzi and Pal, the tags on their collars said. Mitzi
was especially affectionate and I felt welcome, less
like a stranger in this town of endless rain.

The hall opened into a large living area. There was a
TV, VCR, and disc player, all the comforts. Just off
the big room was a dining room, with a mahogany
table that seated eight, and beyond that was the
kitchen.

In the middel of the table was a cassette tape player,
with the door flipped open.

Near the tape player was a note, telling her friend
Judy Maples how much to feed the dogs and where
things were. The dogs came and went, I saw, through a
doggie door that opened off the kitchen into a
groundlevel deck, and from there into a backyard.

I opened the refrigerator, which was well stocked
with beer; I fetched myself one and sat at the counter
sipping the foam. I took the tape out of the bag and
snapped it into place in the machine.

"Hi," she said. "Isn't this cozy?"

She paused as if we were there together and it were
my turn to talk. I said, "Yes ma'am, and I thank you
very large."

"You'll find beer in the fridge," she said, "but
knowing you, you already have. Seriously, make yourself at home. The dogs will want to sleep with you, but
they won't pester: if you close your door, they'll whine
for about five minutes, then they'll shut up and go

about their business. They're well behaved; I'm sure you'll get along famously.

"There's plenty of food. The freezer's well stocked, and if you don't see anything there you want, there's a big freezer in the garage. You can defrost just about anything in the microwave. Again I'm anticipating your little idiosyncrasies and impatiences, and assuming that you've never read an instruction booklet in your life. Do yourself a favor and read the two paragraphs I've left open and marked on the table. It's impossible to defrost food without knowing the codes. You could spend years of your life trying to figure it out on your own. I imagine you'll try anyway.

"I thought you'd be most comfortable in the big room on the right at the top of the stairs. It's a man's room—I rented this house from an FBI agent who's now doing a tour of duty in Texas. So that's where you should go—the room upstairs, not Texas—when you're ready to call it a night."

There was another pause. I stopped the tape, looked through the freezer, found a pizza, and put it in the real oven on a piece of tinfoil. The hell with instructional booklets written by committee in Japan.

I pushed the ON button on the tapedeck.

"So," she said, "on to business."

Yes ma'am.

"The cops picked up that kid who was with Pruitt and Carmichael. His name is Bobby John Dalton, date of birth"—I could hear her shuffling through notes—"one nine . . . umm . . . 'sixty-six. He's got a record, nothing major: one or two fights, one assault charge, a drunk and disorderly, carrying an unlicensed weapon, having an open can in a moving vehicle. He thinks of himself as a tough guy, a muscleman. Maybe he is—I mention it so you'll know . . . he'll figure he owes you for what you did to him in the garage. He was a bouncer in a nightclub, a bodyguard . . . Quintana wouldn't tell me much more than that. I'm recording this on Saturday night. My plane leaves in two hours and I don't know at this moment whether they've actually booked this Dalton kid or are just holding him for questioning. He was still downtown the last time I checked, about an hour ago. I don't know if the cops have any new leads on Pruitt after talking to the kid."

Again she leafed through her notes. "Here's a little more personal information on the Dalton kid . . . just a minute."

She read off a home address, on Pine Street east of I-5. "It's a boardinghouse owned by his mother. She seems to be a character in her own right, in fact as mean as he thinks he is. His father's been dead for years, though probably not long enough. The old man was a gambler and a drunk and was probably abusive. It's no wonder Bobby's on a fast track to nowhere.

"This should make you feel pretty good. At least the cops are doing their part. They're looking at Rigby as a serious abduction, so you've accomplished what you wanted without coming in. However, comma, be advised that Quintana is still on your case."

I heard a click, then another, as if she had turned the machine off then on again. "As you would imagine, the cops are playing it close to the vest on the particulars at the murder scene. I did find out, from a source inside the department, one strange bit of information. At this point they think the woman in the house was killed sometime earlier than Carmichael . . . maybe as much as two hours. They'll know more when the lab gets through and, hopefully, so will I. But assuming that holds up, don't you find it strange?"

Yes ma'am.

"That's all I have on it. I guess you should burn this tape. I've set a fire for you in the living room: all you've got to do is light it and toss this in. In fact, I don't know if you'll get in touch with Judy, or if you'll hear this tape, or if you do hear it, when that might be."

She took a deep breath. "I should be back in Seattle by Tuesday night . . . earlier if I get lucky."

I could hear doubt in her voice now, as if she had come to a new bit of business and wasn't sure how much if any of it she wanted to tell me.

"Have you read my book yet? Did you like it?"

Yes ma'am.

"I guess you could say I'm rewriting the final chapter."

I heard her breathe: she had moved the microphone closer to her mouth and was fiddling with it, trying to set it up straight.

"Help me, Janeway, I'm not having an easy time here. Send me some vibes, give me a clue. I'm trying to tell you some things you should probably hear, but I'm still a reporter and this is the big story of my life. I've lived with it a long time and I don't share these things easily."

I waited. The tape was hot and running.

"I'll tell you some things I put in my original draft and later had to take out. But I won't name names or places here, and I don't want to tell you yet where I've gone. We'll talk about it next week, when I get home, and we'll see where we are then.

"There was a man I wanted to interview, back when I was doing my research. He lived in the city I'm going to tonight. He probably wasn't important. His connection to Grayson was slender—all he did was collect and love Grayson's books. I don't think they ever met, and to tell the truth I'm not sure what my original intent was in seeking him out . . . to see his books, maybe, or get some insight into the quintessential Grayson collector. I didn't think he'd contribute more than a line to my book, but I was in his town, I had his name and a few hours to kill. So I tried to look him up.

"Turned out he was dead . . . he'd been murdered years before, in 1969 as a matter of fact, a few days after the Graysons died. This in itself might mean nothing, but it put an uneasy edge on my trip. I decided to stay over an extra day and ask around. The investigating officer had since retired from the police. I found him running security for a department store. He didn't mind talking about it—it was an old case then, nothing had been done on it for years, and the old cop told me things about the scene that he might not've said a few years earlier. One thing in particular stood out, and I thought of it this morning when you were telling me about the scene at Pruitt's. This Grayson collector was found dead in a room full of books twenty years ago. Right beside his body was a pile of ashes."

37

I opened my eyes to a blinding sunrise. It was six forty-five, the clock radio had just gone off, and the sun was shining.

I shooed the dogs off the bed and hit the shower. Wrapped in steam, I considered Trish and the tape she'd left me. The fire had eaten the tape, but the chimney had gagged on the words. They hung in the air and chilled the morning.

Traffic was reaching its rush-hour peak, a freeway horror show that made I-25 in Denver seem like a solo flight. But the sun was shining: the city sparkled like a crown jewel in a setting of lakes and mountains, and there wasn't a speck of pollution in the air. I felt better than I had in days, better by far than a confirmed fuckup had any right to feel. Damned if this wasn't the first day of the rest of my life. Good things lay off in the distance, waiting to be discovered; I could feel the potential as I crawled off the exchange at Interstates 90 and 5. It was so strong that even having to fight traffic all the way downtown and back again couldn't sour the moment.

By the time I picked up Amy and we got her kids dropped off at day care, it was after eight o'clock. She caught my upbeat mood and we crept back along the freeway with hopeful hearts. She had been enchanted by her night in the hotel: when you're young and poor and the best thing you've ever slept in was a $20 room by the railroad tracks, the Hilton must seem like Buckingham Palace. We chatted our way into Issaquah, ate breakfast in the same Denny's where Eleanor and I had eaten a lifetime ago, and made the final run into North Bend a few minutes shy of nine o'clock.

It was the first time I'd had a good look at the town: I had only been here at night, in a misty rain, or on the fly. Now I saw what Grayson had seen when he'd first stepped off here in 1947: a land of swirling mists and magnificent vistas and above it all that incredible mountain, looming like a sleeping giant. As a rule mountains do not impress me much: I grew up in Colorado, and I had seen many that were higher, deeper, bigger in every way. But I'd never seen one that so dominated its landscape, that commanded without being majestic. It pulled at you like a vast black whirlpool: it stood alone over the town and defined it. "Impressive, isn't it?" Amy said. "Mamma came here as a child in 1942 and never wanted to go anywhere else. She told me once that she got here when they were tearing up the streets for the new highway and the town was nothing but mud. But right from the start, she wanted to live her life here."

"It's the mountain. It gets a grip on you."

"People say there's an Indian in the mountain. If you look on a clear day, like today, you're supposed to be able to see his face. The knee's about halfway down. I never could do that, though. Can't see diddly."

The sister towns, North Bend and Snoqualmie, were connected by narrow back roads. We came into Snoqualmie past the high school, Mount Success, which Amy followed with her eyes as we circled around it.

"My whole history's tied up in that stupid building," she said sadly.

"Amy, you haven't lived long enough to make a statement like that. Your history's hiding out there somewhere, in the next century."

She smiled. "You're a good guy, aren't you, Mr. Janeway?"

"Just one who's lived a fair piece of his own history . . . enough to wish for a little of it back."

She gave the high school a last lingering look. "In the ninth grade they gave us an IQ test. I got one twenty-eight, which surprised a few people. For a week or so I thought I was hot stuff. I asked Eleanor how she'd done, but she kinda blew it off and said not very good. I found out about a year later, when Crystal let it slip one day."

She directed me along a road to the left.

"Her score," she said, emphasizing each digit, "was one . . . eighty . . . six."

She laughed. "She's a genius, sealed and certified."

Somehow I wasn't surprised.

Amy, suddenly moved to tears, said, "God, I love her."

Snoqualmie was just a few blocks of businesses, two bars, stores, a laundry, a Realtor, and a bowling alley. Many of the shops were named for the mountain: There was Mt. Si Hardware, Mt. Si Video, and the Mt. Si Country Store, which had a sign in the window that said THIS FAMILY SUPPORTED BY TIMBER DOLLARS. Begone, spotted owl: never mind what your habits are, you'll have to find another place to have your habits. We were on the town's main drag, looking for a gas station. The street was called Railroad Avenue: it skirted the train tracks, with an old-time railroad station (was this where Moon had stepped out all those years ago and been drawn by Grayson into his new life?) and a historic log pavilion that boasted a log the size of a house perched on a flatbed. As if on cue, Amy said, "There's Archie's place," and I saw a dark shop with the letters THE VISTA PRINTING COMPANY painted on glass and under it, in smaller letters, THE SNOQUALMIE WEEKLY MAIL. He put out a newspaper, I remembered. I got a glimpse of him through the glass, talking to someone I couldn't see. Again I thought of a timber wolf, lean and wiry, and I had the feeling he'd be a good man to know, if I ever had the time.

I stopped at the Mt. Si Sixty-six. Amy filled the tank while I checked in with Denver from a pay phone.

Millie answered at my store. She had been worried, she said: the Seattle police had been calling. Business was lousy, she said. On the other hand, there was an appraisal job in the works, almost twenty thousand books, a job that could run weeks at $50 an hour. But they needed me to start next week.

I told her to give them my regrets and refer the job to Don at Willow Creek Books. If the cops called back, ask for Quintana and tell him I'd buy him a pitcher at his favorite watering hole when this was all over.

We backtracked through town. If Quintana doesn't get me, the poorhouse will, I thought.

Selena Harper had lived just outside town. "There's a helluva waterfall a few miles that way," Amy said. "Supposed to be half again higher than Niagara." But we weren't on a sight-seeing trip and she turned me off on one of those narrow blacktops running west. I saw a marker that said SE 80TH: we hung a left, then another, and doubled back into SE 82ND. There was a mailbox at the end, but the lettering had long ago worn away and had never been replaced. "Mamma never believed in doing any unnecessary work," Amy said. "Everybody in both towns knew her, so why bother putting a name on the box?" The mailbox was empty.

A dirt road wound back into the trees. The woods were thick and undisturbed here; the road was rutted and muddy from last week's rain. I didn't see a house anywhere, but soon it appeared as we bumped our way through the brush. A clearing opened and a ramshackle building shimmered in the distance like a mirage. There had once been a fence, but it had long ago crumbled, falling section by section until now only a few rotting posts and an occasional tangle of wire marked where it had been.

"Welcome to my castle," Amy said. "The only real home I've ever known."

I pulled into a dirt yard, slick with mud and ringed

by weeds. The house was indeed in a sorry state. "I just don't know what to do with it," Amy said: "it's become a white elephant. I've been told the land's worth something, but not as much as Mamma owed. I doubt if I'll break even when I sell it, if I can sell it. I'm having a real problem with that, you know. How do you cut your losses on a piece of your heart?"

She got out of the car and stood looking at it. "The last big thing she went into debt for was a roof. Right up to the end, she wanted to protect all that stuff in the attic, make sure it didn't get ruined by a leak. So about five years ago she borrowed the money and had a guy come out and fix it. She's been paying the interest on the loan ever since, but hasn't made a dent in the principal. So what we have here, ladies and gentlemen, is a ten-dollar tablecloth for a two-dollar table. Let's go inside."

We picked our way up to the porch, where she found two notes taped to the door. On one was scrawled the word *BITCH;* on the other, which had been there longer, *Amy you whore you better stop this shit.* She tore them down and crumpled them in her fist: "Well, I see my ex has been here. Now my day is complete."

I heard the jingle of keys. She opened a door, which creaked on rusty hinges, and I followed her into the most jumbled, crowded, disorganized room I had ever seen. "Don't say you weren't warned," Amy said over her shoulder. "My mother was constitutionally unable to throw out anything. This is just the beginning." She turned and leaned against a doorjamb, watching me as I beheld it. The first problem was the magazines—years of such extinct publications as *Coronet, Collier's, Look, Radio Mirror . . .* they were piled in every corner, on the chairs, at both ends of the sofa. As a book dealer I had made house calls on people who had survived their family pack rats, but I'd never seen anything quite like this.

"The funny thing is, she really did write for some of these magazines," Amy said. "She really was a good writer, she just had trouble deciding what to write, and then making the time to do it. She got five hundred dollars once from one of these jobs. I think that's when she began to talk to Grayson about doing his life in a book. She had worked for him, you know, she was the first person he hired when his shop began doing so well back in the fifties. She answered his phone, wrote his letters, kept his business records. And at work she was neat as a pin . . . or so she said. She never left work without putting everything where it belonged, then she'd get home and throw her own stuff on the nearest pile."

She led me through the hall to the kitchen. The cupboards too were clogged with papers, magazines, clippings.

"Happy New Year," she said.

She pointed to a stair that led down into darkness: "Cellar. More of the same down there. Whatever's there is pretty well ruined by the moisture . . . the whole place has got a mildewy smell. I never go down there without getting depressed and wanting to douse the whole thing with gasoline and burn it to the ground."

The kitchen opened on the other side into a back bedroom. There was another short hall, with steps to the upper floor.

"What you want's up there. You won't even need a flashlight on a sunny day like this. There's a big window in the attic that faces east, and the sun'll light you up like the Fourth of July. Do you need me for anything?"

"Let me go on up and see what I find."

261

"I'll putz around down here. Stomp on the floor if you want me."

Sunlight beamed down the stair like a beacon. The air was heavy and filled with floating dust. I went up past the second floor, up a narrower stair to the top. Light from the east flooded the room, giving you the notion of being a sample on a slide under a microscope. It wasn't an unpleasant feeling—after the days of rain, you were willing to be a bug if it bought you a little sunshine—and I stood there for a moment with my head poking up into the attic before going the last few steps. The attic felt crowded, like the rest of the house, but the room was small and an immediate difference was apparent up here. There was order . . . there was purpose . . . there was care. The boxes were all of one size, fitted together in one large block. They were neatly stacked on pallets in the center of the room, far away from the walls. Each had been wrapped in polyethylene and sealed with clear tape; then the whole bundle was covered by a sheet of the same plastic, making it as nearly waterproof as possible.

It was one of those moments that only a bookman can appreciate, that instant of discovery when you know without opening that first box that you've just walked into something wonderful. Your mouth dries up and your heart beats faster, and the fact that none of it belongs to you or ever will is strangely irrelevant. I walked around the stuff, taking its measure. It was a perfect cube—four high, four deep, four across: sixty-four cartons of Grayson lore.

I stripped back the plastic cover and leaned down for a closer look. I could read the words she had written on the cardboard with a heavy black marker. *Richard/Letters, Poems, Miscellany*

Sketches for Christmas Carol/Correspondence with Benton
Tape Recordings/Darryl Grayson and Selena Harper
Worksheets/Logs of Days
Correspondence/1950-55
Ideas for Phase Two

I took down the box marked *Richard's Letters* and broke open the seal. It was packed tight with original notes, all of it handwritten on legal pads. Selena Harper had probably done his typing and kept the originals, maybe without the author's permission or knowledge. I put the box off to one side and opened the one marked *Correspondence.* It was full of carbon copies, letters Grayson had written and typed himself during the formative years of the Grayson Press. Here was the man's life and philosophy . . . you could plunge in almost anywhere and be caught up in whatever had engaged his mind at the time. He wrote impressions of history to old friends in Georgia; he had long discussions on art with a teacher he'd had in high school and wrote rambling letters on almost any topic to people he'd never met. He was a faithful and generous writer. If you wrote to him praising one of his books, he would answer you, even if he'd never heard of you till that moment. He had a Southerner's sense of chivalry and honor: women would get more consideration than men, warm, chatty greetings to ladies who loved his work. He had a lengthy correspondence of more than five years with a woman in Knoxville: it was a romance of the mind, as they had apparently never met. I picked up a handful of pages, several hundred, and came upon a correspondence with Bruce Rogers that ran through much of 1953. It was hard-core typography, incredible stuff. Grayson had saved all of Rogers's originals along with copies of his own replies. At one time they had sent drawings through the mail, the old master illustrating his points to the prodigy in that language that only they and others like them could read. This will be published someday, I thought—some university press will bring it out in two volumes, *The Letters of Darryl Grayson*, with scholarly footnotes and an index, and some expert—maybe Huggins—would write a long introduction setting Grayson in his proper significance. Grayson was an average speller, and the editor would probably apologize for that and leave it alone. In the final analysis, writing and spelling don't have much to do with each other.

Behind this box was another, *Correspondence/ 1956-58,* and behind that was another covering the next year. Grayson liked to write. He seemed to have written at least one letter a day, sometimes more. I thumbed through the year 1957 and saw many letters headed *Dear Laura.* It was his old friend Laura Warner, who had not, it seemed, been lost in the blitz after all. She had moved to New Orleans after the war and was following his career from afar. In one letter she teasingly called him *My Pyotr,* to which he angrily replied that, Goddammit, he was not Tchaikovsky and she was not his goddamn patron saint, and she laughed in her next letter and called him *my darling boy* and said one of the characteristics of genius was temper. Huggins would die to get into this, I thought. So would Trish. How different their books would've been.

The box labeled *Tape Recordings* was just what it said—a dozen reels of fragile-looking recording tape, sandwiched between sheaths of notes. *Selena Harper and Darryl Grayson: October 4, 5, 6, 1958.* The master's voice, if it could be retrieved, was apparently preserved right here. The oldest recordings seemed to be from mid-1953, brown on white, oxide on a paper backing, and the oxide was beginning to flake. I kept digging. It didn't take long to figure out what *Ideas for Phase Two* was. The material dated from 1968 and 1969—notes, letters, and lists of possible projects, along with rough sketches of new alphabets. There was a list of artists whose work Grayson had admired, who might have been invited to collaborate on future projects. I remembered something Huggins had said, that Grayson had seen his career enclosed by those two *Ravens,* like definitive parenthetical statements, but Huggins had only been half-right. Grayson in no way considered his career finished. He was still a young man with much great work to do: a successful *Raven* would simply write an end to his youth and launch him into his major phase.

I found a box of letter sketches, hundreds of free-hand drawings on thin paper. He couldn't be sitting still, I thought—if he had dead time on his hands, he'd draw letters. Some were signed, some were not. All were originals.

There was too much. I began to skim.

I tore down the block and scattered the center cartons around the room. In the exact middle was the box with the photographs. There were pictures of Grayson's childhood home, of the high school, of the parents, . . . but again, nothing of the brothers themselves. There were copies of the newspaper that Grayson had worked on in school and pictures of old girlfriends. In a separate folder was the North Bend stuff—Grayson's shop under construction, his house, the finished shop, the ancient-looking Columbian press with its cast-iron ornamentation—eagle, sea serpent, snakes—alive in the hard light that poured in through the window. Then there was a run of people shots. Rigby and Crystal: she convulsed over some long-forgotten joke, he slightly uncomfortable in coat and tie, politely amused. Moon in his element, hiking in the high country. Moon again, standing at the edge of a mountain cabin with the alpine scenery stretching out behind him. And there she was, the woman who looked like Eleanor Rigby, posed in the woods with a man I had never seen. She had her arm around him and both of them were laughing into the camera, exuding sexuality. In the background was another woman, obviously unhappy. If looks could kill, the woman in the background would kill them both. There were no names, just that faint inscription in Selena's hand, giving the location and date, always May 1969. But there was something about the two women that drew them together and kept them that way in your mind.

Then there was the snapshot, shoved deep in the file between papers and obviously taken by a much less sophisticated camera. The Eleanor-woman, fat with child, standing on the mountain at Moon's cabin: Grayson's handwriting on the back (I could recognize it now at a glance) giving a date, Sept. 28, 1968, and a short caption, *Queen of the world*. She had that same seductive smile, a wanton, sexual animal even in the last days of pregnancy. She pointed at the picture-taker with her left hand, at her swollen tummy with the other. I could almost hear her teasing voice in the room: *Oh, you nasty man, you naughty boy, you.*

Eleanor's voice.

I heard Amy bumping up the stairs. "Hey," she called. "You gonna die up here? . . . It's almost two o'clock."

She came through the trap and sat on one of the boxes. "Now maybe you've got some idea what I'm up against." She got up, paced, and sighed. "What am I gonna do with all this stuff?"

I broke it to her softly. "You're gonna get rich with it."

38

She couldn't imagine such a thing. "I'd probably feel pretty rich if somebody wanted to walk in here and give me a hundred dollars for all of it," she said. When I didn't bite, she let it go. Just as well, I thought: there was no use speculating, she'd probably faint if I told her half of what I was thinking. But she looked at me across the room and a sense of it began filling up the space between us. The air seemed brighter: the sun had a different aura as it beamed through the window on the west side and lit up a million floating particles of dust. Amy moved out to the middle of the room and flipped up one of the flaps.

"Mamma never told me anything," she said, fingering the papers in the box. "Not once did she ever say she thought this stuff might even be worth the paper it's printed on."

Maybe she didn't know, I thought. Maybe value to her had nothing to do with money. Maybe she figured she'd talk about it someday and just ran out of time. You can't plan a heart attack.

"I guess I should've figured there was something to it," Amy said. "The way she never wanted me to let on it was here, not even to Archie or the Rigbys. I think she was always afraid somebody would come and take it away from her."

"Yeah, but where'd it come from? How'd she get it?"

"Just like she got everything else. Piece by piece, starting way back when she first went to work at Grayson's. I think that's when they started talking about her doing his book someday. And he read some of the things she'd published, and he liked what she'd written, and he said okay, but it's too early. He hadn't done enough yet. But he gave her this stuff, sometimes just a few pages a day, to read and think about. She'd bring 'em home with her—a few letters, some sketches he'd thrown aside—just stuff, you know. I never paid any attention when she told me about it."

"And over the years it became this."

Amy was reading. Whatever was on top was working its way through her brain as she tried to understand its larger significance. "This looks like a plain old letter. He's talking about fishing . . . what's so special about that?"

"It's something other people will have to decide."

"And these other people will want this stuff?"

"You can count on that. They'll want this stuff."

"And you know who they are?"

"I do now."

She picked up the pages and read it all—the three-page letter that Grayson had written on January 4, 1954, I saw as I crossed the room and looked over her shoulder. I moved on to the window and stood staring down at the muddy yard, letting her read in peace. When I turned again, her eyes were fixed on mine. She gave a little smile, naive and worldly all at once. Do what you want, she seemed to say: I won't fuss, I'll go along.

The only thing in my mind was that it all had to be moved. It had been here twenty years and I couldn't leave it even one more night. "The real question is, how does this help us find Ellie?" Amy said. I didn't

268

know, it was too vast, like standing at the edge of a forest on a hunt for one tree. But it had to be moved and then maybe we could start asking questions like that.

Now a funny thing happened—Amy lit into the work with a kind of driving impatience, as if she could clear the house all at once. She had put it off forever, but moving that first box had a galvanizing effect. "You go on," she said, "I'll keep working on it." We had filled up the car. It would take six loads and a full backseat when we made our last run out of here. It was three o'clock, her children had to be picked up by seven, and I still had no idea where I'd make the stash or how long it would take us to get it all moved.

"Go," she said, insistent now. "Go, dammit, you're wasting time."

I drove through Snoqualmie and out along the road to North Bend. Clouds moved in from the west and the air grew ripe with the promise of rain. It came, hard and furious, washing away the hope of the morning. I didn't know how I felt anymore, I wasn't sure of anything. I had made a colossal discovery, but I was no closer to Eleanor than I'd been yesterday. Overriding everything was the depressing thought that I could be saving one life and losing another. Amy Harper wouldn't ever be going back to Belltown, but where was Eleanor?

I settled for the North Bend Motel, one of those older places with the rooms laid out in a long single-story row. I rented a room at the far end, where it might not be so evident to the guy in the office that I was using it for a storage locker. I paid two days in advance. The room was small—piled four high around the table and bed, the boxes would fill it up. I unloaded fast and started back. The rain had come and gone, but the clouds hung low and you could see there was more on the way. I turned into the Harper place at quarter to four. Amy had moved a dozen boxes and was still running hard. She was slightly giddy, confirming what I'd thought earlier, that the act of moving things had given her some badly needed emotional release. Her shirt was dark with sweat, soaked across the shoulders and under the arms, and her face was streaked with dirt. "Don't forget to check the mail," she called as I was going out with the second load.

But again the mailbox was empty.

At the end of the fifth load I ran into trouble. I stopped at the road and knew something was different.

The mailbox was open. I knew I had closed it.

I got out and crossed the road. The box was empty, but a cigarette had been thrown down and was still smoking on top of the damp grass. A beer bottle had been dropped in the mud. Beside it was the print of a man's shoe, an impression that hadn't yet begun to fill with water.

I felt the fear. Night was coming fast, fingers of fog wafted across the land, and Amy was alone in the house.

I splashed along the road with my lights off. I could see a flickering light in the trees ahead. It took on bulk and form and became a car, idling in the clearing.

I stopped and reached under the seat where my gun was. I clipped it to the front of my belt near the buckle. I got out of the car and walked up through the trees.

Headlights cut through the mist at the edge of the porch. Two men sat there in the dark.

I started across the clearing. A voice came at me from somewhere.

"Hey! . . . Where you going?"

I looked at them across the gap. "Going to see Ms. Harper."

"Ms. Harper's dead."

"Ms. Amy Harper wasn't dead, when I left her here half an hour ago."

"That's *Mrs.* Amy *Willis* to you, dum-dum. You can't see her now. She's busy."

"She's having a re-yoon-yun with her old man," the other one said, and they both laughed.

I started toward the house. They got out of the car. They were punks, I had seen their kind many times, I had sweated them in precinct rooms when I was a young cop working burglary. When they were fifty, they'd still be seventeen.

The one riding shotgun had the James Dean look, dark, wavy hair over a fuck-you pout. They thought they were badasses and I was an old fart. That made two surprises they had coming.

"This asshole don't hear so good," the James Dean act said.

His partner said, "What'll it be, Gomer? . . . You wanna walk out of here or be carried out strapped over the hood of this car."

"I'll take the hood, stupid, if you two think you can put me there."

I veered and came down on them fast. I caught little Jimmy a wicked shot to the sternum that whipped him around and juked him across the yard like Bojangles of Harlem, sucking air till he dropped kicking in the mud. His partner jumped back out of range. My coat was open and he'd seen the gun, but he'd already seen enough of what went with it. I stepped over Little Jimmy as the ex loomed up on the porch.

"Who the hell're you?" he growled.

"I'm Rush Limbaugh. Who the hell're you?"

"I don't know you."

"I'm taking a poll to see who's listening to the Asshole Radio Network. Maybe you'd better get out of my way."

"Maybe what I'll do is come down there and kick your ass."

"Maybe what you'll do is shit, if you eat enough."

He started to launch himself off the porch. He balked, almost slipped, and stood tottering at the top.

Then he came, with too little too late. His pal yelled, "Look out, Coleman, he's got a gun!" and he balked again, missed his step, and splashed face-first in the mud.

I went around him in a wide circle. "So far you boys are terrifying as hell," I said. He struggled to one knee. I asked if he could sing "April Showers." I hate to waste a line like that, but I know he didn't get it. I walked past him, close enough for him to grab my leg, but he didn't. I knew he wouldn't. By the time I got Amy to open the door, they were gone.

Amy stood at the window and watched them go. It was the last vestige of her childhood, the beginning of a long and wonderful and fearsome journey.

"C'est la vie," she said to the fading day.

I thought about the woman in Irwin Shaw's great story of the eighty-yard run. I told Amy to read it sometime and take heart.

She had never heard of Shaw. I felt a twinge of sadness, not only for the fleeting nature of fame but of life itself. I told her what a powerhouse Shaw had been when he was young, and how the critics had come to hate him and had made him the most underrated writer of his day. She didn't understand why people would do that, so I explained it to her. Shaw made a lot of money and they never forgive you for that. She asked what the story was about and I said, "It's about you and the damn fool you married, when you were too young to know better." I didn't want to diminish it by telling her any more than that.

We gathered ourselves for the trip to town. I'd be leaving fourteen boxes under Selena Harper's roof for one more night.

"I don't think we made much headway," Amy said.

"We didn't find Eleanor. Maybe we found you, though."

She didn't say anything. She gave me the key and I locked the house. She sank back in the car and closed her eyes, a picture of sudden weariness.

I told her what I had in mind as we drove. "I'm going to call a man who knows all there is to know about this stuff. If I'm right, he'll want to fly up from Los Angeles and look at it."

"It's in your hands. I trust your judgment and I won't go back on you, whatever you decide to do."

I pointed out the motel where I'd made the stash. She gave it a polite look and we swung west with the night, into the freeway, into the driving rain.

39

The night was full of surprises. The first came when I called Leith Kenney from Amy's room at the Hilton. She sat behind me, discreetly nursing her child while I punched in the call.

It rang three times in L.A. and a woman answered.

"Mr. Kenney, please."

"I'm sorry, he's not here."

"Do you know when he'll be back?"

"I really can't say." There was an awkward pause. "He's gone in to a meeting tonight and it'll probably run late. Then he's going out of town."

I blinked at the phone but recovered quickly. "I'm calling from Seattle."

"That's where he's going. Is this Mr. Pruitt?"

I felt my heart trip. I looked at Amy in the mirror, but she was busy changing breasts and didn't notice anything.

"Yes," I said, thinking on my feet. "Yes, it is."

"Has there been a change of plan? This is Mrs. Kenney. Lee will be calling me when he gets there. I could give him a message."

"I don't know . . . I might have to change things."

There was a brief silence. It would really help, I thought, if I had the slightest idea what the hell I was talking about.

"Well," she said, "would you like to leave a message with me?"

"I'll catch him here. Is he staying at the same hotel?"

"Yes, the Four Seasons. They should get in early tomorrow morning."

"Is Scofield coming with him?"

"I don't think you could keep him away, Mr. Pruitt."

"I'll see them then. Thanks."

I hung up and stared at the floor. Pruitt stared back at me.

Amy was looking at me in the glass.

"Something wrong?"

"No," I said. "Everything's fine."

She went across the room and put her children down. I headed for the door and got the second surprise of the night.

"I remembered something today," she said. "I thought of the man who came and looked in the attic just after Mamma died. His name popped right into my head. I knew I'd forget it again, so I wrote it down."

She fished in her jeans and came up with a paper. "His name was Otto."

Again I walked through that cluttered bookstore. I held a bag of Ayn Rand and wondered why the man wasn't there. I looked up a dark stairwell leading to . . . what?

"Otto Murdock."

She looked at me hard. "How'd you know that?"

40

I headed north on the freeway and hoped I'd remember where Murdock's was. I found it after twenty minutes of trial and error. I arrived on a wave of déjà vu. It looked exactly as I'd last seen it—the same dim light shone from deep in the building, the same OPEN sign was propped in the window and tilted at the same slight angle—even the rain was the same, as if the world had turned back on its axis and erased the last seventy-two hours. I pushed open the door and called his name. There was no sound. If any customers had come in since last Friday night, they had left no evidence of their presence. They had come, looked, and left as we had, perhaps with a slight sense of unease. Those who knew Murdock would figure it as another bout with demon rum: the others would mind their own business.

I crossed the store and looked in the back room. Everything was the same . . . the dim light in the corner . . . the rolltop desk with its piles of magazines and papers . . . the canvas briefcase pushed off to one side with my note still taped to the handle . . . the rickety stacks of books and the thick carpet of dust, undisturbed where we hadn't walked and already filming over where we had. I followed our three-day trail across the room and into the stairwell. I looked up into the black hole and called him, but I knew he wasn't going to be inviting me up. My voice felt heavy, like a man shouting into a pillow.

I touched the bottom of the stair with my foot. I leaned into it, took a deep breath, got a firm hold on my gun, and started up. The light faded quickly: there was none at all after the fifth step and I had to go by feel, knowing only that the next step would be onward and upward. I had a sense of movement coming from somewhere . . . *music!* . . . and now the feeling that it had all happened before was as sharp as a scream. I planted each foot, letting my fingers slip along the inner edge of the wooden banister and guide me up. *Don't screw up again,* I was thinking: *don't make the same mistake twice.*

Now I could hear the melody, some classical piece on a radio. I saw a thin line of light . . . the crack at the bottom of a door. It dropped below eye level as I climbed higher, and a kind of sour dampness lay over the top. And I knew that smell, better than the people of Seattle knew the rain. In my old world it came with the smell of Vicks, the stuff homicide cops use to help them get through the bad ones.

I was standing at the top with an old memory playing in color and sound. My partner was a skinny guy named Willie Mott, who was giving me the lowdown on Vicks VapoRub. *This one's ripe . . . put a little glop of Vicks up each nostril and you won't notice it so much.*

I stood at the door of hell and nobody had brought the Vicks.

I touched the wood with my knuckles. Found the knob. Gripped it carefully by the edge, with the joints of my fingers and thumb.

The latch clicked: the door creaked open and the warm moist air sucked me in.

I retched.

I backtracked and stumbled and almost fell down the stairs.

On the third try, I made it into the room. I cupped my hand over my nose and got past the threshold to the edge of a ratty old sofa.

A single lamp near the window was the only source of light . . . a forty-watter, I figured by the dim interior. Dark curtains covered the window. I couldn't see the body yet, but the room was full of flies. The music poured out of an old radio. It wasn't "Rigby," just something he'd been listening to when he finally ran out of time. I moved toward it, still fighting my gut. I hadn't seen much of anything yet.

There was the one window.

A closed door across the room.

A pile of books on the table.

A typewriter . . . a pile of magazines . . . a roll of clear sealing tape . . . and a bottle of lighter fluid.

I moved around the table, watching where I walked. A wave of rotten air wafted up in a cloud of flies.

I tasted the bile. What I didn't need now, after compromising the first scene, was to throw up all over this one.

The lighter fluid might help. I know it's an evil solvent; I've heard it can get in your blood through the skin and raise hell with your liver. But it's stronger by far than Vicks, and even the smell of a cancer-causing poison was like honeysuckle after what I'd been smelling.

I put my handkerchief on the table, then turned the plastic bottle on its side and pried open the squirt nozzle. Liquid flowed into the rag. I touched only the ribbed blue cap, so I wouldn't mess up any prints on the bottle itself.

I made the wet rag into a bandanna. Found a roll of cord and cut off a piece, then tied it over my mouth and nose.

I was breathing pure naphtha. It was cold and bracing and it had an immediate calming effect on my stomach.

If it didn't kill me, I could function like a cop again.

I found him sprawled on the far side of the table. He had been there most of a week from the looks of him. His face was gone, but I could guess from the wispy white hair that he had probably been Otto Murdock.

I didn't know what had killed him: there wasn't enough left to decide. What there was was hidden under a carpet of flies.

Let the coroner figure it. Whatever they pay him, it's not enough, but let him earn it . . . and in the end tell supercop what I already knew.

Murdock hadn't keeled over and died of old age.

And Janeway hadn't done it. This would break his super heart, but when the reaper came calling, Janeway was still in Denver, doing what came naturally. Trying to fit John Gardner into his proper shade of orange, with murder the last thing on his mind.

I didn't see any weapon. Nothing on the table looked promising as a motive or a clue.

There were no ashes.

No sign of a struggle. Even the chair he had been sitting in was upright, pushed back slightly as if he'd been getting up to greet a visitor.

I went to the far door and opened it.

His bathroom. Nothing out of place there.

I was feeling lightheaded by then: the naphtha was doing its dirty work. The skin under my eyes felt like blisters on the rise.

I ripped off the rag and got out of there.

Downstairs, I looked through his rolltop.

Some of the notes in the pigeonholes were three years old.

I looked through the drawers.

Bottle of cheap bourbon, with not much in the bottom.

Letters . . . bills . . .

The sad debris of a life that didn't matter much to anybody, not even, finally, to the man who had lived it.

Pushed off to one side was the canvas bag. Eleanor had wanted to look inside, but I wouldn't let her.

I opened it now and hit the jackpot.

A thick notebook, old and edgeworn . . .

I seemed to be holding Darryl Grayson's original subscriber list. With it was a manuscript, a dozen pages of rough draft on yellow legal paper. I knew the handwriting, I had seen it on other papers in Amy's attic. The top sheet was a title page, aping Victoriana.

THE CRAVEN
*A Tragic Tale of a God's Downfall
Told in Verse by Richard Grayson,
A Witness*

I took it all and went back to Aandahl's and read it.
I read it many times. I was reading it again at
midnight when Trish came home.

41

She had returned almost a full day early. There was
a click and the dogs swarmed her at the front
door.

She looked at me across the room, as if she hadn't
expected me to be there and didn't know whether to
be disappointed or relieved. "You've changed," she
said, and I gave her an old man's grin. She threw her
raincoat over a wicker basket, came slowly around the
couch, and sat facing me with an almost schoolmarm-
ish primness.

"I've been thinking about it," she said. "Been
running it through my head all the way home from
Albuquerque, trying to figure out what I ought to do."

"What's the verdict?"

"I'm in it now."

"I thought you always were."

"It's different now. I'm in it with you."

This was happy news. I felt a warm glow at the
sound of it.

She said, "Whatever happens, we go together."

We didn't need to hash out the ground rules. When you connect with someone, things like that are understood. Suddenly we were like police partners, comparing notes, poring over evidence. There was a lot to be done, and the first commandment was the test of fire. You never hold out on your partner.

We ate a late supper and talked into the morning. For the first time in a long time I broke bread with a good-looking woman without thinking of Rita.

42

She had covered a lot of ground in two days. She had flown out of Sea-Tac at nine-forty Pacific time on Saturday night. Her destination was St. Louis, where she arrived in light snow at two-twelve in the morning. She had a room reserved, but her old companion, insomnia, was along for the ride. She filled the dead time reading. At nine A.M. she was in the homicide room downtown, looking at photographs and evidence from an old murder case. Stuff that was once under tight wraps was shared with her, off the record, by the man on duty Sunday morning. It had been a long time, years, since anything exciting had been added to the file, and they didn't have much hope of cracking it now. She had flown two thousand miles and that impressed them. She had observed the proper protocol, speaking first by telephone with the chief, and they let her see the file.

The victim was Joseph Hockman, fifty-two, a bachelor. She looked at the pictures, including the closeups. It didn't bother her: she had been a reporter for a long time and had seen it all many times.

The victim lay in a pool of blood in a library room. Pictures had been taken from every angle, so she could see the shelving and the arrangement of books on all four walls. The black and whites were vivid and sharp, clear enough that the titles could be read and the jacket formats identified. Her eyes traveled along one row and she saw some famous old books.

All the King's Men.

Elmer Gantry.

Miss Lonelyhearts.

Manhattan Transfer . . .

She began to make notes. Mr. Joseph Hockman collected so-called serious fiction—no mysteries, no fantasy, nothing that smacked of genre. He liked his literature straight, no sugar, no cream. He did have a weak spot for fine limiteds: a shot over the body toward the window wall showed a good-sized section of books in slipcases. She asked for a magnifying glass, and the detective, fascinated, got her one from a desk drawer.

Grapes of Wrath in two volumes.

Anthony Adverse in three . . .

"Looks like Limited Editions Club," she said.

The detective said, "Oh," the way people do when they have no idea what you're talking about.

Near the end of the shelf was a gap where some books had been taken out but not returned.

"Looks like there's fifteen or twenty books missing here," she said.

The detective, who had been reading the reports from the original investigating officers, said, "There was some discussion at the time about the possibility of theft being the motive. They thought that was pretty weak, though. Who'd kill a man that way just to steal a bunch of books?"

"Any indication in the file whether the books ever turned up?"

"Not that I can see."

"Or what they were?"

"Nope. One of the officers pursued that thought as far as he could take it, but the guy didn't keep records like that. He kept it all up here." He tapped his head.

"Somebody took those books and the officer knew that—that's why he pursued it," she said. "Look in this shot, you can see a book on the floor, right under that empty place in the bookshelf. When he pulled the books out, this one came out with it. But he didn't bother to pick it up."

"What does that tell you?"

"It tells me he didn't want that book, just the ones that filled about this much shelf space." She held up her hands about two feet apart. "He didn't care about any of the others."

She went book by book with the glass. Some of the titles were unreadable, but there wasn't a Grayson book that could be identified as such anywhere in the room.

"That's funny," she said. "I heard this guy had all the Grayson books."

The detective said, "Oh," again, as if he hadn't quite made up his mind whether he cared enough to ask her who Grayson was. "They tossed the book angle back and forth but it didn't excite them much. The feeling was, yeah, the perp might've taken a few books, but that wasn't the prime motive."

"But they never found a motive."

"Early in the investigation, the feeling was it might've been personal."

"Did Mr. Hockman have any enemies?"

"Looks like he'd had some words with people. He was becoming a crusty old bastard. But, no, they never got anything they could pin on anybody."

"Did their thinking change later?"

"Like it always does with crimes like this that you can't solve. Some nutcase." He flipped a page and went on reading. "Here's something about a book."

She looked up.

"They interviewd a woman named Carolyn Bondy, who did secretarial work for Hockman. Once a week she'd come over and take dictation, do his correspondence. The week of the murder he sent a letter to a book publisher. He'd gotten a book with a mistake in it and it seemed to ruin his week."

"Really?"

"Does that interest you?"

"Yeah, you bet."

"Too bad they didn't take it much further than that."

"They didn't ask her what the book was or who published it?"

"It just seemed to come up in the course of things."

"Or what the mistake might've been?"

"Just that he was annoyed. He'd been looking forward to this book . . . something special, I guess. Nobody thought it was much of a motive for murder. The woman did say Hockman was a good deal more annoyed than he let on in his letter. The letter he wrote was pretty soft and that surprised her. It was almost like Hockman was apologizing for telling the guy he'd screwed up."

"Anything else?"

"Just this. The reason Hockman was annoyed was because it was the same mistake the guy had made before."

"Is that what she said? . . . The same mistake . . ."

"That's what's in here."

284

"Is there an address or phone number for this woman—what's her name?"

"Carolyn Bondy." The detective read off an address and phone number. "Doubt if she still lives there. It's been twenty years."

She looked through more evidence. She picked up a clear plastic bag that was full of ashes.

"I'll have to ask you not to open that," the detective said. "I mean, we do want to cooperate, but, uh . . ."

"Hey, I appreciate anything you can do. May I just move it around a little?"

"I don't guess that'll hurt anything."

She took the bag with both hands and made a rotating motion like a miner panning gold. Slowly a fragment of white paper rose through the charred silt on the top.

She peered through the filmy plastic and saw two letters.

"Look at this . . . looks like a capital *F* . . . and a small *r* . . . part of the same word."

The detective leaned over her shoulder.

She looked up in his face. "Are you in the mood to do me a huge favor?"

"I won't kill ya for asking."

"Is that a Xerox machine over there? . . ."

She called Wilbur Simon, an assistant managing editor at the *St. Louis Post-Dispatch*. As a young reporter from Miami, she had won a National Endowment for the Humanities fellowship, a year of study and meditation at the University of Michigan at Ann Arbor. Simon had been one of her teachers. They had had good rapport and he had pursued her for his own paper ever since.

She sat in the empty newsroom on Sunday afternoon, reading the clip file on the Hockman case. She and Simon had coffee in a diner not far away and talked about old times, the rain in Seattle, and the Hockman case. Simon had vivid recollections of Hockman. He had been the paper's news editor then and had done the layout on the first-day story and on most of the follow pieces. It stuck in his mind as the beginning of the crazy age. He had said as much in a diary he had kept then and had dug out and reviewed just after she had called him this morning. He had written about life and work and his personal evolving philosophy. The thing about Hockman was, you never thought much about random killers before then and you were always aware of them since. Suddenly you couldn't pick up hitchhikers without taking your life in your hands. The day of the serial killer had come.

"I don't think this was a serial killer, Wilbur," she said.

At least not the kind of serial killer people meant when they used the term, she thought.

They parted with a hug and Simon offered her a job. She smiled and said she was flattered, but it would take more than rain to get her to give up Seattle for St. Louis.

She looked up Carolyn Bondy in the telephone book. There was a George Bondy at that address. The man who answered said Carolyn Bondy, his mother, had died just last month.

She ate dinner alone in the city and caught a ten-o'clock flight to Albuquerque.

She slept on the plane, just enough to keep her awake the rest of the night. A rental car got her into Taos at three o'clock in the morning, mountain time, thankful that she had reserved a room and secured it with a credit card. She had made photocopies of the *Post-Dispatch* clips, but it was that single sheet from homicide with the shadowy image of the two connected letters shot through plastic that she looked at now as she faced the new day. She had done her homework: she knew that Charlie and Jonelle Jeffords lived in the hills fifteen miles from town. She had studied the maps and knew where to drive with only occasional stops to refresh her memory. She bumped off the highway and clattered along a washboard road, leaving a plume of dust in her wake. The road twisted up a ridge and skirted a valley. She saw patches of snow in the high country as the road U-turned and dipped back into the hills. There were washouts along the way, but each had been repaired and the drive was easy. She reached the gate at nine o'clock. A sign nailed to a post said KEEP OUT, and she thought that hospitality at Rancho Jeffords was like the weather, chilly with a chance of sudden clouds. She slipped the rope loop off the gate and drove in. The house was a hundred yards away, shaded by trees and hidden from the road by hilly terrain. It was a splitlevel mountain home with a deck that faced west. There was no sign of life. She pulled into the yard and decided to go ahead with caution, remembering the inclination of the cheerful Mr. Jeffords to greet trespassers with the business end of a gun.

She walked out in the yard and stood in the sun.

Called out to whoever might hear.

"Hello! . . . Is anybody here?"

The hills soaked up her voice.

She tried again but got nothing for it.

She went up the walk and knocked on the door. There wasn't a sound inside.

It had been a gamble coming here without an appointment, but she knew that when she booked the flight. She walked along a flagstone path to the edge of the house. The path led around to a garage, whose side door beckoned her on.

She knocked on the door. "Anybody in there?"

No one.

She touched the door and it swung open.

A workroom, long ago surrendered as the place for cars.

There was clutter, but also a staleness in the air. It was a shop set up for a working man but unused for some time now. The walls gave off a feeling of dry rot and musk.

She saw some equipment she recognized and it drew her into the room. A heavy iron bookpress had been set up on the edge of the bench. A much older bookpress, made of wood, stood on a table behind it.

The tools of a bookbinder.

As she came deeper into the room, her impression of disuse deepened. The place was deep in dust and heavily cobwebbed. The chair at the bench was ringed with spiderwebs.

She was nervous now but she came all the way in, wanting to see it all with a quick look. Again she observed the bookbinder's tools: the rawhide hammer lying on the floor where he'd dropped it long ago, covered with dust; a steel hammer at the edge of the bench, a few feet from the bookpress; balls of wax thread; needles; paper. There was lots of paper, fine marbled stock for endsheets, standard stock for the pages, colored papers and white sheets and some with a light creamy peach tone. Against the wall was a paper rack. And there were leathers, very fine under the dust, and edging tools that looked like cookie cutters and were used, she knew, for laying in the gilt on a gold-trimmed leather book. There was a hot plate to heat the edging tool on, and behind the hot plate was a row of nasty-looking gluepots. She opened one and smelled PVA, the bookbinder's glue. A newspaper, open on the table, was a year old.

She went outside and closed the door. The wind whistled down from the hills. She walked back to her car, opened the door, and sat with her feet dangling out, hoping they'd come home soon.

An hour passed and the sun grew hot. The arroyo baked under the glare of it and the chill melted away. Slowly she became aware of a creepy sensation, like the feeling you get driving on the freeway when the man in the next car stares at you as he comes past.

She looked at the house and saw curtains flutter upstairs. This might be nothing more than the temperature control blowing air up the window, but her sense of apprehension grew as she looked at it.

She wanted to leave but she couldn't. She had come a long way, and though the chance of failure had always been strong, she had never failed at anything by default.

The curtain moved again. No heating flue did that, she thought.

She got out and walked across the yard. She went up the path to the door and gave it another loud knock.

There was a bump somewhere. Her unease was now acute.

She circled the house. Out back was a smaller deck with steps leading up to a door. She went up and knocked. Through a filmy curtain she saw movement, as if someone had crossed from one room to another.

"Hey, people," she called. "I've come a long way to talk to you. Why don't we hear each other out?"

Nothing.

Not a sound now, but the presence behind the door was as tangible as the purse slung over her shoulder. She had a vision of something sexless and faceless, holding its breath waiting for her to leave.

"It's about the Rigby girl and the burglary you had here."

She could feel her voice soaking through the old wood around the window sash. There wasn't a chance of them not hearing her.

"It's about Darryl and Richard Grayson, and the book Grayson was working on when he died."

Even the house seemed to sigh. But the moment passed and nothing happened, and in a while she wondered if the sound had been in her mind.

"It's about the Graysons and their friends . . . you and the Rigbys." She took a breath and added, "And Nola Jean Ryder."

As if she'd said a magic word, the door clicked and swung inward. Someone . . . a man, she thought . . . looked through a narrow crack.

"Mr. Jeffords? . . . Is that you? . . . I can't see you very well."

"Who are you?"

It was the same voice she had heard on the telephone recording—the same only different. The recording had rippled with macho arrogance: this man sounded tired and old and shaky.

"What do you want here?"

"I came down from Seattle to talk to you. I'm a reporter for the *Seattle Times.*"

She told him her name, but he seemed not to hear. Technically, ethically, it didn't matter. The rules only demanded that she give him fair warning. He was talking to a reporter and they were now on the record. She could use him if he said anything worth using.

But she had never played the game that way. "I'm a reporter, Mr. Jeffords." It still meant nothing to him. He heard but did not hear. He listened but his mind heard only words and blipped out meanings. She had done too many interviews with people like him, private souls who suddenly found themselves newsworthy without understanding how or why it had happened. They were always appalled when they opened their newspapers the next morning and learned what they had said.

"Trish Aandahl, *Seattle Times*," she said, loud and clear.

She still couldn't see him. He stood just beyond the doorway, a shadow filling up the crack, his face reduced to an eye, a cheek, part of a nose.

"D'you think it would be possible for me to come in and talk to you for just a minute? I promise I won't take up much of your time."

He didn't seem to hear that either. He leaned closer to the door and in a voice barely louder than a whisper said, "Did you say something about Nola Jean?"

This was the key to him, the only reason he had opened his door to her. Blow this and you lose him, she thought.

"We can talk about Nola," she said as if she'd known the woman all her life.

He opened the door wide and let her in.

She had to squeeze past him in the narrow hall. In that second they shared the same space, close enough to bristle the hair on her neck. She brushed against his arm and felt the soft flannel of his long-sleeve shirt. She smelled the sun-baked male smell of him. She smelled tobacco, the kind her father used to smoke, that Edgeworth stuff with the hint of licorice.

She moved quickly past him, through the dim hall to the big room at the end. The door clicked shut behind her and she heard the lock snap in. His footsteps came along behind her, and for a strange moment she fought the urge to run on through and out the front door.

His house was orderly. The hardwood floor gleamed under a coat of varnish, and there were rugs with what looked to her like Navajo designs in the places where people walked the most. It was not a new house. The floor creaked under her weight and she could see faint ceiling stains where the roof had leaked. The room was steeped in ancient smoke. It had soaked into the drapes and walls and furniture, and in here it had no hint of flavor. They were both chain-smokers, she thought, remembering her parents and what her childhood had smelled like. They smoked what they liked when they had it, but if times were tough, they'd sweep the dust off the floor and roll a tobacco paper around that.

He had a homemade going in the ashtray and a coffee cup that still had almost a full head of steam. His living room was narrow and long. It opened out to the front deck and a secondary hall led away to the right, probably to a bedroom. She turned and looked at him. He was a rugged guy in his sixties. His hair was slate gray, his skin the leathery brown of a cowboy or a farmer. His demeanor was flat, the last thing she expected after hearing his forceful voice on the telephone recording. He had a curious habit of avoiding eye contact: he almost looked at you but not quite. He seemed to gaze past her left shoulder as she told him her name for the fourth time. He sat without offering her a chair and made no move to offer coffee as he leaned forward and sipped his own.

She grappled toward an opening. "I've heard a lot about Nola."

What a bad start, she thought, but it seemed to make no real difference to him. His eyes lit up at the mention of the name; then his mind lost its focus and he looked around the room. He flitted his eyes across her face, stopping on a spot somewhere behind her head. But he didn't say anything and she came toward him slowly and sat on a hard wooden chair facing him. His eyes followed her down, but he kept looking slightly behind her, always picking up something just behind her left ear. *There's nothing back there,* she wanted to say, but she didn't.

Then he spoke. "Who . . . did you say you are?"

"Trish Aandahl . . . I write for the *Seattle Times.*"

"Why did you come here? Did you bring Nola back with you?"

There's something wrong with this guy, she thought. He acted like the prototype for all the dumb jokes you heard kicking around. *One shovel short of a full load.* She didn't know how to talk to him, but she made the long reach and said, "I'm going to try to find her, Mr. Jeffords."

"Good." He gave what passed for a smile. "Real good."

He blinked at whatever held his attention behind her head and said, "I want to see her real bad."

"I want to see her too."

"She was here."

"Was she?"

"Yeah. Nola Jean."

"When was she here?"

"Soon."

This guy's from the twilight zone, she thought. She leaned back in her chair and smiled. "When will Mrs. Jeffords be home?"

"She's gone to the store."

"When will she be back?"

"Grocery shopping."

She would have to wait until Mrs. Jeffords returned and, hopefully, gave her something coherent. The thought of entertaining Jeffords until then was less than thrilling, but she had done heavier duty for smaller rewards than this story promised.

Then she looked in his face and knew what his problem was. She had seen it before, and the only mystery was why it had taken her so long to figure it out.

The recording on the telephone was an old one—a year, maybe two years or more.

Charlie Jeffords had Alzheimer's.

Her next thought chilled her even as she thought it.

She was thinking of the gunplay the night of the break-in, and what Eleanor had said. *I never fired a gun in my life . . .*

She thought of Mrs. Jeffords and the temperature in the room dropped another ten degrees. Goose bumps rose on her arms and she hugged herself and leaned forward in the chair.

"I don't think I'll be able to wait for your wife."

"Aren't you gonna bring Nola Jean back?"

"I'd like to. Would you like to help me?"

He didn't say anything. She took a big chance and reached for his hand.

He looked into her eyes, his lips trembling.

"Nola," he said.

She squeezed his hand and he burst into tears.

He sobbed out of control for a minute. She tried to comfort him, as much as a stranger could. She held his hand and gently patted his shoulder and desperately wanted to be somewhere else. This was the curse of Alzheimer's: even as it eats away your brain, you have times of terrible clarity. Charlie Jeffords knew exactly what was happening to him.

"Mr. Jeffords," she said.

He sniffed and sat up and released her hand.

"The night the trouble happened. Can you tell me about that?"

He didn't say anything. She pushed ahead. "That girl who broke in. Do you remember what she wanted?"

"Her book."

"What book?"

"Came for her book back."

"What book?"

"She wanted her book back."

"What was the book?"

"I been holding it for her."

"Whose book was it?"

"Nola's."

"Wasn't it Grayson's book? Wasn't that Darryl Grayson's book, Mr. Jeffords?"

"It's Nola's book. Gave it to me to hold."

She leaned forward. He tried to look away but she wouldn't let him.

"I'm tired," he said.

Damn, she thought: don't know what's real anymore.

She tried again. "Mr. Jeffords . . ."

But that was as far as she got. Through the front curtain she saw a pickup truck pull into the yard.

Mrs. Jeffords was home.

She left Charlie Jeffords there on the couch. She hurried down the hall and let herself out the back way.

There'd be time enough later to think back on it. She'd have a lifetime to wonder if she'd acted like a frightened fool.

Now all she wanted was to put some distance between herself and the woman in the truck.

She stood on the back porch, flat against the wall, listening for some hint of how and when to make her break.

She heard the woman yell.

"Charlie!"

Then, when he didn't answer, a shriek.

Charlie!

She heard the thumping sounds of someone racing up the front steps. At the same time she soft-toed down the back and doubled around the house.

She stopped at the corner and looked out into the

yard. For reasons she only half understood, she was now thoroughly spooked.

There was no time to dwell on it. The truck sat empty beside her rental car: the woman had jumped out without closing the door or killing the engine.

Go, she thought.

Run, don't walk.

She sprinted across the yard, jumped in her car, and drove away fast.

43

She looked at me across the table and said, "It seems silly now, and yes, before you ask, I do feel like a fool. I've never done anything remotely like that. To break and run just isn't my nature. I can't explain it."

"You don't have to. I've done a few things that I can't explain either."

"Charlie Jeffords never shot at anybody, and I don't think the Rigby girl did either. Where does that leave us? All I can tell you is, the thought of being there when that woman came home was . . . I don't know. The only thing I can liken it to is having to walk past a graveyard at night when I was a kid."

"It's like me walking through the blood at Pruitt's house, and every dumb thing I've done since then. Sometimes you do things."

"I don't know, I had this feeling of absolute dread.

My blood dropped to zero in half the time it takes to tell about it, and I was just . . . gone, you know?"

"So what did you think about it later, when you had time to think about it?"

"I kept thinking that one of the people who's missing in this story is a woman, this Nola Jean Ryder. She's always been the missing link."

"You didn't have much about her in your book."

"I didn't know much about her. She was just a girl Richard met and brought home. I couldn't find out where she came from and nobody knows where she went. It's like she dropped off the earth when the Graysons died."

"How much work did you actually do on her, trying to track her down?"

"Quite a bit. Probably not enough. By then it was obvious even to me that I wasn't going to get it in the book. I was still making more changes on the galleys than the publisher wanted to live with, and we were up against a horrendous deadline. The book was already scheduled and promoted as a March title and publishers want everything done yesterday."

She shrugged and poured herself more coffee. "I had to let her go. Then, after the book came out, I tried to keep up with it, but I had a living to make. I wasn't exactly Robert Ludlum, flush with royalties. It made me some money, but not enough to stop being a working gal."

I reached for the coffeepot. "So what do you think about it now? Are you thinking this missing woman is hiding out down there in Taos?"

"When I saw the truck pull up, I didn't think at all, I just wanted to get out of there. Halfway back to town I realized that, yeah, I had been thinking of them as one. In my head, Ryder had become Jeffords."

"Which is at least possible, I guess."

297

We looked at each other.

I said, "If you had to make book on it now, what do you think happened twenty years ago?"

"I think Nola Jean Ryder set fire to that shop and killed the Graysons. I've always thought that."

"Okay," I said in a semidoubting voice. "Make me believe it."

"I probably can't, unless you're willing to give me some veteran's points for intuition."

"I'll play with you up to a point. But you've got to have something concrete, you can't just pull this intuition act out of thin air."

"I've got three things and that's all, you can take it or leave it. First, I talked to the fire investigator who worked the Grayson fire. This man is extremely competent, and he's convinced it was arson. He's got my slant on life, if you know what I mean . . . we talk the same language, he gets the same vibes I do. You don't meet many people like that, and when you do, you listen to what they say. And he knows that fire was set, it just killed him not to be able to prove it. In a thirty-year career you get maybe half a dozen like that, so strong yet elusive. It sticks in your craw and you remember every bloody detail till the day you die. That's my first point.

"Here's the second. Nola Jean Ryder was very much in evidence at the Grayson place all through the last year of their lives and was never seen again afterward. She was there the day of the fire. Archie Moon saw her arguing with Grayson. Her relationship with Grayson was volatile, very stormy: he couldn't seem to live with or without her, and toward the end it got so bad it affected his work. One man I talked to saw Ryder in the North Bend pub that afternoon, drinking with some guys. She went off with one of them and was gone a couple of hours. Then she was seen walking back to Grayson's in the early evening, in a light rain. That's the last time anybody ever saw or to my knowledge heard of Nola Jean Ryder. A few hours later the Graysons died and she dropped off the edge of the earth.

"Last point. Nobody who knew her doubts that she was capable of doing it. She had a temper that went off like a firecracker and burned at a full rage for hours. Even today it makes people uneasy to talk about her. Archie Moon told me some stuff, then he clammed up and called it ancient history and said he didn't want to talk anymore. Rigby wouldn't talk at all. Crystal at least was willing to give her the benefit of the doubt, for a while anyway. Nobody could understand the hold she had on Grayson: it was as if, after a lifetime filled with women, he had met the one who brought him to his knees."

"This is Darryl Grayson we're talking about now."

"Absolutely. Richard's the one who first met her, but it was Darryl Grayson who wound up with her. I guess things like that can't be explained, how a woman can get under the skin of even a strong man and make him do just about anything."

"And vice versa."

"Yes. There isn't much that separates us when you get down to what counts."

I sat thinking about what she'd told me, then it was my turn to talk. I told her about Amy Harper and she listened like a bug-eyed kid, trying to imagine that treasure hidden all those years in the Harper woman's attic. "I never understood why she was so hostile when I tried to interview her. Now I know. She considered Grayson her own personal territory. She was going to write her own book."

Then I told her about Otto Murdock. I watched the sense of wonder drain out of her face, replaced by horror and dread.

"Did you call the police?"

"Sure. I seem to spend a lot of my time doing that."

"Where'd you call them from?"

"Phone booth not far from Murdock's."

"Did you talk to Quintana?"

"He didn't seem to be there. Supercops in this neck of the woods have a different work ethic than I used to have."

"Did you tell the dispatcher this was part of Quintana's case?"

"I had to. I've told you how important that is, for the main guy to know that stuff right out of the gate."

She took a deep breath. "Sounds to me like you did everything but give them your name."

"I did that too. I wanted to make sure it got to him right away. That part of it doesn't matter anymore, he'd know it was me anyway. They've got me on tape twice now and I've never been much of a ventriloquist. They'll also have the paper I left."

"What paper?"

"Last Friday when I went to Murdock's with Eleanor, I took some pricey books out of his store. I left an offer taped to the canvas bag."

She closed her eyes, then opened them wide. "Let's see if I've got this straight. You left him a note and signed your name to it. Then you went back there tonight and the note was still there but he was dead, and you left the note there for the police to find. Is that about it?"

"It's a bookseller's code, Trish—thou shalt not steal thy colleague's books. I owed the man three thousand dollars. Now I owe it to his estate, wherever that goes. Maybe he was one of those nuts who left everything to his pet cat, but that doesn't change my obligation to him. If I walked out with that note, I'd be stealing his books, in the eyes of the law and in my eyes too."

She looked at Grayson's notebook but did not touch it. "What about this?"

"I didn't steal that, Murdock did. When I'm finished with it, it goes back to Amy Harper."

She gave me a long, sad look.

"All right," I said, "what would you have done?"

"I can't even imagine. I'm not making light of it, it's just that I'm starting to worry about your chances of ever getting back to Denver as a free man."

"I'll worry too if you think that'll help. But I'm still going to pay off Murdock's cat, so I can own those books with a clear conscience and not add grand theft to all the other stuff I've got hanging."

She didn't say anything, but I knew what she had to be thinking.

"If this is getting too dicey for you, I can understand that. If you want to change your mind, I'll understand that."

"No," she said too quickly. Then, after a few seconds' thought: "No, I'm fine."

She gestured at Grayson's notebook. "But look what you've done, you've messed up another crime scene. Quintana will have your head on a stick."

"Maybe I'll get lucky and he won't have to find out."

"I hate to break this to you, Janeway, but luck is not the first word that crosses my mind when I think of you."

"Then you'll have to admit that I'm due for a break."

"You're hanging by a thread. You're walking a tightrope with deep trouble on both sides of you. It had to occur to you that this little notebook just might be the motive for that old man's murder."

"Then why didn't the killer take it?"

"How should I know? . . . Maybe he couldn't find it . . . you said yourself the place was a mess."

"He didn't even *look* for it, that's what I'm telling you. The place was a mess, but it was an accumulated mess. There weren't any drawers emptied, no papers thrown around. I didn't see any ashes on the floor. I don't think the killer even knew this notebook was there."

"Then why was Murdock killed?"

"I don't know that. All I can tell you is, it's different than the others."

"Different killers? . . . Is that what you're saying?"

"No, it's the same guy, and if you dig deep enough, you'll find one motive at the bottom of it. But he was drawn to these guys for different reasons. Carmichael was killed for what was in Pruitt's house. Same thing with Hockman, years ago: he was killed for what he had. Murdock was killed for what he knew."

She leaned over and looked at the notebook close up. But she avoided touching it, as if whatever lay beneath its cover had been hopelessly tainted. "It's still a wonderful motive for murder. Imagine what someone like Huggins would pay for it. He'd sell his house to get it. It's the map to Treasure Island, the only thing a Grayson freak would ever need for the scavenger hunt of his dreams."

I was thinking the same thing, with Scofield playing the Huggins role. A rich man could chase down the subscribers or their heirs and suck the market dry in no time. Each year fewer Graysons would appear at auction and no one would quite know why. Suddenly dealers would list them in catalogs as *rare* and mean it. In ten years the prices on the few odds and ends would be stratospheric.

I told her about Scofield and Kenney and about the interesting talk I'd had with Mrs. Kenney earlier in the evening. She listened with her fingers to her lips and came to the same conclusion I had reached a few hours before.

Kenney and Scofield were flying in to meet Pruitt.

That meant Pruitt had been in touch, sometime since I last spoke with Kenney, probably well within the last twenty-four hours.

"My God, he's found the book," Trish said breathlessly.

"That . . . would seem to be the case."

"What else could it mean?"

"I don't know what it means. Or might mean for Eleanor."

"What are you going to do?"

"I'm gonna be there when the deal goes down. After that it's up for grabs."

She said something under her breath that sounded like "Jesus."

I nudged Grayson's notebook in her general direction. "Maybe you should break down and give this a look. It tells us some things we never knew before."

"Such as what?"

"It turns out that Grayson did a tiny lettered run for each of his books. A superlimited series that went to a few select customers."

"I don't remember seeing that in Huggins."

"It wasn't in Huggins. I looked."

"Huggins would never leave something like that out."

"Unless he never knew about it. Or maybe he did know and couldn't verify it, like the fact that Grayson was working on another *Raven.*"

"This is different than another *Raven.* The *Raven* might not even exist. But if there was a lettered series, Huggins would have to have it."

"But the limitation was so small it was next to nothing. None of the books has ever turned up to prove their existence, and until now it was assumed by everybody that Grayson's records all went up in the fire."

She still made no move to pick up the notebook. I picked it up for her and opened it to the first page.

"Each title had five hundred numbered copies. There were also five lettered copies. These were for customers who had been with Grayson from the beginning . . . the faithful. They loved his books way back when everybody else could care less."

I watched her eyes. It was beginning to come to her now, she was starting to see the dark road we were heading into.

"These lettered copies usually preceded the regular run by a month or so," I said.

Suddenly she knew where we were going. I could see it in her eyes.

"*A,*" I told her, "was a fellow named Joseph Hockman, of St. Louis, Missouri."

She didn't say anything. She reached across the table and took the notebook out of my hands. She read the name in Grayson's own hand, as if nothing less would make her believe it. She put it down on the table, looked across at me, picked it up, and read it again.

"*B,*" I said, "was Mr. Reggie Dressler of Phoenix, Arizona. *C* was Corey Allingham of Ellicott City, Maryland. *D* was Mike Hollingsworth, looks like a rural route somewhere in Idaho. *E* was Laura Warner of New Orleans. That's all there were. The faithful five."

She finally got past Joseph Hockman and let her eyes skim the page. "He knew Laura Warner from Atlanta."

"I know he did. I read your book."

"Jesus! . . . Have you checked these other names yet?"

"I've only had the damn thing a couple of hours. I didn't want to make any police checks from this telephone, even to departments a thousand miles from here. There are other offices I could check, but they won't be open at midnight."

"No, but the newspapers will be."

She sat at her telephone and made some calls: to night city editors at the *Arizona Republic,* the *Baltimore Sun,* the *Idaho Statesman,* and the *Times-Picayune* in New Orleans. While people in distant cities chased down any clip files that might exist, we sat at the table drinking coffee.

Now that she had begun on Grayson's notebook she couldn't leave it alone. "I've interviewed some of these people. Look, here's Huggins . . . number twenty-three of the regular run. He got in early."

A minute later she came to Otto Murdock, number 215.

"Let's look at what else we've got," I said. "I hear dawn cracking."

We had our physical evidence spread out on the table between us. We had Richard's poem, which Trish had yet to read. We had the paper chip from Pruitt's house, and the sheet she had brought back from St. Louis with the two dim letters standing out in the soot. And I had brought in from the car an envelope containing the photographs I had found in Amy Harper's attic.

Trish opened the envelope and looked at the first picture—the Eleanor woman, shot at Grayson's printshop in May 1969.

"Imagine how the kid must've felt, finding this," she said. "You grow up thinking you know where you come from. Your home and family are the real constants in life. Then in one second you see that nothing's what you thought it was."

She turned the picture down and looked at the one beneath it. Three people walking in the woods: the Eleanor woman, another woman, and a man.

"Look at this," she said. "There's Charlie Jeffords."

"Really?" I took the picture out of her hand. The guy was standing in a little clearing, smirking at the camera. The Eleanor woman was posing with him in the same sleeveless blouse, her arm over his shoulder. The other woman stood a few feet away, clearly unhappy.

"This is Jeffords?" I said. "You're sure of that?"

"Sure I'm sure. He's got dark hair here and that horny leer of his'll never be there again, but yeah. Same guy I talked to in Taos."

"I wonder who the other woman is."

She shook her head. "This bothers me a lot. It's fairly obvious now that Jeffords was a player of some kind in Grayson's life and I missed it. Damn."

I wanted to move her past it, beyond her own shortcomings. I took the handle of my spoon and changed the subject, nudging the chip of paper until my words *still* and *whisp* lined up opposite her *Fr*.

"I'm no expert," I said. "But this typography looks the same to me."

"They seem to be the same point size. But the letters are different so it's hard to be sure."

I unfolded the library copy I had made of the original "Raven" and showed her the words *still* and *whisp* where I had circled them in the fifth stanza. "Here's where your *Fr* comes from. Fourth line, second stanza, first word. 'From my books surcease of sorrow—sorrow for the lost Lenore.'"

But I could see she had already accepted the inevitability of its being there. She picked up the yellow pages and read Richard's poem. I watched her face as she read it, but she went through the entire thing deadpan.

"What do you make of this?" she said, putting it down.

I told her what I thought, the obvious supplemented with guesswork. It was a rough draft of something, hand-dated July 1967, two years before the Graysons died. There were numerous strike-outs and places where lines had been rewritten between lines. In the margins were long columns of rhyme words, many keyed to the dominant suffix *ore*. Mixed among the common words—*core, store, door, lore*—were exotic and difficult possibilities such as *petit four, centaur,* and *esprit de corps.*

"Whore," she said, looking up from the page. "That's one Poe couldn't use."

In technique it was like "The Raven," written out in eighteen full stanzas with the Poe meter and cadence. The tone was allegorical, like the old Orson Welles version of *Julius Caesar* in a blue serge suit. You couldn't quite be sure what was real and what had been skewed for effect, or how much might just be the author's own grim fantasy.

The style was in part mythic. It told the story of two young gods, one fair, the other dark: brothers forced to choose between good and evil when they were too young to understand the consequences. The road to hell was an orgy without end, lit up with laughter and gay frolic. Salvation came at a higher price.

One took the path of least resistance and tumbled into hell. The other chose the high road, finding strength in purpose and contentment in his work. But temptation was a constant, and in the end the darkhaired god was his own undoing.

Rigby was the symbol of blind youth. His was the only proper name in the tale. Richard had chosen to write it that way, the entire eighteen stanzas a lecture to youth.

On paper he could do that. He could sit Rigby down and make him listen. He could turn whores into saints and make the dark-haired god bow at the devil's feet.

"There are a couple of lines crossed out," she said, "as if he had changed his mind about something and took off in another direction."

"He wanted to take his brother's name out. You can still read it, though: all he did was draw a squiggly line through it."

She read aloud.

Rigby was a fresh young boy when he arrived like
  Fauntleroy
And took his bashful place beyond the shadows of
  the Grayson door;
Little did he know that Grayson had a legendary
  place in
Bedrooms: everywhere he'd hasten, wives and
  daughters to explore.
Grayson had them everywhere; on the stair and on
  the floor,
              Grayson lusted, evermore.

"Why take that out?" she said.

"It's too blunt. He wanted it to flow differently, he wanted that godlike flavor. He felt he could do that better by keeping himself and his brother nameless."

The telephone rang. She picked it up and said a few words, scribbled a few notes, asked a few questions about when, where, and how. "That's great, friend," she said. "Yeah, do send me copies of those clips, and listen, that's one I owe you if you ever need a Seattle angle."

She hung up and looked at me. She didn't say anything and I didn't need to ask. She looked down at the poem and said, "I think you're right, if it matters. Richard had a well-honed sense of bitter satire. A frontal attack was never as much fun as a hit-and-run."

"The title was blatant enough."

308

" 'The Craven.' What an insult that would've been to a man like Darryl Grayson."

"It belittles his genius. It reduces Grayson's life to the level of his own. And yet it has moments of real . . . what?"

"Love."

"Read it again."

She read aloud from the top: the world according to Richard, first revised version.

> One night sitting with dear Gaston, as the night
>   fell deep and vast in
> All its blackened glory: such a night to chill him
>   to the very core;
> A colder wind I blew upon him, one I thought
>   would shake and stun him
> And might even break and run him far away from
>   sorrow's door.
> But the child remained undaunted: all his faith
>   again he swore
>   Was in his god forevermore.

"I don't believe this," she said. "It doesn't square with what I know about Richard or Rigby."

"You can't take it literally, you'll end up doubting it all. I admit it strikes a false note at the top. We know Rigby wouldn't sit still for what comes later, but that doesn't mean other parts of it aren't true."

She read two flashback stanzas telling of the gods' humble origins.

"I had it right," she said. "If anything, I underwrote it."

The father was a mean drunk and drunk much of the time. The mother was dead and unforgiven. If she wanted understanding, she'd have to find it in the next world because the son she'd left on earth had none to give her.

Lines in the middle of the third stanza made short work of these two and the sorry life they'd given their sons.

Brute and whore together spawned 'em; then
*   forsook 'em, tossed and pawned 'em*
To the devil who upon them did his vile and
*   wicked powers pour . . .*

I joined her reading, quoting from memory.

One would join Old Scratch the devil, while he
*   watched the other revel*
In himself, and gaze with level eyes upon the
*   predator . . .*

"I don't see that in here."

"He squiggled it out. But it's there, off to the side of the verse he kept. You can read it through the squiggle."

"Yeah, I see it now."

Up to this point Richard had worshiped his brother blindly, much as Rigby would do a generation later. "At that time, he was buying his own god scenario," I said. "Grayson was his protector, the only real constant in his life."

"Then it all changes. The god proves false."

"He has his first serious romance, and Richard rankles with fear and jealousy."

"Cecile Thomas," Trish said. "I talked to her. She had gone to grammar school with the Graysons, then her parents moved away to North Carolina and came back to Atlanta when she was a teenager. A classic coming-of-age romance. Grayson thought of her as a brat when they were kids. Then suddenly there she was again, eighteen and lovely."

"There's a squiggled-out verse, just partly finished,

when Richard was still trying to do it in a half-modern idiom, with names and all."

She read it.

> *Grayson had with him a harlot, who had come to*
>   *him from Charlotte,*
> *Though Atlanta, Georgia, was her domicile of*
>   *yore* . . .

"There's another line I can't read," she said.

"It says, *Who, you ask me, could this pig be, who so got the goat of Rigby.* If you look at it under a glass, you can make it out."

"He's doing it again, mixing his own role with Rigby's."

"But he catches it before the stanza's done and squiggles it out."

Her telephone rang.

She took back-to-back calls, from Phoenix and Baltimore. She made her notes with a poker face, as if she were working a rewrite desk assembling facts for a weather report.

She looked up from the phone without a word, pushed her notes off to one side, and again took up Richard's poem.

"You can see the words changing as it goes along. The tone gets darker, angrier."

"He was a clingy kid," I said. "He was what? . . . thirteen, fourteen years old. His brother was four years older, the difference between a boy and a young man. Richard counted on his brother to be there when things in his life went wrong."

"Then it got to be too much." She flipped a page. "We can only guess how Darryl felt, when all we've got is Richard's side to go by."

"My guess is the same as yours. He was being suffocated by his father on one side and by Richard on the other. So he ran away with his girlfriend to the coast, only his friend Moon knew where."

"And Moon wasn't telling."

"And Richard settled into a cold rage. He had already lost his mother, and now the unthinkable was happening, he was losing his brother. To a kid that age, the feeling of abandonment was probably enormous."

"He hated Moon for obvious reasons."

"Moon was everything he could never be. Strong, independent . . . the kind of man Grayson would want for a brother."

"In South Carolina, Grayson found that sense of purpose that would carry him through life. He'd fought Old Scratch and won."

She read it.

*And when the young god chose to fight, he waged
    a battle that was mighty;
Purpose kept his honor far away from Satan's
    harsh and blust'ry roar.
This was how he rose above it: did his work and
    learned to love it,
And his skills made others covet everything he
    made and more.
'Tis some deity, they marveled, living there
    beyond that door:
        He'd joined the gods, forevermore.*

For three stanzas the god walked on water, could do no wrong. All he touched was blessed: he was on a spiral ever upward.

Then came *The Raven.*

*And when it seemed that none could daunt him,
A sepulchre rose up to haunt him
Stuck in there as if to taunt him, all the more to
    underscore*

That he who'd walked among the gods
Had tumbled down to hell's back door,
        A-burning there, forevermore.

"The misspelled word," she said. "But it's all out of sequence. He's giving his brother all that success before *The Raven,* when it really didn't happen till five or six years later."

"Creative license again. He thought it worked better dramatically. But the real question is, what is this business of the misspelled word? What the cop in St. Louis told you, that Hockman had just gotten a new book with a misspelled word . . . that's damned interesting."

"And not just any word. The same word."

"How could Grayson make that mistake again?"

"If we knew that, we'd know something, wouldn't we?"

"Whatever happened, it was disastrous."

"The god begins to fail. He starts doubting himself, becomes obsessed by a vision of his failure. He tries to put it right, but he can never do it well enough."

"Nothing he does can satisfy him now."

"It can never be good enough."

"He sinks into despair."

"And takes refuge in alcohol and sex."

And Rigby heard in disbelief the Craven's method
   and motif
Of luring maidens into wretchedness behind his
   bedroom door.
One poor fool she filled herself with fantasy, then
   killed herself,
Unable to instill herself into his craven heart
   before
She turned up high the unlit gas and died upon
   her father's floor:
        To irk the Craven nevermore.

"God, there was a girl who killed herself," Trish said. "I kissed her off with a paragraph. I didn't think it had that much to do with Grayson, it was months after their affair and she seemed despondent over everything, not just him."

She looked at me, riddled with doubt.

"Who knows what it had to do with," I said. "Maybe it's just Richard again, trying to blame some circumstantial tragedy on his brother."

"What about Laura Warner?"

"You did what you could with her. You chased her pretty hard."

"Not hard enough."

"Then that's what revised editions are for."

We were in the last lines now. The dark-haired god idolized in the early verse had suddenly been reduced to ridicule.

The time had come to resurrect the ancient failure
*   that infected*
Every facet of his life . . .

She looked at me and I gave her the next line from memory.

But his second task was tougher; it was Poe who
*   made him suffer . . .*

"Poe defeated him," she said. "He never did get it right."

"Then where'd the book come from?"

She shook her head.

"And the ashes . . ."

"I don't know."

"If Grayson was such a failure at the end of his life," I pressed, "why is his book still causing so damned much trouble?"

"I don't know. I just don't know."

We didn't speak again till the phone rang. The late man at the *Times-Picayune* in New Orleans.

She talked for a while and hung up.

"He burned her house," she said flatly. "Killed her, then set fire to her house."

"Laura Warner."

She nodded. "They're all dead. St. Louis, Phoenix, Idaho . . . all dead. All but a blind, crazy woman in the Maryland case."

BOOK III

THE RAVEN

44

It was raining again. I heard two things, the steady drumming of the rain and the click of my bedroom door as Trish came in. I lay still for a moment, listening to her footsteps as she approached my bed. I had been in a deep sleep for all of ninety minutes: the digits on the clock beside the bed told me it was now 4:52. I blinked my eyes and gradually came awake, aware of her presence a foot or two away. She stood for a long minute, then leaned over and touched my shoulder, shaking me gently.

"It's time," she said.

"Yeah, I'm awake."

"We gotta get going."

She went away and I lay there for another minute, thinking about what we had discovered in the night. I thought about five old murder cases in five different cities, and about the blind woman the killer had left alive in Maryland.

I hit the shower. Thought about it some more as I stood in the steam.

I smelled bacon as I came downstairs. She stood in the half-dark kitchen, cooking by the light from the smoke hood over the range.

"Didn't we just eat?" I asked in a surprised tone of voice.

"Such as it was."

But my appetite is always good in the morning and

I was hungry again. I sat at her kitchen table and let her pamper me.

"Scofield and Kenney are due in at six-thirty, more or less, according to the flight plan they filed in L.A.," she said. "We should play it safe and be there with time to spare."

I agreed with that. We were probably safe if we could leave in another ten minutes. We were already slightly south of town, and that would give us a full hour to make the few miles to Sea-Tac before the rush hour began.

I asked if she'd gotten any sleep. "Didn't even try," she said, handing me a plate of food. She sat across from me with her own plate and said, "I can't sleep with stuff like this going on."

She had been thinking about the sequence of those five old murder cases and had come up with a point of logic that had escaped us at midnight. "The cases all followed the Grayson lettering sequence, in precise order. *A* came before *B,* then came *C, D,* and *E,* all within days of each other. Think about that a minute. Picture a map of the United States and ask yourself, if you were going to kill people in five different parts of the country, how would you go about it? I'd do the two in the West first because I'm out here already and it's closer. Do Idaho first, then fly to Phoenix. Then go east and do the others, St. Louis, then New Orleans and Baltimore, in either order. What the killer did, though, was St. Louis first . . . *A.* Then he went to Phoenix, *B;* then he flew clear back across the country to *C,* Baltimore. Then back across the country again to Idaho. Then back again to New Orleans. Does this make sense? Not unless you've got Grayson's list and can see the connections."

"It's like he couldn't see anything beyond the list."

"Just get there, do it, and move on the next one."

"Whatever it was, the urgency was so great he didn't even think about geography."

She shivered. "This is a real crazy one we've got here."

"And he's still out there doing it."

Forty minutes later we were sitting in a maintenance truck at the end of a concourse where the smallest airline carriers and various private flights were routed. Our driver was a cheerful fellow named Mickey Bowman, who ran the airport's public relations office and didn't seem to mind being roused from bed when Trish had called him at three-thirty. I knew a little about the odd relationships that sometimes develop between PR people and the press—the Denver cops had a public affairs specialist with the rank of division chief, and depending on who held the job, you could sometimes see the good and bad of what he did on the front pages of the Denver newspapers. If he stonewalls, they dig out the facts anyway, only they write them in such a way as to make his boss look stupid, silly, or devious. A good PR guy knows when to promote and when to back off and do the gal a favor. He is always in when the press calls: he never gives her the feeling that, all things considered, he'd rather be in Philadelphia than sitting in a maintenance truck at six o'clock on a rainy morning talking to her. He is an expert at damage control, and if the story is going to be critical, he sometimes earns his pay more for what's left out of a piece than what's put in.

Bowman had been a reporter himself in a previous life and he knew the routine. He knew what her deadlines were, just as he knew that she seldom did stories of that nature. "We'd like to meet a guy at the airport, Mickey," she had said, "and we're not sure yet whether we'll want to announce ourselves after he gets here." Bowman's dad had been in the Seabees in the big war, she told me later: he had passed along that can-do mentality to his son. Bowman was waiting when we arrived. He got us through security, verified when and where Scofield's plane would be coming in, and now we sat with Trish wedged tight in the seat between us, the airport VISITOR tags clipped to our lapels.

I sat quietly splitting my concentration. One side of my brain listened to the shoptalk between Aandahl and Bowman while I thought about our killer with the other half. I thought about a blind woman in Baltimore who had been left alive in the middle of a nine-day rampage, who had later gone mad and been committed. Trish was telling Mickey Bowman about a great public-relations man she knew by phone but had never met. The guy worked for United Airlines in Miami, and he had all but written her first big story for her on deadline. A plane had been hijacked: FBI sharpshooters had gotten under the aircraft without the hijacker's knowledge, and one was trying to crawl up the plane's nose assembly before the gunman figured out where they were. The United man had an office window that looked down on the scene. Trish sat at a desk across town, her phone rigged through a headset, taking verbatim descriptions as the United guy talked the story out to her. "They killed the hijacker," she said, "but I've never forgotten that PR man. You're pretty good yourself, Mick."

This was high praise from someone who never dealt in bullshit, and Bowman knew it. "Mickey used to be a bureau chief for the AP in Indianapolis," Trish said for my benefit. I joined the small talk and learned a few things about wire-service reporters. But I was still thinking about the blind woman in Maryland.

At six-thirty sharp a burst of noise came through

Bowman's radio. "Your bird's on the ground," he said. At almost the same instant a car materialized, a black Cadillac that came slowly up the runway and stopped, idling about thirty yards to our right. The two men sitting in the car would be Scofield body-guards, I guessed. Bowman started his engine and cleared away the steam from our windows with his air blower. I had to hand it to him: he must be curious as hell about the story we were doing, but he never asked.

A sleek-looking jet nosed its way around the corner and came toward us. "Well, what do you think?" Trish asked. I told her I tried not to think, I just react, and Bowman laughed when she did not. She was letting me call the plays, at least for now. It had been my decision to get on Scofield's tail as soon as he touched down at Sea-Tac; I just wasn't comfortable waiting around for him to show up at the Four Seasons. When you're dealing with a fruitcake like Pruitt, a lot can happen in ten miles.

The plane taxied in and came to a stop. The ground crew rolled out a steel stairwell, a door opened, and a man got out and popped open an umbrella. Then Rodney Scofield stepped out in the rain. I didn't need a formal introduction: he was an old man whose snowy hair curled in tufts under the edges of his hat, whose ruddy face—as near as I could tell from that distance—was all business. This was his clambake, he was the boss. The grunt beside him held the umbrella over his head, and the two grunts in the Caddy got out and stood at attention. He was at the bottom of the stairs when Leith Kenney emerged from the aircraft. Kenney looked just as I'd pictured him, which doesn't happen often when all you have is a voice to go by. He had a neatly trimmed beard: he was slender and tall and had the word *bookman* stamped all over him. He was carrying a small suitcase, which he looked ready to defend with his life. He reminded me of a diplomatic courier in wartime, transporting top secrets with the valise chained to his wrist. But I was willing to bet that this suitcase contained nothing but money.

Here we go, I thought.

We went south, a surprise. I was happy to have done something right for a change and picked up Scofield at the airport. The Cadillac whipped into I-5 and headed for Tacoma like a homing pigeon. Bowman followed without question: Trish would owe him a big-league debt when it was over. The Caddy cruised at the speed limit and Bowman kept our truck two or three cars behind it. We didn't talk: just sat rigid, tense in the seat. After eight or ten miles, the Cadillac turned off the highway and took to a two-lane, state-numbered road. Bowman dropped back but kept him in sight, cruising along at forty.

The rain had stopped and the sky was breaking up into long streaks of blue. A stiff wind blew down from Rainier, buffeting the truck as we rocked along. I thought we must be due east of Tacoma now, skirting the city on Highway 161. It was small-town suburban, broken by stretches of open country. Snow blew off the mountain in the distance, a swirling gale driven by the same wind that rolled down the valley. We came to a river, crossed it, and arrived in the town of Puyallup.

The Cadillac stopped. Pulled off to the side of the road.

We drove on past and I got a glimpse of Scofield and Kenney confering over something in the backseat.

"They're looking at directions," Trish said. "Double-checking."

"Then we're almost there."

Bowman hung a left, did a quick U-turn, and came cautiously to the corner. We could see the Cadillac still parked off the road in the distance. We sat at roadside and waited.

They came a minute later. Bowman allowed just the right gap to develop, then swung in behind them. I wasn't too worried: none of the guys in the Caddy looked like pros to me, meaning the only way they'd make us was by accident. The Caddy hung a right, into a road that ran along the river. The place they were going was about half a mile along, a small café well back from the road. There was a gas pump out front and a couple of junk autos at the east side of the building. The yard was unpaved, puddle-pocked from all the rain. "Pull in," I said, and Bowman did, taking a position between cars on the far end. Scofield and Kenney got out and went in, leaving the two grunts alone in the car.

"Well," I said. "Looks like we fish or cut bait."

"Let me go in," Trish said. "At least if Pruitt's in there he won't know me on sight."

"Okay, but do it quick. Get us three coffees to go, then get back out here and tell me what's going on."

She clutched her raincoat and struggled through the wind to the front door. I got back in the truck and waited. Bowman didn't say anything, and in a minute I forgot he was there. I thought about Pruitt and Grayson, and about the blind woman in Baltimore. And I was suddenly very nervous.

One of Scofield's grunts got out of the Caddy and tried valiantly to light a cigarette. No smoking allowed in the old man's car, I thought. But the wind was fierce and at last he had to give it up.

The café got busy. It was a workingman's joint, the customers coming and going in blue jeans and flannel.

The slots in front of the building were now filled in with cars, and another row had begun out near the road behind us. A young couple brushed past, then two farmers, then a guy in coveralls who looked like the town grease monkey. They all converged at the front door, just as the door swung open and Trish came out.

She stepped aside, clutching a brown paper bag against her breast. I got out and let her into the truck and she gave me the news. Our friends had taken a booth at the far end of the dining room and were sitting there alone, waiting.

Trish gave out the coffees. "Hope you don't have to be anywhere," she said by way of apology to Bowman. He just grinned, well aware of the points he was piling up with her, and said his time was her time. He'd need to call in at nine and make sure a few things got done: other than that, he was all hers. More people came and went, old men in twos and threes mixed with the occasional loner. They would fill up the tables in a corner, eat their soft-boiled eggs and gripe as old men in small towns have always done about the thieves and sons of bitches running things in Washington. I could fit right in if they'd let me: a helluva lot better that would be than sitting out here like three bumps on a log. This was a difficult place for a stakeout. But you'd be much too conspicuous out on the road, so you took what the situation gave you and hoped you blended in. I hunched down in the seat till my eyes were level with the dash. I could still see everything that went on at the front door.

Bowman and Trish were talking shop again. I listened but did not hear. Then we all settled into that quiet restlessness that always seems to come in the second hour. I replayed the case in my head, trying to remember everything from the top. Slater walked into my store and we did our little macho dance. I crossed swords with Pruitt, came to know Eleanor and the Rigbys, absorbed the legend of the Graysons, met Huggins and Amy Harper. But through it all I kept thinking about a woman I had never met and probably never would, a blind woman who had gone crazy in Baltimore.

I got my chance at her when Bowman went to make his phone call. "The guy in Baltimore," I said. "When he called you back, did he say anything about the particulars of that particular case?"

"He read me some stuff from the clips. I made some notes." She opened her purse and got out her steno pad. "I spent more time with him than the others because of the blind woman."

"Yeah, the blind woman."

"What're you thinking?"

"I don't know yet. Go on with what he told you."

"The victim's name was Allingham. He lived with his wife on the outskirts of Baltimore, a suburb called Ellicott City. Nice house, secluded neighborhood, well-to-do people in their midfifties."

"And the wife survived."

"Not only survived, she seemed to've been deliberately left alone. He came into the room with her. She could hear him breathing."

"*Him* . . . did she say it was a him?"

"That's how the clips had it. *He* came in . . . *he* stood there breathing hard. She knew what was happening, too: knew they had an intruder and he had just killed or seriously hurt her husband. Blind people see better than we think."

"What else?"

She flipped a page. I looked at her notes and saw a cryptic brand of shorthand, probably something of her own making that was unreadable to the rest of the world. "Her name was Elizabeth. She was never a credible witness. She just sank into darkness after that. But who could blame her?"

I closed my eyes and tried to see it. Trish said, "The cops thought it might've been her dog that saved her. She had this German shepherd Seeing Eye dog, very protective. They say the dog raised hell when the cops arrived. They had to bring in a dog man to muzzle him before they could interview the widow."

"I don't think the dog had anything to do with it."

"How so?"

"Dogs don't usually discourage that kind of killer, at least not for long. If he'd wanted her, he'd go through the dog to get her."

"Maybe the noise scared him off."

"Maybe. And I can't help wondering how she could hear the killer breathing if the dog was barking."

"Who knows what she really heard? But look, are you going somewhere with this?"

"I don't know yet. It's just nagging at me. Did any of your news guys mention ashes at the scene?"

"No, but that wouldn't be in the clips. The cops never . . ."

"But you did say the house in New Orleans was torched and burned."

"Yeah, the cops there thought it was done to cover up the murder."

"They may've told the press that, but I'll bet there were some cops down there who didn't believe it."

"What're you thinking?" she asked again.

"Might've been somebody burning a book. He left it burning and the fire spread and burned the house."

Bowman had come out of the restaurant, standing off to one side to grab a smoke. I looked at Trish and the question that had nagged at me all morning bubbled up and out.

"Why would he leave the blind woman alive?"

"You tell me."

"Because of her blindness. That's the one thing all the others had in common that made her different. They could see."

"He knew she couldn't see him. Couldn't identify him."

"That's the logical answer. But this bird wasn't thinking logically. And I can think of another possibility."

She shook her head. "I must be dense."

"There was something in the book. Something they could see and she couldn't. Something that had been put in or bound in by mistake. Something so awful in the killer's mind that it had to be retrieved, and anybody who had seen it killed."

"I don't know, Janeway."

"I don't know either. I'm just doing what cops always do in murder cases, I'm playing it through in my head. Maybe he never intended to kill anybody. But he went to St. Louis to get his book back, and Hockman wouldn't play. Now we get into the collector's mentality. Hockman suddenly knew he had something unique. He wasn't about to give it up, not for Jesus Christ, not for Daryl Grayson himself. The only way to get it from him was to kill him."

"Keep going," she said, but her voice was still laced with doubt.

"The killer was single-minded, you figured that out yourself. He flew from *A* to *B,* and so on. He had one thing on his mind, getting that book. There was a desperate urgency to it, the cause transcended geography, transcended everything: he couldn't think about anything else. So he gets to St. Louis and Hockman won't give it to him. He whacks Hockman, maybe in a fit of rage. Now he's a killer."

I let that thought settle on her for a few seconds.

"Let me tell you something about killers, Trish . . . something you might know but never thought about. There are people who never kill till they're forty, fifty, then they kill a dozen times. That first one pushes them over the edge, sets them on a dark path they never intended to travel. The first one's the catalyst: there's no question after that. He goes to Phoenix and this time he doesn't even ask. He wades in, kills the people, takes the book. And so it goes."

"Until he gets to Baltimore . . ."

"And he walks into the room and there's this woman, obviously blind, with a dog and all, maybe a cane leaning against a table. She's blind, she didn't see anything, she's not part of this. He leaves her alive."

"But who'd go to such a length? Who'd do something like that?"

"Only one guy I can think of. The guy who made it."

Her eyes opened wide. "Jesus, Janeway, what're you thinking?" she asked for the third time, her voice now an urgent whisper.

"Did you ever talk to the coroner who did the Graysons?"

"No," she said in a tiny voice. "There was never a reason."

"There was never any doubt that it was really Darryl and Richard Grayson who died in that fire?"

She never got to answer because Bowman came back and got in beside us. We sat in the car, still as death, thinking about it.

All this time we've had the wrong motive, I was thinking. We've been thinking money, but that was never it. All the specter of money had done was cloud it. Only after Scofield had begun to collect Grayson and the books had become so avidly sought and eagerly paid for did money become a credible possibility. But this case had begun long before that.

The clock pushed ten: the breakfast rush was over. Scofield and Kenney had been inside more than two hours.

"They must be getting discouraged by now," I said.

It was on that weary note that Pruitt arrived.

45

He was the invisible man, leaving footprints in the snow. *Watch out for old ladies,* Slater had said, but you still couldn't see him except that he was carrying Scofield's suitcase. The suitcase was like the snow in that old horror film: it lit him up, made his tracks visible so you could pop him as he ran across the yard. It danced of its own volition, as if the arm clutching it against the gingham dress had vanished. He had tried to cover it with a shawl, which was too small. I sat up straight in the seat, so suddenly that Trish jumped up with a jerk of her own. "What's going on?" she said, but I was already out of the truck, splashing after the hooded squaw who moved between cars and headed across the muddy yard twenty yards to our right. He looked like old Mother Bates in *Psycho,* walking with the sure and deadly gait of a man. I fell in behind him and we headed out toward the row of cars parked by the road. The wind whipped at his shawl and clutched the corners of his hood. I got a glimpse of cheek as he half-turned and tried to look back. But he didn't turn far enough: he was caught in the Satchel Paige syndrome, afraid to look, afraid to see how much trouble followed him. If he could make it to his car without having to look upon his enemy, he'd be home free.

He didn't make it.

"Pruitt," I said, and he spun on his heel and locked in my eyes from a distance of six feet.

His free hand slipped down into the folds of his dress. I danced in close and grabbed him. With the other hand I ripped away the suitcase and made him fumble it. It popped open on the ground and the wind sucked up the money, a fluttery gale of greenbacks that blew back across the yard toward the café. He cried out and tried to dive down and save it. I met him coming down with a knee to the jaw, flopping him back on his ass in the mud.

It was all fast motion and unreal after that. I stood over him and said, "Take out that gun and I'll kick your head off," but I knew that wouldn't stop him. He cleared the dress with a handful of iron and I drove my shoe under his armpit. He grabbed at the sky, fired a round in the air, and I nailed him hard with the other foot. He withered, twisting in agony like a deflating balloon, rolling under the wheels with a gaffing, hissing sound. I kicked his gun and it spun off into a puddle. I knew I had hurt him, maybe busted his ribs, but he wasn't finished yet. He still had the knife, and as I dragged him out, he rolled into me with the blade leading the way. I caught his wrist with a wet smack. For a few seconds we strained against each other while the point of the knife quivered like a seismograph that couldn't tell if an earthquake was coming. Then I knew I had him. I saw it first in his

eyes, that chink in the hard shell that comes to all
bullyboys when they play one hand too many. He
didn't look mean anymore. He looked small and tired
and astonished.

"Now you are going to tell me where the girl is." I
said this with the knife at my throat but the tide
turning fast. His arm collapsed and he let the knife
fall away as if surrender could save him. I hit him
hard with my fist so he'd know better, and I hit him
again, then again, then I lost track as I battered his
face back and forth. I could hear my voice pounding
at him as well, "Where is she . . . where is she," with
every punch, and after a while he stopped saying he
didn't know. I felt Trish on my back, heard her
screaming at me to for Christ's sake stop it, but for
that long minute stopping was just not possible. I had
slipped over the edge and become every bad cop who
ever took up a rubber hose or swung a billy club in
anger.

Trish grabbed me around the neck. I shrugged her
off and went at Pruitt again.

Then I did stop. I lunged at him one more time, a
reflex, but I pulled back without letting that last fist
fall. I looked at him, bloody and cold, and I knew he
wouldn't be telling anybody anything for a while.

I got up and looked around. Trish was sitting in
mud ten feet away. Bowman was standing far back,
watching as if he couldn't quite believe what had just
happened. Farther back, people were running out of
the diner as word spread that hundred-dollar bills
were falling out of the sky.

In the babble of the crowd I heard the word *police*. I
had a few minutes on the long end to do what I had to
do and get out of there.

I dragged Pruitt around the car, took out Slater's
handcuffs, and locked him to the door handle. I didn't

see Trish when I looked for her again: I didn't know where she'd gone, but Bowman was still there. I went over to him and said, "Gimme the truck keys, Mickey," and he looked at me as if I was not a guy to argue with and he gave me the keys. I handed him the keys to the cuffs and told him to give them to Trish.

I headed toward the café. The crowd at the door pushed back and gave me a wide berth.

I heard voices as I moved through. Again the word *police*. Somebody else said they were on the way. A woman asked what the hell was going on and a man said, "Some crazy guy beat up an old lady in the parking lot."

I pushed past the waiting area and saw Scofield and Kenney sitting at the booth in the corner. They were looking at something on the table between them, studying it so intently they couldn't even hear the commotion up front.

I walked right over and pulled up a chair. Scofield jerked back, as startled as if I'd attacked him. He grabbed a book off the table and put it out of sight on his lap. Kenney looked at me with unruffled eyes and I jumped into the breach as if we were all old friends.

"I'm glad to see you didn't come all this way for nothing."

"Do I know you?" Kenney was wary now, but in his manner I caught a glimmer of recognition.

"That's a good ear you've got. I'm the guy you've been talking to on the phone."

He didn't say anything. I could see he was with me but he tried to shrug it off. This was all a moot point: they had what they'd come for.

"Before you go flying back to Tinseltown," I said, "I should tell you there's a lot more where that came from."

"Lots more what?"

"I don't have time to draw you a picture. I'm talking sixty cartons of Grayson ephemera. I'm talking notes, diaries, letters, sketches, photographs. You name it, I got it."

Kenney took the news like a world-class poker player. But Scofield began to tremble.

"And, oh, yeah," I said as an afterthought: "I also happen to have picked up Grayson's original subscriber list along the way . . . if something like that could be of any interest to you."

Scofield fumbled in his pocket and got out a vial of pills. He took two with water. Kenney looked in my eyes and said, "What do you want?"

"Right now just listen. You boys go on up to Seattle and wait for me in your room at the Four Seasons. I'll either come to you or call you later today or tonight. Don't talk to anybody about this till I get back to you. Are we all on the same page?"

They looked at each other.

"Yes," Scofield said in a thin voice. "We'll be there."

I got up and left them, pushing my way through the crowd. Outside, the yard looked like a convention of lunatics. People ran back and forth, crawled under cars in the mud, screamed at each other. Two fistfights were in progress off to the side, and in the distance I heard a siren.

I didn't see Bowman or Trish and didn't have time to look. I got in the truck and drove away.

I was well up the highway when I realized that something was clinging to my windshield. It was a crisp C-note. Franklin flapped madly against the glass as I banked north into I-5. I didn't stop even for him. In a while he lost his hold and blew away.

46

I was waiting at a table in the Hilton coffee shop when Huggins came in. He glanced around nervously, scanning the room twice before he saw me. A flash of annoyance crossed his face, but he chased it away and put on a passive mask in its place. I didn't move except to raise my eyes slightly as he crossed the room in my direction.

"Mr. Hodges," he said, sitting down.

"My name isn't Hodges, it's Cliff Janeway. I'm a book dealer from Denver."

If this surprised him, he didn't show it. His eyes had found the bait that had lured him here, that charred paper chip that had been haunting his dreams since Saturday night. I had put it out on the table, on top of the sheet Trish had brought back from St. Louis.

He leaned over the table and looked at it. "May I?"

"Carefully."

He picked up the fragment and again gave it the long, hard look through the eyepiece. His breath flared out through his nostrils as he looked. When at last he put the paper down, his eyes looked tired, as if he'd just gone halfway round the world.

"What do you think?"

He grunted. "It's hard to say."

"Come on, Mr. Huggins, let's not play around. The day is going fast and I've got lots to do."

"I'm not sure what you want from me."

"Let's start with this." I shoved the paper from St. Louis across the table and under his nose. "That look like the same alphabet to you?"

It pained him to look: you could see it in his eyes, the sure knowledge that he had something here but he'd never be able to keep it.

"Mr. Huggins?"

"Yes . . . I guess I'd have to say it probably is."

We looked at each other.

"So," he said: "now you can go tell Scofield and that'll be that."

I was finding it hard to argue with him. A part of me knew where he was coming from and sympathized with his viewpoint. As a bookman I was offended at the prospect of Scofield buying up every remaining scrap of Grayson's work. But I had Amy Harper to consider. This stuff was her future.

Suddenly Huggins was talking, one of his now-familiar monologues. But the tone was different: his voice had taken on the soft weariness of the defeated. "Twenty years ago, Grayson was an incredibly fertile field for a collector. He had just died and his books could still be had at almost every auction of fine-press items. I built my own collection piece by piece, scrap by scrap. It was so satisfying. You carve out your expertise, you shape and define it, and because of your scholarship others come into it and find the same pleasures and satisfactions you have. But you remain the leader, the first one they think of when they've taken it as far as they want to go with it and they're ready to sell. Then a man like Scofield comes along and everything changes."

He sipped his water and gave me a hard look. "I haven't been able to buy anything now for more than seven years. Only isolated pieces here and there, things that fall into my lap. You can forget the auction houses . . . Scofield's man is always there, always. And you can't outbid him, you'd have to be Ross Perot. . . . I don't know, maybe it's time I donated what I've got to a library and got out of the Grayson business. The trouble is, I don't know what else there is in life. I've never known anything that can give me the thrill of finding a Grayson variant . . . the thought of not having that is almost more than I can bear. Now, with my wife gone, the notion of clearing out my Grayson room and giving it all away . . . and yet, I've always been a practical man. When something's over, it's over."

"You could try taking pleasure in what you have."

He gave me a bitter smile. "I think you know better than that. The thrill is in the hunt, sir."

"Of course it is. And I wish I could help you."

"But in the end you're just what I feared most . . . Scofield's man."

"Not quite that. I wasn't lying to you, I didn't know who Scofield was."

"But you do now, and that's where you'll go. I don't blame you, understand, but I can't help fretting over it and wishing money didn't rule the world."

We seemed to be finished. Then he said, "How did you find it? Was it Otto Murdock?"

I sat up straight. "What about Murdock?"

"That's what I'd like to know. Obviously you know the name."

"How does he figure into it?"

"The same way everyone else does. He's been chasing it."

"You mean the Grayson *Raven?*"

"That, or anything else that'll keep him in potato water for the rest of his life."

"I understand he was a pretty good Grayson man once."

"Second only to yours truly," he said with a sad little smile. "Otto really had the bug, fifteen, twenty years ago."

"And had a helluva collection to prove it, I've been led to believe."

"Until he started selling it off piece by bloody piece to pay the whiskey man."

"Where'd he sell it?"

He gave a little laugh. "That shouldn't be hard to guess."

"You bought it."

"As much of it as I could. Otto was going through periods of trying to straighten himself out. Then he'd fall off the wagon and have to sell something. He sold all the minor stuff first. Then, just about the time he was getting to the gold-star items, along came Scofield with all the money in the world to buy them from him. I was like a duck shot right out of the water. Scofield paid him fifteen thousand dollars for a Benton *Christmas Carol* that wouldn't get fifteen hundred at auction. How do you compete with somebody like that?"

I let a couple of heartbeats pass, then I said, "Have you seen Murdock recently?"

"Hadn't seen him for years, till about a month ago."

"What happened then?"

"He called me up one night and asked if I could get some money together."

"Was he trying to sell you something?"

"That's what it sounded like. I never could get him to be specific. All he'd say was that he was working on the Grayson deal of a lifetime. Stuff he'd known about for years but had never been able to get at it. Whoever owned it was unapproachable. But that person had died and now somebody else had come into it, somebody who didn't know as much or care as much about it. He needed some money to approach her with."

"How much money?"

"He wasn't sure. He had seen this person once and he couldn't tell if she was as naive as she seemed or was just taking him for a ride. My impression was, she wasn't a heavyweight, but you only get one shot at something like that. Misjudge her and you lose it. Pay too little, lose it. Pay too much, you still lose it. What he asked for was five thousand."

"He was going to try to steal it."

"I figured as much. If he was going to pay five, it had to be worth fifty. God knows what a madman like Scofield would pay."

"Why wouldn't Murdock go to Scofield for the money in the first place?"

"Who knows what Otto was thinking? If this really was a once-in-a-lifetime Grayson score, you'd want to try to buy it yourself and *then* sell it to Scofield. That's how I'd do it, if I was Otto and had a little larceny in my heart."

"So when he came to you for the five, what'd you tell him?"

"What do you think I told him? I said I'd need to know exactly what I'd be getting for my money. You don't just hand over five thousand dollars to a man who's fully capable of drinking it up in a lost weekend."

Now he wavered. "I made a mistake. I can see it in your face."

"You both did. He could've bought it all for a hundred dollars. She might've given it to him just for hauling it out of there."

He looked ready to cry. He didn't want to ask, didn't dare ask, but in the end he had to.

"What the hell are we talking about?"

"You don't want to know."

"No," he said dryly. "I probably don't."

"So Murdock came and went. Was that the last time you saw him?"

"Saw him, yes."

"But you heard from him again."

"He called me about ten days ago. He had been drinking, I could tell that immediately. He was babbling."

"About what?"

"He was raving about some limited series of Grayson books that I had missed in my bibliography. He seemed to think Grayson had made a special set, just a few copies of each title, at least since the midfifties."

"What did you tell him?"

"To find a good hangover cure and go to bed."

"Did he say anything else?"

"They're all dead. That's what he said, they're all dead, all five of 'em."

"What did you make of that?"

"Nothing. He was hallucinating."

"Was that the end of it?"

"Just about. He rambled on for a while longer. Talked about getting himself together, becoming a real bookman again. Said he was going to write the real story of Darryl Grayson: said it had never been told but he was going to tell it, and when he did, the book world would sit up and take notice. It was all drunken balderdash."

He looked weary, suddenly older. "If you want to chase down a drunk's pink elephants, be my guest. Archie Moon and the Rigbys might know something. Otto said he'd gone out to North Bend and talked to them about it."

"What did he say?"

"I don't know. I couldn't take any more."

He was ready to leave now. As he pushed back his chair, I said, "By the way, did you know Murdock was dead?"

He blinked once and said, "No, I didn't know that."

"I'm sure it's been on the news by now."

"I don't read newspapers and I never watch anything but network news on television. I can't stand these local fools."

"Anyway, he's dead."

"How? . . . What happened?"

"Murder."

He blinked again. "What the hell's happening here?"

"Good question, Mr. Huggins. I don't know, but I'm gonna find out."

47

Amy Harper had brushed out her long red hair and put on her one good dress. She looked less all the time like the doe-eyed schoolgirl I had rescued from Belltown. She had found someone to stay with her children overnight: a good thing, because this was going to run late.

She wouldn't be doing any lifting and toting today. She was going to sit in a chair and supervise while a billionaire's handyman did the work for her.

We zipped along I-90 in the Nash and I told her what the game plan was. Somewhere on the road, ahead of us or just behind, Scofield and Kenney were heading for the same destination: I had called them from Amy's room and told them where to go. She listened to what I was telling her and demanded nothing. She had a Spartan nature, patient and gutsy and uncomplaining, and I liked her better every time I saw her.

A kind of muted excitement filled the car as we flew past Issaquah for the run into North Bend. I was anxious without being nervous. I knew what we had: I knew the power it would hold over Scofield, and even Amy felt the strength of it as the day gained momentum. I had taken on the role of Amy's guardian, her agent, in the talks to come. But a murder case was also on the fire: the fate of another woman I cared about greatly was still in doubt. *It's not about money,* I thought again. I believed that now more than ever. But money had become so mixed up in it that only the moneyman could help me untangle it, and I wasn't above using the Grayson papers as a wedge on him.

It seemed impossible but it was still only one o'clock. I thought about Trish and wondered how she was doing with Pruitt. I had left Bowman's truck at her house and changed over to the Nash before meeting Huggins at the Hilton.

Now I banked into the familiar North Bend off-ramp. The day was lovely, chilly like a mountain pool, and the wind swirled clouds behind the mountain in the distance. For a moment I thought I saw the Indian in the mountain, but when I blinked and looked again, he was gone. I headed down toward the main street and turned into the motel where I'd left the stash.

The black Cadillac was there in the yard.

"They're here," I said.

I got out, went to the office, and asked for Rodney Scofield. Room four, the man said, and I walked up the walk and knocked on the door.

Kenney opened it. He had a cocktail glass in his hand, ice bobbing in amber liquid.

We went in. I drew up a chair and Amy sat on the foot of the bed. "This is Miss Amy Harper. She's running this show. My name's Cliff Janeway, I'm a book dealer from Denver."

"Leith Kenney." He shook hands, first with Amy, then with me.

"Where's Scofield?" I asked.

"In the bathroom. He'll be out. Want a drink?"

"Sure. What're we having?"

"Can you drink Scotch?"

"I'm a William Faulkner bourbon man. That means between Scotch and nothing, I'll take Scotch."

He smiled: he knew the quote. Suddenly we were two old bookmen, hunkering down to bullshit. He looked at Amy and said, "Miss Harper?"

"Got a Coke?"

"7-Up."

"That'll be cool."

Kenney and I smiled at each other. He took a 7-Up out of a bag, filled a glass with ice, and poured it for her. He asked how I wanted my drink and I told him just like they shipped it from Kentucky.

A door clicked open and Rodney Scofield came into the room.

He was thin, with a pale, anemic look. His white hair had held its ground up front, retreating into a half-moon bald spot at the back of his head. His eyes were gray, sharp, and alert: his handshake was firm. He sat at the table, his own 7-Up awaiting his pleasure. He had a way about him that drew everyone around to him, making wherever he chose to sit the head of the class. He was a tough old bird, accustomed to giving orders and having people jump to his side. Now he would sit and listen and take orders himself, from a girl barely out of her teens.

It was up to me to set the stage, which I did quickly. "Everything I told you in the restaurant is true. Gentlemen, this is the Grayson score of your lifetime. This young lady here owns it, and she's asked me to come and represent her interests."

"Whatever you pay me," Amy said to Scofield, "Mr. Janeway gets half."

I looked at her sharply and said, "No way."

"I won't even discuss any other arrangement." She looked at Kenney and said, "If it wasn't for this man, I'd've given it away, maybe burned it all in the dump."

"Amy, listen to me. I couldn't take your money, it'd be unethical as hell, and Mr. Kenney knows that."

"Lawyers do it. They take half all the time."

"So do booksellers, but this is different. And you've got two kids to think about."

"Maybe I can help you resolve this little dilemma," Kenney said smoothly. "Let's assume for the moment that you've really got what you think you've got. That remains to be seen, but if it's true, Mr. Janeway would have a legitimate claim for a finder's fee."

I felt my heart turn over at the implication. I had come here chasing five thousand dollars, and now that jackpot was beginning to look small.

"What does that mean?" Amy said.

"It's a principle in bookselling," I told her. "If one dealer steers another onto something good, the first dealer gets a finder's fee." I looked at Kenney and arched an eyebrow. "Usually that's ten percent of the purchase price."

"That doesn't sound like much," Amy said.

"In this case it could be a bit more than that," Kenney said.

I leaned forward and looked in Amy's face. "Trust me, it's fine."

"Let's move on," Kenney said. "Let's assume we're all dealing in good faith and everybody will be taken care of. Where's the material?"

"It's not far from here," I said. "Before we get into it, though, I need to ask you some questions. I'd like to see that book you bought back in the restaurant."

Kenney was immediately on guard. "Why?"

"If you humor me, we'll get through this faster."

"What you're asking goes beyond good faith," Kenney said. "You must know that. You've told us a fascinating story but you haven't shown us anything. I've got to protect our interests. You'd do the same thing if you were me."

I got up and moved around the bed. "Let's you and me take a little walk." I looked at Amy and said, "Sit tight, we'll be right back."

We went down the row to the room at the end. I opened the door and stood outside while he went in alone. When he came out, ten minutes later, his face was pale.

My first reaction to the Grayson *Raven* was disappointment. *It's been oversold as a great book,* I thought as Kenney unwrapped it and I got my first real look. It was half-leather with silk-covered pictorial boards. Grayson had done the front-board design himself: his initial stood out in gilt in the lower corner. The leather had a still-fresh new look to it, but the fabric was much older and very fine, elegant to the touch. In the dim light of the motel room it gave off an appearance of antiquity. The boards were surprisingly thin: you could take it in your hands and flex it, it had a kind of whiplash suppleness, slender and tough like an old fly rod. The endpapers were marbled: the sheets again had the feel of another century. You don't buy paper like that at Woolworth's and you don't buy books like this on chain-store sale tables. The slipcase was cut from the same material that had been used for the boards: the covering that same old silk. A variation of the book's design, but simpler, serving only to suggest, was stamped into the front board of the slipcase. My first reaction passed and I felt the book's deeper excellence setting in. The effect was of something whisked here untouched from another time. Exactly what Grayson intended, I thought.

I opened it carefully while Kenney stood watch. Scofield hadn't moved from his chair, nor had Amy. I leafed to the title page where the date, *1969,* stood out boldly at the bottom. A plastic bag containing some handwritten notes had been laid in there: I picked it up and moved it aside so I could look at the type without breaking my thought. The pertinent letters looked the same. Later they could be blown up and compared microscopically and linked beyond any doubt, if we had to do that. For my purpose, now, I was convinced.

I flipped to the limitation page in the back of the book. It was a lettered copy, *E,* and was signed by Grayson.

E was New Orleans. Laura Warner's book.

"Well," I said to Scofield. "How do you like your book?"

"I like it fine."

"Then you're satisfied with it?"

"I don't know what you mean." His eyes were steady, but there was something about him . . . a wavering, a lingering discontent.

"Are you satisfied you got what you paid for? . . . That's what I'm asking."

"It's the McCoy," Kenney said. "If it's not, I'll take up selling shoes for a living."

"Oh, I don't think you'll have to do that, Mr. Kenney," I said. "But something's wrong and I can't help wondering what."

They didn't say anything. Kenney moved away to the table and poured himself another drink.

"On the phone you told me something," I said. "You said Scofield had touched the book and held it in his hands."

I looked at Scofield. "What I seem to be hearing in all this silence is that this is not the book."

"It's not the one I saw," Scofield said. "I don't know what this is. It may be some early state or a variant, maybe some experiment that Grayson meant to destroy and never did."

Kenney sipped his drink. "It's a little disturbing because we know that Grayson didn't do lettered books."

"So the hunt goes on," I said with a sly grin.

Scofield's eyes lit up. This was what kept him alive as he headed into his seventh decade. The hunt, the quest, that same hot greed that sent Cortez packing through steamy jungles to plunder the Aztecs.

I fingered the plastic bag.

"That's just some ephemera we found between the pages," Kenney said.

I opened the bag and looked at the notes. One was from Laura Warner, an enigma unless you knew how to read it. *Pyotr,* she had written, *don't you dare scold me for teasing you when you yourself tease so. It does please me that you can laugh at yourself now. Was this a test to see if I'd notice? How could you doubt one who hangs on your every word? I'm returning your little trick, lovely though it is, and I await the real book with joyful anticipation.*

348

None of us rehashed the words, though the last line hung heavy in the room. I opened the second note, a single line scratched out on notebook paper. *Hang on to this for me, it'll probably be worth some money. Nola.*

"What do you make of it?" I said.

"Obviously it's passed through several hands," Kenney said. "People do leave things in books."

I turned the pages looking for the poem "Annabel Lee." I found it quickly, with the misspelled word again misspelled.

Kenney had noticed it too. "Strange, isn't it?"

I held the page between my fingers and felt the paper. I thought of something Huggins had said: there's no such thing as a perfect book. If you look with a keen eye, you can always find something. I pressed the page flat against the others and saw that the top edge trim was slightly uneven. There's always something.

"Just a few more things and we can get started," I said. "I know you boys are dying to get into this stuff, but you have to help me a little first."

"What do you want?" Scofield said.

"I want to know everything that happened when you saw that other *Raven* and held it in your hands. I want to know when it happened, how, where, who was involved, and what happened after that. And I want to know about Pruitt and where he came from."

"I don't understand what any of this has to do with you."

"I've got a hunt of my own going, Mr. Scofield. I'm hunting a killer and I've got a hunch you boys are sitting on the answers I've been looking for."

48

Twelve years ago, Pruitt had been a hired gun for Scofield Industries. He was a roving troubleshooter whose job took him regularly into fifteen states, the District of Columbia, Europe, South America, and the Far East. Within the company he was known as the Hoo-Man, an inside joke that had two cutting edges. *HOO* was short for his unofficial title, head of operations, but in private memos that floated between department heads it was often spelled *WHO*. Pruitt knew who to see, who to avoid, who would bend, who would bribe. In third-world countries, Scofield said without apology, bribery was a way of life. If you wanted to do business in Mexico, it was grease that got you through the doors. You could play the same game in the Philippines, as long as you played by the Filipino rule book.

The remarkable thing about Pruitt was his ability to function in foreign countries without a smattering of language. There were always translators, and Pruitt knew who to ask and how to ask it. He was fluent in a universal tongue, the whole of which derived from half a dozen root words.

Love and hate. Sex. Life and death. Fear. Money and politics.

The stuff that gets you where you want to go, in far-flung places that only seem different from the town you grew up in. A military junta has a familiar look to a guy who's gone before a mom-and-pop city council in Ohio, asking for a liquor license.

Grease rules the day, from Alabama to Argentina.

This was a big job and Pruitt was good at it. He was always at the top of his game when the specs called for double-dealing and mischief. He was a shadow man whose best work could never be preplanned or monitored. He was judged strictly on the big result, success, while the boss insulated himself in a glass tower high over Melrose Avenue, never to know the particulars of how a deal had been set up.

"I wasn't supposed to know these things," Scofield said. "But I didn't get where I am by not knowing what's going on. I have a remarkable set of ears and I learned sixty years ago how to split my concentration."

Pruitt had witnessed Scofield's Grayson fetish from the beginning. He watched it sprout like Jack's beanstalk, exploding in a passion that was almost sexual. Pruitt knew, without ever understanding that attraction himself, that this spelled money.

With cool eyes he saw Scofield's collection outstrip itself ten times during the first year. By the end of year two it resembled a small library, with the end nowhere in sight. Scofield was no green kid, to burn bright and burn out when his whim of the day withered and left him dry. Scofield knew what he wanted for the rest of his life. He was a serious player in the Grayson game. Pruitt may have been the first of the Scofield associates to understand the old man's real goal: to be not just a player but the only player.

By the middle of the third year, Scofield had acquired many of the choice one-of-a-kind items that push their owners into paranoia. He had moved the collection from the office to his mansion in the

Hollywood hills, where it was given an entire room in a wing on the second floor. Scofield was nervous. He summoned his security people, discussed plans for a new system, impregnable, state-of-the-art. Pruitt, who was expert in such things, was brought in to consult and was there to help supervise the installation.

Thus sealed in artificial safety, Scofield breathed easier. But no system is better than the men who create it.

Pruitt waited and watched, biding his time.

"That year I began buying books from Morrice and Murdock in Seattle," Scofield said. "My dealings were all with Murdock, who was then considered the country's leading dealer in Grayson books."

It was the year of the Morrice and Murdock break-up, when Murdock stumbled out on his own in an alcoholic stupor. "He still had a lot of books," Scofield said, "things he had hoarded over the years. But he was cagey, difficult. He knew Grayson was on an upward spiral, but the books were his ace in the hole. He also knew that I was the market: if I happened to die or lose interest, it would stabilize and Grayson would settle into his natural level, still upward bound but at a much slower rate. Murdock wanted to make all he could on every book, but even then he was afraid of selling. No matter what I paid him, he seemed to go through it at an unbelievable clip.

"He was the kind of man who would promise the moon and give you just enough real moonbeams that you couldn't help believing him. He talked of fabulous things, hidden in places only he knew about, and all that time he dribbled out his books one or two at a time. I bought everything he showed me and paid what he asked. I knew the day was coming when he'd get down to brass tacks and I'd see what he really had. I've had experience with alcoholics. Eventually they lose everything."

In the fourth year the big break came. Murdock called, claiming to have a client who owned the only copy of Darryl Grayson's last book.

But the deal had to be handled with tenterhooks. The woman was extremely nervous. She would only meet with Scofield under mysterious conditions, in a place of her choosing, with her identity fully protected.

"Did you ever find out," I asked, "why this was?"

"It was fairly obvious to me," Scofield said, "but Murdock explained it later. His client knew Darryl Grayson personally. They had had an intimate relationship. She had been a married woman then, still was, and if any of this came out, her marriage might be jeopardized."

"Did you buy that?"

"Why not, it was perfectly feasible. Have you read the Aandahl biography on the Graysons?"

I nodded.

"Then you know how Grayson was with women. The fact that a pretty young woman was married to someone else wouldn't have slowed him up much. She wouldn't have been the first woman to have carried on with Grayson while she was married to someone else. And Grayson was known to have given his women presents—books, notes, charts . . . mementos of completed projects. It was part of the pleasure he took in his work, to give out valuable pieces of it after the main work was finished. Once a project was done, Grayson wasn't much for keeping the records or hanging on to his dummy copies. For years it's been assumed that these were all destroyed, but I've never been convinced of that."

"So what happened?"

"We flew to Seattle."

"Who is we?" I looked at Kenney. "You?"

Kenney shook his head. "I hadn't been hired yet."

"I took Mr. Pruitt," Scofield said.

"Surely not," I said in real dismay.

"There was no reason to doubt him then."

"But what purpose did he serve?"

"He was what he always was: a bodyguard. I learned long ago that it pays to have such men with you. When you've got money, and that fact is generally known, you get accosted by all kinds of people."

"But you had nobody with you to function as an expert . . . nobody like Kenney?"

"Murdock was my expert. He had already had one meeting with this woman and had examined the book himself. There was no doubt in his mind what it was."

I didn't point out that the ax Murdock was grinding would've given Paul Bunyan a hernia. It wouldn't help to beat that horse now.

"So you took Pruitt," I said. "What happened when you got there?"

"Murdock met us at the airport and took us straight to the meeting place. I wasn't at my best: I'm prone to colds and flu, and I felt I was coming down with something. The weather was bad: I remember it was raining."

"What else does it ever do in this town?"

"We went to the place she had picked out, a restaurant downtown. She wanted to meet in a public place, probably for her own protection. Murdock had reserved a table in a far corner, where she'd told him to go. It was dark back there, but that's how she wanted it. We did it her way . . . everything, her way."

He sipped his drink, gave a little cough. "She was late. We waited half an hour, maybe more. Murdock and I had little to talk about. It seemed like a very long wait, and I was not feeling well."

"Where was Pruitt all this time?"

"Posted at the door, up front."

"So when she finally did get there . . ."

"She had to walk right past him."

"And he'd have seen her."

"But not to recognize. She wore a veil . . . black coat, black hat . . . and a deep red dress. The veil did a good job. I never saw her face and neither did Murdock. With the veil, and the darkness at that table, she could've been anyone."

"Did she bring the book?"

"Oh, yes." He trembled at the memory of it. "It was superb . . . magnificent . . . completely lovely. Beyond any doubt, Grayson's masterpiece."

"You could tell all this in the dark?"

"Murdock had come prepared. He had a small penlight and we examined the book with that. You can't be sure under conditions like that, but there we were. I still didn't know what she wanted. She didn't seem to know either. She seemed in dire financial need one moment and unconcerned the next, as if her two greatest fears were selling the book and losing the deal we had come there to make. The ball was in my court: I felt I had to do something or risk losing it. I had brought some cash—not much, about twenty thousand dollars in thousand-dollar bills. I offered her this for the opportunity to examine the book for one week. The money would be hers to keep regardless of what we finally decided to do. We would sign a paper to that effect, handwritten by me and witnessed by Murdock. In exactly one week we'd meet back at that same restaurant. If the book passed muster, she would be paid an additional fifty thousand. Her reaction was palpable: it was more than she'd dreamed . . . she took it, and I felt I was home free."

The room was quiet. Kenney stood back like a piece of furniture. Amy sat on the edge of her chair. I held fast to Scofield's pale eyes.

"So you had the book," I said. "Then what?"

"We flew back to Los Angeles with it. I wrote Murdock a check for his work, and at that point I decided to have some independent appraisers fly in and look at it. I called Harold Brenner in New York."

He looked at me expectantly. I had heard the name, had seen Brenner's ads in *AB*, but I had never had any dealings with the man. Kenney said, "Brenner's one of the best men in the country on modern small-press books."

"But Brenner couldn't come out till the end of the week," said Scofield. "This would still leave us time to have the book examined and get back to Seattle for our meeting with the woman in red, early the following week. Then I got sick—whatever I had caught in Seattle got dangerously worse, and on my second day home I was hospitalized as a precaution. That night my house was burglarized. My choice Grayson pieces were taken."

"Including *The Raven*, I'm sure," I said. "How long did it take you to realize that Pruitt was behind it?"

"The police were surprisingly efficient. Pruitt had been out playing cards that night: four other men would swear that the game had gone on till dawn and he'd only left the room once or twice to use the facility. But from the start, one of the detectives knew it was an inside job. How could it be anything else? . . . Who else would know how to defeat the system and get in so easily? The big problem was proving it . . . they had to catch the perpetrator and make him talk. Within forty-eight hours they had questioned everyone remotely connected with the installation of the security system, including all of Pruitt's local cronies. Early on the third day they made an arrest, a petty hoodlum named Larson, who had known Pruitt for years. When he was picked up, he still had one of the break-in tools in his possession."

I gave a dry little laugh. Even after my long police career, the stupidity of some criminals amazes me. This is why the jails are full.

"It was a screwdriver," Scofield said. "One of those extra blades that comes on a utility knife, you know, a six-tools-in-one instrument. He had used it to break open the bookshelf locks. This was easy: once he'd gotten into the house, then into the library, breaking open the cabinets themselves was relatively simple— he just wedged his screwdriver into the metal lock and pried it open. But it left a scrape mark, which was identical to the sample police made later with the same tool. He also left a partial heelprint in the garden outside the house. His heel fit it perfectly. We had just fertilized that flowerbed, and a chemical residue was found in the nail holes of his heels. I was getting that fertilizer from Germany, it wasn't yet widely available in the United States, so the odds of finding that precise mix of ingredients in any other garden would have been quite long. We didn't even have the analysis back from the crime lab yet, but Mr. Larson—and more to the point, Mr. Pruitt—must have known what it would show. Larson was a two-time loser who was looking at a long trip up the river. His incentive to deal was getting better by the hour."

"To give them Pruitt's head on a platter."

"You could put it that way."

"I can almost guess the rest."

He nodded. "Suddenly my attorney got a call from Larson's lawyer . . . Larson's *new* lawyer. We were told that full restitution might be made if the case could be discreetly dropped."

"I'll bet the cops loved you for that."

"The detective who had made this case was not thrilled, to say the least. He fumed and yelled and said this was not my call to make."

"But he soon learned better, didn't he? Grease runs the world in L.A. too."

"You've got to understand something. This was never said, but there was a strong implication that if I didn't agree right then, on the spot, my books might end up in the Pacific Ocean. What was I supposed to do? I agreed to have the case dropped, and on Monday morning a note was delivered to my office. If I showed up at a certain corner at a certain time, a taxi would arrive and the driver would have my books in two big boxes. And that's what I did. I never saw Pruitt again until just this morning. End of story."

"Not quite, Mr. Scofield. You left the woman in red hanging from a cliff."

"I flew back to Seattle that same night. There wasn't time to have the book examined by Brenner or anyone else. I went on my gut, as they say, not the first time I've done that in my life. I was still weak from my illness, and the stress of having lost the book for the better part of a week had also taken its toll. I went against my doctor's orders, had to be helped to my chair in the restaurant. She was already there when I arrived. She seemed quite nervous, unsure. But even then I had no idea anything was wrong. We chatted for perhaps three minutes. I had the money all ready for her, in a small valise, just as I brought it to Pruitt this morning. The book and the valise were there on the table between us. I felt so sure . . . and then . . ."

"What?"

"I remember I had a coughing attack . . . a bad one. And it was almost as if that was what finally made her balk and call the deal off. She reached out and picked up the book, not the money, and for a minute I still didn't realize what it meant. Then she apologized and said she just couldn't sell it after all. I tried to persuade her . . . if it was more money she needed . . . but no, it was more like . . ."

I waited, my eyes on his.

"I don't know how to put it exactly . . . an act of conscience maybe. I guess that's it, she was overcome by conscience and guilt. She reached in her purse and brought out the money I'd given her. I made her keep it. I thought maybe it would give me a claim on the book if the day ever came when she'd change her mind again."

He looked around from face to face. "Then she walked out. We never heard from her again."

No one said anything for a long moment.

"Just like Dillinger," I said.

None of them seemed to know what I was talking about.

"You and John Dillinger," I said. "Both laid low by a woman in red."

49

I left them there, Kenney and Scofield to their work and Amy watching them from a chair near the door. I drove into North Bend alone. I had fish to fry.

This is where it all happens, I thought: it doesn't have anything to do with Baltimore or Phoenix or even Seattle except that those cases all spun out of here. I was thinking of Grayson, doing the work he

loved without having to compete with his own fame
and glory. We do get older: sometimes we even get
wiser. Fame and glory don't mean as much when
we're fifty, when they're finally within reach, as they
did when we could only dream about them at twenty.

The gate was locked at the Rigby place so I went on
past to Snoqualmie. Fingers of sunlight led the way,
beaming down through pockets of mist that wafted
across both towns. The area bustled with commerce
in the middle of the afternoon. Tourists drifted along
the avenue, going or coming to or from the waterfall.
A mailman moved along the block, stopping in each
store. Near a corner a team of glaziers was busy
replacing a broken storefront.

I drove past Smoky Joe's Tavern and turned a
corner, pulling up at the curb. Archie Moon's printshop was dark and locked. I got out and went to the
door, cupped my hands, and peeped through the
glass. Somewhere back in the shop a faint light shone,
but I rapped on the glass and no one came.

"I think she's gone for the day," a voice said.

I turned and said hello to the mailman.

"If you're looking for Carrie, she usually takes half
a day off on Tuesdays," he said.

"Actually, I'm looking for Archie."

"Carrie can tell you where he's at: she rides herd on
him like a mother hen. But you'll have to catch her
tomorrow."

I thanked him and got back in the car. I watched
him sort some mail and drop it through the front-
door slot. Then he moved on down the street and I
drove out of town, on to Selena Harper's house.

Things were soon looking up. Trish was sitting on
the front porch steps when I turned into the yard.

"I figured you'd turn up here," she said. "The only
hard part was finding this place. And psyching myself
up for a long wait."

360

I wanted to hear all about the other theaters of war, about Pruitt and the cops and all that had happened since I'd seen her five hours ago. But her mood was cool, almost hostile as she watched me come toward her.

"Sorry I had to run out on you like that. Things got kinda hectic."

"Didn't they though," she said, unforgiving. "You're quite an act, Janeway. But I can't say I wasn't warned."

She cocked her head to one side, showing a long bruise under her left eye. "Pretty, huh?"

"What happened to you?"

"Think about it a minute. You're a bright boy, you'll figure it out."

I thought about it and came up with nothing.

"You were trying to turn Pruitt into next week's dog food. I grabbed you around the neck. Next thing I knew I was flat on my back in the mud."

"Wait a minute, hold it. Play that back again."

"You slugged me, you son of a bitch."

I was, for once in my life, speechless.

"Wanna hear it again?"

"No . . . I really don't think I do."

"Do you know what I did to the last man who tried to raise a hand to me?"

"I've got a feeling I'm about to find out."

"Think of a hot-oil enema and maybe you can relate to it."

"Ayee." Beyond that I didn't dare laugh. I tried to reach out to her, but she looked at my hand the way you'd look at a spittoon.

"Come on, Trish."

She stared off at the graying sky.

"Come on."

She didn't move.

"Come on. Please."

"Please what?"

"Get up, tell me it's okay, and let's get on with it."

"Is that the full and complete text of your apology? Now I know why you're so successful with women."

"I am sorry. I really am."

She didn't respond, so I said it again. "I'm sorry."

"How sorry are you?"

"I don't know. How sorry do you want me to be?"

"I want you to do something for me."

I didn't say anything. I seemed to know what she wanted.

She gripped my wrist and I pulled her up. She smoothed her skirt with her free hand and said, "I want you to go in and talk to Quintana."

I moved on past her to the top of the porch.

"I'm serious about that," she said, losing no ground behind me.

I turned and she was right there, so close we bumped together.

"He's gonna treat you right. But you've got to do it now."

I unlocked the front door and stood aside so she could go in first. The house smelled musty and looked golden and gray. A light rain had begun, with the sun still shining off to the west, the dark places broken by splashes of streaky sunlight. She came in reluctantly, like an infidel desecrating a holy place, and I followed her on through the front room toward the kitchen. She stopped for a moment, seemed to be listening for something, then turned and looked at me across a shaft of watery yellow haze. "Am I imagining this," she said, "or is something happening between us?" The question was sudden and improbable, infusing the air with erotic tension. I thought of the midnight supper we had had and how easily she had done the impossible, taken Rita's place at the other end of the table. "It does seem to be," I said. But I didn't yet know the shape it might take or where it might go from here. She lived in Seattle and I lived in Denver, and neither of us had had time to give it much thought.

She looked away, into the clutter of the kitchen. I came up behind her, close enough to touch. But she was not a woman you did that to until you were very sure.

She sensed me there behind her, took a half-step back, and pressed herself lightly against me.

I put an arm around her, then the other. She leaned her head back and I hugged her a little tighter.

"Something's certainly happening," she said. "I know *that*'s not my imagination."

"In Rome they had a term for it."

"Lustus profundus," she said, stealing it.

"The next best thing to a chariot race."

She laughed and pulled herself away, moving across the room. "God, I don't know what to do with you. I wish I knew."

"Whatever you want. It's not that complicated. I don't come with a Japanese instructional booklet."

She took a long breath. "I've been celibate almost two years."

"I can't imagine why. It can only be by choice."

"I got hurt. I mean really burned. I swore off men. And meant it, too, until . . ."

She blushed. Her skin looked hot.

"I don't know what I want to do," she said.

"But, see, you don't have to know. You can figure it out in your own good time. Nobody's pushing you."

"Now that I'm over here," she said, and we both laughed.

She asked where the Grayson stuff was and I led her back to the stairs and up to the loft. I crawled up into the room and reached back for her. We clasped hands and I helped her up. It was all as I'd left it, the two remaining rows separated by a three-foot gap and draped by a sheet of clear polyethylene. I walked out on the plastic and held up my hands like Moses going through the Red Sea.

Behind me, she said, "Who the hell am I kidding?"

When I turned, she had pulled her blouse out of her skirt and had taken loose the top buttons.

"So what do you think?" she said brightly. "Is that plastic cold?"

50

I've always hated plastic, the symbol of everything phony in the world.

Not anymore.

It was hot and quick, intense. We were both long overdue.

I buried my face in her hair, loving her, and she clawed the plastic down and sealed us inside it. We slipped around like a pair of peeled avocados twisted together in Saran Wrap.

Then we lay on top and cooled off, and in a while, when she was ready, she told me about Pruitt. They had parked him in the Pierce County Jail on a hold order from Seattle. Quintana would be sending some-one down, maybe as early as tonight, to pick him up. Trish was vague on the possible charges. What Quin-tana wanted now was to talk to him and see how his story compared with the version they had gotten out of the kid, Bobby John Dalton. "I had a long talk with

Quintana on the telephone. He actually talked to me.
I must be living right."

"Cops tend to do that when they think you know
more than they do."

"He seemed almost human. I got some great background out of him, off the record."

"What did he tell you?"

"Off the record. That means you tell no one without
my permission, under penalty of death."

Sure, I said: I could play her reporter game.

"Bobby's version of that night remained constant
through two days of questioning. You broke his jaw,
by the way—the cops had to take his statement
through clenched teeth. He's eating through a straw,
which is hard work for a meat eater."

"I'll send him a get-well card."

"Bobby and Carmichael took the Rigby girl to
Carmichael's house. That's just off Aurora Avenue,
not far from downtown. By the time Pruitt got there
Rigby had been trussed up, gagged, and stashed in a
room off the kitchen. There was an argument over
what to do with her. Carmichael was worried about
Pruitt—he had this sudden fear that Pruitt might go
too far and hurt her if she didn't come up with the
book. I take it Pruitt doesn't always know when to
stop once he gets started."

I thought of Slater's battered face and told her
Carmichael had good reason to worry. "Where was
Bobby in all of this?"

"By then he was hurting so bad he wasn't worrying
about anybody but himself. Carmichael was the one
sweating it. If Rigby was going to come to any real
harm, Carmichael didn't want to know about it—and
he sure didn't want it happening there in his house.
But he couldn't stand up to Pruitt. At one point Pruitt
lost his temper and knocked Carmichael back into the
kitchen table and broke off one of the legs. Pruitt

yelled at him and said he was worse than Slater. If it
hadn't been for Slater, he'd have taken the girl last
week and they'd have the book by now."

"Which is probably true."

"Pruitt went into the room with Rigby alone. There
wasn't a sound, to hear Bobby tell it. He said it was
spooky, the two of them standing in the dead silence
looking at each other and not knowing what was
happening in the other room. Then Pruitt came out
and said he was going to get the book."

"He scared it out of her. He was her bogeyman,
Slater said. I don't know why."

"Maybe why's not important. It was in the bus
station, in a locker. She had put it there the first day
she got to town."

I gave a little laugh and shook my head.

"That's about it. Pruitt told Carmichael to take
Rigby on up to his house, he'd be along himself as
soon as he could get downtown and get the book.
Then he'd settle up with them and they could both go
to hell. Bobby took off for the nearest emergency
room, and that's the last he saw or heard of them till
he read about Carmichael in the newspaper."

"We can finish the story ourselves from there.
Carmichael took Eleanor on to Pruitt's alone. Olga
was already dead in the house and the killer was still
inside waiting. The only thing about it that I can't
believe is that Quintana would tell it all to you."

"He wants you to come in."

"He's moved on in his thinking. He's past Pruitt
now, same as I am. He knows it's not Pruitt and he
knows it's not me. He told you this stuff to send me a
message. This goddamn man is one pretty good cop."

"Go see him, Cliff. Do this for me, please, do it
now, before it gets any worse. Who knows when the
moon will turn and Quintana will start drinking
blood again."

"I'll make you a deal. If I don't wrap this mother up by tomorrow, Quintana can have me. Solemn word of honor."

She lay there weighing it, clearly unhappy.

"I've got to follow this one out, Trish. If I'm wrong, Quintana can have everything I've got and you can come visit me every third Tuesday of the month in the crowbar hotel."

"You're chasing a ghost."

"I'm betting all those deaths were set off by something in those books. Something that humiliated him beyond any imaginable reason. It attacked him in his guts, in his heart, where he lived: it made his life unbearable to imagine them out there for someone else to see. It threatened to destroy the one thing that made life worth living. The Grayson mystique."

"But you're hanging all this on the blind woman."

"It's not just the blind woman, it's far more than that now. We've got the chronology, with the homicides following the Grayson lettering schemes to the point of making no geographic sense. We've got the ashes at Hockman's and Pruitt's, and what do you want to bet there weren't ashes at all the others too? The house in New Orleans caught fire, there were lots of ashes there. We know he didn't go there to burn old newspapers, we know exactly why he was there and what he'd come to burn. Why do I have to work so hard convincing you of this?—it's even in your book, that scene when he wanted to burn those 1949 *Ravens* because of the misspelled word. Now the injury was ten times worse. This was to've been his masterpiece, the book to put that old one to rest at long last. And somehow he messed it up again, and the masterpiece turned to dust. And that offended him so deeply that he couldn't even wait to get those books outside the murder scenes to destroy them. Who else would do that but Grayson himself?"

"He would kill people, you're saying, because of the mistake he'd made."

"No. He kills people because he's a killer. He just didn't know that till he'd done the first one."

This is how it works. You get an idea. Usually you're wrong. But sometimes you're right. In police work, you follow your idea till it pays off or craps out.

One thing leads to another . . .

And suddenly I knew where Eleanor was.

"There's a cabin in the mountains," I said. "She goes there when she wants to be alone."

I kicked into my pants, tore into my shirt, got up, sat on a box, and pulled on my shoes.

"What're you thinking now," Trish asked, "that she's free to come and go?"

"I don't know. But I'm betting that's where she'll be."

"Where is this cabin?"

I stopped short. I didn't know.

"So what do you know about it?"

"Moon's supposed to own it, but they all use it. It's an hour's drive from here."

"Maybe still in King County, though."

"Moon said he built it forty years ago and gradually it's been surrounded by national-forest lands."

"But he still owns it."

"That's the impression I had."

"If it's in his name, I can find it. There's a title company the paper uses when we're doing stories that deal with land. They can search out anything. If I can catch them before quitting time, we can plot it out on a topographical map."

We agreed to coordinate through Amy at the motel. Then we split up, Trish on a fast run back to Seattle, me to Snoqualmie, to stake out Archie Moon's print-shop.

51

I waited but he didn't come. Eventually I headed on over toward North Bend. It was almost six o'clock, almost dark, and almost raining when I drove up to the Rigby place and found the gate open. The sun had gone and the night rolled in from the Cascades, pushing the last flakes of light on to the Pacific. The house looked smaller than I remembered it. Crystal had left the front porch light on, casting the yard in a self-contained kind of glow that was almost subterranean. You got the feeling that divers would come down from the hills, swim around the windows and eaves, and wonder what strange creatures might be living there.

Behind the house the printshop was dark. Beyond that, a stretch of meadow ran out to the woods. For a brief time, perhaps no more than these few moments on this night only, the field caught the last of the day's light in this particular way and spread a silver-blue blanket at the foot of the trees.

Crystal heard me coming and was standing at the door. I clumped up the stairs and she opened the door.

"Well, Janeway, I didn't expect to see you here. You look like an old man."

"I am an old man, and getting older by the minute. Have the cops been back?"

"Just once, that same night. They decided not to

tap the phone. They don't seem as worried about you as they were at first."

"That's good to know. Can we talk?"

"Sure. Come on in."

The house was dark, like the first night I'd seen it, except for the one light coming out of the kitchen down the hall. I went on back like one of the family. She came in behind me and motioned to the table, and I pulled out the same chair I'd sat in earlier.

"Where's your husband?"

"Out in the shop working."

"I didn't see any lights out there, that's why I wondered."

"You can't see the lights when he's in the back room."

She poured coffee from a pot on the counter and offered second-day rolls. They microwaved instantly, she said, and were about as good the day after. I shook my head no and she sat across from me, her face etched with the sadness of the ages. She sipped her coffee, looked at me through her glasses, and said, "What's on your mind?"

"Nola Jean Ryder. We could start with that, go on from there."

Her face didn't change, but I could sense her heartbeat picking up to a pace something like a jackhammer.

"I haven't heard that name in twenty years."

"Really?"

"Well, that woman who wrote the book about Darryl and Richard did want to ask me about her. I couldn't help her much. That's something Gaston and Archie and I never talk about."

"Why not?"

"It wasn't what you'd call a pleasant association. It's something we'd all rather forget."

370

I waited her out.

"Nola Jean was Darryl's . . . I don't exactly know how to put it."

"Huggins called her his whore."

She stared off at the dark window. "So who the hell's Huggins and what does he know about it? Was he there? I only met the man once or twice, years ago, and he didn't seem much interested in Nola Jean then."

"Well, was she a whore?"

"If you mean did she walk the streets and hook for her supper, the answer's no."

"There are all kinds of whores, though."

"Are you talking from experience?"

"You seem to forget, I was a cop. I did my time in vice."

"Of course. You've probably seen whores in their infinite variety, and all in the line of duty. Somehow I don't think you ever met anyone quite like Nola Jean. She was the kind of dark-spirited gal people write books about."

She got up and went to the coffeepot but did not pour. Looking out across the meadow, she said, "She could get men to do anything. I never knew how she did it. The only one she couldn't touch that way was Gaston. She sure tried, but none of it worked. I guess that's why she hated him."

She rinsed out her cup and turned it bottom-up on the counter. Again she stared through the window, past the edge of the printshop to the meadow. She turned her head toward me and said, "This is all ancient history. I don't see what she's got to do with anything today."

"Do you have any idea where she went?"

"No idea at all. Just drifted away, seems to be what everybody thinks."

The room was heavy with the presence of this long-lost woman. Crystal hugged herself as if that would make her warm again.

"I don't think about her anymore." But she looked away. She was not a woman who lied easily.

"I can't even remember what she looked like," she said, trying to shore up one lie with another.

"It shouldn't be this hard. Just think of Eleanor."

She jerked around and smacked her coffee cup into the sink, breaking it. Surprise became anxiety, then dismay, finally despondence.

"How did you know?"

"Saw some old photographs. There's really not much doubt."

"Oh, God." She gave a mighty shiver. "Oh, Jesus Christ."

"Crystal," I said as kindly as I could. "We've got to stop the lies now. Get your husband in here so we can talk it out."

"No! . . . No. We don't talk about these things to Gaston."

"We're gonna have to start. It can't stay buried any longer."

"Oh, don't do that. Please don't do that. Ask me . . . whatever you want, ask me."

"Why would Gaston Rigby raise Nola Jean Ryder's daughter?"

She gave a little cough and took off her glasses. Dabbed at her eyes with trembly hands.

"Crystal . . ."

"Why do I get the feeling you already know these things? You ask the questions but you already know the answers."

"There's only one answer that makes sense. Grayson's her father."

She looked out at the shop and said nothing.

"What did Gaston think when she started to grow

up? When every time you looked in her face you saw this evil woman you all hated?"

"It wasn't like that."

She turned and looked at me straight on, wanting me to believe her.

"Truly," she said, and I did believe her.

"Then tell me how it was."

"I don't know if I can. You'd have to've been part of it, watched them together when she was growing up. She didn't look anything like Nola then, all we could see was Darryl in her face. And Gaston thought the sun rose and set on that child, she just lit up his life. I've never heard that song "You Light Up My Life" without thinking of Gaston and Ellie. He loved her to pieces. Read to her nights, took her over to Seattle to walk along the waterfront. He was so crazy about that child, I actually envied her sometimes. He'd take her walking and later tell me it was like Darryl himself was walking with them. So that's how it was. She's ours but she came from Darryl, the last living part of him. It was like he'd made her, like a book, without any help from any woman, and left her here for us. And what's in a face? I mean, really, who cares what someone looks like? Ellie's really nothing like Nola Jean in any way that counts. She didn't get her heart from her mamma, or her mind . . . we all know where that came from. And when she started to grow up and look like Nola, Gaston didn't seem to notice at all. To him she was Darryl's little girl, and I don't think he ever worried or even stopped to consider who her mother was."

"What about you, Crystal? Did you think about it?"

She didn't want to answer that. She had thought about it plenty. "She's got nothing to do with Nola Jean Ryder anymore. You can't raise a child from the cradle and not love her." She fidgeted with her hands.

"Only two things have mattered in my life—first Gaston, then Eleanor. Anybody who thinks I didn't love that child is just full of it, and they'd better not say it to me. I had her almost from the day she was born. Nola never cared: as soon as Ellie was born, she was out of here, gone on the road with some bum she met down at the tavern. We started thinking of Ellie as ours, right from that first winter. Even when Nola came back here in the spring and took up with Darryl again, she couldn't care less about her daughter. And after Darryl died, she never came back."

We looked hard at each other. I leaned across the table so she couldn't escape my eyes. "I hate to break this to you, Crystal, but you're still lying to me."

Another shock wave rippled across her face. She touched her lips with her fingers and seemed to be holding her breath.

"You keep talking about Darryl Grayson as if he's really dead."

"Of course he's dead. Everybody knows that."

"I think he's alive and well."

"You're crazy."

"I think he's alive and still working after all these years."

She shook her head.

"And you and Rigby and maybe Moon have devoted your lives to his secret. You've created a safe haven where he can do his stuff in peace and seclusion, back there in that shop, in that back room where nobody ever goes."

"You are out of your mind."

"Then I might as well tell you the rest of it, since you feel that way anyway. I think Grayson is obsessed by the idea of his own genius. I think after a while it became all that mattered to him. The mystique, the Grayson legend, the almost religious following that's coming along behind him. I think that's what this case is all about. You tell a guy often enough that he's a god, after a while he starts to believe it. And it led him straight over the edge, till he became as cold-blooded a killer as I've ever seen."

"You must be mad."

"Let me ask you this. Have you ever heard of Otto Murdock?"

She tried to shake her head. I wouldn't let her.

"He's a book dealer, or was, but you know that. He's dead now. Murdered."

"I saw it . . . in the newspaper."

"Ever hear of Joseph Hockman?"

She made a little *no* movement with her head.

"What about Reggie Dressler? . . . Mike Hollingsworth?"

"I don't know what you're talking about."

"What about Laura Warner?"

Nothing from her now. Her face looked like stone.

"They were book collectors. Grayson killed them."

"I want you to leave now," she said numbly.

"You remember your stalker? . . . The guy named Pruitt?"

Her eyes came up and gripped mine. Oh, yes, she remembered Pruitt.

"He'd be dead now too if he hadn't been lucky. Somebody else took the knife that was meant for him."

"Will you leave now?" she said thickly.

"Yeah, I'm finished. And I'm sorry, Crystal, I really am. I liked you all."

I got up from the table. "I suppose you'll tell Grayson what's been said here tonight. I imagine he'll come after me next."

I gave her a last sad look. "Tell him I'm waiting for him."

I walked out.

* * *

375

Down in the yard, where the night was now full, I turned away from the car and went along the path to the printshop. I looked back once, but Crystal was nowhere in sight. I was confident now, strong with faith in my premise. The old bastard was out there somewhere, his return as inevitable as the rain. I remembered the night I'd spent here, squirreled away in the loft, and the constant feeling that some presence was close at hand. Someone downstairs. Someone a room away. Someone walking around the house in the rain at four o'clock in the morning. Bumps in the night. You feel him standing in the shadows behind you, but when you turn to look, he's gone. Cross him, though, and he will find you and cut your heart out.

I stood in the total dark of the printshop door. I put my hand in my pocket and took hold of the gun. Then I pushed open the door and went inside.

I crossed to the inner door. It made a sharp little click as I pushed it in.

"Crystal?"

It was Rigby's voice, somewhere ahead. I stepped into the doorway and saw him, perched on a high steel chair halfway down the long worktable. No one was in the room with him, but that meant nothing. People can be anywhere, for any reason.

"Who's there?"

I came all the way in, keeping both hands in my pockets. My eyes took in the length and breadth of it, from the far window to the locked door on this end that looked like nothing more than a storage room. Then, when I was sure he was alone, I came around the end of the workbench so he could see my face. I felt a chill at having my back to the door.

He took off his glasses and squinted.

"Janeway. Well, gosh."

He'd been doing something there at the table,

working on a sketch of some kind. He pulled open a thin, flat drawer, dropped his work inside, closed and locked it. Then he put one foot down from the chair he sat on and leaned forward into his knee.

"You look different," he said.

"It's this case. It's aged me a lot."

"Case?"

"Yeah, you know. Your missing daughter."

He didn't say anything for a long moment. "These are hard days," he said after a while.

"I'm sure they are. Maybe it's almost over now. You could help . . . answer a few questions maybe?"

"Sure," he said, but he was instantly uneasy. He was not a great talker, I remembered. He was private and sensitive and reluctant to let a stranger see into his heart.

He smiled kindly through his beard and gave it a try. "What do you want to talk about?"

"Grayson."

His smile faded, replaced by that shadow of distress I had seen in him that first night. "That's a long time ago. I don't know what I could tell you that would make any difference today."

I waited, sensing him groping for words. Let him grope it out, I thought.

"I have a hard time with that."

"What about Nola Jean Ryder?"

His eyes narrowed to slits. I never found out what he might have said, because at that moment the outer door slammed open and Crystal screamed, "Gaston!" and I heard her charging through the dark front room.

She threw open the door and vaulted into the back shop.

"Don't say another word!" she yelled at Rigby.

"What's—"

"Shut up! . . . Just . . . *shut up!* Don't tell him anything."

She came toward me. I moved to one side.

"I told you to get out of here."

We circled each other like gladiators. By the time I reached the door, she and Rigby were side by side.

"Don't you come back," Crystal said. "Don't ever come back here."

"I'll be back, Crystal. You can count on it."

I went through the shop with that chill on my neck. The chill stayed with me as I doubled back toward Snoqualmie. I thought it was probably there for the duration.

52

Headlights cut the night as Archie Moon turned out of Railroad Avenue and came to a squeaking stop on the street outside his printshop. For a time he sat there as if lost in thought: then, wearily showing his age, he pulled himself out of the truck's cab and slowly made his way to the front of the building. A key ring dangled from his left hand: with the other hand he fished a pair of glasses out of his shirt pocket, putting them on long enough to fit the key in the lock, turn the knob, and push the door open. He took off the glasses and flipped on the inner light, stepping into the little reception room at the front of the shop. He stopped, bent down, and picked up the mail dropped through the slot by the mailman earlier in the day.

He rifled through his letters with absentminded detachment. Seeing nothing of immediate interest, he tossed the pile on the receptionist's desk and moved on into the back shop.

I got out of the car across the street, where I'd been waiting for more than an hour. I crossed over, opened the door without a noise, and came into the office.

I could hear him moving around beyond the open door. The back shop was dark with only a single light, somewhere, reflecting off black machinery. Shadows leaped up in every direction, like the figures in an antiquarian children's book where everything is drawn in silhouette.

I heard the beep of a telephone machine, then the whir of a tape being rewound. He was playing back his messages, just around the corner, a foot or two from where I stood.

"Archie, it's Ginny. Don't be such a stranger, stranger."

Another beep, another voice. "Bobbie, sweetheart. Call me."

And again. "Mr. Moon, this is Jewell Bledsoe. I've been thinking about that job we discussed. Let's do go ahead. And, yes, I would like to have dinner sometime. Very much. So call me. Tomorrow."

Moon gave a little laugh laced with triumph. "Ah, Jewell," he cried out to the empty room. "Ah, *yeah!*"

He was a busy man with a heavy social docket. He was much like his pal Darryl Grayson that way. In great demand by the ladies.

There was another message on the tape. She didn't identify herself, didn't need to. It was a voice he had heard every day for twenty years.

"Oh, Archie, where are you! Everything's gone crazy, I feel like I'm losing my mind. Call me, please . . . for God's sake, call me!"

He picked up the telephone and punched in a number. Hung up, tried again, hung up, replayed the message.

"Goddammit, honey," he said to the far wall. "How the hell am I supposed to call you if you're over there blabbin' on the goddamn phone?"

He tried again and hung up.

I heard him move. I stepped back to one side, leaning against the receptionist's desk with my left hand flat on some papers. I rolled my eyes around and looked out to the deserted street. My eyes made the full circle and ended up staring down at the desk where my hand was.

At the stack of mail he had thrown there.

At the letter Eleanor had mailed from the Hilton.

I touched the paper, felt the lump of something solid inside. A federal crime to take it: not much time to decide.

"Janeway." He was standing right there, three feet away. "Where'd you come from? You look like you been rode hard and put away wet."

"You got the wet part right." I leaned back from the desk, trying not to be too obvious. "And, yeah, I been rode pretty hard, too."

"How'd you get in here? I didn't hear the door."

"Just walked right in. Saw the light, came in, heard you back there on the phone . . . thought I'd sit on the desk and wait till you're done."

"Half-blind and now I can't hear either. What's on your mind?"

"I've been thinking some about that cabin of yours."

"I guess I told you I'd give you a tour of God's country, didn't I? Can't say I expected you tonight, though."

"Just thought I'd come by and see if the offer's still good."

"Yeah, sure it is. Why wouldn't it be? If you're still around in a few days . . ."

"You get up there much?"

"Not anymore, not like I used to. It's too hard to make a living these days; I gotta work Saturdays and sometimes Sundays and I'm gettin' too damn old and too slow. Two or three times a year is all."

He held his hand up to his eyes. "Let's step on back in the shop. That bright light's playing hell with me."

I followed him around and leaned against the doorjamb, keeping my hands in my pockets and letting my eyes work the room. It was a busy printer's printshop, cluttered with half-finished jobs and the residue of last week's newspaper. Long scraps of newsprint had been ripped out and thrown on the floor. Paper was piled in rolls in the corner, and in stacks on hand trucks and dollies. A fireman's nightmare, you'd have to think. He had a Chandler and Price like Rigby's, a Linotype, and an offset press that took a continuous feed of newsprint from a two-foot roll.

He stood in the shadows a few feet away. "Crystal said you're still trying to find Ellie. Havin' any luck?"

"As a matter of fact, I'm having a helluva time just getting people to talk to me."

"Maybe you're asking the wrong people."

"I don't know, Archie, you'd think the people who're supposed to love her would be knocking me down to help. But everybody seems more interested in pandering to the vanity of a dead man than finding that girl."

This bristled him good. I thought it might.

"Who's everybody? Who the hell are you talking about?"

"Crystal . . . and Rigby."

"Hell, that's easy enough to understand."

"Then make me understand it."

"Why do I smell an attitude here? It oughta be obvious what their problem is, if you came at them the way you just came at me."

"Rigby's relationship with Grayson, you mean."

"Yeah, sure. You don't walk in that house and say anything against Darryl . . . not if you want to come out with your head in one piece. And the same is true over here, by the way, so let's back off on the rhetoric and we'll all be a lot happier."

"And I still don't get my questions answered."

"You got questions, ask 'em. Let the sons of bitches rip."

"Let's start with this one. Do you think Nola Jean Ryder set the fire?"

He rocked back in his tracks. But he kept on moving, trying to cover his surprise by making the sudden movement seem intentional. He climbed up on a high steel chair at the table where the answering machine blinked its red light and looked at me from there, leaning in and out of the shadow.

I wasn't going to ask him again. Let him stew his way through it. Finally the silence got to him and he said, "The fire was an accident."

"Some people don't think so."

"Some people think the world is flat. What do you want me to do about that?"

Who's got an attitude now? I thought. But I said, "Give it a guess."

"Darryl died, that was the end of it. That's my guess. There wasn't any reason for Nola Jean to be here anymore. I doubt she ever stayed in one place more than six months in her life till she came here. Why would she stick around after Darryl died? Everybody here hated her."

"Did you hate her?"

"I never gave her that much thought."

I grunted, the kind of sound that carries a full load of doubt without the bite.

"Look," he said, annoyed that I'd caught him lying. "She was Darryl's woman. That made her off-limits to me, no matter what I might've thought from time to time or how willing she might've been to play around."

"Did she come on to you?"

"That woman would come on to a green banana. Look, I'm having a hard time understanding how any of this old shit's gonna help you find Ellie."

"This sounds like the stone wall going up again, Arch."

"Well, fuck, what do you expect? This stuff hurts to talk about."

"Who does it hurt? Grayson's dead, right? Can't hurt him."

He didn't say anything.

"Who does it hurt? . . . You? . . . Rigby? . . . Crystal?"

"Hurts us all. When you lose somebody like that, it hurts."

"But real people get over it. At least they move on past that raw hurt and get on with life. I'm not saying you forget the guy: maybe you love him till you die. But you don't carry that raw pain on your sleeve for twenty years."

He rocked back, his face in darkness.

"So what's the real story here? Why does Rigby get the shakes every time Grayson's name comes up? Why does Crystal go all protective and clam up like Big Brother's listening? You'd think the man just died yesterday."

"Gaston . . ."

I waited.

"Gaston thought Darryl walked on water. Damn

near literally. Haven't you ever had somebody in your life like that, Janeway?"

I shook my head. "I've got enough trouble with the concept of a real god. Don't ask me to deal with men being gods."

"Then how can you expect to understand it?"

I reached into my jacket where I'd tucked the envelope under my arm. Took out the glossy photograph and held it up in the light so he could see it. "Can you identify the people in this picture?"

He made a show of it. Took the picture and grunted at it. Leaned way back in his steel chair. Put on his glasses, squinted, and finally said, "Well, that's Nola Jean Ryder there in the front with her arm around that fella."

"Are you telling me you don't know the others?"

"I don't seem to recall 'em."

"That's strange, Archie, it really is. Because here's another shot of all of you together. I believe that's you over there in the corner, talking to this fella you say you can't remember."

"I can't remember everybody I ever talked to. This has been a long time ago."

"Try the name Charlie Jeffords. Does it ring a bell now?"

"That's the fella down in New Mexico . . ."

"Whose house Eleanor burgled. Now you've got it. Maybe you see why it bothers me so much, the fact that all of you know exactly who Jeffords was right from the start. The minute she got arrested and the name Jeffords came up, you knew why she went down there and what she was trying to find out. You could've shared that information with me when it might've meant something, last week in court. But for reasons of your own, you all hung pat and let that kid take the fall."

The room simmered with rage. "I'll tell you,

Janeway, you might be thirty years younger than me, but if you keep throwing shit like that around, you and me are gonna tear up this printshop."

"Who was Charlie Jeffords?"

He was still rocking slightly. The steel chair made a faint squeaking noise as he moved back and forth on it.

"Charlie Jeffords," I said.

"Leave it alone."

"Who's the other woman in this picture with Jeffords?—the one standing back there glaring at them from the trees?"

He shrugged.

"I seem to be doing all the work here. Maybe I can figure it out by myself; you can sit there and tell me if I go wrong." I gave the picture a long look. "The first time I saw this, something struck me about these two women. They look too much alike not to be related. They've got the same hairline. They've both got Eleanor's high cheekbones."

He leaned forward and looked at the picture as if such a thing had never occurred to him. "That damn Ryder blood must be some strong shit."

"Keep trying, Archie, maybe you can find somebody you can sell that to. Me, I'm not buying any more. When you've worked in the sausage factory, you try to be careful what brands you buy."

"What do you want?"

"The only thing that's left. Everything."

"I don't think I can help you with that."

"Then I'll tell you. Charlie Jeffords was Darryl Grayson's binder."

He took in a lungful of air through his nose.

"Grayson never wanted that known, did he? That's why you're all so tight about it, you're still protecting the legend, pushing the myth that every book was created from dust by one man only, start to finish.

The mystique feeds on that. Even Huggins can't understand how Grayson could turn them out so fast and so perfect and with so many variants. Well, he had help. That's not a capital crime, the man was human after all. Most of us would be proud of that, being human. But not Grayson."

"I don't think we should talk about this anymore."

"I'm not guessing here, you know. A friend of mine went to Taos to see Jeffords. What do you think she found there? A garage full of binding equipment. Very fine leathers, a bookpress or two . . . do I need to go on? Charlie Jeffords was a bookbinder by trade, right up till last year when he got sick. Jeffords did the binding on every Grayson book that came out of here."

"That's not true."

"Then what is?"

"Darryl did a lot of it . . . a helluva lot. I did some. Gaston did. Richard did, before he started making so much money with his own books. But Charlie was the best . . . him and Gaston. Those two could bind a book you'd want to take home and eat." He leaned forward, slapped his knee, and said, "Ah, shit," with a sigh.

He shook his head, hating it. "You can't take anything away from Darryl just because he turned some of it over to other people at the end. He did *all* the conceptual stuff. The design, the lettering, the layout—that's where the real genius is. And he told all of us how he wanted 'em bound and we did 'em that way to the letter. And he looked 'em over with an eagle eye and tossed back any that weren't right. I'm not saying the binding's not important, it's damn vital, it's the first thing you see when you look at it. But it's a craft, it can be learned. What Darryl did came from some goddamn other place, who knows where. Ain't that what genius is?"

"I guess."

"You know damn well."

"Well, we'll leave it at that. You wanna tell me now who the other woman was?"

"Jonelle."

"And she was . . ."

"Nola Jean's sister."

He got off the bench and I tensed. But he sat back down again, pushed back and forth by restless energy.

"Richard played around with both of 'em at one time or another. Then he brought 'em over here and the trouble started. I guess it appealed to his sense of humor. Two screwed-up sisters and two screwed-up brothers. I remember him saying that one time. Nola thought it was funny as hell."

"Did anybody ever ask Jonelle what became of her sister?"

"She didn't know either. That's what she told the people that investigated the fire. Me, I didn't give a damn. Good riddance, we all thought. Then Jonelle moved away too."

"And she and Jeffords landed in Taos."

"Apparently so."

"And ended up together."

"I guess that proves some damn thing. Fairy tales come true or something. Jonelle always had this crazy lust for Charlie Jeffords. But Nola Jean always took Jonelle's men away from her. It came as natural as breathing. She tortured Charlie Jeffords and drove that poor bastard nuts. Diddled and teased him and never even gave him a good look at it."

The telephone rang. He didn't want to answer it. But we both knew who it was, and he picked it up just as the recording started to kick in.

"Yeah," he said. "Yeah, he's here now."

Then Crystal told him something that made his mouth hang open.

He held the phone away from him, looked at me, and said, "I've got to take this."

"Sure."

"Shut that door but don't go away. We're not done yet."

I stepped back into the front room and closed the door. I couldn't hear anything. Crystal seemed to be doing all the talking.

I looked down at the desk, at Eleanor's letter. Picked it up and put it in my pocket.

What's a little federal crime at this stage of the game, I thought, and I walked out.

I crossed the street and stood in the dark place between buildings. I watched his storefront and I waited. He seemed to be back there a long time. When he did come out, he came slowly. He came to the front door and out onto the sidewalk.

"Janeway," he called up the empty block.

I didn't move.

"Janeway!"

He jumped in his truck and drove away, leaving his door wide open. I let him get well ahead. I wasn't worried. I knew where he was going.

53

*A*rchie, she wrote.

I've done it again. Took one of the books thinking I'd put it back in a day or so. Then got busted and the book's still in my car, wrapped in a towel under the front seat. I know, you've warned me about it, but he never seems to miss them and it brightens my life when I've got one with me. I love them so much. I wish I could love people that way but I can't. The books never disappoint me. They are eternally lovely and true, they've been at the core of my life for as long as I can remember. Even when I'm far away, just knowing they're there can lift me out of the gutter and make me fly again. Just the possibility that he might destroy them fills me with despair. I think I would die if that happened, especially if the cause was some stupid act of my own. So please get the book and put it back in the room, so he won't notice it's gone. Here are my keys so you can get in. Think good thoughts and smile for me. Love ya. Ellie.

There were three keys in the envelope—one for a car, two for more substantial locks. I put them in my pocket, got out of the car, and started across country through the woods.

It was easy going. The ground was damp but hard: the underbrush sparse. I followed my flashlight till the trees began to thin out and a clear beam of moonlight appeared to light the way. I saw the Rigby house in the distance as I approached from the east, moving along the edge of the silver glade. Dark clouds drifted across the moon in wisps, and the meadow seemed to flutter and undulate in the stillness around it. The light from the kitchen window stood out like a beacon, the darkened printshop squatting like a bunker behind it. I stayed at the edge of the trees, skirting the dark wall to blend in with the night. As I walked, the printshop seemed to drift until it slowly covered the light from the window like an eclipse. When the blackout was full, I turned and walked straight across the meadow.

I came up to the back of the shop and eased along the outer wall. The clouds had covered the moon and again the night was full. The glow from the kitchen was a muted sheen at the corner of the shop, a suggestion of radiance from some black hole. I turned the other way, circled the building from the south, and came to the front door at the corner where there was plenty of dark cover.

I was looking into the front yard and, beyond it, down the side of the house. Rigby's truck was gone but Moon's was there at the front steps. The only light anywhere was the one cast out of the kitchen. I slipped along the front of the shop, keeping in shadow as much as I could. A clock had begun ticking in my head, a sense of urgency that drove me on.

I reached the door with the keys in my hand. Fished out the car key and dropped it in my other pocket. The heavy brass key slipped in easily on the first try and the lock snapped free. I put that key away too and stepped inside the shop. The smell of the leadpot, faint but unmistakable, was the evidence that Rigby had been here plying his trade. I flipped up the switch one notch on the flashlight, so it could be flicked on and off at a touch. I flicked it once, satisfied myself that nothing stood between me and the back room: then I locked the front door, crossed the room, and went into Grayson's workshop.

Funny to think of it that way, as Grayson's, though that had been my thought the first time I'd seen it. I knew the back-room lights could not be seen from the house, but it was not a chance I wanted to take. I flicked my light, three quick flashes around the room. Saw the high steel chair where Rigby had been sitting three hours ago and the open space where Crystal and I had squared off as if in battle. Across the room was the door I had noticed with the half-frivolous thought *perhaps it's in there, the answer to everything.*

The padlock was a heavy-duty Yale, the same color as the third key in my hand. I snapped it open, gave a soft push, and the door creaked inward.

It's a wine cellar, was my first thought.

A cool, windowless room, perfect for storing things away from heat and light. But something else, not wine, was aging on those shelves.

Books.

Dozens of books.

Scores . . .

Hundreds . . .

Hundreds!

And they were all *The Raven.*

A Disneyland of *Ravens,* row after row, elegantly bound and perfect-looking, all the same, all different. Some so different they seemed to mock the others for their sameness.

Funny thoughts race through your head.

Eureka!

Dr. Livingstone, I presume . . .

And Stewart Granger, buried alive in that African mountain, crawling into a treasure chamber with a torch over his head and the miracle of discovery on his lips.

King Solomon's Mines!

That's how it felt.

I took down a book and opened it to the title page.

1969.

I looked at another one.

1969.

Another one . . . and another one . . . and another one . . .

1969 . . .

         . . . 1969 . . .

                  . . . 1969 . . .

A year frozen forever, with no misspelled words.

I try not to presume too much in this business. That's how mistakes are made.

But it was probably safe to say I had found the Grayson *Raven.*

54

I couldn't shake the thrill of it, or chase away the faceless man who had made it. I stood at the dark front door, watching the house and not knowing what to do next. Then the second impact hit and I had to go back for another look. The room was different now, transposed in a kind of shivery mystical brew. It was alive and growing, nowhere yet near whatever it was trying to become. Twenty years ago it had been empty. Then the first book came and life began.

But where was it going? When would it end?

I supposed it would end when the artist died and his quest for the perfect book had run its course. Maybe he had even achieved that perfection, reached it a hundred times over, without ever accepting what he'd done.

It would never be good enough. He was mad, crazier than Poe. He had locked himself in mortal self-combat, a war nobody ever wins.

Again I watched the house. A shadow passed the kitchen window, leaping out at the meadow.

A light rain began.

I stood very still but I wasn't alone. Grayson was there. In the air. In the dark. In the rain.

Across the yard I heard the door open. Two shadow figures came out on the porch and I moved over by the hedge, a few feet from where they stood.

"Archie." Her voice was low and full of pain. "How could this happen to us?"

He took her in his arms and hugged her tight.

"Were we so evil?" she said. "Was what we did that wrong?"

"I got no easy answers, honey. We did what seemed best at the time."

Now she cried. She had held it in forever and it came all at once. She sobbed bitterly and Moon patted her shoulders and gave her what comfort he could: "We'll get past it. I'll go find Gaston and bring him back here so we can figure it out together." But she couldn't stop crying and Moon was not a man who could cope with that. Gently he pulled away and turned her around, sending her back to that desolate vigil inside the house. He hurried down the steps and got into the truck, and I stepped behind the hedge and stood there still until his headlights swung past and he was gone.

I hung around for a while: I didn't know why. Crystal was alone now but that wasn't it. She was shaken and vulnerable and I thought I could break her if I wanted to try again. But I didn't move except to step out from the hedge to the corner of the house. In a while the kitchen light went out and the house dropped into a void. Pictures began with color and sound and the case played out, whole and nearly finished, the way they say a drowning man sees his life at the end. A chorus of voices rose out of the past— Richard, Archie, Crystal, Grayson—battling to be heard. I couldn't hear them all, only one broke through. Eleanor the child, growing up as that room grew and the bookman worked in his solitude. She read *The Raven* and read *The Raven* and read *The Raven,* and with each reading her knowledge grew and her wisdom deepened. Her entire understanding of life came from that poem, but it was enough. She heard the bump at the door and looked up from the table where she read *The Raven* by candlelight. *'Tis some visitor,* she muttered, *tapping at my chamber door* . . .

The visitor was me.

She was six years old, what could she know? But her face bore the mark of the bookman: her mother had not yet returned to claim her. I hung there in the doorway, waiting for her statement, some tiny insight that had escaped us all. What she had for me was a sassy question.

Don't you know what a cancel stub is? . . . How long have you been in business?

I trudged across the meadow in a steady rain. I was wet again but I didn't care. I was locked in that book room with Eleanor, caught up in its wonder and mystery. I stopped near the edge of the trees and looked back at the house, invisible now in a darkness bleached white. I wished Crystal would turn on a lamp. A powerful army of ghosts had taken the woods and the rain bore the resonance of their voices. In a while I moved on into the trees. The light from the house never came, but I could follow the bookman's wake without it.

55

The cabin was fifty miles north, far across U.S. 2 near a place called Troublesome Lake. It was a wilderness, the access a graveled road and a dirt road beyond that. "There's no telling what the last five miles is like," Trish said, spreading the map across the front seat. "It shows up here as unimproved. That could be okay or it could be a jeep trail."

She asked about police and I told her what I thought. There might be a sheriff's substation at Skykomish, a hole-in-the-wall office staffed by one overworked deputy who wouldn't move an inch without probable cause. Unless we could lay out a case for him, we were on our own.

Trish was tense and trying too hard to fight it. We both knew I should take it from here alone, but somehow we couldn't get at it. She was my partner, she had earned her stripes, I wasn't about to insult her with macho-man bullshit. I had never had a female partner in my years with the Denver cops. I'd always thought I'd have no problem with it—if a woman was armed and trained and tough, I could put my life in her hands. Trish was not trained and she was unarmed. You never knew about the toughness till the time came, but that was just as true of a man.

It had to be said so I made it short and straight, well within the code. "If you have any doubts about going up there, this is the time to say so. It's your call. But you've got no gun, we don't know what's there . . . nobody would think any less of you."

She gave me a doleful smile. "I'll be fine. I get nervous before anything that might put me on the spot. That's all it is. If something starts, I'll be fine."

She had borrowed a press car equipped with two-way radio to her city desk. She had left a copy of the map, sealed in an envelope, with her night city editor. At least her common sense was alive and kicking. The problem was, the radio might not work at that distance, she said: its effective range was about forty miles, but mountains played hell with the signal and could cause fading at any distance. Once she had called in from Bellingham, a hundred miles north: another time she had barely got through in a thunderstorm from Issaquah. You never knew.

She asked for some last-minute ground rules. "If we find your friend up there, we wrap her up and bring her down. No theatrics, no cowboy heroics, no waiting around for whoever might come. We bring her down. Period, end of story. You go see Quintana and we let the cops take it from there."

Life should be so simple. I said, "Deal," and I hugged her and I truly hoped it would work out that way. She held me tight for another moment. "I'm fine," she said, and that was the end of it. There would be no more said about nerves or rules, no more second-guessing.

She started the car and drove us north on Highway 203.

For about twenty miles we headed away from where we wanted to go. The map showed the cabin off to the northeast, but the road drifted northwest. The entire middle part of the country was mountainous backwoods with no main roads, so we had to go around. We stopped for coffee, took it with us, and pushed on. I wasn't tired: I was running on high octane as the case played out and I was drawn to the end of it. The night had been a revelation. I had broken the problem of the misspelled word after taking another long look at Scofield's Laura Warner book at the motel. One thing leads to another. Once you knew how that had happened, you could make a reach and begin to imagine the rest.

How the fire might have started.

The who and why of the woman in red.

What had happened to Nola Jean Ryder.

What the face of the bookman looked like.

I rode shotgun and let the case play in my head. I ran it like instant replay, freeze-framing, moving the single frames back and forth. I peered at the blurred images and wondered if what I thought I saw was how it had all happened.

The road dipped and wound. The rain beat down heavily.

Somewhere on the drive north, I began to play it for Trish.

"Richard sabotaged his brother's book. I should've seen that long ago. The bitterness between them was obvious in your own book, and there was plenty more in that 'Craven' poem he wrote. There's one line in 'The Craven' that even tells how he did it. 'And when it seemed that none could daunt him, a sepulchre rose up to haunt him.' The line after that is the one I mean. 'Stuck in there as if to taunt him.' That's exactly what he did—came down to the shop, unlocked the plate, scrambled the letters, printed up some pages on Grayson's book stock, then put the plate back the way it was, washed the press, took his jimmied pages, and left. This is a simple operation. A printer could do it in a few minutes.

"Remember how Grayson worked. He was an old-time print man who liked to lay out the whole book, make up all the plates before he printed any of it. This is how he got that fluidity, the ability to change things from one copy to another: he didn't print up five hundred sheets from the same plate, he tinkered and moved stuff throughout the process. And he cast his own type, so he always had plenty even for a big book job. So here they were, Grayson and Rigby, ready to print *The Raven*. They did the five lettered copies. You can imagine the back-and-forth checking and double-checking they went through. No nit was too small to pick—never in the history of the Grayson Press had pages been so thoroughly examined. There must be no flaws, no hairline cracks, not even the slightest ink inconsistency, and—you can be damn sure—no misspelled words. The finished books were examined again. Rigby probably did the final look-over and pronounced them sound. He was the one with the eagle eye—remember you wrote about that, how Grayson had come to count on him to catch any little thing. Boxing and wrapping them was the point of no return. Once those five books were shipped, *The Raven* was for all practical purposes published. This was it, there'd be no calling it back: he was telling the world that this was his best. And he knew he'd never get a third crack at it, he'd look like a fool.

"I don't know how Richard got to the books. I imagine they were right there on an open shelf in the printshop the night before they were shipped. The shop would've been locked, but Richard had a key. His big problem was that Rigby was living in the loft upstairs. Maybe Grayson took Rigby out to celebrate and that's when it was done. Maybe Richard waited till he was sure Rigby was asleep, then came quietly into the shop, lifted the books, took them to his house, and did the job there. It doesn't matter where he did it—the one thing I know now is what he did. He sliced that one page out of each book and bound in his own page. And the misspelled word was misspelled again."

"You make it sound simple."

"It is simple. It's like outpatient day surgery for a world-class doctor. It's even been done for commercial publishers by people a helluva lot less skilled than he was. You cut out the page with a razor, trim the stub back to almost nothing, give the new page a wide bead of glue so the gutter seals tight and the stub won't show at all. I think I could do it myself, now that I know how it was done, and I'm no bookbinder."

"When did you figure this out?"

"Eleanor saved me from buying a book that had been fixed like that. It wasn't uncommon for publishers in the old days to do it. And later, when I examined the book that Scofield had bought from Pruitt, I noticed that the top edge was just a hair crooked. It didn't impress me much at the time, but when I looked at the book again a while ago, it was just that one page that was off. When I looked down at it from the top, I could see the break in the page gathering where the single sheet had been slipped in past the stub. Even when you know it's there, it's not easy to see. He did a damn good job of it and the book is the proof. The whole story is wrapped up in that book—the only surviving copy of the five Grayson *Raven*s.

"Laura Warner's note tells us how the book got back to North Bend. She saw the misspelled word and thought Grayson was joshing her. She should've known better—Grayson didn't kid around, not about this stuff. In St. Louis, Hockman had already seen the mistake and had sent Grayson a letter about it. What would Grayson do when he got such a letter? Stare at it in disbelief for a minute, then get right on the phone to St. Louis. He wanted the book back, but Hockman had had time to think about it. He was a collector first of all, and it had crossed his mind that he might have something unique, maybe some preliminary piece never intended to be released. It was ironic—he had sent the letter wanting Grayson to take the book back, but he ended up refusing to part with it."

"At that point Grayson would go out to his shop. Look at his plate . . ."

"And see what?" I let her think about that for a few seconds. Then I said, "If you were Richard and you wanted to drive your brother crazy, what would you do? I'd wait till the books were shipped, then I'd go back in that shop and change the plate back to the mistake again. Talk about diabolical—you'd have Grayson doubting his sanity. He wouldn't be able to believe his eyes, but it would be right there in front of him. In trying so hard not to make a mistake, he'd made the same old one again. Such things do happen in printing. It's the stuff you think you know that comes back to bite you."

"So then Grayson did what? . . . Went to St. Louis? Killed Hockman?"

"I don't know. I'm not so sure of that anymore."

"Well, somebody did."

"Let's keep following the natural order of things. I think Richard set the fire. One thing leads to another. If Richard did the book, he also did the fire. Whether he knew his brother was passed out drunk in the back room is something we can argue till shrimps learn to whistle. Richard was a screwed-up, pathetic man and everybody knew it. Nobody knew it better than he did. No one has ever made a case that this guy had even one happy day in his whole lousy life. He hated his brother but he loved him too. What he'd done to him had him jumping for joy one minute and despising himself the next. But it was done and you can't undo something like that. He couldn't get it off his conscience—he'd never find the courage to confess. He had wrecked his brother's dream, destroyed his vision, and left his masterpiece in ruins. He'd been planning it for years, probably since Grayson had made the decision to do another *Raven*. We know he was thinking about it at least two years before the fact: his *Craven* notes are dated 1967, and he writes of it then as a fact accomplished. Now he'd done it and he was glad, but in the end he couldn't forgive himself. He cashed his chips, but he still had enough rage to take Grayson's printshop with him."

A small town sprung up on the wet road. I saw a sign for U.S. 2 and she turned right, heading east.

"The story should've ended there," I said, "but the dark parts of it were just beginning. Laura Warner's book had arrived back in North Bend. The sequence of events was tight—the book may've come a day or two either side of the fire, or maybe on the day itself. In any case, the scene at Grayson's was chaotic, and it all centered on this one book. The book arrived and Nola Jean Ryder lifted it and passed it on to her sister for safekeeping. My guess is that Nola got the book before anybody even knew it was there. Then something happened, I don't know what, that caused her to drop off the face of the earth. Hold that thought for a minute. Something happened, we don't know what. And it set our killer off on a chain reaction that's still going on."

"He killed her."

"That's what I think. She was the first victim. That's what made him snap, and he hasn't drawn a sane breath since."

"He killed her," Trish said again. Her voice was a strange mix of certainty and doubt. "Have you got any evidence?"

"Not much, not yet. Nothing you'd want to take into court without a body. But the argument still packs a lot of weight. Turn the question around. What evidence do we have for her being alive? There isn't any. She's been missing twenty years, three times what the law demands for a presumption of death. That seven-year-wait didn't get established in law by itself. When people go missing that long without a

401

trace or a reason, they're almost always dead. Damn few of them ever turn up alive again. Add to this the fact that Nola was self-centered and greedy—you know she'd come back for that book if there was money in it. But her own sister hasn't seen her— Jonelle still had the book, after all, twenty years later. Charlie Jeffords told you Nola'd been there, but that wasn't Nola, it was Eleanor. That's what got him so upset. That's why Jonelle was so upset when Eleanor popped up without any warning on her doorstep. What a shock, huh? There stood Nola Jean in the flesh. The woman who'd always driven Charlie a little crazy, whose memory still does on the bad days. And damn, she hadn't changed a bit."

We stopped at the side of the road and I sat with my eyes closed while Trish looked at the map. I was thinking of the sequence again, probing it at the weak places. Laura Warner sent her book back, but by then the killer was on the road, coming her way. Hockman had mailed his letter from St. Louis, as much as a week earlier. Hockman was already dead and the killer was somewhere between St. Louis and New Orleans, taking the scenic route. The killer arrived in New Orleans after stopovers in Phoenix, Baltimore, and Idaho. He killed Laura Warner but couldn't find her book. So he burned the whole house down, figuring he'd get it that way.

We were moving again: I heard Trish give a nervous little sigh and the car regained its steady rhythm. "Not much further now," she said, and I answered her with a grunt so she'd know I was still among the living. I was thinking of the woman in red, nervous about selling her *Raven,* willing to consider it because of the money but finally backing out in a jittery scene that Scofield would remember as a sudden attack of

402

conscience. And I thought of the Rigby place where all the *Raven*s were, and I thought again how one thing leads to another in this business of trying to figure out who the killers are.

We had stopped. I opened my eyes and saw that she had turned into a long, straight forest road, a mix of mud and gravel that stretched out like a ribbon and gradually faded to nothing. She was looking at me in the glow of the dash, and I had the feeling she was waiting for me to laugh and say the hell with this, let's go back to town and shack up where it's dry and warm. I reached over and squeezed her hand.

"Let's go get her," I said.

Her mouth trembled a little. She put the car in gear and we started into the woods.

56

It was desolate country, the road rutted and water-filled. We banged along at fifteen miles an hour and it seemed too fast, and still we got nowhere. I sat up straight, watching the odometer move by tenths of a mile. The road would run north by northeast for seven miles, I remembered from the map: then we'd come to a fork and the branch we wanted would run along the creek and climb gradually past the lake. The cabin would be in the woods at the top of the rise. Our chances of making it would depend on the condition of the road beyond the fork. Down here the gravel kept it hard, basic and boring, one mile-slice indistinguishable from the next. We would come to a bend, but always the ribbon rolled out again, winnowing into a black wall that kept running away from us. I had a vision of a vast mountain range off to my right, though nothing could be seen past the narrow yellow shaft thrown out by the headlights. We could be anywhere in the world, I thought.

I put an arm over Trish's shoulder and stroked her neck with my finger. She smiled faintly without taking her eyes off the road. I touched her under the left ear and stirred the hair on her neck. She made a kissing gesture and tried to smile again. Her skin felt cool and I noticed a chill in the air. She had started to shiver, perhaps to tremble—I had never thought about the difference until then—but she made no move to turn on the heater, and finally I reached over and did it for her. "Don't pick at me, Janeway, I'm fine." In the same instant she reached up and took my hand, pressed it tightly against her cheek, kissed my knuckles, and held me tight. "Don't mind me," she said. "I'm fine."

Incredibly, we had come just two miles. It seemed we had been on this road to nowhere half the night. The odometer stood still while the clock moved on, flicking its digit to 1:35 in the march toward a gray dawn four hours away. We had already debated the wisdom of coming in the dark, the most significant of the pros and cons being the possibility of getting in close before anyone could see us coming versus groping around in an alien landscape. Best to stay loose, I thought: see what we found when we got there. We could park and wait in the trees if that seemed best. Given my temperament, neither of us could see that happening.

The road had begun to rise gradually out of the

valley and the rain was now little more than a fine mist. The headlights showed a wall of rock rising up from the right shoulder and a sudden drop-off on the left. We came to a short steep stretch, then it leveled off again and the climb went on at its steady upward drift. "I think the lake's over there," Trish said, nodding into the chasm. "The fork's got to be right here somewhere."

We reached it a few minutes later, as the clock turned over at 2:04. Now the tough part would begin. But it wasn't tough at all. The rain ceased to be a factor up here as the road faded into simple ruts on a grassy slope. The grass held the earth firm even in the rain. We could make it, but it was going to be slow going on a road well-pocked with deep holes. The car rocked, sloshed through what seemed like a gully, and then began to climb again. This continued until we crested on a hill. "Probably lovely up here on a sunny day," Trish said. God's country, I thought. I hoped God was home to walk us through it.

"Let's do it," I heard myself say. "Let's get it on."

This was a stupid thing to say and she laughed a little. She said, "Jesus," under her breath, and the name seemed to come up from some ethereal force in the car between us. How did we get here, defying logic, with no viable alternatives in sight? I wanted to get it done now, pull out the stops and get on down the road. But we rocked along at a crawl. It was 2:30 A.M.

Then we were there. I knew it. She knew it. There were no signs posted and no cabins in sight, but something made her stop on the slope and let the car idle for a long moment. "I think we're very close," she said in a voice just above a whisper. The terrain had stiffened in the last hundred yards as if in a last-ditch effort to push us back. We were sitting on a sharp incline, her headlights pointing into the sky. "Careful when you go over the hill," I said. "Better cut your lights and go with the parking lights." She pushed the switch too far and the world plunged into a darkness so black I had nothing in my experience to compare it to. She pulled on the parking lights and the only relief from the oppressive night was that the dashboard light came on and lit up our faces. "Not gonna be able to see a damn thing with these parking lights," she said. But we didn't dare make our final approach any brighter.

"Let's see how the radio's doing," she said.

She lifted the little transmitter off its hook, pressed a button, and said, "Car six to desk, car six to desk."

Static flooded the car.

She sighed and tried again.

Nothing.

"No offense to you, sweetheart," she said, "but I can't remember ever feeling quite this alone."

"Let's get going."

She eased the car over the hump. The road made a severe dip to the right, and I braced against the door with my foot and leaned against her to keep her steady behind the wheel. We straightened out and went into another dip. The floor scraped against the rocks as we straddled deep holes at the bottom. Up we went again, Trish hunched tight over the wheel, fighting shadows and ghosts that hadn't been there before. The parking lights weren't much better than nothing. "God, I can't even see the road now," she said. "I don't know how much longer I can do this."

"Hold it a minute."

She stopped and I told her I was going to get out and lead her along on foot. She didn't like that, but she didn't like this either. I took my flashlight and opened the door and stepped out on a rocky hillside.

Underbrush grew thick on the slope beneath me: I could see an almost impenetrable blanket of it in the faint glow of the parking lights. The rain was steady but light: it didn't bother me at all. I flicked my flashlight and motioned her on, walking slowly three feet ahead. The ground rose again and we took it easy and gradually worked our way to the top.

Something flashed off through the trees. She killed the lights and I felt my way back to the car.

We sat in the dark, listening to the rain drumming lightly on the roof.

"Looks like somebody's home."

It was my voice, rising out of nothing. I moved over next to her and we sat for a while just looking at the light from the cabin.

"Whoever's there keeps late hours," I said.

I put my gun on the seat beside my right leg, along with the flashlight. It was hard to know what to do, to do the wise and right thing. It would be a grope, going up there in the dark, and I couldn't take a chance on using the light. Slip on the rocks and maybe break a leg. But I knew I couldn't sit here till first light either.

Trish was trying the radio again. "Car six to desk."

A broken voice came at us from the dash. ". . . esk . . . ix . . . you . . . ish?"

"Stand by, please." She turned her face and spoke in my ear. "I don't know if he's really reading me. What should I tell him?"

"Whatever you want."

It doesn't matter, I thought grimly. It's up to us.

Correction. It was up to me.

I felt a little sick thinking about my predicament. Trish had no place in this action except to complicate it. Should've seen that, Janeway, and read her the rules accordingly. You see things differently at the bottom of the hill. You play by her rules, bending over to be politically correct, and you bend too far and put your tit in a wringer.

But it wasn't my call anymore because that's when the killer came for us.

57

These things happened in less time than it takes to tell it.

I felt his presence. I knew he was there, and then he was there.

The windshield smashed and shards burst in on us. I heard a clawing sound, someone tearing at the door on the driver's side. I brought up the light and saw a flash of steel, and I killed the light and fell across Trish as two slugs came ripping through the door glass.

The back glass blew out, crumbling into hundreds of little nuggets. I reached behind me and slammed down the lock—just in time, as he grabbed the handle and yanked it hard, rocking the car with his power. Something heavy came down on the roof: the car took a rapid-fire pounding as if some giant had begun battering it with a log. He was kicking at the door with his boots, as if he could smash it in and tear us apart with raw power. I heard the side window break: another kick and it came completely out of its frame, and I knew in seconds he'd have his hand inside grabbing for the lock. I couldn't find my gun—in the scramble on the seat it had fallen somewhere and I didn't have time to fish for it. What I did was instinct: I grabbed the gearshift, jerked it down, and hit the accelerator with my fist. The car bumped down the slope, driverless and blind, clattered off the road, hit a deep hole, and threw us together with a punishing jolt. Trish took the brunt of my weight: her breath went out like a blown tire, and the car careened again and she took another vicious hit. I thought we were going over, but no—there was a tottering sensation and a heavy thud as the wheels came down. I heard the sound of bushes tearing at us: we were plunging through the underbrush, spinning crazily on a quickening downward course. I was going after the brake when the crack-up came—a thud, a crunch, and a shattering stop, flinging me against the floor with Trish on top. I felt a tingle in my legs, and in that moment my great fear was that I had broken my back.

I kicked open the door and slipped out on a carpet of wet grass. I lay there breathing hard, listening for approaching footsteps. I heard Trish move inside the car, a few feet away. "Where are you?" she said thickly, and I shushed her and pulled myself close. I reached back into the car, felt along the seat and down to the floor. I felt her leg, her thigh, her breast, her arm . . . and under the arm, my gun.

"Hold tight," I whispered. "Don't move."

I pulled myself around to the end of the car, facing what I thought was the upslope. Now, you son of a bitch, I muttered. Come now.

Now that I can bite back.

But of course he didn't come, he was too cunning for that. I sat in the rain and waited, guessing he could be anywhere. He could be ten feet away and I'd never know it till too late. This worked two ways—he couldn't see in the dark any better than me, I could

hope, and in any exchange of gunfire my odds would
have to be pretty good. I had been in gunfights and left
two thugs in cold storage: all he'd done was kill
people.

I felt better now. The gun was warm in my hand,
like the willing flesh of an old girlfriend. Sweetheart, I
thought, papa loves you. I looked back where I knew
the open door was: wanted to say something that
would cheer her up but didn't dare. I didn't know
where he'd gone: couldn't risk even a slight bit of
noise that might stand out in the steady drip of the
forest. He'd have to assume I was now armed. He'd
have missed his chance to overpower us and now he
would know—if he knew anything about me—that
I'd had time to get out my piece. If not, it was a big
mark for our side. Maybe he'd even come after us in
that same reckless, frenzied way. Come ahead, Fagan,
I thought—come and get it. I willed him to come and
I waited in the grass like a scorpion. But he wasn't
there.

I felt a great sense of calm now. He had tried and
missed—tough luck for him. He had taken his shot
but I was still here, huddled in the cop mode with my
gun in my hand. I heard something move behind me.
Trish was out of the car, coming on her hands and
knees. I shushed her again, took her in my arm, and
pulled her down against me. I told her it was all right
now, it was going to be fine. I was goddamned
invincible and I wanted her to know it, to help quiet
the desperate fear I thought must be eating her alive.
Then she whispered, "What do you want me to do?"
in a voice so wonderfully calm it pushed me up
another notch, past the cop mode to a place I'd never
been.

It wasn't just me anymore, protecting some helpless
woman. She was my partner again and I drew on her
strength.

"Janeway."

"I'm thinking."

"Well, knock it off."

I made a little laughing sound through my nose and hugged her tight.

Don't get too cocky, I was thinking: don't try to be Doc Savage or Conan the Barbarian. You don't need to be now, she's here with you.

Gotta plan, I thought. Gotta be more than strong, gotta be smart.

Draw him out. Use the environment, whatever the hell it is out there. Bloom where you're planted, in the country of the blind.

See him first and you've got him. Draw him to the place where he thinks you are, then be somewhere else.

H. G. Wells had it right when he lifted that proverb. *In the country of the blind, the one-eyed man is king.*

Light might do it.

Noise might.

I put my mouth against her ear and said, "I'm going back to the car. Keep alert."

I crawled to the door and up to the front seat. Static poured out of the radio, through the open door, and blended into the rain. I wasn't sure yet what I was doing: the first bit of business was to find out what was possible. I needed to see. I took off my jacket to make a shield against the light, then I reached over and turned the light switch back so the dash would light up. A voice came through the radio—"Desk to car six"—and I jumped back against the seat, startled. But the voice broke up and disappeared in the static. I opened the glove compartment. There wasn't much inside—a few papers, the registration, an ownership manual, a screwdriver, some road maps, and a roll of electrical tape. What could I make of that?

The radio said "six" and faded, and I had an idea. I

leaned out and hissed. Trish crawled over and I told her what I was going to do. The static on the radio was now a jumble of voices, low enough that it couldn't be heard much beyond the open door, but the noise was constant. It wouldn't matter, I thought: he wouldn't hear it. I tore one of the road maps apart, wadded up a quarter section, added some spit, and made it into a gummy mass, a spitball about half the size of my fist. It would fit well enough into the slight recesses of the steering wheel spokes where the horn buttons were. I picked up the electrical tape and leaned out into the rain. "Here we go," I said.

I blew the horn. Twice . . . three times.

"Scream," I said, and she screamed my name at the black sky.

I mashed the wadded paper into the horn button and the steady wail began. I whipped the tape tight around it, three, four, five times, and left it dangling. The horn blared away: it would drive a sane man crazy and a crazy man wild. He'd have to come now, I thought: he'd have to.

I took her hand and we moved away from the car.

Carefully . . . one step at a time.

Eight steps . . . ten . . .

Underbrush rose up around us.

"Get down here," I said. "Lie flat under those bushes and don't move."

She dropped to the ground and was gone. I stood still and waited.

I tried to remember what little I had seen of the terrain. The car had tilted right as it clattered down the slope. We had gone a hundred yards, I guessed, which would put the cabin somewhere to the left and above us.

The horn filled the night with its brassy music. I felt as if I were standing on top of it, it was that loud.

Off in the distance a light flashed. It flicked on and off twice. I said, "Uh-huh," and waited. He was gambling, hoping he could find his way without tipping his hand. You lose, I thought. His flashlight came on again, swung in a quick semicircle, dropped briefly down the slope, and off again. I now knew that the road was about fifteen feet above me, that the ground was steeper than I'd thought, and he was forty to sixty yards away, moving along to my right. He wouldn't dare use the light again, I thought, but almost at once he gave it another tiny flick, as if he'd seen something he couldn't quite believe the first time. Yes, he had caught a piece of the car in that swing past it: he saw it now, and if he raised the beam by a few degrees, he'd see me too, standing by the trees waiting. If he moved the light at all, I'd go for him right from here. Knock him down and he's done for . . . give him a flesh wound, a broken arm, a ventilated liver. On the firing range I'd been a killer—shooting from the hip, in a stance, close up or distant, it didn't matter. I could empty a gun in three seconds and fill the red with holes. It's an instinct some cops have and sometimes it saves your life.

I should've taken him then, but the light was gone now and it didn't come back. Minutes passed and I battled my impatience. Think of the hundred and one stakeouts in a long career: waiting in a blowing snow for fifteen hours and not being bothered by it. I had learned how to wait: I'd learned the virtue of patience—and had unlearned it all in minutes. I saw the bookman's face pass before me in the dark.

Rigby.

Who else fit the Grayson pattern all up and down the line?

Who did Grayson count on? Who would be this destroyed by a misspelled word? Who would take that failure so personally and torture himself and take up the sword against those who'd tarnish Grayson's memory?

Who had the skills and the single-mindedness to spend the rest of his days trying to finish Grayson's book?

He had the greatest hands, Moon had said. He had the finest eye.

Rigby.

That's what happens when you make gods out of men, I thought.

And now he was here. I felt my hand tremble slightly, uncharacteristically. Chalk it up to the dark: I still couldn't see him and I strained against the night, trying not to make that big fatal mistake. We were a few feet apart, microorganisms, deadly enemies who would kill each other if we happened to bump while floating through the soupy ether that made up our world.

There wasn't a sound. The blaring horn had ceased to exist. It can happen that way when it's constant, no matter how loud it gets.

I was betting my life on a shot in the dark.

Be right with your own god, I thought, and I opened fire.

In the half-second before the gun went off I had a flash of crushing doubt. Too late, I wanted to call it back. Instead I pumped off another one, took his return fire, and the slope erupted in a god-awful battle in the dark. I went down—didn't remember falling, didn't know if I'd been shot or had slipped on the wet slope. Something hard had hit my head. I rolled over on my back, only then realizing that my gun was gone and he was still on his feet. There was light now, bobbing above me. I saw his shoes, heard the snap of the gun as the pin fell on an empty chamber, saw the log he'd hit me with clutched in his other hand. He dropped the gun and got up the knife. I tried to roll to my feet but couldn't quite make it. Got to one knee and fell over, like a woozy fighter down for a nine count. He loomed over me, then something came out of the dark and hit him.

Trish.

It wasn't much of a fight. The light dropped in the grass and they struggled above it. He knifed her hard in the belly. She grabbed herself, spun away, and, incredibly, spun around and came at him again. He knifed her in the side and this time she went down.

She had bought me a long count, fifteen seconds.

I was up on one knee with the gun in my hand, and I blew his heart out.

58

I carried her to the car and put her down on the seat.

Don't die, I thought. Please don't die.

I worked her clothes off . . .

Gently.

Everything was blood-soaked. The frontal wound was the scary one. The knife had gone in to the hilt, just at the hairline above her crotch. Her navel was a pool of blood, like an eight-ounce can of tomato paste. The cut was raw and ugly. I dabbed at it and tried to push the blood back, but it welled up again like a pot flowing over. I covered it with my hand. The last thing I worried about, now, was infection.

Blood oozed between my fingers and kept coming. She was going to die, right here on this car seat, and there wasn't a thing on earth I could do to save her.

There wasn't anything to be done. Even if I could get the hole plugged, she'd be hemorrhaging inside. I was watching her die.

She smiled. Her face had a peaceful, dreamy look.

"Tam-pons," she said. "Almost that . . . time of month."

Tampons. Jesus Christ, tampons.

I got them out of her bag. The package looked small in my hand. It was what it was.

I tore the electrical tape off the steering wheel. There wasn't enough left to go around her. But I had my belt, my shirt . . .

I ripped off the shirt and rigged her up the best I could. I cut a hole in my belt so it would fit her tight, and I pulled the shirt up between her legs, tying it to the belt front and back. It would be like a crude chastity belt and would work about as well as that ancient device ever had.

I shoved the tampons in and it took the whole package to stop the flow in the front. The wound on the side had sliced through her flesh, but the entire layer was still hanging there. I laid it back and drew the shirt tighter so it would hold.

A work of art.

A waste of time and we both knew it.

Then I got on the radio. I called nonstop for two hours and had no idea if I was getting through.

I held her hand and told her to be brave. These were just words. Who the hell was I to tell her about bravery?

She slipped into a deep sleep.

I was losing her.

Dawn was breaking as the helicopter came over the trees.

Now the medics had it. I had to get away from there: my guts were in turmoil.

I climbed the hill. The cabin rose up suddenly, the lights still blazing. A woman stood in shadow at the window.

Eleanor.

I clumped up the steps and walked in. One look at my face and she knew. She cried and I held her and I looked down the slope with its aura of death and its red lights flashing.

In a while one of the medics came up the hill. "They're taking her off now," he said. "She's awake and she wants to see you."

I asked him to sit with Eleanor while I climbed back down the slope. Someone had covered Rigby with a blanket and I stepped around him on my way to the copter. I got inside and sat on the floor beside the cot where Trish lay pale as death.

She didn't say anything, just held my hand a moment. "We gotta get moving," the medic said, and his eyes met mine and I knew what he meant. It was touch and go.

"You boys ride her easy," I said. "She's got a bigger heart than all of us put together."

I met the second medic coming down the hill. I stood on the bluff and watched the copter rise slowly over the woods. In the distance I could see police cars coming.

I went into the cabin to look for Eleanor, but she was gone.

59

I was sitting in the precinct room on the perp's side of the table when I finally met Quintana. He came into the room with a steaming cup in his hand, sat across from me, and doled out the evil eye.

"You dumb fuck," he said after a while.

The coffee was for me. I drank it black, same as he did.

They interrogated me for two hours. His partner, Stan Mallory, brought in some Danish and we went till noon. Twice during the questioning Quintana let me phone the hospital, where nothing had changed.

At twelve-fifteen he said, "Let's get out of here."

He seemed to be talking to me, so I followed him out to the parking lot, where he shuffled me to the shotgun side of a late-model Ford.

"This is supposed to be my day off," he said as he drove the wet streets.

I waited a moment, and when he didn't follow his thought, I said, "There aren't any days off, Quintana. Don't you know that yet?"

He knew it. He was just about my age and going through the same brand of burnout that had made my last year on the job so restless.

"I hear you were a good cop," he said.

"I was okay."

"A damn good cop. That's what they all say. I made some calls."

"I put a few assholes away."

"I hate to see a cop take a fall. Especially a good cop."

He was up on the freeway now, heading north. But he dropped off on the John Street ramp. We drove past the *Times* building, where the clock on the Fairview side said quarter to three.

"We need to talk to Eleanor," he said.

"You'll never find her. She could be anywhere by now."

"You remember where you left her car?"

"I think so."

"Show me."

We went north, and after a bit of double-tracking I found it. He opened the door and looked under the seat and took out the *Raven* she had left there.

"What do you think, maybe she took this out to compare it with the other one?" he said.

"I think that's part of it. And some of it's just what she said. She just loved having them."

He touched the book with his fingertips. "Isn't that a lovely goddamn thing."

"Rigby was no slouch. They say Grayson was good, but there ain't no flies on this."

We drove back downtown. A voice came through his radio, telling us Miss Aandahl was out of surgery. Her condition was guarded.

"I got a guy at the hospital keeping tabs," Quintana said. "We'll know what he knows as soon as he knows it. If I were you, I'd get some sleep. Where've you been holed up?"

I looked at him deadpan. "At the Hilton."

"You son of a bitch," he said with a dry laugh.

Surprisingly, I did sleep. Six hard hours after a hard shower.

I came awake to a pounding on the door. It was Quintana.

"I didn't say die, Janeway, I said sleep. Get your ass dressed."

I asked what he'd heard from the hospital.

"She's been upgraded to serious. No visitors for at least three days, and she won't be climbing Mount Rainier for a while after that. But it's starting to look like she'll live to fight another day."

He took me to dinner in a seafood place on the waterfront. It was superb. He paid with a card.

We didn't talk about the case. We talked about him and me, two pretty good cops. He was going through burnout, all right, it was written all over him. At thirty-eight he was having serious second thoughts about decisions he had made in his twenties. He had been a boxer, a pretzel baker, a welder, a bodyguard, a bartender, and, finally, at twenty-three, cop. He was solidly Roman Catholic, a believer but unfortunately a sinner. In his youth he had studied for the priesthood, but he had repeatedly failed the test of celibacy. A guy could go crazy trying to do a job like that. Now, after spending a few hours with me, he was charmed by something he'd never given a moment's thought. Quintana was the world's next killer bookscout.

"This stuff is *just* goddamn fascinating," he said.

"My world and welcome to it." I didn't know if he'd make the literary connection, so I helped him along. "That's a line from Thurber."

"I know what it's from. You think I'm some wetback just crawled over the border? *Walter Mitty*'s from that book."

"Good man."

He had a leg up on the game already.

I asked if he had a first name.

"Shane," he said, daring me not to like it.

But I couldn't play it straight. "Shane *Quintana?*"

"I see you come from the part of Anglo-town where all brown babies gotta be named Jose."

"Shane Quintana."

"I was named after Alan Ladd. Kids today don't even know who the hell Alan Ladd was." He deepened the Chicano in his voice and said, "Ey, man, Shane was one tough hombre, eh? He knock Jack Palance's dick down in the mud and stomp his gringo ass."

"I think it was the other way around. And Shane was a gringo too."

"Don't fuck with Shane, Janeway. I can still put you in jail."

"That's your big challenge in the book world, Quintana. *Shane*. Find that baby and it gets you almost two grand."

We went to a place he knew and shot pool. Neither of us would ever break a sweat on Minnesota Fats but we took a heavy toll on each other. He had a beeper on his belt but nobody called him. I could assume Trish was alive and holding her own.

Late that night we ended up back downtown in the precinct room. Mallory was still there, two-fingering some paperwork through an old typewriter.

We sat and talked. Eventually Mallory asked the big question.

"So what're you gonna do?"

About me, he meant.

Quintana shrugged. "Talk to the chief. I dunno, Stan, I don't see where we've got much evidence for a case against this man."

Mallory gave him a you've-got-to-be-kidding look.

"We'll see what the chief says tomorrow," Quintana said.

In a little while Mallory left. Quintana said, "If I get you out of this shit, it'll be a miracle. The Lady of Fatima couldn't do it."

421

I followed him into an adjacent room. He sat at a table with some video equipment. "I talked to Mrs. Rigby today. You interested?"

"Sure I am."

He popped a cassette into a machine and Crystal's haggard face came up on a screen. "Most of this's routine. Stuff you already know. The kicker's at the end."

He hit a fast button and looked in his notebook for the counter number where he wanted to stop it. "Her problem was, they never had any money," he said. "They owned the property they lived on, they'd bought it years ago before prices went out of sight. And she had a piece of land in Georgia that she'd inherited. I guess that's gone now. She'd given it to Eleanor and they put it up for the bail."

The machine whirred.

"Rigby wasn't interested in anything that generated their day-to-day income. He was always doing his *Raven* thing. But she loved him. So he sat out in that shop and made his books, and they just kept getting better and better. After a while she thought they were better than Grayson's. One day Rigby went down to Tacoma to look at some equipment in a printshop liquidation, and Crystal brought Moon over to see the books. Moon couldn't believe his eyes. He thought Grayson had come back to life, better than ever.

"The temptation to sell one was always with her after that. She started hearing what people were paying—all that money changing hands out there and they had none of it. If she could just sell one, for enough dough. She could hide the money and dribble it into their account and they wouldn't be so damn hard up all the time. Rigby didn't seem to notice things like that. As long as there was food on the table and a roof over their heads, he didn't spend a lot of time fretting. He didn't care much about the books either. He'd finish one and toss it back in that room and never look at it again. Sometimes he talked about destroying them, but he never did because Eleanor loved them and he couldn't stand to hurt her. But all of them knew—Crystal, Moon, Eleanor—they all knew that if he ever made one that satisfied him, the others were all history.

"The temptation killed her. But she was afraid, scared to death. If Rigby ever found out . . . well, he'd never forgive her, would he?"

"If she was lucky."

"Yeah, except she didn't think of it that way. She'd be betraying Grayson in his eyes and that scared her silly. It came to a head about seven years ago. They had a string of money problems all at once and she started making some calls. Eventually she got funneled to Murdock, who was then the leading Grayson dealer in the country. The rest of it's pretty much like Scofield told it to you. When he had that coughing attack, that's what scared her off. It dawned on her what an old man she was dealing with. If Scofield should die and the book get out . . . well, that would make news, wouldn't it?"

"It would in the book world."

"And there was a chance Rigby would hear about it and go look and see the book was missing from that back room."

"Eleanor might even tell him. She'd read it in *AB*, a new Grayson book found, and tear it out and show it to him."

He stopped the tape, ran it back slightly to the spot he wanted, and leaned back in his chair. "That's when Pruitt came into it. When he lost his job with Scofield, it was all downhill from there. He thought if he could find this woman in red, he could do two things—get back at Scofield and put himself on easy street. But he figured wrong. He thought it had to be one of

Grayson's old girlfriends, and for most of a year he chased down that road, trying to track 'em all down."

"What a job."

"That's what he found out. This Nola Jean—he worked on her for months and came to the same dead end everybody else came to. He went out and interviewed the Rigbys one time, even went to Taos, tracked down her sister, tried to talk to her. None of it panned out. Finally he ran out of leads and had to give it up. But he never stopped thinking about it.

"In the last five years, Pruitt really descended to his natural level in the order of man. He was a cheap hood, dreaming of glory. Then Eleanor got busted in New Mexico. That was the catalyst, that's what started this new wave of stuff. There was a little article in one of the Seattle papers, not much, just police-blotter stuff. There wasn't any what they call byline on the story, it was just a long paragraph, Seattle woman arrested in Taos heist and murder attempt, but your friend Aandahl says she wrote it. Pruitt saw it. Suddenly Grayson was back on the front burner again. The Rigby girl had broken into the Jeffords woman's house. What could that mean? Maybe Jeffords had been Scofield's woman in red. The only thing Pruitt knew for sure at that point was that Jeffords had had something the Rigbys wanted, and he had a pretty fair idea what that thing was. He called Slater and sent him to New Mexico to watch Rigby. Then Pruitt went to North Bend to confront Crystal, but she wouldn't admit anything. He harrassed her for a day or two, but that didn't get him anywhere. So he flew down to New Mexico and turned up the heat on Eleanor. He stalked her, called her at night with threats. He'd call at midnight and hum that song. Anything to rattle her, to get her to give up the book."

"This was when she was out on bail."

"Yeah, there was a period of about a week there

when Pruitt and Slater were hard on her case. She didn't have the book then but she knew where it was. Charlie Jeffords had told her, it was Nola's book. So she went back and took it and made her run. The funny thing is, she might not've done any of that if the Jeffords woman had just talked to her."

"All she wanted was to find her mother."

"So they get back up here and Pruitt starts in on Crystal again. Stalking, calling. There were some death threats. He'd call her at night and play that song, just a snatch of it, just enough of it, just enough of it. But loud, menacing. Then he started on Rigby too, and that was his big mistake. He was messing with the wrong dude. Rigby wound up at Pruitt's house and you know what happened after that. He ransacked the joint and found the photocopies of Grayson's *Raven*—that what you found burned in the wastebasket. I figure Pruitt made that copy when he stole Scofield's book, years ago.

"There wasn't even a misspelled word in that one."

"I'll bet he didn't even look."

He punched the tape. Crystal's voice filled the room.

"We stood around in shock," she said, faltering.

Quintana leaned back in his chair. "She's talking about the morning after the fire."

"We were over at Archie's shop, in Snoqualmie," she said. "We were like three dead people. Gaston and Archie were beside themselves. Gaston was inconsolable. It was the worst day of our lives . . . until this one. I don't think we said a word to each other the whole time. What could be said? Then we heard the door open . . . someone had come into the shop. And I remember Archie yelling out that he was closed . . . go away, just . . . go away. But the footsteps came on, and then she was there. Nola. I kept waiting for her to say something . . . maybe to cry. But she looked at

Gaston across the room . . . she looked straight at him and said, mean as hell, 'Cry if you want to, suckers. I'm glad the son of a bitch is dead.'"

Crystal sniffed and dabbed her eyes. "I knew she didn't mean that, it was just spite. She'd had that awful fight with Darryl the day before . . . and she'd always hated Gaston because she could never move him the way she always got at other men. When she said it, I felt sick. I turned away from her, I couldn't look at her . . . and then . . . then there was this thump, or a kind of . . . crushing sound . . . and when I turned around, she was lying there with her brains . . . and Gaston stood over her with the bloody hammer and Archie . . . Archie'd kinda shrunk back to the wall and we all just . . . just . . ."

Her face was pale. She looked faint.

Quintana's voice came in. "Take your time, Mrs. Rigby. Would you like some water?"

"No."

But she took the glass he handed her and gulped it.

"Then what happened?"

"Archie said . . . something like . . . it's a good thing you did that or I woulda. But that was just talk, it was Gaston who'd done it. And he'd sat down and there was no concern or . . . anything . . . on his face . . . and somebody mentioned the police. And I said no . . . can't call them, they'll lock him up and what would I do without him? He was my life, how would I live? So we rolled her in a rug and that night Archie and I took her off in the truck and we buried her."

Off camera, Quintana said, "What about the other people he killed?"

"I don't know." She began to cry again.

"Should we believe that, Mrs. Rigby?"

"I don't care what you believe. My life is over."

Quintana snapped off the machine and rewound the tape. Neither of us spoke until it clicked.

"Did she know Rigby had taken Eleanor?"

"I don't think so. She says no. I believe her." He put the cassette away and pushed himself back from the desk. "I found out a few more things while you were out playing the Lone Ranger. It was Rigby who made that call at four o'clock in the morning. He called the cops on his own kid. I think he was afraid of himself, what he might do if it turned out that Eleanor really had that flawed book. Hell, he was right to be afraid, he'd killed everybody else who ever had one. He tried to hide his voice, but I've got the tape and it was him. He was on long enough for the number to get logged, so we know the call came from that phone. I think he turned on the record at Pruitt's for the same reason. There was a part of him that wanted us to catch him."

I thought of Crystal and Archie and asked what he thought would happen to them now.

"Whatever it is, it won't be anything compared to what they've already been through. We'll see if the facts bear out her story. I doubt if they'll do any jail time; the only charge would be rendering criminal assistance, and the statute's probably run on that. They don't seem to care right now. They waived their rights to a lawyer, gave us statements of their own free will, and the statements jibed and I believe 'em."

He turned up his palms. "You might as well be in on the payoff if I can swing it. There's just one thing. You've got to teach me this bookscouting stuff. Call it one you owe me."

"I'll give you the two-day crash course, teach you all I know."

"I'm a quick read. One day will do it."

In the morning he came to get me. Trish had a restless night but was upgraded to fair. She was asking for me but her doctors told her not yet, maybe tomorrow.

Quintana and I ate breakfast together and then did a couple of bookstores. I watched him buy without comment, and afterward we sat in a coffee shop and I told him what he'd done wrong.

Never buy a bad copy of a good book. The better the book, the more the flaws magnify.

Condition, condition, condition . . .

We drove to the jail and picked up Moon. He looked old in his jail clothes, and he looked strangely small sitting between the two deputies in the back-seat.

We arrived at Rigby's in brilliant sunshine. Moon walked between us as we crossed the meadow. We went along the path I had followed up from the house, dipped into the trees, and stopped a hundred yards into the woods.

An hour later, the deputies dug up the rug containing the bones of Nola Jean Ryder.

In the spring they flew into Denver for Quintana's long-postponed book odyssey. Trish was looking good and I was thrilled at the sight of her. We ate that night in a Mexican place on a hill near Mile High Stadium, and in the morning we lit out for Nebraska, Iowa, and points east. The trouble with Denver is it's a light-year from everywhere, a hard day's ride to any other city with bookstores. The landscape is bleak, though there are those who love the brown plains and the dry vistas and the endless rolling roads. We filled the day with shoptalk, of books and crime and the people who do them. We laughed our way across Nebraska, drawn by the Platte and bonded by the good companionship that makes book-hunting so special and rich. We prowled in little towns where thrift-store people are uncorrupted by the greedy paranoia of the big-city stores. It was in such a place that Quintana made the first good strike of the trip, a sweet copy of Alan Le May's *The Searchers*. It wasn't *Shane*, but it was a solid C-note, which is not bad for thirty-five cents.

We scouted Lincoln and found some gems at Bluestem, an oasis of books just off downtown; then we moved on to Omaha. The weather was grand all the way, and we laughed about it and Trish swore it had not rained a drop in Seattle since I'd been there last October. Quintana made a dubious cough but had to agree that the winter had been unusually dry. We swung north into Minneapolis and spent a day tramping around with Larry Dingman of Dinkytown Books. I still had the picture of Eleanor that Slater had given me long ago, and in every stop I showed it to bookpeople in the hope that someone had seen her.

In Chicago I saw a guy brazenly doctor a Stephen King book, just the way Richard Grayson had done *The Raven.* He sat at his front counter and tipped a first-edition title page—sliced out of a badly damaged and worthless book—into a second printing. The book was *The Shining,* an easy deception because the second printings are so much like the firsts in binding, jackets, and stock. The only notable difference is on the title page verso, the magic words *first edition* are at the bottom of a real one and missing from the others. The entire operation took less than five minutes, and when it was done, even a King guy would have a hard time telling. The guy marked it $200. Quintana leaned over his counter and called him a crook and a few other things before Trish managed to pull him away and we headed for Indianapolis.

I had a dream that night about the first Grayson *Raven.* In the dream Richard fixed that one too: changed two letters of type after Grayson had quit work and gone to the pub for the evening. It would've been easy then, in 1949, when it was just the two brothers working alone and a mistake was easy to miss. No glue, no tip-ins to tell a tale years later: just switch the letters and it would always be assumed, even by Grayson, they'd been set that way. At breakfast in the morning I told Trish and Quintana and none of us laughed. For a long time we couldn't shake the notion that the whole Grayson tragedy had been for nothing.

We were out ten days, in all a great trip. They stayed

with me another three days in Denver, and the house felt empty when I put them on the plane and watched them fly away.

A year has come and gone. It's winter in Denver, late on a snow-swept Saturday night as I sit at my front counter writing in the little diary that I've begun keeping of my life in books. Far up the street a shrouded figure comes out of the snow, battling a wicked wind that howls in from the east, and I think of Eleanor Rigby. I still have a delusion that one of these days she's going to walk into my bookstore and help me write a fitting end to the Grayson case. Grayson was my turning point as a bookman. I came home with enough of Scofield's money that, for now, I can buy just about any collection of books that walks in my door. I still have Grayson's notebook: Amy gave it to me. Kenney calls once a month and asks if I'm ready to sell it. I should probably do that: the money they're throwing around is just too good to keep turning it down. But Kenney understands when I laugh and tell him how it would diminish the old man's life if suddenly he had that roadmap to everything.

Among the fallout from the Grayson papers were letters indicating the real identity of Amy Harper's father. The name Paul Ricketts had been one of the pseudonyms used by Richard Grayson in his early writings, and the letters revealed an affair of many years' duration between Richard and Selena Harper. "So we're first cousins," Amy wrote of herself and Eleanor. "Imagine that." The news from the Northwest gradually tapered off. I had to return the Ayn Rand books to Murdock's estate as his last two relatives could never agree on anything. The best guess, the one that seemed most likely to me, was that these were the last of Murdock's really good books, gathered for a wholesale run so he could get some money together to make Amy an offer. The cops found a big batch of real Graysons'—all the lettered copies of everything but the 1969 *Ravens*—in the rafters above Rigby's shop. He couldn't resist taking them, holy books made by the hand of God, as he traveled through St. Louis, Phoenix, Baltimore, Boise, and New Orleans. As for his own, they are called the Rigby *Ravens* now and are widely admired by people who have seen them. Scofield wants them but his woman in red doesn't seem to care so much about money anymore. The books will belong to Eleanor, wherever she is.

The New Mexico case is still open. Charlie Jeffords died not long ago and it remains to be seen who fired the gun, if and when the cops find Eleanor. I've just about decided that it's too easy for people to disappear into that street-level book subculture. I keep showing her picture around when I'm on the road. There's a lot of money waiting for her and Scofield's not getting any younger.

It's ten o'clock—time to get the hell out of here and go home. The figure in the street has reached my door, and in this moment, in less than an instant, I think, *hey! . . . maybe . . . maybe.* At the edge of her hood I see the facial features of a young woman. She turns her head, our eyes meet through the plate glass and she smiles faintly. It's the neighborhood's newest hooker, heading on up to the Safeway after a hard day's night. I give her a friendly wave and turn off the lights fast. In the yard behind the store I look at the black sky and wonder what books tomorrow will bring.